"If you have an appetite for evil, you'll love sitting down to *Ghost Road Blues*, which is deliciously creepy."
—Richard Sand, author of the award-winning Lucas Rook mystery series

"Jonathan Maberry is writing big, scary books that feel just right."
—Bill Kent, author of *Street Legal, Street Fighter,* and *Street Money*

"A wild mélange of soulful blues music and gut-wrenching horror!"
—Brinke Stevens, horror actress and author

"Terrifying. Maberry gets deep into the heads of his troubled characters—and ours."
—Jim Fusilli, author of *Hard, Hard City* and *Tribeca Blues*

"Maberry . . . delivers scare after scare."
—Scott A. Johnson, author of *An American Haunting*

"Unputdownable!"
—Michael Penncavage, editor of *Dark Notes from New Jersey*

"Jonathan Maberry delivers! Echoes of King, Bradbury, Poe, Wellman, and Straub."
—C. Dean Andersson, author of *I Am Dracula* and *Raw Pain Max*

"This is the best book I've read this year!"
—Dave's News and Reviews

"Teeming with demons, brutality, and madness, but equally brimming with beauty, love, and wisdom."
—Kim Paffenroth, Ph.D., author of *Gospel of the Living Dead*

"Dark, scary, and so darn well written, one might think this book was something Stephen King wrote and forgot about many years ago."
—Michael Laimo, author of *Dead Souls* and *The Demonologist*

"*Ghost Road Blues* reminded me why I'm afraid of the dark."
—Charles Gramlich, author of *Cold in the Light*

## Other books by Jonathan Maberry

FICTION

*Ghost Road Blues*

NONFICTION

*Vampire Universe*

*Cryptopedia*

# DEAD MAN'S SONG

## JONATHAN MABERRY

**PINNACLE BOOKS**
Kensington Publishing Corp.
www.kensingtonbooks.com

*To my wife Sara and my son Sam*

SO MANY PEOPLE TO THANK . . .

To my first readers: Arthur Mensch, Randy Kirsch, Charlie Miller, and Greg Schauer . . . for your comments, observations, and insights.

To my experts: Chief Pat Priore of the Tullytown Police Department; Larry Kaplan, DDS; Dan Noszinski; Richard F. Kuntz, First Deputy Coroner of Bucks County; and Jim Gurley. Any errors that remain in the book are purely the author's doing.

To the publishing folks: Michaela Hamilton, Sara Crowe, Elizabeth Little, and Doug Mendini.

To my fellow writers: Tess Gerritsen, Stuart Kaminsky, J. A. Konrath, John Lutz, Yvonne Navarro, Steve Hamilton, Richard Sand, Bill Kent, Michael Laimo, Charles Gramlich, Simon Clark, David Housewright, Jeremiah Healy, Bev Vincent, Jemiah Jefferson, Stephen Susco, Tim Waggoner, H. R. Knight, Gary A. Braunbeck, Ken Bruen, Kealan Patrick Burke, Nate Kenyon, David Wellington, Bryan Smith, Katherine Ramsland, Scott Nicholson, Don D'Ammassa, W. D. Gagliani, Bruce Boston, Gregory Frost, Fred Wiehe, Noreen Ayres, and Kim Peffenroth for endless support.

To my guest stars: Stephen Susco, Ken Foree, Tom Savini, Jim O'Rear, James Gunn, Brinke Stevens, Debbie Rochon, and Joe Bob Briggs for dropping by to make an appearance in this book and the next.

To the Bluesmen, Mem Shannon and Eddy "The Chief" Clearwater, for allowing me to use their wonderful blues lyrics in this book and the next.

My colleagues at Career Doctor for Writers (www.career

doctorforwriters.com) and Writers Corner USA (www. writers cornerusa.com).

And to the superstars of my Novels for Young Writers class, Brett Knasiak, Aly Pierce, Ali Dowdy, Charlie Patton, Richard Wang, Lee Biskin, Jack Inkpen, Rachael Lavin, and Julie Hagopian.

# THE GUTHRIE FARM

And I think I'm gonna drown
I believe I'm gonna drown
I think I'm gonna drown
Standing on my feet.

—Mem Shannon, *Drowning on My Feet*

Sing it like the midnight wind,
Sing it like a prayer;
Sing it on to the way to hell,
Them blues'll take you there.

—Oren Morse, *Dead Man's Song*

## (1)

It was October when it happened. It should always be October when these things happen. In October you expect things to die.

In October the sun shrinks away; it hides behind mountains and throws long shadows over small towns like Pine Deep. Especially towns like Pine Deep. The wind grows new teeth and it learns to bite. The colors fade from deep summer greens to the mournful browns and desiccated yellows of autumn. In October the harvest blades are honed to sharpness, and that's when the sickles and scythes, the threshers and combines, maliciously attack the fields, leaving the long stalks of corn lying dead in haphazard piles along the beaten rows. Pumpkin growers come like headsmen to gather the gourds for the carvers' knives. The insects, so alive during the long months of July, August, and September, die in their thousands, their withered carcasses crunching under the feet of children hurrying home from school, children racing to beat the fall of night. Children do not play out-of-doors in the nights of Pine Deep.

There are shadows everywhere—even in places they have no right to be. The shadows range from the purple haze of twilit streets to the utter, bottomless black in the gaping mouths of sewers. Some of the shadows are cold, featureless—just blocks of lightless air. Other shadows seem to possess an unnatural vitality; they seem to roil and writhe, especially as the young ones—the innocent ones—pass by. In those kinds of shadows something always seems to be waiting. Impatiently waiting. In those kinds of shadows something always seems to be watching. Hungrily watching. These are not the warm shadows of September, for in that month the darkness still remembers the warmth of summer suns; nor were they yet the utterly dead shadows of bleak November, to whom the sun's warmth is only a wan memory. These were the shadows of October, and they were hungry shadows. When the dying sun cast those kinds of shadows, well . . .

This was Pine Deep, and it was October—a kind of October particular to Pine Deep. The spring and summer before had been lush; the autumn of the year before that had been bright and bountiful, yielding one of those rare and wonderful Golden Harvests that are written of in tourist books of the region; and though there had been shadows, there hadn't been shadows as dark as these. No, these shadows belonged to an autumn whose harvest was going to be far darker— these were the shadows of a Black Harvest October in Pine Deep. So, it was October when it happened. It should always be October when these things happen.

In October you expect things to die.

## (2)

"They said they'd send us some coffee and hot sandwiches in about half an hour," called Jimmy Castle as he trudged back into the clearing a quarter mile from the Guthrie farmhouse. Yellow crime scene tape was strung from post to post along the rows of towering late season corn, the ends anchored to the wooden rails of the fence that marked the boundary of the big farm. Tarps were pegged down over the spot where Henry Guthrie had been gunned down just a few days ago, and the criminalists and other crime scene investigators would be back in the morning to finish up their comprehensive search of the area. Of the three gunmen who had come into town after fleeing a bloody shoot-out in Philadelphia, two were dead and one—Kenneth Boyd—was still on the loose. That meant that the scene had to be secured until the CSI team was completely done, and it also meant a long cold night for Castle—who was still on loan from Crestville to help with the manhunt—and his partner, Nels Cowan, who was local PD.

Castle had his hands jammed deep into the pockets of his blue Crestville PD jacket, fists balled tight in a losing battle to try and hold on to some warmth. He walked briskly, shoulders rounded to keep the wind off his ears, his straw-colored hair snapping in the stiff breeze. "I told them to send some of those pocket hand-warmers, too . . . getting pretty freakin' cold out. . . ."

His words trailed off to nothing as he entered the clearing and all thoughts of warmth were slammed out of his brain.

He stopped walking, stopped talking, stopped breathing. The world imploded down into one tiny quarter-acre of unreality; time and order and logic all were smashed into one chunk of madness. All sound in the world died; all movement failed; all that existed was the tableau that filled his eyes as Jimmy Castle saw the two *things* that occupied the clearing. His mouth sagged open as he stood there rooted to the spot, feeling all sensation and awareness evaporate into smoke as the seconds fell dead around him. All of his cop reflexes, all of his training in crisis management simply froze into stillness because nothing at the Academy, nothing he had seen on the streets of Pittsburgh, where he'd done his first years, and nothing since he'd moved to Crestville could have prepared him for what he saw there in the moonlight darkness of the Guthrie cornfield. His mind ground to a halt and he just stood there and stared.

Nels Cowan lay on the muddy ground, arms and legs spread in an ecstasy of agony, head thrown back and lolling on what little was left of his throat. Cowan's mouth was open, but any scream he uttered echoed only in the dark vastness of death; his eyes were open as if beholding horror, but that look was frozen onto his face forever, like an expression carved onto a wax mask. Blood glistened as thick and black as oil in the moonlight. The ghastly wounds on Cowan's throat were so savage that Castle could even see the taut gray cords of half-severed tendons and the sharp white edge of a cracked vertebra. The dark shape hunched over Nels Cowan raised its head and looked at him without expression for a long moment, and then the bloody mouth opened in a great smile full of immense darkness and hunger, lips parting to reveal hideous teeth that were grimed with pink-white tatters of flesh. The teeth gleamed white through the streaks of red as the smile broadened into a feral snarl; its features were a mask of lust and hate, the nose wrinkled like a dog's, the black eyes became lost in pits of gristle. A tongue, impossibly long and purplish-gray, lolled from the mouth and licked drops of blood from the thing's chin.

Jimmy Castle opened his mouth, mimicking the silent scream of Nels Cowan; however his scream escaped, ran shrieking out into the night air and soared disjointedly up into the night. The frozen moment of time melted and he sagged to his knees, still screaming as his fingers scrabbled at the butt of his gun, his fingernails making scratching sounds in the silence. He was only distantly aware that the gun was coming free of the holster. With no mindful awareness of his actions he racked the slide, flicked off the safety, held the gun out and up in both hands, pointed. Fired. Actions performed a thousand times in practice, performed now with absolutely no conscious control, machinelike and correct. The barrel of the heavy 9mm rose, sought its target, and screamed defiance at the man-shape that was rising, tensing, readying itself to spring.

He tried to say the word "Freeze!" and though his mouth worked at it he could not manage any sound. Then his hands, operating independently of his brain, squeezed the trigger.

Thunder boomed and lightning flashed in the clearing as Jimmy Castle tried to blast the thing back into nightmares.

He fired straight, aiming by instinct alone at the centerline of the creature's body. He fired fast. He fired true. He fired nine times, each boom as loud as all the noise in the world, sending nine tumbling lead slugs directly into the thing, catching it as it rose, catching it in belly and groin and chest. He hit it every single time.

And it did him no damn good at all.

# PART ONE

# BLOOD HUNT

The hellhounds dogging my steps, everywhere I go
The hellhounds following my tracks, everywhere I go;
Caught my scent at the crossroads
And chasing me through the corn
Hellhounds dogging me everywhere I go.

—Oren Morse, *Lost and Lonely Blues*

I don't mind them graveyards,
and it ain't 'cause I'm no kind of brave;
Said I don't mind no graveyard,
but I ain't no man that is brave.
'Cause the ghosts of the past, they are harder to face
than anything comes from a grave.

—A. L. Sirois, *Ghost Road Blues*

# Chapter 1

## (1)

The morphine should have kept him out for hours, down there in the darkness where there was no pain, no terror. After the doctors had stitched up his mouth and lip and the nurses had inserted replacement IV needles in his hand and shot the narcotics into his blood, Malcolm Crow should have just gone into that dark nowhere where there are no memories, no dreams. But that didn't happen.

He only slept for a few hours while Officer Jerry Head—on loan from the Philly PD and part of the combined task force that had been formed to hunt down Kenneth Boyd, Tony Macchio, and Karl Ruger—sat in a plastic visitor chair and watched.

In his dreams Crow walked through the cornfields of the Guthrie farm, looking for Val, searching for her everywhere but finding nothing. As he hunted through the dreamscape he could hear a whispering echo of music buried beneath the hiss and rustle of the moving cornstalks—faint, but definitely there. He knew it was blues because it was always blues in his dreams; he knew that if he could get closer to it, if he could find its source, then he would be able to tell the name of the song. Somehow that mattered, though he did not know why. The dreamer never questions the logic of the dream.

Crow pushed through the corn, wincing now and then as the sharp blades of the leaves nicked his face and palms. He was barefoot; his hospital gown flapped open and the cold stung his ass. The ground was hard, his feet were blistered and bleeding, but he did not stop, did not even look down. The breeze stilled and for just a second he could hear the song more clearly. Damn, he *did* know it, but he just couldn't pull the name out of his head. Something about a road. Something about a prison. What the hell was it?

He turned, orienting himself, and looked back the way he'd come. Behind him the corn was smashed down and broken aside as if his passage through the field had been like a bulldozer's. He could see the trail leading in a twisted line going back so far that it vanished into the distance. The music was stronger now and he moved off to his right, humming as he went. It was in his head, in his mouth, and then he *knew* it. It was an old prison blues song, something someone had taught him long ago, back when he was a kid; and this time it came to him: "Ghost Road Blues." A song from down South, something to do with prisoners suffering in Louisiana's Angola prison and praying for release—even if it was the Angel of Death who unlocked their chains.

Crow stopped and listened to it, one ear hearing the song drifting along the breeze and the other listening to the song play inside his head from a long time ago. That had been on a warm early autumn afternoon on Val Guthrie's porch, with Val sitting on the swing next to Terry and Terry's little sister, Mandy. Crow's brother Billy—good ol' Boppin' Bill—had a haunch propped on the whitewashed rail, tossing a baseball up into the air and catching it in his outfielder's glove. Val's dad was there—old Henry—and Henry's wife, Bess. There were others, too—farm folks and field hands, brothers and cousins of the Guthrie clan, all of them smiling, clapping hands or snapping fingers, tapping their toes as the man with the guitar played his songs. Crow could see the guitarist so clearly: a stick-thin guy with a nappy Afro and dark eyes that sparkled with equal measures sadness and humor. Dark skin and loose clothes, skinny legs crossed with one work-booted foot jiggling in the air along with his music. A dime with a hole in it hung from a string tied around his brown ankle. Scars on his hands and face, shadows in his eyes, laugh lines around his mouth. Crow remembered the nickname he, Val, and Terry had given him because he was so skinny: the Bone Man.

On some level Crow knew that he was dreaming all of this, just as he was aware that he had dreamed of the Bone Man many times. Standing motionless now, adrift in sea of waving corn, Crow closed his eyes and listened to the gentle voice of the singer. The song was a lament for the prisoners in the infamous Red Hat House at Angola Prison in Louisiana who were imprisoned more for their skin color than for any real crime; they were beaten and humiliated by the guards, tortured, degraded—yet enduring. Then at the end of their days in that hellish place they stood tall and proud as they strolled that last mile to where Ol' Sparky waited—knowing the other prisoners loved them for it and the guards hated that they could never truly break their spirits.

The song ended and the last mournful notes were sewn like silver threads through the freshening breeze, leaving Crow feeling lost and abandoned out there in the field. He opened his eyes and looked around. It was darker now, the sun hidden behind storm clouds as long fingers of cold shadow reached from the mountains in the north across the fields toward him. He clutched the inadequate hospital johnnie around himself, trying to conserve its meager warmth.

"Are you there?" he said aloud, and he wasn't sure if he was calling for Val or for the Bone Man. As if in answer the corn behind him rustled and Crow spun toward it, his heart suddenly hammering. The Bone Man pushed aside the dry stalks like a performer parting the curtains to come onstage. He had his old guitar slung across his back, the slender neck hanging down behind his right hip. His skin was no longer dark brown but had faded to an ashy gray, and his eyes had a milky film over them, making him look dead.

"I heard you playing . . ." Crow said, his voice as dry as the Bone Man's eyes. The Bone Man opened his mouth and said something, but there was no sound at all, not even a whisper. He smiled ruefully and gave Crow an expectant look, obviously waiting for an answer. "I . . . can't understand you," Crow said. "I mean . . . I can't hear you."

The Bone Man licked dry lips with a gray tongue and tried again. Still no sound at all, but Crow could at least read the man's lips well enough to make out two words. Little Scarecrow. He understood that. Little Scarecrow was what he had once been called, years ago—a nickname given him by a man he'd given a nickname to in turn. Tit for tat. The Bone Man and Little Scarecrow. What he was called when he was nine.

Thunder rumbled far away to the northeast, and they both turned to look. There was a flash of lightning beyond the fields, over past the lover's lane by the drop-off that led down to Dark Hollow. Crow saw the Bone Man nod, apparently to himself, and when the gray man turned his milky eyes were filled with a fear so sharp that it bordered on panic.

"I knew someone who lived down there once," said Crow, and he was amazed to hear that his own voice had changed. It was the voice of a child. Maybe nine or ten. "There was a bad man who lived down there a long time ago."

Narrowing his eyes, the Bone Man peered at him. Apparently he, too, heard the change in Crow's voice. Little Scarecrow's voice.

"He killed my brother, you know. He killed Billy and ate him all up."

Now even Crow's body had changed. He was nine years old, wearing pajamas and holding a tattered stuffed monkey. The Bone Man towered over him and little Crow—Little Scarecrow—looked up at him. "He ate Billy all up. He did it to my best friend's sister, too. He made her all dead and ate her up. He does that, he . . . eats people all up."

A tear broke from the dust-dry eye of the Bone Man and cut a path down his cheek.

"The bad man wanted to eat me all up, too . . . and he was gonna, but you stopped him! You came and stopped him and he went running off." Little Scarecrow shuffled his feet and hugged his monkey tight to his chest. "Val's dad said that you killed that man. Did you? Did you kill the bad man?"

The Bone Man opened his mouth, tried to say something, but the thunder boomed overhead and both he and the boy jumped. Red lightning veined the clouds, souring the breeze with the stink of ozone. The storm was centered over the drop-off to Dark Hollow, but it was coming their way fast with thunder like an artillery barrage. Without thinking he reached out and took the Bone Man's hand. It was dry and cold, but it was firm, and after staring down at the boy in apparent shock for a long minute, the gray man returned a reassuring squeeze. Little Scarecrow looked up at him—and deep within the morphine dreams the adult Crow felt the surreal quality of the moment as he saw a dead man through his own youthful eyes. It was like watching a movie and being a part of it at the same time.

Officer Jerry Head looked up from his copy of *Maxim* as Crow shifted uneasily, twisting the sheets around his legs. "Bad dreams," he murmured, then grunted. "No surprise there." He went back to the article he was reading. Outside the window, in a totally cloudless sky, there was a flicker of distant lightning that Head did not consciously notice, but as he read his right hand drifted down and he absently began running his thumbnail over the rubber ridges of his holstered pistol's grip.

In the cornfield, Little Scarecrow and the Bone Man stood hand in hand, watching the storm; it was a big, angry thing—flecked with red and hot yellow and sizzling white, lumped with purple and black. A cold wind came hard out of the northeast, heavy with moisture and smelling of decay. Above them a cloud of black night birds flapped and cawed their way toward the southwest, racing to outrun the storm, but the lightning licked out and incinerated three of the birds. They fell, smoking and shapeless, into the corn.

Tugging the Bone Man's hand, Little Scarecrow looked up at him, puzzled and frightened. "I thought you killed the bad man. That's what Val's dad said . . . that you killed the bad man."

There was a final terrible explosion of thunder and a burst of lightning so bright that it stabbed into Little Scarecrow's eyes like spikes and he spun away, clamping his hands over his face—

—and woke up with a cry of real pain and genuine terror.

"Griswold!" he screamed as he woke and then there was a big dark shape looming over him and hands on his shoulders. Crow was blind with sleep and morphine and he tried to see, tried to fight, but the hands were too strong.

"Whoa, man," said the voice of the man standing over him. "You're gonna pop your stitches you keep that shit up."

Abruptly Crow stopped fighting, blinking his eyes clear to see the big cop standing there. Broad-shouldered with a shaved head and an easy grin. It took Crow a second to fish his name out of the dark. "Jerry . . . ?"

"Yeah, man, it's just me." Head smiled at him, but there was concern in his eyes. "You were having one hell of a nightmare there."

"Christ," Crow muttered, "you don't know the half of it."

Head helped Crow settle himself and he arranged the sheets and plumped his pillow as tidily as any nurse, gave him a sip of water through a straw, and settled back in his chair, scooping his magazine from off the floor where it had fallen.

Crow rubbed his eyes. "What time is it?"

"Almost six. Sun'll be up in a bit. You weren't out more than a few hours, though. You want me to get the nurse to bring you something, help you sleep?"

"God, I don't think I ever want to go to sleep again." With the tip of his tongue he probed the stitches inside his mouth, wincing. He sighed and settled back against the pillow but there was no getting comfortable. Everything hurt. Even his hair felt like the ends of brittle pieces of straw stuck into his scalp. "You on shift all night?"

"One of the local blues is supposed to relieve me at six-thirty." He hesitated. "I can stick around if you want, though—"

Crow waved it off. "Thanks, man, but it's cool. Tell me, though, did, um, anything else happen last night? I mean, after . . ."

Last night had been the second chapter in a nightmare that had begun two days before, on September 30. The whole thing had started when a trio of Philadelphia mobsters had forced a drug deal to go sour so they could make off with both the money and the cocaine, and had left behind a warehouse littered with dead men—their own cronies, a posse of Jamaicans, and at least one cop. Karl Ruger led the crew, and if there was ever a sicker, more violent, more vicious son of a bitch on planet Earth, then Crow had never heard of him. Ruger had been the directing force behind the buy, and he had made it go south because he needed enough money to flee the country—not just to elude the police man-hunt, but to escape the wrath of Little Nicky Menditto, the crime boss of Ruger's own outfit. Rumor had it that Menditto had learned that Ruger was the man hunted nationwide as the Cape May Killer—a psychopath who had slaughtered a group of senior citizens at the lighthouse on the Jersey Shore. Little Nicky's grandparents had been on that tour.

The slaughter had been a bizarre by-product of a mob war in Philly, but Ruger had gone way past his instructions of "doing something to hurt Little Nicky." Ruger had committed atrocities that were being written about in books and made into movies. Ruger was the kind of real-world killer than made Ted Bundy look like a genial neighbor. His identity had remained hidden for years, but then the whisper stream had started and Ruger knew that he had to run or die. The mob was never known for understanding or forgiveness.

How or why Ruger's crew had crashed their car was something neither Crow nor the interjurisdictional police task force had been able to determine, and the ensuing man-hunt was massive. Unfortunately their car had crashed on a remote edge of the Guthrie family farm. Every time Crow thought about how Ruger invaded the Guthrie house, brutalized the family, and nearly killed Val—*his* Val!—Crow felt his guts turn to ice.

It burned Crow that he hadn't been there in time to stop Ruger before he moved like a killer storm through the lives of Val and her family. Crow's best friend, Terry Wolfe, mayor of Pine Deep and owner of the country's largest Haunted Hayride, had begged Crow to drive out to the attraction and shut it down, fearing what would happen if Ruger and his men showed up there. Crow had wasted way too much time getting that job done, and not really taking the job all that seriously. Mobsters and police manhunts just didn't seem real in Pine Deep, and violence on that scale was something safely buried in the town's past, not its present. Not now.

So, while Crow was tooling around, taking his time, Karl Ruger was beating the hell out of Val, her father Henry, her brother Mark, and Mark's wife, Connie. Ruger tied everyone up except for Val and Henry and forced them at gunpoint to go out into the fields to help him fetch one of his injured men, Kenneth Boyd. By the time they got back to where Ruger had left Boyd, there was no trace of him, the cash, or the drugs. Boyd had split and taken Ruger's lifeline with him. Ruger went totally off his rocker at that point, and, as Val later told Crow, Henry had seen just one chance to save his family. He shoved Val away from him, urging her to run while he ran the other way to draw Ruger away from the house. Ruger, snapping out of rage and into cold efficiency, simply shot Henry in the back as he ran and left him to die out in the rainy darkness. It was so callous that Crow felt bile in his throat.

Ruger headed back to the farmhouse, but Val wasn't there. So he vented his anger on Mark—beating him, knocking his teeth out, totally humiliating him—and then forcing him to lie there on the floor and watch as he set about raping Connie. If Val had been even two minutes later it would have been too late for Connie, but Ruger was just starting to tear at her clothes when Val snuck in and tackled him, then immediately fled, taking a cue from her father's sacrifice by tricking Ruger into chasing her. She had hoped to outrun him, to lose him in the darkness of her farm and then circle back to the house and get one of her father's guns, but Ruger was as fast as he was sly and he caught her before she had taken a hundred paces. He was strangling her, trying to crush her throat to satisfy his dark need to hurt, to destroy, when Crow finally arrived. Too late to save Henry, almost too late to save the others.

The only thing that had gone right that night was that Ruger had underestimated Crow. Ruger was a big man, two hundred pounds of sinewy muscle packed onto a wiry six-foot frame. He had incredibly fast hands and he had never lost a fight in his life because there was nothing in his psychological makeup that could accept any reality except one in which he dominated. When Crow stepped out of his car, what Ruger saw was a short, thin man who looked about as threatening as a shopkeeper, which what Crow currently was. What he did not see were the years upon years of jujutsu training; what he did not see were the years on the Pine Deep police force as one its most decorated officers—all of that in the past, but not long past. Ruger made one of the worst mistakes anyone can make in a fight: he underestimated his opponent, and it had cost him.

They fought in the rain and the mud and it was the most vicious fight of Crow's life. No mercy, no rules, no hesitation. It was eye-gouging and groin-kicking and throat-crushing. It was a life-or-death back-alley brawl between two men who *had* to win. Quitting or surrender were impossible concepts for both of them because to lose the fight was to lose absolutely everything.

In the end, Crow had won the fight, though he looked like he'd been trampled by horses. He was bloodied, winded, nearly blind with pain, but he was on his feet and Ruger was down. Which is when Crow had made *his* mistake, and it was every bit as foolish and dangerous as Ruger's. Crow had not finished Ruger off. He left him there, down and apparently unconscious, and had run straight to Val to see if she was okay. It was around that time that the first patrol car had arrived, with Jerry Head at the wheel and a young local cop, Rhoda Thomas, riding shotgun. Head had gone into the house to check on Mark and Connie, Rhoda stayed in the yard to help Crow and Val. No one paid enough attention to Ruger. No one saw him struggle to his knees, no one saw him fish in the mud for the gun Crow had dropped at the beginning of the fight, no one saw him wash it clean in the heavy downpour. Only luck, or perhaps a little bone thrown to them by providence, gave Crow just enough warning to react when Ruger opened fire. Rhoda went down with a bullet in her shoulder and Crow was grazed by two bullets, one on each side of his torso, as he scrambled to pull Rhoda's sidearm. He returned fire and emptied the Glock's entire magazine into Ruger, watching as the bullets knocked the man into a weird puppet dance. Head appeared on the porch and added his fire and Ruger went down in a storm of bullets.

Val went down a moment later, the damage to her throat blending with shock and dragging her down into darkness. Crow tried to stay conscious, but after the beating he had taken, and the two bullet wounds, he had nothing left. He dropped.

His next memory was of waking up in the hospital, with Terry Wolfe telling him that Henry was dead but Val was alive. Mark and Connie were deeply hurt, both physically and psychologically, by Ruger's sick games. Rhoda was in surgery, but was expected to make it. And Karl Ruger . . . well, somehow, with all the commotion as cops and paramedics flooded the place, he crawled off and vanished. A dozen bullets in him, Crow was sure of that, and yet he crawled away and simply dropped off the face of the world.

That should have been it. Crow assumed that it *was* it, that Ruger's bones would one day be found out there in the woods beyond the Guthrie farm. Yeah, we all know about assumptions. Ruger was far from dead. Last night—could it be just a few hours ago?—just shy of midnight, Karl Ruger broke into the hospital. He attacked and nearly killed the fa-

cilities engineer, shut down the main and backup genera-
tors—plunging the hospital into total darkness—and while
everyone was screaming and staggering in blind panic, the
killer made his way to Crow's room, beat the shit out of
Crow's police guard, and attacked Crow again, looking for
serious payback. Val had been with Crow in the room, and
Ruger struck her a terrible blow to the head, fracturing the
bone above her eye socket.

Crow was sewn together with stitches and badly bruised
from their last fight, but even with all that he *should* have
been able to defeat Ruger a second time because Ruger
should have been a short step away from dead, but Ruger
was not a shambling hulk, he was not dying on his feet. Instead he faster than before, and far stronger. Unnaturally
strong, like nothing Crow had ever seen. He threw Crow
from one end of the room to the other and was a heartbeat
away from crushing his throat when Val—dazed and bleeding—crawled over and got the pistol from the fallen officer's
duty belt. She opened fire, and that gave Crow a tiny window
of opportunity to scuttle over and grab the small throwdown
strapped to the cop's ankle holster. From point-blank range
they emptied both guns into Ruger, and this time there was
no doubt—every shot went home.

In a bizarre encore of the night before Ruger went down,
almost immediately followed by Val.

And still it wasn't over. In the brief period between Val's
collapse and the arrival of doctors, nurses, and a lot of cops,
there had been a moment of complete insanity when something impossible happened, and no one but Crow had witnessed it. He had bent to reach across Ruger's dead body
toward Val when Ruger opened his eyes and grabbed Crow's
wrist with unbelievable force, pulling him close long enough
to whisper five words. Just five, but they had punched holes
in Crow's mind.

"Ubel Griswold sends his regards."

Then Ruger had laughed the coldest laugh Crow had ever
heard, the light went out of his eyes, and he sank back to the
floor. Dead for sure this time.

From that moment to this those words kept echoing through his mind. All through the process of being stitched, bandaged, moved to another room, Crow kept hearing that icy voice.

There was no way Karl Ruger could have known that name, Crow was sure of that. Griswold was thirty years dead, killed by the Bone Man and left to rot down in the wormy swamps of Dark Hollow. No one in Pine Deep even mentioned his name anymore, and yet Karl Ruger had used his dying breath to speak the name of the only person to have shed more blood, done more harm, destroyed more lives, than Ruger himself had.

Ubel Griswold sends his regards.

Jerry Head said, "No, after all that shit, what else could happen?" He laid his magazine on his thighs. On the cover Eva Longoria was wearing next to nothing and looking happy about it. Crow nodded and they both sat there for a moment watching the second hand on the wall clock tick its way around from 5:54 to 5:55.

"Jerry? Are they sure Ruger's dead?"

"You kidding me?" Head asked, grinning; then he saw that Crow wasn't kidding. "Yeah, that evil son of a bitch is dead for sure. You and your lady popped enough caps in him to kill him five times over."

"You're sure? I mean really sure?"

"Man, if he ain't then I'm going to get myself a hammer and pound a stake through his heart." There must have seen something in Crow's face—in his lack of a responding smile—because he spread his hands and said, "Just kidding, man. You want me to go ask a doctor to double-check on Ruger, be more than happy."

"No . . . no," Crow said, letting it go. "No, it's cool, man. I guess after everything that's happened I'm just paranoid, you know?"

The cop looked at Crow for a moment, the nodded, and smiled a bit more gently. "Yeah, I guess you are. I been on the job eleven years and I never had a run-in with anyone like Ruger. Met some pretty bad dudes, but this Ruger guy was somethin' else—and you had to take him down twice. Must have scared the living shit out of you."

*You have no idea,* Crow thought. He said, "Guess I'm still a bit twitchy."

"Shit, you got every right to be. I know a lot of tough guys—and I'm no pussy myself—but I don't know anyone could have taken Ruger down like you did."

"Hooray for me," Crow said dryly and twirled one finger over his head.

"No, I'm serious, man. Some guys go their whole life never knowing what it's like to really be tough, but you *know,* man. No one can take that away from you."

However, in Crow's mind Ruger's voice whispered *Ubel Griswold sends his regards,* and there was no part of him that felt either heroic or tough.

"Thanks, Jerry. That means a lot."

"Look . . . why don't you try to get some sleep."

Sleep was an unappetizing concept, but Crow faked a yawn anyway. "You're right, Jerry . . . I'm roadkill. Let me see if I can catch a few hours." He closed his eyes and turned away and pretended to fall asleep. After a few minutes he could hear the officer shift uncomfortably in his chair, sigh heavily, and then begin turning the pages of his magazine. The minutes crawled by as Crow lay there, eyes shut, staring at the inner walls of his brain, trying not to see Karl Ruger's face grinning at him. *Ubel Griswold sends his regards.* By the time Head went off shift and a stone-faced Tow-Truck Eddie Oswald took up the post in the guest chair, Crow was feeling like he wanted to rip out his IV and go screaming down the halls.

Crow opened his eyes to bare slits and saw that the hulking part-time police officer was hunched over with his elbows on his knees reading the Bible, his lips moving and his face alight. Crow didn't feel like a sermon from the village religious nut, so he closed his eyes and really tried to sleep. That didn't work. So to pass the time he tried to catalog the damage to his body without actually moving. He could feel the stitches in his mouth, and by probing with his tongue he could feel three loose molars. The two bullet grazes on his sides—improbably one on each love handle—itched more than they hurt, but the rest of his body made up for it by hurting quite a lot. He felt like he'd been run over by a trolley.

Crow lay there in bed, in the false darkness of closed eyes, and relived all that Ruger had done. So much wreckage, so much harm. He heard a faint rustle as Tow-Truck Eddie turned the page of his Bible. *Ubel Griswold sends his regards. Dear God,* Crow thought.

### (2)

Tow-Truck Eddie read and reread the same page and not one word registered. None of the elegant and symbolically complex phrases of St. John's Revelations made a lick of sense to him even though he'd read every one of those pages over and over again to the point that his lips formed the words before his eyes even scanned them, but his conscious mind was not dwelling on the End Times or the opening of the Seals. Instead of Bible or page or word, what he saw was the face of the Beast. Not as he first saw it in a holy vision—disguised as it was in a costume of flesh with curly red hair and freckled apple-red cheeks and a child's body—nor as he had seen it the other night on the road, a figure in hooded sweatshirt and jeans pedaling a bicycle along the black curves of Route A-32. No, the image that swam before Eddie's eyes was the image he had seen just yesterday, right there in Pinelands Hospital, walking bold as the devil—and why should he not be as bold as that?—right out of the front doors just as Eddie and his partner, Norris Shanks, were coming in to sit a guard shift. The Beast had walked right past him, within reach, within arm's length. Eddie could have killed him right there. *Should* have killed him.

*I am the Sword of God,* he thought, and was it not the very truth? Yet he had not done anything, had not acting out his own holy purpose because God Himself had spoken in

his head and stayed his hand. *Wait! Wait until you are alone!*
And he had stayed his hand, though it burned him that the
end of his most sacred mission had been right *there*. What
did it matter that there were other people around? Surely
once the Beast had been killed his true nature and face
would be revealed to all. Wasn't that the point? To reveal the
Beast so that the righteous would see and understand?

He wanted to drop to his knees while Malcolm Crow
slept and beat his head on the floor seven times, to beg his
Father to explain why his hand had been stayed. Could he
risk it? Tow-Truck Eddie looked at the man in the bed and
wondered if he was really asleep. A few minutes ago he had
moved, but that could have just been shifting in his sleep. He
was supposed to be drugged. Surely, he wouldn't wake if
Eddie went to his knees to pray. The nurse had already done
her rounds and wouldn't be back for an hour. He'd only need
a few minutes, just a simple abasement and then his prayers.

There was the sound of footsteps and then a voice spoke
in greeting just outside the door followed by a response. A
conversation started, muffled by the closed door, but it was
right outside. *No,* he thought, *don't risk it, too dangerous.
Just wait, just wait, Father will speak to me. He will make
His will known. Wait. You were told to wait. Be a good son.
Wait. Wait.* Then, like the taste of water on a parched tongue
he heard his Father's voice.

*You are my son and in you I am well pleased.*

Tow-Truck Eddie nearly cried aloud. He wanted so much
to throw himself down on his face and weep, to tear at his
clothes and hair, to beg forgiveness for his weakness and
failure. His hands trembled and he almost dropped his Bible.
"Father . . ." he whispered in his softest voice. "Forgive a
sinner his transgressions."

*You are my beloved son.* The voice rang in his head. *You
are my faithful servant, and you are my holy instrument on
Earth. Do you know this?* It was part of their litany and he
knew it so well that tears filled his eyes.

"I—failed you, my Lord, my Father . . ."

*You are the Sword of God. Do you know this?* The words hit his brain as if the fist of God had punched right through his skull. Eddie had to bite his tongue to stifle the cry that rose like a boiling bubble in his chest. He dropped the Bible on his lap and clamped both hands over his mouth, staring at Crow, who stirred briefly and then settled. After a long minute while he watched to see that Crow was going to remain asleep and as the searing agony of God's displeasure ebbed away like a reluctant tide, Eddie remained frozen there on the edge of his chair.

More gently now, God said, *You are the Sword of God. Do you know this?*

"Yes . . . yes, my Lord!" Eddie said in the tiniest of whispers.

*When the Hand of Righteousness beholds the Beast, what is thy holy purpose?*

"To destroy him, my Lord! I am the servant of God!"

*And to this holy purpose do you dedicate yourself?*

"I am the instrument of the Lord and His will is as my own. With my body, my heart, and my immortal soul shall I serve the will of the Lord."

*Then in my servant I am well pleased. But be ever vigilant for the Beast is clever and the Beast is quick, and to destroy him will be a test and a trial to you. Be not overconfident, be not complacent even in your power. The Sword of God is patient and he is strong.*

"I will be patient as well as powerful, my Lord."

*The servants of the Beast are many and they are strong. Be silent, be secret. Be patient, and do not be deceived. The Beast may wear a child's flesh but it is the Son of Perdition.* There was a pause and Eddie tensed, certain that some great truth was about to be imparted. *It is not death, not blood that will destroy the Beast. It is ritual.*

Joy blossomed in Eddie's chest as he finally, completely *understood.* Now he knew why God had stayed his hand yesterday. He could have killed the skin-suit the Beast wore, but unless he performed a blood ritual then the Beast's spirit would simply find a new host. He closed his eyes against the welling of his joyful tears, nodding as understanding rose like a new sun in his heart. No, he had to take the Beast to some quiet place and then perform the ritual to its utmost conclusion, to the point where he tore the Eucharist from the Beast's chest and tasted it, sealing the Final Covenant.

God whispered silkily into his mind. *You are the Sword of God, and in you I am well pleased.* Gratitude flooded through Eddie and he wept silently, his face in his hands.

### (3)

Crow kept his eyes closed and listened to the faint mumblings as Tow-Truck Eddie spoke to himself. *Is he praying? Of course he is,* he told himself.

Then a few minutes later he thought, *Is he crying?* He listened and after a while he could clearly make out Eddie's nearly silent sobs. *Oh, that's just peachy,* Crow thought.

### (4)

Mike Sweeney was fourteen years old. In eighty-eight days, on December 28, he would be fifteen, but he wasn't entirely sure he would ever live that long. Until recently Mike seldom thought about the future because the future had always seemed like an impossible concept—the future was something that people got to if they had a sane life. There was nothing about Mike Sweeney's life that was sane. Or safe.

He wasn't a handsome kid, though others thought he would grow into it. He had the makings. Curly red hair that was garish now but would darken to reddish-brown if he lived into his twenties, good bones, a splash of freckles, blue eyes. Those eyes were his best point, and certainly the thing that Anna Marie Hellinger, who was in his English class, thought made him look brooding and mysterious. She wasn't wrong. Mike knew a thing or two about brooding. He did it well, he did it often, and he had reason.

When Mike was still in diapers, his father, Big John Sweeney, had gone sailing through the guardrail up on

Shandy's Curve and had been cooked in his car at the bottom of the ravine. Before grass had started to grow on Big John's grave, Mike's mom, Lois, had let local mechanic Vic Wingate move in, and shortly after that they were married. Though Mike was never aware of it, this was a major town scandal. Big John was well liked and there was always a little suspicion surrounding the crash—the official report was that he had fallen asleep at the worst possible place on Route A-32, but the expression "Oh, horseshit!" was thrown in the face of almost anyone who said that, especially if it was said over beers at the Harvestman Inn, where Sweeney's friends still hung. Suspicion even fell briefly on Vic Wingate, but that was something folks kept to themselves, even at the Harvestman, because Vic was not the kind of guy you made comments about, not unless you wanted to eat puréed food through a wired jaw. Vic Wingate, you see, was a hitter.

Vic was forty-seven years old and except for his eyes— he had the cold and patient eyes of an old crocodile—he could have passed for a fit thirty-five. He was rawboned and flat-bellied, with arms and shoulders that held a promise of quick and ugly power though not bulky muscles like Tow-Truck Eddie, nor the sculpted physique of Terry Wolfe, the town's charismatic and handsome mayor. Vic Wingate had wrestler's muscles and boxer's hands. Vic was battlefield tough and would take a bad hit just to land a crippling blow, though very few hits ever got past him. Vic chose his fights with care, he hit first and hardest, and knew where to hit. Since Mike was four Vic had used him to practice the art of hitting, flicking out with apparent laziness to knock Mike sprawling, or rapping him hard enough on the top of the head to drop him to his knees. If Mike had a dime for every time he'd felt Vic's hand he could have saved all the struggling farms in the borough of Pine Deep.

Until last night, all of those blows—blows beyond counting—had been slaps. Hard, yes, painful, yes, but open-handed. Now all that had changed. Last night Mike, at the ripe old age of fourteen-going-on-never-grow-up, had graduated to the fist.

It had started after Mike had been late delivering the last of his newspapers and had been hurrying home along the darkened stretch of A-32 when a monstrous wrecker had come barreling down the road and had very nearly run him down. To save himself from being ground to roadkill under the twenty-four-inch wheels, Mike had swung his bicycle off the road with an agility and speed that was a surprise to him even while it was happening. The wrecker had missed him by inches and Mike had gone ass-over-heels into a pumpkin patch, cracking a rib, bruising his skin, and banging his head. It wasn't the most graceful landing, but it was a landing, and you know what they say about landings you walk away from.

By the time Mike had peeled himself up from the ground and struggled his wheezing way to the road, the wrecker had gone and Mike was even further behind Vic's curfew. He'd been picked up (actually, almost run down again) by Malcolm Crow, the guy who owned the store where he bought his comics and model kits, and had tooled around with him for a while, winding up all the way out at the Haunted Hayride. Crow had called his friend, Mayor Wolfe, who had in turn called Vic to come pick him up. Vic drove out to get him and when Mike had opened his mouth to greet Vic, his stepfather had silenced him with a punch to the stomach that was so hard—so shockingly hard—that Mike thought that his guts were being smashed against his spine. Then Vic grabbed him by the hair and the back of his belt and had flung him into the car and driven home. That alone would have been bad enough, but once they were inside the door, Vic had really gone to work on him. That first blow to the stomach was followed by an encore of punches to just about every part of Mike that Vic could reach. He beat him from the front hallway all the way into the kitchen and when Mike was tucked into a corner Vic had dragged him out into the open and continued beating him.

It was right about that point where something very odd had happened to Mike, and in the space of a heartbeat Mike felt everything *change*. It was as if he just stepped outside of his body and stood apart, indifferent to the blows that rained down on him, separated from the pain and terror as surely as he was separated from the flesh and nerve endings that were under assault. It was the weirdest feeling in his life. He was aware of an actual physical shift as his consciousness lifted and moved to another place, just a few feet away, watching Vic as he grunted and sweated and hit. He watched Vic and saw the man's muscles bunch and roll, saw his hands move up and down, saw him shift to put power behind each blow. It was fascinating, like watching a machine on an assembly line, and he found that he could study it with a total lack of emotional involvement. The hands rose and snapped down, sometimes as slaps, sometimes as punches, and as he watched, Mike saw something else, too. He saw Vic's face grow steadily more red, saw sweat burst from his pores, saw his hands redden with tissue damage each time a blow struck one of Mike's elbows or his forehead, saw the labored heave of his chest as the beating took its toll on Vic. Mike saw Vic, the forty-seven-year-old man, not Vic the indestructible machine.

As revelations went, it was a monster. All night long Mike worked it out. Vic was forty-seven. Mike was fourteen. If he lived—*if*—then in ten years he would be twenty-four and Vic would be fifty-seven. Vic was getting older and from now on he wouldn't be getting stronger; Mike, on the other hand, *would*. Though Mike often doubted that he would really live to be twenty-four, knowing that he *could* outlive and outlast Vic was enough. Of course, the thought that he might die was an equal comfort, because Vic couldn't do much to him then, either. The key was that if he lived long enough, he would outlast Vic Wingate. One day Mike would be a fully grown adult man and Vic would be—*old*. All Mike had to do was endure. Vic was human. It was Mike's version of a win-win scenario.

That was the first part of the revelation and it wasn't until dawn this morning that Mike had gotten the second wave of the revelation, which was equally comforting but in an entirely different way. Or, perhaps it was comforting to an entirely different part of Mike Sweeney—for, truth to tell, there were a lot of different parts to that boy.

At dawn he'd gotten up and had staggered on wobbly legs into the bathroom to piss blood. He didn't bother to turn the light on. There was a faint dawn glow coming in through the frosted glass of his bathroom window, but he knew the smell. Uric acid mixed with copper. It wasn't the first time he'd pissed blood strong enough to smell it. Vic was a treat to live with. He finished urinating, washed his hands, and as he turned to go back to bed he rubbed his hand across his stomach, probing at the mound of the massive hematoma that had blossomed from Vic's punch. It was gone. His probing fingers pushed into the pale skin of his belly and found no hard swelling at all. He stopped in the doorway and pressed harder. Ah, yes, it was there, but smaller, deeper. An *older* pain, like a wound that was going away.

Mike stopped and turned, reaching out for the light switch, flooding the bathroom with a blue-white glow that made his mirrored image look as pale as a ghost. He closed the door and stood before the full-length mirror on the inside of the door, squinting at his reflection. In pajama bottoms and no shirt, he was a mass of bruises, to be sure, and the ones on his face were the worst. One eye was puffed nearly closed and there were blood crustings under both nostrils, more of it under his left earlobe that had been torn by a punch, and a ridge of knuckle marks on his jaw and lips. He turned and looked at his side, where he'd landed on a pumpkin, and the bruise glowed a fierce purple over the cracked rib. All of that was as it should be, as he expected. Nevertheless the bruise on his stomach, which was the worst of all the injuries, was now nothing more than a faintness of red, like a blush, not even as scarlet as the red from a belly flop into a pool. Last night—not eight hours ago—it had been a swelling mound, a volcano about to blow with a dark purple fist-size core surrounded by every shade of blue and red. Now it was almost gone.

Mike Sweeney stared at the bruise—at the absence of a

bruise—and then looked into the mirror image of his own blue eyes. He looked and looked, searching for answers in those familiar eyes—and then just like that flick of a switch that had made him step out of his body last night, those eyes were not familiar at all. One second he was looking into the eyes of Mike Sweeney, fourteen going on fifteen, teenage paperboy and favorite punching bag of the town's meanest son of a bitch and the very next second he was looking into the eyes of someone he didn't know at all. These new eyes were older, deeper, *stranger.* The blue was the same shade but it was flecked with red as if tiny drops of blood were sprinkled throughout each iris. The pupils were huge, like a cat's at night, and the whites were veined with red. The face was different, too. Still bruised, but now the bruises looked superimposed over a different face, which was also older, with a stronger jaw and skin that was gaunt and stretched over brow and cheekbones. The lips of this stranger's mouth were thin and hard as if he was fighting a grimace of pain, and the upper lip was cut by a thick white scar. The hair had, indeed, turned reddish brown.

Mike Sweeney stared at this face for a long time and the longer he stared the clearer the image in the mirror became, and the less clear the look in the flesh-and-blood face was. Those eyes, his real eyes, dulled into glass as if they were the eyes of a mannequin. Anyone looking at those eyes would have said that there was no one home.

At fourteen, Mike had never heard the expression *fugue state* before. Had he been in any way cognizant of what was happening at that moment—which would be a paradoxical impossibility—he would have seen a true fugue state. For the moment, however, Mike Sweeney was indeed not home. At that moment there was no Mike Sweeney. There was something *else.* Call it a chrysalis.

He turned and went back to bed, his body functioning with reflexive efficiency even to the point of turning out the bathroom light. He climbed into bed, pulled the covers up, and lay there, staring up at the ceiling and seeing absolutely nothing. Certainly he didn't see the ghostly figure of a gray-skinned man with a guitar sitting on the chair of his computer table.

When he woke later that morning, he would remember nothing at all about what he had seen in the mirror, and the thought that the bruise on his stomach had healed too fast would not even enter his mind.

As the boy slept, the figure sitting on the chair sat and stared at him, leaning forward, elbows on knees, eyes intent on the lines of the boy's face, wondering if he should be filled with hope or despair.

It was a toss-up.

### (5)

Detective Sergeant Frank Ferro of the Philadelphia Police Department's narcotics division was a tall middle-aged man with dark hair going gray, dark brown skin, and a face that generally looked as dour and lugubrious as a funeral director's. Exhaustion was painted on his features and evident in the droop of his broad shoulders. It had been a long couple of days since he and his partner, Vince LaMastra, had followed Ruger's trail to Pine Deep and had stayed to oversee the manhunt. Hours of grueling work as well as exposure to the killer's grotesque handiwork had burned Ferro down to a weary, shambling shadow of himself. He had only recently come back to his hotel room after the incident at the hospital, and was heading into the bathroom to take a shower, when his cell phone rang. When you're a cop, a call before dawn is never going to be good news, and he paused for just a moment, giving the cell phone an accusatory glare as if it was a friend who had kicked him when he was down; then he bent and scooped up the phone from the bedside table and flipped it open. "Ferro."

"Frank?" It was Vince LaMastra, sounding tired but stressed. "I just got a call from Chief Bernhardt . . . those two officers we left at the Guthrie Farm to maintain the crime scene . . . ?" He ended it like a question.

"What about them?"

"Frank . . . they're dead. Both of them."

*"What?"*

"I don't have the details, Frank. Got to be Boyd, though. There's no one else . . ."

"No . . ." he breathed, squeezing his eyes shut against the immensity of the news and against his own tottering weariness. He took a deep breath. "Two minutes, Vince. In the lobby." He disconnected and stared at the middle distance for a long moment.

"Jesus Christ," he said and reached for his gun.

# Chapter 2

## (1)

"Hi, is this Lois Wingate?"

"Yes?"

The voice on the phone was soft, cautious, and Crow could picture her pale and timid face, the eyes that always looked afraid. No wonder, he thought, being married to Vic Wingate must be a real treat. "Lois, this is Malcolm Crow. You remember me from high school? I own the—"

"Yes. That store where Mike gets his comics."

"Right, and sorry for calling so early. I don't know if Mike told you yet, but I offered him a job at my store starting tomorrow."

"He has his paper route."

"I know, but I think I can pay him a bit better than what he makes delivering papers, and he'll get a discount at the store. Plus," and here he was careful not to let any of his contempt for Vic into his voice, "he won't be out as late."

There was a pause and Crow knew she was making the connection. Crow suspected that Lois had probably felt the back of Vic's hand more than once, and shared awareness might work in Mike's favor.

"That would be fine," Lois said at last. "Do I need to sign something . . . ?"

"Work papers, yeah, and I'll send some home with Mike."

There was another pause. "I heard about you on the news last night. And about your friend, Val Guthrie. I was sorry to hear about your troubles."

"Thanks. I'll pass that along to Val."

A final pause. "I'll pray for you." She hung up quietly.

Crow looked at the phone for a bit, touched by that last comment, as hurried as it was. "Right back atcha," he said softly.

His second call was to Terry Wolfe, but all he got was voice mail. He called Terry's office, his home, his cell, and even his wife Sarah's cell. Nothing. He tapped the cover of his cell phone with his thumb, thinking; then he dialed the numbered for the deputy mayor, Harry LeBeau, a fussy little man who had taken the unpaid job only because no one else wanted it. LeBeau answered on the third ring. "Harry? It's Crow."

"Crow! Dreadfully sorry to hear about—"

Crow cut him off. "Thanks, Harry . . . look, I'm trying to find Terry. Any idea where he is?"

"Heavens, no. I've been trying to get him since last night. Gus has been calling me every fifteen minutes since—well, since what happened to you at the hospital—but no one's seen hide nor hair."

"Crap. Look, if he gets in touch have him call me on my cell." He closed his phone and mulled that over. Where the hell was Terry?

**(2)**

Four floors below where Crow sat in bed making calls, Dr. Saul Weinstock leaned back in the creaking wood swivel chair of the morgue attendant's office, hefted his legs to prop his sneakered heels on his desk, crossed his ankles, and stirred six packets of raw sugar into the coffee that he steadied on his thigh. Starbucks Venti dark roast, and piping hot. A bag with two chocolate croissants lay on the desk by his feet and the office CD player was tinkling with a live recording of *Jim West at the Maiko II*. Carefree stuff, improvised and witty. Weinstock was constructing the moment to be as casual and relaxed as the piano jazz that filled the air, consciously stage managing his own mood because the alternative was to run screaming through the halls, and he did not think that would be good for his patients.

His cell phone chirped and he pulled it from its belt clip, saw that it was his wife, and flipped it open with a smile. "Good morning, sweetie." He looked at the wall clock. Six-fifty-four. "What are you doing up this early? The kids okay?"

"They're fine. I just couldn't sleep, thinking about Val and Crow." Rachel sounded tired. "How are they?"

"Sleeping, which is a mercy." He filled her in on Val and Crow's injuries and the prognosis, though he didn't tell her that Val was pregnant—something only he and Val knew—and that because of it she was having to tough out the pain with nothing stronger than Tylenol. "They'll be okay, though. The real thing is that I have to schedule two autopsies."

"On Yom Kippur?" Rachel said, and Weinstock winced, then flicked a glance at the calendar. He had totally forgotten.

"I'll be done long before sunset, honey," he said quickly. "But even so, with all that's going on, I don't think God is going to single me out for punishment if I don't atone enough. I think he's concentrating on the entire town at once."

"Are you fasting at least?" she asked just as Weinstock reached for a chocolate croissant, and he yanked his hand back as if he'd been burned.

"Sure," he said.

"Saul . . . ?"

"Well, fasting-ish, anyway. Just coffee." He reached over and folded the bag closed, considered, and then put a file folder over the bag to hide it.

"Saul, my folks are expecting us at schul this evening. Can I tell them you'll be there?"

"Rachel, honey . . . with what's going on in town . . . I'm just not sure I can make that promise. Like I said, I have two autopsies to do today, and both of them are important to this police thing that's going on."

She made a sound like she had tasted something nasty. "Henry and that Ruger character?"

"Uh huh, and I don't mind slicing Ruger, but I have to tell you, honey, I just can't bring myself to take a scalpel to Henry Guthrie. It'd be like cutting up my Uncle Stanley." Weinstock set his cup down and rubbed his eyes. "It's weird . . . I never thought of what I do as gruesome before, but the thought of cutting open Henry is just plain creepy."

"Then don't do it," Rachel said. "Let Bob Colbert handle it. He didn't even know Henry."

He sipped his coffee. "This is just all too crazy, Rache. Just too frigging weird for Pine Deep." The real kicker had been the autopsy he had performed the day before on the body of Tony Macchio, one of Ruger's accomplices. For some reason the cops had not been able to discern Ruger had first shot Macchio and then tore him apart. Literally tore him apart, apparently with his bare hands. And his teeth. Weinstock had never seen anything like it, even in medical texts, and outside of slasher films he had never even heard of anything like it. Ruger was a monster, and one that was scarier than anything that Crow had ever cooked up for the town's famous Haunted Hayride. No fangs, no bat wings or bugeyes, and seeing his handiwork, actually being wrist deep in the bloody leavings, had shaken Weinstock to his core. He knew it, too, hence the stage dressing to affect an air of calm before starting today's postmortems. He closed his eyes and sighed. "You're right, honey, Bob can do it."

"Good. No sense putting yourself through anything more if you don't have to."

"Okay, sweetie, let me go make some calls. Give Abby and David a kiss for me. Tell them I'll be home later, and, honey, I promise I'll be there in time for synagogue. Hand to God."

"I love you," Rachel said, a lot of meaning in her voice.

"Me, too, sweetie. Bye." He snapped the phone shut, took a long sip, and sat there with his eyes closed for a while listening to the music, letting the notes play over his nerves like a masseuse's fingers. He opened his eyes and stared at the file folder that hid the croissants, pushed it aside, grabbed the bag and opened it, and stared into it with naked longing. Then he scrunched the bag up and threw it in the trash can, uttering a string of expletives that would require some heavy-duty atoning.

Abruptly he sat up, set his coffee cup down on the desk, and walked with forced calmness into the cold room where the double row of stainless-steel drawers gleamed in the bright fluorescent lights. He went to drawer #14, jerked the lever down and swung open the door, then grabbed the hard plastic handle on the slab and pulled it out along its rollers. A body lay under a white sheet, the cloth tented on nose, chest, and toe-tips, but Weinstock whipped the sheet down to reveal the corpse beneath. The killer's skin was blue-white and waxy, the eyelids half-open showing shark-black eyes. The body had not yet been prepped for autopsy and was still clothed in shirt, jacket, and trousers that were filthy and pocked with bullet holes crusted with blood that had dried to a chocolaty thickness. Even in death Karl Ruger wore a twisted smile, his lips curled away from the jagged stumps of his broken teeth. Weinstock considered. Maybe it was a grimace of pain, he conceded, but damn if it didn't look like a shit-eating smile.

Weinstock was alone in the morgue—his nurse, Barney, was working the three to eleven—so there wasn't a living soul to hear Weinstock when he leaned over Ruger's body and said, "You are a total piece of shit and I hope you burn in hell!"

He spat on Ruger's dead face and then slid him back into his cold box with a grunt of effort that sent the slab slamming against the wall, then he swung the door shut hard enough to send echoes bouncing off all of the tiled walls. He sagged against the bank of stainless-steel doors, closed his eyes, folded his arms tightly across his chest, and concentrated on beating down the hatred in his brain, muttering, ". . . Shit, shit, shit . . ."

When the intensity finally ebbed, Weinstock rubbed his eyes with the heels of his palms and then pushed himself away from the wall of doors, walked slowly across the morgue floor, paused once in the doorway to the office and threw back a look that was half embarrassed and half venomous, then swept his hand down over the light switches and left, heading back to his coffee and jazz and his cell phone.

Inside the cold drawer, Karl Ruger lay in the silence of death, still and breathless. There were no longer any drops of spittle on his face. He'd already licked them off.

### (3)

By the time Frank Ferro and Vince LaMastra got to the Guthrie farm, there were twenty officers, two full ambulance crews, four press vehicles erecting microwave towers, and a crowd of rubberneckers who were trying to get past the yellow crime scene tape. It was frosty cold and a frigid mist floated a foot above the ground. When LaMastra asked a uniform where the chief was, the officer pointed down a lane that had been trampled through the corn. Though the sun was rising, there were still thick shadows clustered around the base of the cornstalks and all along the path. Surrounding the scene Coleman camping lanterns had been placed. The shadows leaned back away from the lanterns, but they did not fully retreat.

Jerry Head hurried up to them as they walked along the path to where the bodies had been found. He looked bleary eyed with exhaustion. "Sarge, I was about to turn in when I got the call. My motel's right up the road, so I was able to get here in a hot minute. I secured the scene best I could, but we're ass deep in civilians around here. Okay if I run some of them off?"

"Good call, Jerry. Thanks," Ferro said, clapping him on the shoulder, and a second later he could hear Head's deep voice booming out behind them. He nodded to LaMastra and they moved forward through the throng of officers until they stood at the edge of the clearing and saw what lay there.

"Holy Mother of God," LaMastra said, and actually took a half-step back as if he hoped he could step back out of any reality where what he saw was possible. He gagged and turned away, staring at the tops of the nearby corn while he worked his throat. "Jesus Christ, Frank . . . what the hell is *wrong* with this town?"

Ferro looked at his partner for a moment, finding that easier to bear while he composed his face into one he'd want the local cops to see. Now was not a time to come unglued. Breathing in and out through his nostrils, Ferro turned slowly back to the clearing and forced himself to take in every detail, trying to access that part of his mind that could be cool, detached, clinical. It was a struggle not to yell. "It's not the town, Vince. This is our mess—Ruger and Boyd."

LaMastra gave a single fierce shake of his head. "You're wrong there, Frank. It is this goddamn town."

Ferro had nothing to say to that. There was a twenty-foot square that was formed partly by the intersection of two access paths through the corn, but which had been expanded by many of the stalks being trampled down. The far side of the clearing was edged by a white slat fence that trailed away to either side into the shadowy fields. A tall post reared up above the fence and a raggedy and headless scarecrow hung in limp cruciform over the scene. On the ground at the foot of the post was the better part of a shattered jack-o'-lantern with a wicked grin. Below the scarecrow lay the first of the two bodies. Officer Nels Cowan, late of the Pine Deep Police Department, lay in a rag-doll sprawl that spoke of arms that had been wrenched nearly out of their sockets. His head was tilted back at an impossible angle on a splintered spine; the backward tilt revealing a savage tear in the throat that exposed a severed windpipe and the knobbed inner edge of the spine. His service sidearm lay on the ground inches from his hand.

Near him, with one outstretched hand reaching up to lay across Cowan's left ankle, was what had once been Jimmy

Castle, late of Crestville PD. His throat was also a raw and shredded mess, as if dogs had been at him. Castle's eyes bulged from their sockets with a terminal and everlasting astonishment at what he had seen.

There was blood everywhere and pieces of torn red matter that could have been cloth from the uniforms of the officers or it could have been their own flesh. Scattered around Castle's body were at least a dozen shell casings, and the faint bite of cordite still hung in the air. As he and LaMastra pulled on latex gloves, Ferro stood there and read the scene, fighting back the ache in his chest that made him want to take LaMastra's cue and flee this insane town. He fished a pack of gum from his pocket, unwrapped a stick slowly—his trick for controlling the shaking of his hands—and then placed it on his tongue. Chewing would give his mouth something to do other than gape, and the mint fought off the nausea.

The scene was a puzzle, and he stood there, chewing, evaluating the details. Two bodies, savagely torn. Worse than what had been done to Ruger's buddy Macchio. That killing had, at least, a sense of ritual about it, but this looked to be less . . . what was the word? Controlled? *Animals?* It seemed unlikely. Not in this part of Pennsylvania. Shell casings everywhere. That meant that Castle had nearly emptied his magazine. Castle was ex-Pittsburgh PD—it seemed pretty unlikely he's have fired off that many rounds without hitting something, but there was no other body around. No trail of blood, either, or at least no blood trail beyond the spatters that filled the clearing. So if Castle hit anything, there was no immediate visible evidence of it.

It was a mystery and Frank Ferro hated mysteries. He hadn't joined the police force to solve them, and he hadn't welcomed the promotion to detective division to pursue them. Ferro preferred order. He had a hunter's nature, and that was something he liked: the hunt for clear answers, not for the unexplainable. When he and LaMastra had come to Pine Deep on the trail of Karl Ruger and his accomplices, they'd both thought it was going to be a straightforward hunt. Difficult, yes, dangerous, to be sure—but in essence a hunt. Now, after two days in this town he knew that the hunt had tangled itself into the weirdest set of circumstances he'd ever encountered. The most brutal murders of his career, killers who can take a chestful of bullets and still have the strength and power to lay siege to a hospital and nearly kill three people. Dead civilians, dead policemen. Ferro unwrapped a second stick of gum and chewed it as he stood there, his face giving nothing away, his dark eyes flat and apparently emotionless as he worked the scene in his head. He saw something else that puzzled him. The blood. There were smears and splashes, sprays from opened arteries that painted the corn and the slat fence . . . but throat wounds like that, even if the hearts of the men had stopped quickly, should have spilled a lake of blood. There wasn't nearly enough of it. He stepped forward and took a pencil from his pocket, then knelt and probed the ground as close to Cowan's shoulder as he could reach without risking the integrity of the crime scene. The pencil slipped easily down into the soft earth. Despite the chill, the rain of two nights ago still left the earth very muddy and yielding. He pushed the pencil down three inches and then withdrew it to examine it like a dipstick. There was a little blood and a lot of damp earth. Not enough blood, though, not enough by a long shot. It should have seeped deeper than this. He rose, looking around for other anomalies. That was the smart thing to do—to be a scientist, a criminalist, not a gawking bystander, and he could feel his detachment creeping back by slow degrees. He caught LaMastra's eye and then jerked a chin toward the blood splashes. "You reading this?"

The younger man had seen Ferro probe the ground with his pencil and understood the implications. "The blood?"

"Uh huh."

"Maybe the ME will figure it out." He pointed with his Maglite to a spot in the clearing where bare earth showed through the mess. "You see that?" There were several footprints clearly pressed into the mud. He glanced at the shoes of both dead officers, then grunted. "Gotta be the perp's."

"Make sure the lab guys take castings. See how they match up against the ones we got from Ruger and Boyd." Ferro rose, his knees creaking a little.

"Not going to be Ruger's," LaMastra said.

"No," Ferro agreed.

"So . . . you make Boyd for this shit?"

Ferro gave a small half-shrug. "Who else? Macchio's dead. Ruger's sure as hell dead. Unless there was a fourth man in that car, the only suspect we have left is Boyd."

"Yeah," LaMastra said dubiously, "but I don't like the feel of that, y'know?"

"No kidding, Vince." With a sour-faced LaMastra in tow, Ferro walked the perimeter of the crime scene, noting everything, working the catalog into his brain, fighting the mixture of revulsion, hatred, and fear that was boiling in his gut. LaMastra tapped him on the shoulder, and jerked his head toward the far side of the clearing, where Chief Gus Bernhardt was standing next to a young man carrying an oversize medical bag. Gus waved him over and the two detectives circled back to them.

"Frank, this is Dr. Bob Colbert from Pinelands College," Gus said, pointedly looking at Ferro rather than at what was behind him. "Bob teaches anatomy and forensics at the college and fills in for Saul Weinstock on ME work once in a while." They were all wearing latex gloves, so they just nodded to one another as Gus introduced the detectives.

The doctor looked to be a young forty with black hair and a pronounced Gallic nose. "Saul couldn't get out here," he said in a thick northern Minnesota accent. "I'm, uh . . . kind of sorry I was available."

"I heard that," agreed LaMastra. "This is some of the sickest shit I ever saw."

"I'll pronounce them so you can get your lab team to work. I can only imagine how badly you want to get whoever did this."

Ferro met his gaze. "You have no idea, doctor." He ordered everyone out of the clearing except for the ME. The other cops moved back reluctantly, their faces white with shock and grim with frustrated anger. Chief Bernhardt turned a face to Ferro that was gray and sweaty. He tried to say something but it stuck in his throat. There were tears brimming in his eyes and he looked ten years old. Ferro just nodded to him and left him alone for the moment.

Ferro drifted along behind the ME, making the young doctor nervous by peering over his shoulder as he examined the wounds, palpated the flesh on the throats of each victim, and took temperature readings. As the doctor worked Ferro continued to read the scene himself, not liking what he was seeing for a hundred different reasons. "Well?" Ferro asked after the ME had finished his cursory examination.

"Well, I guess I have to officially say that they're dead. They are. Boy are they." The doctor's face was as sweaty as Bernhardt's.

"Cause of death?"

The doctor pursed his lips. "I'm going to let Saul Weinstock do the post, but I've lived in hunting country my whole life, and I've hunted bear in Potter County here in Pennsylvania and in Minnesota, where I grew up."

Ferro frowned. "What are you saying? That a bear did this?"

"A bear? No, the bite radius doesn't look big enough, but if I was to make a horseback guess here, Detective, I'd say that yeah, *some* kind of animal was involved."

"You're calling this an animal attack?"

"Detective, I'm not calling this anything but two dead guys. I mean, two dead officers. What I'm saying is that from a superficial analysis—lacking the specifics of a postmortem—the wounds *appear* to be bite marks, which *suggests* animal attack."

Ferro stepped closer and dropped his voice. "Has Dr. Weinstock shared with you the nature of the wounds he identified on the victim found yesterday?"

"Tony Macchio? Yes. Among other things he was bitten."

"It was Dr. Weinstock's opinion that the bites were made by human teeth. He lifted impressions. No trace of animal attack, according to him."

Colbert nodded. "Right, I know, but that's not what I think we have here, and mind you, it is possible that an animal came upon the bodies after they'd already been killed, but what I see—what I *think* I see—are different kinds of bite marks. And before you ask, no, they are not human bites. No way. Human bites are nasty but the teeth are pretty blunt. The skin is bruised more because human teeth aren't used to biting through living skin, there's more blunt tearing and ripping than we have here. Plus, it's generally easy to differentiate between human and animal bite patterns just from observation. Look at an apple that's had a bite taken out of it, you can tell if it was a man, a dog, a cat, whatever."

Ferro looked over at the clear impressions made by a set of shoes other than the pairs worn by the cops—marks that almost certainly had to have been left by the killer—and then looked down at the bodies. He looked around for animal prints and saw nothing. "So what kind of bite do we have here?"

Colbert mopped frigid sweat from his face. "I don't know. Maybe a dog. It's big enough for a dog, if we're talking dog. A German shepherd or something bigger. Nothing smaller, that's for sure."

"And you're sure these wounds aren't postmortem. I mean . . . it seems pretty clear that there was a third man here, and there's a good chance it's one of the fugitives involved in the manhunt. Are you saying that this wasn't a murder but that these two armed officers were instead attacked by an animal?"

"Detective, I'm not sure of anything. I said that this was a horseback guess—I don't want you to hold me to it. Whatever left the bite marks could have come along postmortem, sure. The state forest is a stone's throw away from here, something might have smelled blood and come prowling after your fugitive killed them. Bottom line is I don't really know."

Ferro nodded. "Fair enough. One more thing, doctor . . . what do you make of the amount of blood?"

Colbert looked at him for a moment, then looked around,

opened his mouth to say something, then stopped and looked at the scene again. "Hunh," he said.

"Tell me what you're thinking."

"Well," Colbert said, nodding at the bodies as he stripped off his latex gloves, "there is certainly a great deal of visible blood spill and spatter . . ."

"But?"

"But given the severity of the injuries—to two grown men—the amount of visible blood is less than you would expect." He cut a look at Ferro. "That's what you're referring to, isn't it?"

Without directly answering, Ferro said, "I would appreciate it if you noted that in your preliminary report." When the doctor nodded, Ferro added, "Dr. Colbert, I'd prefer you only spoke with Dr. Weinstock about this, and no one else. Are we clear on this?" His brown eyes bored into Colbert's and the ME nodded, then moved away without another word.

As the doctor left LaMastra ushered the police photographer and the techs onto the scene. The photographer's flash was popping wildly as Gus Bernhardt lumbered heavily up, his eyes now dry but still looking hurt. He had a cell phone in his hand and was flipping the lid closed as he approached.

"A word with you, Frank?" murmured Gus, touching his elbow and then guiding him to one side out of earshot. "Frank, we're losing control of this situation." Ferro gave him the kind of look a comment like that deserved, but Gus shook his head. "No, what I mean is that we really don't have the manpower and resources to do this. Half the men we have on the force are local shopkeepers and gas station attendants dressed up like cops, and you know that as well as I do. They're beat from working double shifts. These two poor sonsabitches—Cowan and Castle—they were local boys. No way we should have stuck them out here alone."

"They were two well-armed and well-trained professional police officers," Ferro said quietly.

"Yeah, okay. Maybe." Gus wiped his mouth with the back of his hand. He was a massive, sloppy fat man in a poorly tailored uniform that was all decked out with whipcord and silver buttons. No matter what the temperature his face was perpetually flushed red and shining with sweat, though at the moment he was even redder and wetter than usual. He looked like he wanted to say something, but he didn't have the words to express what he was feeling. Ferro didn't much like the chief, but he felt sorry for him.

"Has the mayor been informed about this?"

"No one seems to know where he is. We've tried everything, but his cell is turned off, he's not in his office, and his wife said that Terry wasn't home."

"That seems odd, doesn't it? Did his wife seem agitated? Was she worried?"

"Well, I didn't think to ask," Gus said, and saying it reinforced for both of them the difference between him and Ferro. The Philly cop would have asked, and would have done it as a matter of routine, and they both knew it. Gus changed the subject. "Could Ruger have done this before he set out for the hospital last night?"

LaMastra, who had just joined them, said, "No, sir. Jimmy Castle had called into your own office at 4:57 A.M. That's what? Just shy of two hours ago. He'd called in a request for coffee and hot food because it was getting cold out here."

Gus's face was screwed up in puzzlement. "That don't make sense. Ruger was dead by then. Macchio's been dead for two days and Boyd was spotted in Black Marsh yesterday, apparently heading southeast. So . . . who's that leave?"

"Has to be Boyd," LaMastra said. "No one else it can be."

"But *why*? From what you guys told me Ruger was the only killer. Boyd was a flunky. What'd you call him? A 'travel agent' . . . he mostly just got real crooks out of the country and stuff like that. Why would a guy like that screw up his own getaway to come back here and kill two cops? It doesn't make sense."

"Christ, Chief, nothing about this case has made a damn bit of sense since Ruger and his buddies wrecked their car here," LaMastra said.

"Wish I could say that I had a working theory about

what's going on," Ferro said, "but I don't. Perhaps the ME's report will give us something we can use."

A few yards behind them, hidden in the lee of an ambulance, was a small, balding man with wire-frame glasses and a handheld tape recorder. Willard Fowler Newton, who doubled on news and features for the tiny *Black Marsh Sentinel,* was staring at Ferro's broad back, and like Chief Bernhardt and the coroner, he was sweating badly despite the cold. He had slipped through the police cordon in hopes of getting enough for a good news story for the morning papers, but he sure as hell didn't expect to get this.

# Chapter 3

## (1)

"Let's go inside. I'm freezing my nuts off out here, Frank," complained LaMastra, shivering in his light blue PHILA PD windbreaker. Ferro didn't seem to mind the cold as much, or at least had more discipline and didn't show it, but he offered no argument when LaMastra repeated his suggestion. They moved into the Guthrie farmhouse, which was already crowded with cops of various kinds. Most of the officers looked expectantly at Ferro, but one glance told them that he had nothing new to say. The detectives went into the kitchen and the local officers seated at the table cleared out as soon as LaMastra gave them The Look. Ferro sat down and sipped his coffee; LaMastra strolled over and peered into the big pot that stood on the stove. The turkey soup was two-days cold and there was a thin film of grease congealed on the surface. "I'll just heat this up a bit," he said, looking at Ferro for approval. "Shame to let it go to waste. Think it's still good?"

Ferro was too tired to care either way, so LaMastra stirred the soup vigorously, replaced the lid and sat down across from his partner. Vince LaMastra was a big blond ex-jock who had played wide receiver for Temple University before entering the police academy. At thirty he still had the narrow hips, broad shoulders, and bulky muscles of a college ballplayer, but now there were the beginnings of crow's feet at the corners of his bright blue eyes and laugh lines etched around his mouth. Not that he was laughing at the moment as he sat hunched over, forearms on the table, frowning at Ferro. "Gus was right—this case is getting away from us, Frank."

Ferro snorted. "We never really had our hands on it. This was a runaway train from the first." Frank Ferro was older and more battered than his partner, his dark brown skin marked here and there by faded pink scars—souvenirs from his days walking a beat in North Philly. His manner was quiet and refined, but his eyes were cop's eyes. Quick and hard.

"Not what I mean," LaMastra said, shaking his head. "These killings, Frank . . . they bother me—and don't give me that look. I'm not talking about how it makes me feel, 'cause I'm just like every other cop here. It makes me sick and angry and I would give my left nut to have five minutes in a locked room with Kenneth Boyd—if he's actually the prick who did this. No, what I'm saying, Frank, is that I just don't get why Boyd *would* have done this."

"Maybe he hung around Ruger too long. Perhaps homicidal mania is contagious. I don't know."

"How sure are you that Boyd is the killer here? You yourself said this wasn't like Boyd. A guy like Boyd shouldn't even have been at that drug bust that went south. I think Ruger probably planned to screw the deal and then take the money so he could split. He must have found out somehow that Little Nicky suspected that Ruger'd killed his grandparents down in Cape May. The mob's not big on due process, so Ruger figured that a suspicion alone is more than enough wind up on a meat hook somewhere. So since he had to get the hell out of Dodge anyway he set up the drug buy and then deliberately jacked it so that he and his crew could wipe out the Jamaicans and keep the money all for themselves. Main reason to support this is Boyd being there for that buy. He's not a soldier, he's a travel agent. The only reason on earth that Ruger would drag him along is to help him get out of the country afterward. Nothing else makes sense. Boyd's a tool, not a killer. That's one of the things that just doesn't fit." He got up and began stirring the soup.

Ferro shrugged and rolled his coffee cup between his palms, staring at the liquid as it agitated. "Apparently we underestimated Boyd. Maybe he and Ruger partnered because they were cut from the same cloth. Both of them . . . just plain crazy. Just because it's not in Boyd's jacket doesn't mean we really have insight into who he is."

"Let's look at that." LaMastra put the lid back on the pot, turned, and leaned a hip against the counter as he began ticking items off on his fingers. "First, we got Karl Ruger's car breaking down here in Pine Deep. Okay, that makes sense, anyone can have a breakdown. Two, we got Ruger having a serious dispute with Tony Macchio. Who knows why? Maybe he's really, really pissed at Macchio, or maybe he's just a sick psycho son of a bitch and tearing people up is how he unwinds. Either way, he focuses on Macchio and tears him up. Spoils him. *Eats* him, for Chrissakes."

"Perhaps I'll pass on the soup."

"Now, maybe he's trying to scare the living piss out of Boyd at the same time. You know, make a point? Scare him so bad that he won't ever think about double-crossing him."

"But maybe Ruger overdid it," Ferro offered. "From what we were able to get out of Valerie Guthrie, Ruger believed that Boyd broke his leg in a gopher hole and was cooling his heels out in the cornfield, waiting for Ruger to come back with a stretcher. According to her, Ruger was really torn up when he found that Boyd had bugged out, but that whole thing might have been a dodge. Boyd might have pretended to be injured so he could slip away from Ruger."

"Maybe. Point is Ruger's royally pissed and starts blasting away to vent his anger. Shoots Guthrie, beats the shit out of everyone else. Then he dances with that guy Crow and unexpectedly gets his ass handed to him. Okay, so, that leaves Boyd missing. That leaves the money missing."

"And the coke."

"And the coke, right. It also leaves Karl Ruger all messed up and it leaves him as one very pissed-off individual. He goes psycho and maybe he figures that Val Guthrie and Crow are the reasons why his life has suddenly turned to shit, sneaks into the hospital for a little payback, but it turns out bad for him and he gets shot to shit. Exit Karl Ruger from the equation."

Ferro smiled thinly. "Okay, so what is the part you don't like?"

"I'm coming to that. So, Boyd, no matter how crazy he may or may not be, has to be aware that he is being chased down by half the cops on the eastern seaboard. Logic would dictate that he would just cut his losses and split. Which, apparently, he did 'cause he's spotted in Black Marsh heading away from Pine Deep."

"Without the money or the coke," Ferro observed. "Witnesses say he wasn't carrying anything. No bags, nothing."

"Right, because the area is too hot, and no amount of money is going to do him much good in jail or in the morgue. Probably just stuffed his pockets with as much as he could carry and he's gone. Except that he *isn't* gone." He stirred the soup some more. "Now we've got two dead cops and the only criminal in this whole area who has any connection to this place is Boyd. Which is the part I don't like. Think about it, Frank. He comes back to the farm—*why?*"

"Well, for one thing he probably doesn't know Ruger is dead. That hasn't made the papers yet. Maybe he and Ruger had worked out a rendezvous thing. You know—if we get separated meet me at such-and-such place at such-and-such time. Boyd could have been on his way back to the farm thinking that Ruger was going to meet him."

"He'd have to be a complete moron to think that there wouldn't be a police presence at the farm after everything that happened."

"I thought we already agreed Boyd was not the sharpest knife in the drawer."

"Still don't buy it, though."

"Another thought is that maybe he hid the money somewhere around here." LaMastra opened his mouth to speak but Ferro held up a hand. "Consider this, Vince . . . maybe

Boyd let himself be seen in Black Marsh just to establish that he had left Pine Deep. Take the heat off, get us looking in the wrong place. We can assume he knew Macchio was dead, and maybe he witnessed Crow shooting Ruger at the farm the other night and figured that Ruger was dead, too. With the two of them out of the way, and him establishing to witnesses that he was leaving town, then the Pine Deep manhunt is over. Boyd slips back into town to recover the money and drugs he'd hidden."

"Okay, that's a better possibility, though he'd still have to be an idiot to believe it. But why attack the cops? How could that possibly work for him in any scenario?"

"Why not? Maybe they saw him when he came back for his stash?"

"Maybe," LaMastra said and started ladling the soup into a couple of bowls. "But killing two cops? Does that make any sense? Up till now Boyd's been along for the ride and there aren't any murder warrants on him. Even in the video from the shoot-out with the Jamaicans it was clear he didn't even try to hit anyone. Most he's looking at is drug trafficking and flight to avoid. A good lawyer'd have him out in five even without a plea. Why on earth would he want to up the ante against himself by killing two cops? Does that make any sense?"

"Not if he's sane, no. Maybe he's been huffing coke by the handful ever since he hooked up with Ruger. But if Boyd's that wired and desperate, who knows to what extreme he'll go?"

"Okay, but does it make sense to tear them to pieces?" He reached over and placed a bowl in front of Ferro.

"Again, not if you're sane . . . but when it comes right down to it, do we really know that much about Boyd and his psychological makeup?" Ferro shook his head. "Almost everything we have on him is supposition based on known history."

LaMastra sat down with his bowl and for a few minutes he and Ferro said nothing as they started in on the soup, which was a rich turkey stock with lots of chunky vegetables and plenty of meat. The fact that it had been sitting on the stove for two days didn't bother either of them. They'd had much less savory food over the years they'd been on the job.

Ferro nodded. "I don't have a backup plan here, Vince."

LaMastra swallowed and said, "I still don't like it, Frank, because every time I think of it the situation gets worse. I mean, Castle emptied a whole magazine out there. What the hell was he shooting at if not Boyd, and if it was Boyd, how come he missed? And don't try to sell me any bulletproof vest nonsense, because even with a vest at that range that many shots would have broken just about every one of Boyd's ribs."

"Right, and if he didn't miss," Ferro said glumly, "how come Boyd isn't sitting there with a bunch of holes in him? If he was wounded, why was there no visible blood trail leading from the scene?" He sighed. "Maybe we were too hasty about blaming Macchio's death on Ruger."

LaMastra looked at him, his spoon halfway to his mouth. "Jeez-us Christ."

"Just a thought. We know what Ruger was capable of because of Cape May, so we just assumed he'd murdered Macchio, but after what we saw this morning . . . I don't know."

"I don't know either. It's—" LaMastra sucked his spoon for a moment, trying to phrase it, but only came up with, "It's weird."

Ferro thought about that. He finished his soup, got up, walked over to the stove, and stirred the pot for a few moments. "I had thought we'd be heading home today, Vince."

LaMastra looked at the wall as if he could see through it and through the timbers of the house and out into the cornfield. "Those poor bastards. That's no way for cops to go."

"No way for anyone to go."

LaMastra grunted and repeated, quietly, "No way for cops to go."

### (2)

Outside the house, on the other side of the kitchen window, Willard Fowler Newton crouched in the shadows cast by the side of the house. He was flushed from nervousness and the cold wind. He had been leaning against the wall for ten minutes listening to Vince LaMastra and Frank Ferro try to work through the killings. His arm ached from holding a small tape recorder up to the window.

As he crouched there he was trying to make sense of what he'd heard, matching it with the info he'd gotten from that kid, Mike Sweeney, last night. The kid had said something about the man who was the center of the police dragnet being the same guy known in the papers as the Cape May Killer, a mass murderer who was the most wanted man in the country. Newton had been excited at first, but when none of the official press releases had even hinted at the connection, he'd dismissed it. Now, however, what he was hearing from these cops was going off like fireworks in his brain.

Willard Fowler Newton was about to break the biggest story of his career, and he knew for sure that it was going to be a total scoop. No one else had a clue about this stuff. No one.

### (3)

The Bone Man perched like a crow on a slender branch that reached out from the big oak nearest to the house. All the other branches were filled with night birds, their black-on-black feathers rustling drily in the shadows thrown by the house.

The conversation inside the house ended as the two cops got up and headed back to the crime scene and the reporter crabbed sideways along the house, keeping to the shadows until he could make a break and spring for his car parked out on the road. The Bone Man watched him all the way, and then watched the little car cough and sputter its way up the hill and over; then he stood up, featherlight on the branch, which did not even creak under his weight, and leapt down to the ground. He moved in the opposite direction from Newton, deeper into the corn, past policemen who did not see him and the search dogs who did not smell him—though the oldest of them shivered a bit as he passed, heading deep into the field, and then beyond it to the forest. The stink of blood was overwhelming, and he turned in a full circle, his unblinking eyes penetrating the shadows beneath the trees until he found what he was looking for.

The thing that had once been Kenneth Boyd sat on the rotted trunk of a fallen tree, jaw sagging loose, lips rubber, streamers of flesh caught between misshapen teeth, staring stupidly at the smears of dried blood on its hand, eyes as blank as a doll's. The Bone Man stood still for a long time, staring at the thing, then as he moved a step forward the creature raised its gory head and looked around slowly until it saw him step into the sunlight. Instantly the vacuous expression transformed into one of feral hate and appalling hunger. Boyd bounded up and lumbered toward the newcomer, staggering on one broken and twisted leg but showing no flicker of pain. Ragged hands that were tipped with black claws reached out toward him as his mouth opened in a guttural scream of rage and hunger.

The Bone Man said nothing, did nothing, just watched as Boyd rushed at him, watched as he swayed from side to side in a parody of drunkenness. Boyd launched forward with unnatural speed, slashing at him with its claws, snapping at the air with his jagged teeth, rushing forward to try and bowl him over, drag him down, overwhelm him with a savage animal rage. The Bone Man did not try to step aside or run; he merely waited as Boyd leapt the last few yards, snarling with fury—and passed straight through him. The Bone Man turned to see the arc of Boyd's leap end with a bone-snapping impact on the cold ground. Two nails on Boyd's outstretched right hand were torn from their roots, and the creature made no attempt at all to break his fall. Boyd's face smashed into the ground, crunching the cartilage in his nose into pulp and driving a tiny twig deep into the iris of his right eye.

The Bone Man smiled the smallest, thinnest smile. "You thirty years too late trying to kill me, you ugly piece of shit," he said in a voice that was a whispery echo.

The creature bounded forward again, claws tearing the

air, and again he passed through the Bone Man as if he were smoke. The monster tumbled to the ground and once more scuttled around to face him again, mouth wrinkled like a dog's muzzle, eyes blazing with hate. Boyd rose slowly to its feet, standing in a hunchbacked crouch, glaring at him.

"We can keep this shit up all day," the Bone Man said. "I'm a ghost, you dumbass."

Then Boyd froze, head cocked in an attitude of listening, but the Bone Man heard nothing. Boyd sniffed the air with his broken nose, paused and sniffed again. Then as if some unseen hand had reached into his mind and dialed down a rheostat the predatory light went out his eyes and his snarling mouth drooped again into the slack-jawed hang of emptiness. It took two aimless steps backward, turned first to the right and then to the left, both motions apparently without purpose, and after swaying in the sunlight for a full minute, he tottered off across the road back toward the cornfields. The Bone Man watched him go and stood quietly for a long time until even the faintest sounds of his lumbering passage through the corn had faded. He sighed and then sat slowly down on the rotted log, pulling his guitar around so that as he sat it lay across his bony thighs. His long fingers stroked the strings, and as the breeze returned to stir the tips of the tall corn he began to play and sing. It was the old prison blues song, "Ghost Road Blues." The air above and around him seemed heavy and oppressive as it loomed above the farms and forests of Pine Deep. In the clearing near the cornfields where four people had now died, the Bone Man played blues to lament the dead and to preach the gospel of the dark times. Not times coming at the End of Days, but of the darkness here at hand—an October darkness, abroad and hungry.

### (4)

It was a Sunday morning and Mike Sweeney slept late, lost in a dream that played and replayed. In his dream the wrecker that had chased him on Route A-32 didn't miss him;

in his dream the huge black truck with its demonic driver and the ugly gleaming hook caught up with him as he raced along the asphalt. The driver wore Vic's sneering face, though even in the dream Mike didn't think Vic was truly at the wheel. He pedaled his bike faster and faster, his legs pumping insanely, the rubber of the thin tires screaming in a high-pitched wail, the cold wind slicing at him as he fled, but the wrecker kept getting closer and closer. Mike risked a look, daring to glance over one shoulder and there—right *there*!—was the huge silver grille of the truck. He could hear the roar of the engine as it chased him. No, not a roar—it was a growl. Deep, angry, hungry—not at all the sound of a machine but the hunting snarl of a beast. A monster.

"No!" he cried and the sound of his own voice was whipped out of his mouth and blown past him to be gobbled up by the teeth of that gleaming grille. He leaned forward over the bars, his butt up in the air, trying to add more weight and power to his pumping legs and at the same time cut the wind resistance. He flicked another glance over his shoulder and saw that he was pulling away. Inches . . . feet . . . yards. He kept it up, trying to make it to the entrance of the farm just down the road. If he could make that . . . just a few hundred yards now . . . he would be safe. It was Val Guthrie's place. Crow would be there. He'd be safe with Crow and Val.

His chest was an oven that burned up the air as soon as he gasped it in and then set to burning the flesh of his lungs, and still he raced on. Sweat burst from his pores and ran down his face and chest before freezing against his skin, and still he raced on. The growl of the wrecker's engine diminished ever so slightly as he pulled ahead, and still he raced on. Pinwheels of fire exploded in his eyes, and still he raced on. His heart was slamming against the walls of his chest and felt like it was ready to burst, and still he raced on.

Less than a hundred yards now and he began angling wide so that he could make a fast, hard turn left and shoot onto the entrance road. Suddenly there were people lining the side of the road. Silently watching the race as they stood in the shadows. Even in the dark, even at that speed, he could see their faces and read their expressions.

First he passed Terry Wolfe, the mayor, who smiled at him with kindly blue eyes and then reached up to rip his own face off in a sudden splash of blood, revealing beneath the mask of flesh a monster's face, with bloody fangs and blazing eyes.

Mike raced on.

Then he sped by a tall, stick-thin black man in a dirty black suit that was streaked with mud and rainwater. The black man's smile was genuine, and he played a few notes on a beautiful old guitar, picking the notes with the fingers of one hand and stretching those notes out with a gliding touch of a bottleneck slide. The black man said something but his voice made no sound.

Mike raced on.

At the end, as he was about to make his turn, he saw a tall blond man with heavy features and furious eyes step out into the road and grab at his handlebars with both hands. Mike tried to twist free, tried to veer around him, but one powerful hand clamped around the fork tube just below the handles and the bike stopped as surely as if he'd slammed into a wall, and his own momentum sent him flying over the handlebars. He rolled in midair, trying to land on his feet, needing to land running, but he kept turning and slammed onto his back with so much force that he could hear bones break all along his back. He skidded along the blacktop, his hooded jacket shredding, and then his shirt . . . and then his skin. By the time he stopped the long slide, there was a ten-foot smear of red painted on the blacktop. Mike cried out in agony and raised his head to see where the truck was and how much time he had, trying at the same time to read his body to see how badly he was hurt. He raised his head and looked down the length of his body and there, framed between the up-turned toes of his sneakers, was the wrecker.

Three feet away.

It would have been some small comfort to Mike if that had been the point at which he woke up from the dream, but it wasn't. He felt the wheels all the way up his body; he felt and heard each bone splinter and snap, felt the searing pain as his groin and stomach were ground flat under the immense weight of the wrecker, tasted the coppery blood as it burst in a torrent from his screaming mouth, felt every part of him explode into bloody fragments until the rolling wheels smashed his awareness into utter black agony.

Then he woke up, covered in sweat, his body still screaming from every pore, from every nerve ending. His curly red hair hung in seaweed twists down from his bowed head, and his freckles were as dark as bullet holes against his pale skin. His heart was beating so hard in his chest that it hurt, lances of pain shot down his left arm, numbing his fingers. Fiery lights danced in his blue eyes and he bent forward, gagging, almost vomiting. Then . . . it eased. Like a great wave the pain reached its peak and then slid back into the vast sea of his dreams, leaving him awake and alive. Even so, he trembled and shuddered. Mike had once read that the body had no memory for pain, but he knew that wasn't true.

As the dream—and the ghost pain—eventually faded and he settled back against the sweat-soaked sheets, he feared to return to sleep, just as much as he feared being awake in this house. Vic Wingate here in the real world, the wrecker lurking on the black roads of his dreams. At fourteen, Mike Sweeney had cultivated a precise understanding of the nature of hell and an absolute belief in its reality. It was called "his life."

## (5)

When the door opened, Crow expected it to be Terry Wolfe, but it was Saul Weinstock. The doctor wasn't smiling, which was rare for him, and his face showed the same haggard look everyone involved in the Ruger affair seemed to be wearing. A team moroseness tinted by extreme exhaustion. He held a clipboard in one hand and had a folded newspaper under his arm. Tow-Truck Eddie looked up from his reading as Weinstock slouched in.

"Can I have a couple of minutes, Eddie?"

Using a finger to bookmark his place in Revelations, the officer stood, towering head and shoulders above Weinstock, and left without a word. When the door was closed, Weinstock dragged the guest chair nearer the bed and sprawled in it, looking over his shoulder at the closed door. "He's an odd duck," he observed.

Crow grunted agreement. "Always has been."

"Ever have a real conversation with him?"

"I don't know if anyone has. Maybe God. He was on the cops full time when I was, but aside from work-related stuff I doubt we ever said ten words to one another. No, that's a lie. He once asked me if I'd accepted Jesus as my personal savior."

Weinstock looked amused. His features were a dead ringer for Hal Linden in his *Barney Miller* days, a show that Crow remembered watching and Weinstock didn't. "What'd you tell him?"

"Told him I'd think about it, and left it there. He never asked again."

"I'm shocked. I can't imagine you missing the chance for a smartass comment."

"Uh, Saul, have you looked at the size of that sumbitch? He could bench-press Iowa. Guess he never asked you about JC?"

Saul snorted. "Haven't you heard? We Jews are all going to hell. We have a special section, a gated community. Right next door to the Buddhists, the Hindus, and the pro-choice lobby. It'll be a party town." He glanced back at the closed door. "Seriously, though, that guy spooks me a little. I've never met anyone with less of a sense of. . . ." He groped for the word.

"Humor?"

"No. Humanity, I guess. It's just hard to believe that he does ordinary things like watch MTV, eat Fruit Loops, or fart."

"I've done all three at the same time."

"You, Crow, are all too human. Granted, you have a supernatural tendency to be a pain in the ass, but you're human enough. Which reminds me, say ahhhh."

Crow opened his mouth and Weinstock set the newspaper down and leaned forward with a tongue depressor and a pen-light, flicked the light back and inside Crow's mouth, sniffed once, and sat back, tossing the depressor into the trash can. "Looks like the ladies' sewing circle threw a kegger in your mouth."

"Gee, doc, everything you says just paints a picture."

"How do you feel? How're the aches and pains? Any double vision? Blood in your urine? Pins and needles anywhere?"

"Nope. Just your garden-variety every-molecule-in-my-body-hurts kind of pain. Just what you'd expect after getting the shit kicked out of you—twice—and getting shot. Twice."

Weinstock rolled his eyes. "Don't even start with that 'getting shot' bullshit. Both slugs barely grazed you."

"That's as may be, but as far as the shit-kicking went—"

"That I'll grant you." He reached over and picked up Crow's bandaged wrist, gently probing it with his fingertips. "This hurt?"

"Only when some ham-fisted quack is poking it."

Weinstock set it down. "I saw the X-rays before I came in. Nothing broken, but you have a lot of pretty serious bruising. Be careful, 'cause the first time you even tap that thing against something you're going to cry like a five-year-old girl."

"Excuse me? But I never cry like anything less than a ten-year-old."

They grinned at each other, comfortable with the banter, each knowing that it was a splendid way of not really talking about last night even though it was right there in each other's eyes. Crow said, "How's Val?"

"Still sleeping, thank God. On top of what she must be feeling about her dad, that eye socket is going to hurt like a son of a bitch. A migraine is not out of the question. Better to keep her under as long as we can. The MRI can wait until this afternoon, if she's up to it, or tomorrow."

Crow nodded. "Thanks."

Weinstock slapped Crow's thigh. "You're going to have to be her support, buddy-boy, because she's going to have to deal with a lot of pretty hard stuff over the next couple of days. Henry's funeral arrangements, for one, and running the farm. The house is probably a wreck, what with the mess Ruger made and then a zillion cops tramping through it. Anything you can do to get some of this taken care of so she doesn't have to will lighten her load."

Crow nodded. "I called Diego, the farm foreman. Asked him to see to the house and the farm. He's a stand-up guy, been with Henry forever. You've met him."

"Yep." Weinstock frowned. "We all know Val's tough as nails, but nobody's invulnerable and you have to remember that if she has a strong support system then it'll be easier for her to remember her strength, you dig?"

Crow cocked his head and studied the doctor. "It's strange," he said, "but everyone keeps saying you're a heartless bastard. I think they may be wrong."

Weinstock ignored that and picked up the newspaper he'd been carrying, the Crestville *Observer*. "You see this yet? You're famous." He spread it out and Crow glanced at the headlines: MONSTERS IN SPOOKTOWN: MANHUNT ENDS IN SHOOTINGS, DEATH. The article ran through the events at the farm and highlighted Crow's fight with an "unnamed assailant," then chucked in a lot of backstory about Crow's better days as a Pine Deep cop. It was lurid stuff, poorly written and overly dramatic.

Crow made a rude noise and pushed it away. "Typical. Long on hysteria, short on details."

"Well," Weinstock said, "there's still a manhunt going on. Can't expect them to give away too much info. Crooks read papers, too."

"No self-respecting crook would read the *Observer*."

"Good point."

"I notice, though, that there's nothing about the Cape May Killer."

Weinstock shook his head. "I think there's about fifteen

people in the whole town who know about that, most of them cops, and none of them better talk to the press. Gus would have their balls."

"The hell with Gus—that guy Ferro'd have their balls. He's a lot scarier than Gus."

"Yeah, he can be intense. Do him some good to smile once in a while." He looked at his watch. "Better get my ass in gear. I got to do the autopsy on your sparring partner."

Crow felt the skin on the back of his neck contract like wet leather left out in the sun. "You're going to do an autopsy on Ruger?"

"Yep. Want me to save you a souvenir? His heart's probably small enough and hard enough to make a good watch fob." Weinstock's grin turned into a frown. "Crow . . . you just went about four shades of green. Sorry," Weinstock said, patting Crow's knee. "Guess it's too soon to make those kind of jokes."

"Just a bit."

Weinstock cleared his throat and looked at his watch. "Anything I can get you? Something you want brought in?"

"Yeah, how about wheeling Val into see me . . . or cutting me loose so I can visit her."

Weinstock sucked his teeth. "If you behave, I'll have an orderly wheel you down to her room later so you can sit with her. She's sleeping now, but as the day wears on she's going to need you there."

"I know," Crow said. "Thanks. You know I proposed, right?"

"You told me about twenty times." Weinstock said, thinking that Val would be very lucky if all the physical and emotional trauma she'd undergone in the last forty-eight hours didn't cause her to miscarry. He was pretty sure Crow didn't yet know that Val was pregnant.

Crow asked about Connie and Mark, Val's brother and sister-in-law. Weinstock looked dubious. "She's pretty rocky, though physically she's okay. The shrinks are with her now, and will be seeing her off and on all day. I'd rather keep her, and Mark, a couple more days. We had some difficulties with Mark's avulsed teeth, but we were able to clean the sockets and reseat both teeth. They're ligated to the adjoining teeth, and he'll have to be careful for a couple of months. He's on antibiotics and will need root canal to restore the blood supply, but we can get that done, either here or he can see his oral surgeon, though he'll want to check in with an endodontist fairly soon as well. That's all fairly routine. Our residents reseat teeth after every hockey game at the college and twice on Friday nights after the bars let out. Psychologically, though, he might be as shaky as Connie, and the next few days are going to be very tough for them, which is why I'd rather have them here. He has very real grief to deal with, but he also has Connie to attend to. She was very nearly raped, as you know, and neither of them is coping with that very well. They're both acting as if she *was* raped, and Mark's withdrawn from her a bit. Doesn't say much to her, doesn't even ask about her. Connie is even worse, and without Mark's support. . . ."

"Yeah," Crow said softly, "Mark's not Henry." Which said it all.

"Few people are. I'm not a big believer in hell, as you know, but I think Ruger should burn for killing Henry." His cell phone rang and he plucked it out of the pocket of his white lab coat, flipped it open, and said, "Weinstock. Yeah, Bob, what is it?" He listened for over a minute without saying anything, but as Crow watched the doctor's face aged ten years and turned gray. Finally he said, "Okay. Thanks." He sighed heavily and laid the cell phone in his lap.

"What was that all about?"

Weinstock cocked his head at Crow. "You know Nels Cowan and Jimmy Castle?"

"Sure. Why?"

Weinstock rubbed his eyes. "That was Bob Colbert on the phone. You know him. Teaches at the college, fills in for me as ME sometimes."

"I don't like where this is going, Saul. Did something happen to them? Nels and Jimmy?"

"Yeah," Weinstock said wearily. "Something happened."

(6)

Once the sun was above the corn and the bodies of Officers Cowan and Castle were zippered into black plastic body bags and taken away by ambulance, it became easier to search the crime scene and surrounding fields for the blood trails that Ferro and LaMastra knew had to be there. It was LaMastra who ultimately found the line of footprints leading deep into the corn, though there was little actual blood along the wandering path.

Earlier, after they had first viewed the scene, Ferro had put the call out through Gus that they needed a lot more men on the ground, and the request—fueled by early news stories of the manhunt and the killings—flashed through jurisdictions on both sides of the Delaware. By the time LaMastra had picked out the front yard of the Guthrie place was a parking lot, and more cars lined the service road and both sides of the verge on A-32 for a hundred yards north and south. Gus took names and badge numbers from every cop, and LaMastra divided up the teams while Ferro and a ranger from the State Forest Commission pored over regional maps. Cell phone reception was spotty so officers with high-powered walkie-talkies were assigned to each group. Gus Bernhardt made some calls and brought in a dozen men he knew to be top hunters or hunting guides, and he deputized them on the spot, mostly to enforce a confidentiality decree. Three teams of hunting dogs were brought in—the same ones that had failed to track Ruger through the rain two nights ago—and at 9:15 the search began in earnest.

Before the teams headed out, Ferro made it very clear that this was a search and apprehend job designed to locate Boyd and/or his stash of money and cocaine, but there was not one officer there who wasn't reading the situation as a search and destroy. Ferro and LaMastra both knew it. Spotter planes were in the air before the first teams had covered half a mile and they crisscrossed the fields all morning. There was nothing they could do about the forest—the great Pinelands State Forest was too dense for any aerial surveillance, so when they'd swept the Guthrie fields a dozen times they refueled at Doylestown Airport and flew back to start a spiral search that used the Guthrie farmhouse as ground zero.

Ferro stayed at the farmhouse to coordinate, but LaMastra wanted to be out in the fields. He carried a Mossberg Bullpup shotgun with a twenty-inch barrel and an eight-shell clip, and there was nothing in his expression that suggested "cuff-and-arrest." The same hard lines were cut into the faces of every man with him. It had become a blood hunt, and everyone there wanted a taste.

## (7)

They let Crow in to sit with Val later that afternoon, but he had to have his police guard with him—a sullen Sergeant Jim Polk had the afternoon shift. The officer stationed in Val's room was a fierce-looking female cop from Philly named Coralita Toombes, and she showed great tact by pulling her chair outside to allow Crow some privacy. Polk also left, looking pleased to be out of Crow's company. Their dislike of each other went back years. For the next few hours Crow sat by Val's bedside, holding her hand, watching her sleep and praying to God that she was not dreaming. They had been having some particularly nasty dreams lately—both before Ruger's arrival in town, and after.

Val was swathed in bandages and hooked up to machines that beeped and pinged. A bag of saline hung pendulously above her, dripping steadily. The liquid was so clear that it seemed to exemplify purity, and that somehow comforted Crow. Nothing else these days seemed very pure, from the blighted crops to the pollution spread by Ruger and his crew. He hated it that so much of this muck had invaded Val's life, he hated seeing her diminished like this. Val was the strongest person he'd ever known; she was as tough as her father, and to know that she'd been manhandled, pawed at, chased, shot at, and then nearly murdered by Ruger filled Crow with a rage so white-hot that it was, in itself, an example of purity.

At that moment he would have gladly traded his life to roll the clock back a couple of days so that he could have made the choice to go out to the Guthrie farm instead of doing Terry's errand out at the Haunted Hayride first. Had he done so he would have gotten there before Henry had been gunned down. This knowledge was a worm gnawing at his guts.

Crow bent forward and kissed her hand, but she didn't stir. Her face was shrunken by the depth of her sleep and her right eye was covered by a thick gauze pad held in place by a circlet of bandages, but even with all that she was beautiful. Strong jaw, high cheekbones, clear brow. Her nose was a little askew from a motorcycle accident—the same one that had given her scars on her knees, breasts, and belly. Scars Crow knew very well from close study. Val's black hair was fanned across the pillow like a raven's wings. Her left hand was hooked to the IV, her right held in Crow's hands, and both of them looked strong despite the slackness of sleep. Not girlie hands like Connie's, but the tanned, strong, clever hands of a woman who owned and managed the biggest farm in the region. Hands that could be so gentle and yet could turn a wrench or hit a tennis overhand that could chip paint from the foul line.

Crow had loved Val off and on since third grade, even though she was more or less a "rich kid" and Crow was anybody's definition of "wrong side of the tracks." They'd met when Crow and his big brother, Billy, had gone to work for the summer at the Guthrie farm, earning comic book money by picking corn and pumpkins, filling wheelbarrows full of apples, gathering basketsful of strawberries. At nine, Val Guthrie was as tough as a hickory stick and smart as a whip, and her father put in charge of all the kids hired from around the town. Her best friend at the time was another rich kid, Terry Wolfe, and it was pretty clear that Terry was sweet on Val. Crow and Billy had become friends with them and throughout that summer and into the grim Black Autumn that followed they ran as a pack, often with little Mandy Wolfe running along behind to catch up. When that season started it was always Val who called the shots even though

Billy was older. Then things turned bad and by the end of that season Billy was dead, Mandy was dead, and Terry was in a coma, all victims of the Pine Deep Reaper. That left Val and Crow together during those last days before the Reaper was himself cut down. Now, thirty years later, Val and Crow were going to be married—just as another Black Autumn was burning its way through their lives.

*Ubel Griswold sends his regards.*

In his mind he could have sworn he heard the cold whisper of Ruger's laughter. He realized that he was still squeezing Val's hand too tightly and as he relaxed the pressure he nearly jumped as her fingers curled around his as if refusing to let go. He froze, not wanting to wake her and yet willing her to wake. Her one visible eyelid trembled for a moment and her brow furrowed as if she were puzzling out the nature of being awake. Then that eyelid opened and she looked right at him with one single dark blue eye.

All afternoon he'd been rehearsing something witty and clever to say when she finally woke up, but his throat went as dry as sand and he couldn't say a thing.

Instead, Val said, "You look horrible."

He swallowed, smiled, and said, "Whereas you are the most beautiful woman in the world." He kissed her hand.

"Oh, please." She pulled her hand gently out of his and reached up to touch her face, probing the thick bandage over her eye. "Ow. How's this look?"

He peeked under the gauze. "Like an eggplant on a hot summer day, but hey, a few pounds of makeup and nobody'll ever notice." He took a cup of water from the bedside table and handed it to her. She sipped once through the straw, took a breath, and took a longer sip before handing the cup back, her face thoughtful. Crow could imagine the tape machines in her head replaying everything that had happened. He said softly, "Ruger's dead."

"For sure this time?" Equal parts edge and uncertainty in her voice, echoing what he had asked Jerry Head.

"For double damn sure."

"Good," she said and it was very nearly a snarl. She

touched her chest, feeling for her little silver cross, but it wasn't there; the nurses had taken it off. Crow opened the drawer of the bedside table and fished it out. He clumsily managed to place it around her neck and attach the clasp. She seemed to relax a bit more once it was on.

"How are Mark and Connie?

Crow gave it to her straight, repeating verbatim what Saul Weinstock had said. Val listened and then gave a single curt nod, but he knew she was processing it. "There's more," he said, taking her hand again. He took a deep breath and then told her about the new killings out at the farm. He could see the hurt register on her face, but she didn't break.

"Those poor men," she said, her voice hollowed out by shock. "Did they have families?" When he nodded, she shook her head. "My God!"

"They'll catch Boyd soon, though. I saw the news earlier and they have state troopers, forest rangers, every kind of cop . . . even dogs and planes out there."

Her mouth was as hard as a knife blade. "They ought to gun him down and bury him in an unmarked grave. Right next to Ruger." Crow nodded, staring down at her hand, feeling the harshness of her words, but not finding any fault with her sentiments.

A few moments later she squeezed his hand and when he looked at her there were tears in her eyes. "I just want it to end, Crow!" she said, and her chest hitched with the first sob. "I just want it to be over." She started to cry then—deep sobs that made her body spasm and jerk. Crow reached for her and tried to comfort her with his nearness, whispering meaningless words as he held her. When he heard her say, "Daddy!" between the sobs, Crow lost it, too, and they clung together in grief.

### (8)

Sunday was the only day Dick Hangood got to sleep in and he usually didn't crawl out of bed before four in the afternoon, so when his phone rang at three, he leaned over and stared bleary-eyed at the caller ID, saw that it was Willard Fowler Newton, and almost didn't answer. The only reason he even bothered was because Dick's lover, Anton, was still asleep and the phone would wake him up. He slipped out of bed, took the portable phone, and clicked it on as he went into the living room. He slouched down into a leather armchair and immediately his dog leapt into his lap.

"You have one minute and then I'm going back to sleep, Newt, and unless this involves Brad Pitt and gratuitous nudity, I am probably going to fire you. Just so you know." Dick Hangood was the editor and co-owner of the *Black Marsh Sentinel,* a small paper that came out three times a week in the town just south of Pine Deep.

Willard Fowler Newton said just fourteen words: "The guy Malcolm Crow shot and killed last night was the Cape May Killer."

Dick Hangood sat up in the chair so fast he sent his Pomeranian flying off his lap and onto the hardwood floor where—in a fit of pique—he began savaging Anton's socks, which were lying atop his shoes by the sofa. "Newton," he said tiredly, "if you are jerking my chain—"

"Dick . . . I interviewed someone who was involved in what happened the other night." He was stretching that. Mike Sweeney had told him about the Cape May Killer connection, but Mike was on the periphery of what had happened.

For Hangood shifting gears into true newsman mode was an effort, but he managed it. "Who else knows about this?"

"No one."

"I mean, what other papers are there?"

"I'm serious—no one. The cops have been keeping this hush-hush. What I mean is . . . some other reporters know about the cop killings, but no one else knows about the Cape May Killer angle. I've been following the story all day," Newton said urgently.

Hangood was still trying to find sense in this. "But the chief already issued a statement about the shooting at the

Guthrie place. No one said anything about it being related to Cape May."

"Yeah, I know. That's why this is what we in the news business call a scoop."

"Don't get smart with me, Newt."

"Wake up, Dick . . . this is the real thing. We have to go to press right now. We have to get this out in a couple of hours. We'll never have another chance—"

"Shut up and let me think."

"There's more . . ."

"More?"

"Early this morning two police officers were murdered out at the Guthrie farm. I saw the bodies, Dick. I have pics. Long range, sure, but pics. And I, um . . . overheard some conversations between the two lead cops. I know the whole story, Dick, and how it ties back in with the Cape May thing. I have it all."

Hangood felt like the floor was tilting under him. His mouth moved like a Kissing Gourami for several seconds before he managed to say, "Newt—if this is on the level, if this is what you say it is—then this story is going to be picked up on every news service in the world. You could get a Pulitzer for this."

Newton said nothing. He was hyperventilating.

## (9)

"I gotta take a leak," Polk said to Toombes and ambled off down the hall. She barely shrugged. He went down past the men's room, looked over his shoulder to make sure Toombes was out of his line of sight, and then cut into the fire tower. He closed the door and pulled his cell phone out of his pocket, punched in a number, and waited. Vic Wingate answered on the third ring.

"Vic, it's Jim."

"You get yourself switched like I told you to?"

"Yeah, they got me guarding Crow all day."

"He talk to anyone?"

"Just the doctor. Saul Weinstock."

"What did they talk about?"

"I wasn't in the room then, but it couldn't have been much of anything."

"So you don't know when they're going to do the autopsy?"

"Actually, Vic, I do. It's scheduled for this afternoon."

There was silence at Vic's end. "That soon, huh? Shit."

"It's an ongoing criminal investigation. Has to be done fast. That a problem?"

"Of course it's a problem, numb-nuts. We can't let Ruger get sliced up."

"Why not, Vic? He's dead, I don't see how he's important to the Man at this point. He's out of the game, far as I can see."

Vic laughed. "Yeah, well, you've never been too swift at the best of times, Jimmie, my boy. Trust me when I tell you that Ruger is not out of the game."

"But, I don't get it—"

"No. You *don't* get it, and you'd better wake up every day from now on and pray thanks that you continue to not get it. Now shut up for a second and let me think. We have to find a way to get that Jew doctor to postpone the autopsy for at least a full day. You understand me, Jimmie? A full day."

"Why?"

"Because I damn well said so. And because the Man wants it that way—or is that not enough of a reason for you?"

"No, sure, it's cool. I was just asking—"

"Well, don't. Look, they're bringing in some new stiffs for the doctors to play with. If this goes the way I want it to, then they'll autopsy them first."

"Why?"

"Because it'll be part of an active investigation. Ruger's old news, as far as they're concerned. When these other bodies come in they'll be shifting gears—but it might take the better part of the day before that happens, so I need you to stall the Jew."

Polk licked his lips. "Yeah, okay, Vic. I'll think of something."

"Don't get caught, either. You may be be a dickhead, but for the moment you're useful. You get caught, then you're no use to me—or to the Man. No damn use at all, you reading me?"

"I hear you, Vic."

"Good, now get your ass in gear." He broke the connection.

Polk leaned against the cold cinder block wall of the fire tower and stared at nothing for two whole minutes, then he pushed himself away and straightened his clothes.

"Mother of God," he breathed and went back into the hall, but a bad plan was already forming in his head.

# Chapter 4

## (1)

When Tow-Truck Eddie came home from the hospital his mind was racing like the engine of his wrecker. He locked the front door, closed all of the blinds, and yanked the curtains shut, bathing the house in gray-brown darkness despite the sun outside. He peered around the corners of each curtain to make sure that no one outside could see in, and whenever he was uncertain he used strips of duct tape to seal the edges of the curtains to the wall. He finished, paused to consider, and then went and taped up every window in the house, basement to attic. It took three thick rolls of duct tape. That was okay, he had plenty. Lately he'd been using it to pull all of the hair off his arms and legs and torso. For his privates he used a razor.

Once the house was secure, he double-checked the locks on the front and back doors, stripped off his police uniform, and went upstairs to the little shrine he had made to contain the first of the holy relics he would collect. The shrine was a low, flat wooden cabinet that had started out as an IKEA entertainment center but which had been called to a higher purpose by Eddie's needs. He crossed himself seven times as he knelt in front of the shrine, then he opened the doors and removed the vessel that contained the Eucharist, which he placed on top of the cabinet. He went through the entire ritual of blessing the elements, taking his time and getting each step precisely right. Error was sinful, even if by accident. He used a bottle of Evian to fill his chalice—an old boxing trophy he'd won back in his twenties, before he knew who he truly was—and then he lifted the ciborium, which contained the Eucharist. That it was really a Tupperware container did not matter. One day he would have elements made from gold, but for now humility in all things was correct. He took a deep breath, fighting the rush of excitement that shivered upward from where his knees pressed into the floor and where his upturned heels dug into his buttocks. Gooseflesh covered him like a contour map of the Holy Land as he pried off the lid and removed the Eucharist. He blessed it and holding it in both hands lifted it toward heaven. After two days the knotty muscle of Tony Macchio's heart had begun to smell a bit. Bitter and strong, like a man's heart should be. After all, this was the heart of the Baptizer, whom God had directed him to kill so that his energies could be released and consumed by the new Messiah, by Tow-Truck Eddie, who was the Sword of God.

He took a knife and cut a thick slice, praying all the while, phrasing it as formally as he could. "This is the body of Thy servant, sacrificed for Thee and in remembrance of my own sacrifice on the cross in the land of the Jews. This is the flesh that makes the seal of the Final Covenant. I, the Son of Man, the Son of Heaven's King, the righteous and unyielding Sword of God, bless this flesh in Your Holy Name. All glory to God the most high!" Then he ate the meat, chewing it slowly in order to explore the nuance of the taste, and when he had eaten, he took the cup, and after he had blessed it, he drank. He set the cup down and lowered his forehead to the floor and wept for the glory of God.

When he was finished, Tow-Truck Eddie returned the vessels to their places, took the cup and knife to the bathroom and washed them seven times each, put everything in its place, and left the room that held the shrine. Still naked and now fully erect, he went down to the basement where he kept his weights and by candlelight he pushed his body to its

absolute limit, clanking the barbells, pyramiding the weights
so that he lifted heavier weights each time while decreasing
the reps, keeping himself in the haze of the burn, loving the
bite of lactic acid in his bulging muscles, watching the veins
pop and harden, delighting in the shine of sweat on his skin.
Twice he ejaculated while lifting, both times while imagining the death of the Beast, the demon in his sham of a child's
body, writhing and twisting in Tow-Truck Eddie's powerful
hands. Each time, at the point where his dreaming mind
heard the snap of bones in the Beast's throat, he came, spurt-
ing come in gooey ropes over his belly. Both times he stopped,
washed himself, prayed for forgiveness, and did seven Our
Fathers before going back to his weights.

At fifty Tow-Truck Eddie had a thirty-two-inch waist and
at expansion his chest was sixty-eight inches around. His bi-
ceps taped out at twenty-four inches and his wrists at fourteen inches. In his bare feet he stood just over six feet six and
on his weakest days he could bench-press 420 pounds in
twenty-rep sets. He had always been strong, but never in his
life had he been this strong, this blessedly powerful. He
jogged upstairs to the second-floor shower and spent a half
an hour under the hottest spray he could endure, soaping
himself to a high lather, rinsing, soaping, rinsing, until the
bathroom was totally fogbound. He toweled himself dry and
dressed in clean white underwear, sweat socks, a crisp blue
pair of work pants, and a starched work shirt. He pushed a
ball cap down over his short blond hair, strapped a Buck
folding knife to his belt, tucked a leather slapjack in his back
pocket, tucked his feet into work shoes, and then grabbed his
keys as he headed for the door.

The wrecker was parked behind his house and it sat there
like a sleeping dragon. Eddie unlocked a big corrugated tool
chest bolted behind the driver's seat and removed several
flexible magnetic signs that were blank and painted the exact
color of the wrecker. Eddie placed the two biggest ones over
each of the front doors, obscuring the name Shanahan's
Garage. He took two longer but thinner ones and placed
them over the Shanahan clover logo on either side of the

tow-truck's boom. Then he fished in the box and removed a license plate, walked around behind the truck, and pulled off the existing plate, which was held in place by magnets, swapping it for the dummy plate. He knew that he might still be recognized, but with the smoked windows in the cab it wouldn't be very likely, and if someone did . . . well, that's a risk he was willing to take. God would allow him to succeed, or He wouldn't. Satisfied, he relocked the toolbox and climbed behind the wheel. It was time again to hunt for the Beast.

## (2)

Mike Sweeney was crouched behind the hallway railing, listening though the slats as Vic and his mom talked. Vic said that he would be out all day and when his mom asked him where he was going there was a sound that could have been a slap. Mike's hands closed around the slats and gripped them knuckle-white, but he did not hear his mother crying so it must not have been a hard slap, just one of Vic's perfunctory shots. Mike listened to his mom apologize for forgetting her place and then prattle on about how she was going to pack him a nice lunch. There was a space of time filled only by distant noises in the kitchen, and then the slam of the door as Vic left. He heard Vic's car start and drive away. Mike rose from his listening post and went quietly down the stairs, pausing briefly to lean around and peer down the hall. Mom was sitting at the kitchen table pouring gin into her oversized teacup. It was not even noon, but Mike knew she'd be drunk by dinnertime, and passed out by eight.

He moved like a pale ghost down the hall, carefully opened the front door, and slipped out. His bike was around back, beside the garage. Mike had repaired the damage it had sustained when he was nearly run down on the highway. He walked it quickly down the street to the corner before climbing on. The effort of pedaling, even slowly, hurt. His cracked rib were still sore, though he had to admit it did hurt a lot less today than he thought it would, but he had all the bruises that Vic had painted on him with his fists, and every single one of those yelled at him as he started riding the bike up the hill toward the center of town. Except for the big bruise that should have been on his stomach, and wasn't, but that sliver of awareness was stuck in another part of Mike's subconscious, hidden away under the label *chrysalis*.

However, Mike was not thinking about his bruises, but about his new dream—the one with the wrecker. He was smart enough to understand that trauma can gouge a mark in you and leave part of itself there—Mike's life was all about trauma—yet there was something more to this dream, and as he rode into town he tried to suss out what it was. Possibly it was the newness of the dream that made it so intense, and the fact that it was largely a memory of what had just happened. It could have been that, sure. Or, it could be something else. Mike had no idea what the "something else" might be. He didn't believe in prophecy any more than he believed in guardian angels or a loving and protective God. So much of his life had argued too eloquently for the opposite of those concepts. Mike had no cosmology, no metaphysics. Yet there was something else.

He biked along the winding side streets toward Corn Hill, flicking his glance carefully down each side street just in case there was a gleaming wrecker waiting there, engine growling quietly.

### (3)

Tow-Truck Eddie made the turn from Mariposa Lane onto Corn Hill and began climbing toward the business district. Already the streets were filling with tourists. The crowds were heavier than they had been last weekend, and definitely heavier than they had been this time last year. A good year for the town, except for the blight. Eddie did not consider the blight to be the work of an angry God because he had asked God that question and his Father had told him that the spread of disease and pestilence that was crippling the farms surrounding Pine Deep was the work of the Beast.

Eddie could understand that. The Beast was a destroyer and God was a bringer of good things, and those thing included the rain and sun that brought forth the abundance of the harvest. The thought that the Beast had caused such blight in Pine Deep—his town—filled him with a cold rage. It was yet another reason to find the monster and destroy him before all of the farmers Eddie had grown up with were ruined. Destroying the Beast was the same as defending his town, which was the proper work for the Sword of God.

Suddenly he saw a figure in a hooded sweatshirt pedaling a bicycle not more than half a block away. Heading *away* from him. Was it the same bicycle? Eddie couldn't tell, there were people and cars in the way. Tourists were jaywalking, slowing traffic, and Eddie ground his teeth as he saw the figure—*was it the Beast?*—round a corner and vanish from sight. Growling in fury, Eddie edged his wrecker forward and the sheer reality of its massive size made the tourists hustle out of the way until he finally reached the corner of Trencher Street and he made a hard left out of the flow and bustle.

But the street was empty. Wherever the Beast had gone to, he was nowhere in sight. Eddie cursed and punched the steering wheel with the callused heel of his hand.

*Patience,* whispered the voice in his mind. His Father's soothing voice. *Patience.*

Eddie sat there until cars choked the street behind him and began honking, and when he was calm again, he took his foot off the gas and began rolling down the street, continuing the hunt. Patiently.

### (4)

A ragged line of police officers, state troopers, and deputized hunters moved out of the tall corn and passed into the shadows of the great Pinelands State Forest. The trees stood rank after rank, mingling Scotch pine and Norway spruce, pitch pine and Table Mountain pine, and a dozen other varieties, spreading back into the game lands by the tens of thousands, packed so tightly together that men walking nearly shoulder to shoulder were almost constantly separated by the knobby trunks of the trees. The underbrush was heavy, tending toward stunting maple, gnarled scrub pines, and thorny bushes ringed by late-season poison ivy and poison sumac. The ground was uneven and seemed to close like a thousand hungry mouths around the ankles of the searchers. More than one man went down with a twisted ankle and had to limp back to the staging area on Dark Hollow Road. The trees were filled with crows and starlings and other black-eyed night birds who watched with ironic amusement as the men looked for what wasn't there.

Hours hobbled by like cripples and at times the cool October sun seemed frozen into the hard surface of the sky. At the van of one long arm of the search, Detective Vince LaMastra stalked with hungry eyes, an acid stomach, and a fury that had nowhere to go but inside. He had his big shotgun cradled in the crook of his arm and he wanted to use it on that cop-killing bastard, but by three that afternoon he knew in his heart that the gun wasn't going to be anything other than dead weight.

His team made it all the way to the Passion Pit, a flat piece of ground at the top of a steep pitch that tumbled down into the shadows of Dark Hollow. It would be time-consuming and dangerous to climb down that hill all the way to the cleft formed by the feet of three mountains, and LaMastra knew he didn't have enough daylight for that. If Boyd had gone down there, they'd never catch him before sunset, and after dark one man could elude a thousand in that dense warren of twisted gullies, streams, and bogs. If they came back tomorrow to give it a shot they'd need rappelling gear, but by then the trail would be as dead as Jimmy Castle and Nels Cowan.

Standing on the lip of the pitch, LaMastra stared down into the shadows, feeling empty and on edge. He did not notice that all of the trees around him with filled with crows, each of them watching him with bottomless black eyes.

\* \* \*

Back at the staging area, Frank Ferro paced slowly back and forth, hands jammed deep into his pockets, shoulders hunched against the deepening cold, thoughts blacker than they had ever been. Ferro knew that he was something of a control freak. Not really a type-A personality, but close enough. He liked answers, he liked patterns, and he liked cases that stayed within the boundaries of police work. Even when he failed to close a case, his world was balanced on the fact that it was all cops and robbers and sometimes the robbers won. This case, though, seemed to be outside of those boundaries. Vince had put his finger on it earlier when he said that the case was getting away from them. Maybe it already was. He didn't feel that he was in charge of it in any useful way, but he wasn't blasting himself for it because he truly felt that this case would have gotten away from anyone. It was that kind of case. Outside of all normality, beyond cops and robbers.

He tugged his cell phone out of his pocket and tried for the twentieth time that day to get hold of Mayor Terry Wolfe, but there was still no joy. Annoyed, he jammed the phone back into his pocket as he looked out over the sea of waving corn that was stirred by a piercing breeze out of the north. Night was coming on and Ferro didn't like the feel of it.

He thought about that feeling, trying to pick it apart. Ferro was never a deeply emotional person, and certainly not one prone to romantic fancies, either in thought or action, so when he realized that he didn't like the *feel* of the coming night, he felt a tickle of self-disgust. Or tried to but no amount of personal recrimination would make the feeling go away as he looked out over the corn to the forests beyond. He wanted LaMastra and the others to stop, to turn back, to leave those ugly woods.

"You're a fool," he said aloud, sneering at his feelings.

A minute later, though, he used the powerful satellite phone. "Vince? You got anything?"

"Not a goddamn thing, Frank. Nothing, not even a footprint."

"I heard from the lab and they matched the shoe impressions they took this morning to the casts they took from around Ruger's car. Definitely Boyd."

"Shit," LaMastra swore. "What about those teeth marks, though? Don't tell me Boyd's walking around wearing a set of dog dentures."

"No word from Dr. Weinstock yet. The only new intel I have is that, teeth or no, Boyd is our man to about a ninety-nine percent degree of certainty."

"Still makes no friggin' sense, Frank . . . but between you and me, if I saw Boyd right this minute I don't think I'd be wasting time reading him his rights. There's a lot of places out here to bury a—"

Ferro cut him off. "Look, Vince, it's getting late. Let's call it. Bring everyone back."

There was silence on the other end for a moment and Ferro thought his partner was going to argue, but LaMastra just said, "Yeah, okay."

It took an hour for all of the police and the hunters to come back. One tracker, leading a pair of setters on leashes, came stumping out of the woods past large mounds of dirt torn up by Henry Guthrie's foreman in order to sink a new irrigation pipeline. The dirt stood eight feet high, like a small mountain range, and as the tracker past it his two dogs suddenly jerked away from the excavation. The dogs didn't bark, but they moved sharply and nearly pulled the tracker off his feet. The tracker yanked back on the leashes but couldn't get the dogs to walk in a straight line past the dirt and had to let himself be dragged in an arc that went forty feet clear of the nearest mound.

He frowned at the way the dogs were moving and sniffed the air to see if there was skunk on the breeze, but the air just smelled of ozone and wet earth. Had the dogs barked or been more visibly agitated, the tracker would have investigated the mounds, because the dogs knew the scent and would certainly have barked at even the faintest trace of their prey, but these dogs just wanted to move on and move away. That sent a different message to the tracker. Not prey, but something the dogs didn't like. Dogs *liked* prey, and this didn't look like that, so none of his alarm bells really went off. The day was old, the dogs were tired, and maybe there was a skunk hunkered down in the corn poised to spray. He didn't feel like going through all that shit tonight and soon forgot about it. The last of the men passed by, and within minutes even the sound of them moving through the corn to the staging area had faded to a whisper and finally died. Silence settled like dew over the excavation.

An hour passed, and nothing moved. Full dark came on, sliding in tidal waves of shadows across the seas of corn, washing up against the wall of pines. Stars ignited coldly overhead, and there was the faint threat of moonlight far away to the east.

The big mound, the one nearest to the front rank of cornstalks, trembled. The piles of loose dirt shivered for a moment, was still, and then abruptly fell outward from the mound in muddy clumps as the whole side of the mound collapsed. As it fell away, an arm was revealed. Waxy-white flesh in a torn and stained sleeve. Dead fingers lay half-curled like worms around a palm that was caked with dirt. The nails were thick and dark, cracked and crusted with old blood.

A night bird cawed and flapped its way out of the trees and lit atop the mound, staring hungrily down at the dead flesh. It waited for a while, listening to the night, hearing no sound, seeing no movement, then it hopped down the slope driven by hunger at the sight of so much spoiled meat. Two others swooped down and landed on the ground near the base of the mound. The razor-sharp blade of the moon sliced through a distant bank of clouds and bathed the hand in a blue-white light. The night bird cawed again and hopped down another few inches. The other two stood and watched. One more hop and the night bird was close enough to bend down and take a single experimental peck, tearing a tiny scrap of skin away from the bulge of muscle at the base of the thumb. The other birds cried out in appreciation and edged forward. Now all three were close enough to dine. The one on the mound took a final hop and stood by the edge of the hand, its clawed feet an inch from the little finger. It swallowed the first bite and bent for another.

The hand shot out and closed around it with such speed and force that the bird exploded in a spray of bloody black feathers. It had no chance to cry out as it died, but the others screamed in terror and threw themselves into the air, racing up and away as the dead thing under the dirt shoved its way out into the moonlight, still holding the crushed bird in its hand. It rose slowly, using its other hand to paw dirt away from its milky eyes and slack-lipped mouth. For a moment it stood swaying there, staring up at the rising moon with a dreadful expectancy. Then it seemed to notice that it held something in its hand and looked down to see burst meat and fresh blood.

Without a moment's hesitation Kenneth Boyd stuffed the dead crow into his mouth, tearing at it with wickedly long white teeth.

# Chapter 5

## (1)

Crow tapped on the half-open door as he leaned into the room. "Can I come in?"

In a chair by the window, Mark Guthrie laid his newspaper in his lap and looked up. He was a few years younger than Val, handsome like their father, but softer, less rugged, and unlike his father Mark, was starting to lose his hair. He had a thick purple bruise on his right cheek that had already started to yellow around the edges. There was a thin band of bruising across the bridge of his nose, and deep pain vibrating in both of his eyes.

Mark didn't say anything, which Crow took for as much of a welcome as he was going to get. He came in and sat on the edge of the bed.

"How's it going, chief?" he said, pasting an amiable smile carefully on his mashed lips. When Mark said nothing, Crow went on. "Val and I might be getting out tomorrow. What about you and Connie?"

Mark said nothing, but a lump of cartilage began pulsing in his jaw.

Crow said, "I looked in on her, but she was sleeping."

"Yes," Mark said tightly, "she prefers to be asleep. They give her as many sedatives as she wants."

Crow digested that for a moment. "What about you? I

know this is going to sound like a stupid freaking question, but how are you handling this?"

Mark's gaze held for a moment and then wavered and he turned and looked out the window. "How would you expect me to be handling it?"

That was a minefield question and Crow went through about forty replies in his head before he said, "Like a Guthrie, I suppose."

Mark's eyes snapped back and locked on Crow's, searching for mockery. Crow kept his face neutral, trying to convey friendship. They held the contact for a long time and Crow could see Mark's eyes begin to glisten with moisture, then Mark turned away again and went back to staring out the window. After several minutes of complete silence, Crow sighed and left.

### (2)

Vic Wingate was a patient man. Over the last thirty years he had learned the art of waiting, and knew the benefits of thinking before acting. As a result he seldom made a mistake. This was both the greatest of the skills he'd learned from the Man, and the greatest skill he brought to the Man's service. He was a tool, finely made, and one that worked as perfectly as planned. He was completely aware of this, and instead of feeling exploited he believed with every fiber of his being that he was being used in the best possible way and to his fullest potential. How many servants feel that? Or know it to be the truth?

All day long he'd sat on a canvas folding chair and stared at the slowly bubbling surface of the swamp at the bottom of Dark Hollow, a place forever shrouded in purple shadows by the towering pines and the height of the three mountains that formed it. There was a thermos of coffee by his right foot, and an Igloo cooler by his left in which Lois had packed three ham-and-cheese sandwiches, an apple, and two packs of Tastykake chocolate cupcakes. In his shirt pocket was half a pack of Kools. Vic smoked whatever brand was closest to hand; he didn't care as long as it wasn't some low-tar bull-shit. He was smoking now, taking long slow drags, holding the mentholated smoke deep in his lungs until he could feel the muscles in his chest start to spasm and then he would ex-hale slowly, practicing the technique of showing no discom-fort, even to the point of exerting control over the cough reflex. Vic knew a lot about control. Even his rages were preplanned and deliberate. He never did anything that wasn't thought out first, not even smacking Lois around or kicking the shit out of his faggot stepson, Mike. Everything was planned out, and everything fit into a much larger blueprint. The Man's blueprint. The Plan.

As he sat there, smoking, sometimes the Man would speak to him, whispering into his mind, and sometimes not. At the moment the swamp was quiet except for the buzzing of late season flies. There were almost always flies down here, he considered. Probably because there was always heat coming up from the swamp, and—here he smiled thinly through the smoke that leaked out between his clenched teeth—because down here there was almost always something dead.

Such as the young woman who lay with her head and shoulders submerged in the black muck. Vic reached into his shirt pocket and found the plastic cards he'd tucked behind his pack of smokes, pulled them out, looked at them. Amex card, Visa debit card. Once upon a time he'd have driven up to Easton and sell them to a guy he knew, but he didn't really need the money now—not with the huge stash he had gotten from Boyd. He tucked them back in his shirt and looked at the third card, a driver's license. Cecelia Goodchild. Bad photo of a pretty twenty-six-year-old brunette. He flipped the card into the bushes. There were at least forty other cards in there, mostly women. A few men. Some of them were completely faded now, impossible to read even if someone knew to look for them there. Cecelia Goodchild's card would rot with the others before anyone saw it, and even if by some weird and wild chance it was found, no trace of Goodchild herself ever would be. He reached out with one booted foot and pushed against the heel of her shoe. With a stretch he could just reach it. Her body slid forward an inch. Not enough to sink it, just enough to stir the surface of the swamp. Ringing the dinner bell, he thought, and though he did not feel the Man inside his brain, he somehow knew that he would be amused by the gesture. The Man loved a good joke.

The surface of the swamp remained unmoved, the body untouched. No matter, Vic thought, when he's hungry, he'll eat. He sat back in his canvas chair and waited. Vic was very good at waiting.

### (3)

"Mr. Crow," said the nurse, "Dr. Weinstock approved you for a fifteen-minute visit with Ms. Guthrie and you've been in here three hours. Time to go back to your room!" The nurse was barely five feet tall, with curly blond hair and a sweet face and in any other circumstances Crow might have labeled her as "cute," but Weinstock had warned him about Nurse Williams. Around the hospital she was known as the Half-Pint Horror and everyone went in fear of her. "Don't believe that charming little smile, brother," Weinstock had warned. "She's about as cuddly as a scorpion and far less agreeable."

Crow wasn't up to another battle, so he kissed Val and hobbled back to his room with Polk in tow, and when he climbed weakly into bed Polk made no offer of assistance. They had never been friends, even when Crow had been a Pine Deep police officer. He had always taken Polk for a weasel and a suck-up, mostly to town lowlifes like Vic Wingate. He wasn't sure why Polk disliked him, but had never felt interested enough to find out. Polk picked up Jerry Head's copy of *Maxim* and tuned Crow out completely. Fine with him. Crow reached for the TV remote and surfed through the channels until he found the news. None of the towns in that part of Bucks County were big enough to have their own TV station, so he settled for CNN. The multiple murders in Pine Deep were still getting serious play, especially now that two police officers had been killed, but so far no one had made the connection to Cape May. Crow thought that was strange.

A couple of years ago a group of senior citizens who were visiting the famous lighthouse in Cape May, New Jersey, were attacked and slaughtered by person or persons unknown. The attack had been incredibly savage and the killers had literally torn the tourists to pieces. A total of eighteen dead, two of them the grandparents of the head of the Philadelphia mob. The murders at the Cape May Lighthouse had made the papers across the country and throughout much of the world. Books had been written about it, there had been documentaries on the History Channel and Court TV, and Jonathan Demme was already making a movie about it with Don Cheadle and Colin Farrell, but no one had ever been arrested for the crimes or even named in the press.

As of the other night—when everything was going to hell and Ruger was still on the loose—Crow knew only the local cops, the mayor, and Crow were privy to the truth that Ruger was the Cape May Killer. Now that Ruger was dead he didn't understand why the story hadn't broken. He turned to Polk and was on the verge of asking him about it, and decided against it. Instead he reached for his cell phone on the bedside table and speed-dialed Terry Wolfe's cell number, but it went straight to voice mail. He clicked off and dialed Terry's home number. Same thing. He tried Sarah Wolfe's number, but her phone was apparently turned off. "Damn it," he muttered.

Polk looked up. "You say something?" When Crow didn't answer Polk gave a sour grunt and went back to his magazine.

### (4)

Saul Weinstock was not performing the autopsy on Karl Ruger, or on either of the two murdered officers. Instead he was sitting in his office, wringing cold water out of his socks and seething with fury. He had scrubbed and dressed for the postmortems and had come breezing into the morgue only to slosh to a halt ankles-deep in icy water. Water geysered up from a broken pipe by the big stainless-steel autopsy table and the whole morgue was awash.

*"Son of a bitch!"* Weinstock yelled and then splashed over to the valve, but by the time he shut the water off he was completely drenched. Cursing sulfurously, he examined the pipe and saw that it was completely separated from the spigot set, not actually broken but clearly dislodged. How in blue hell had *that* happened? Could water pressure have done it? He doubted it, but there were no obvious signs of tampering. And who would do that anyway? Then he thought of some of the outrageous-verging-on-criminal "jokes" the first-year med students had pulled over the years. For one stunt they had broken in and dressed four corpses as the Beatles, complete with Sergeant Pepper costumes. Another time they had removed the heads from three anatomy cadavers and mounted them like hunting trophies over Weinstock's desk. No one had ever been caught, and it was Gus's disillusioned opinion that the first thing med students at Pinelands learned was how to bypass the hospital's years-out-of-date surveillance equipment.

Weinstock slogged to the office, tore off his clothes, and climbed into a clean set of scrubs, but his socks and shoes were soaked and the paper booties wouldn't do him any good. His feet were freezing. He snatched the phone off the hook and called maintenance and read some poor sap the complete riot act, slammed the phone down, waded barefoot through the pool—which was draining through the floor grille now that there was no torrent to feed the flood—and left a set of wet bare footprints all the way to the elevator, snarling at everyone he met along the way.

### (5)

The Bone Man stood in the shadows of Dark Hollow, at the base of the slope that climbed up through darkness into the wan sunlight hundreds of yards above. Up there was the

Passion Pit, where young lovers came to sweat and grunt, and it was where the police had paused in their search for Boyd. He sighed. It was also the place where, thirty years ago, a gang of local men had beaten him to death.

The Bone Man turned and looked back down the murky vine-choked path that lead through twists and turns to the bog where he had fought Ubel Griswold. He stroked the strap of his guitar, remembering how he had used the instrument to smash the man down, and then had stabbed him with the splintered spike of the wooden neck. Panicked, insane with terror, he had dragged the body deeper into the swampy bottom of the hills and shoved him down into the mud, burying him where—in the words of his Uncle Lester—"God can't even find 'im."

Yeah, he'd done that, and all things considered it was safe to say that God never did find him down there in Dark Hollow. But the devil did, sure as hell, and now Griswold was back.

But so was he, and how, why, and what for were questions he couldn't begin to answer. His very existence seemed like the punchline to some kind of cruel cosmic joke. If he had been brought back to try and save the town as he did once before, then someone up there forgot to tell him how to do it. He was barely more than a shadow, more invisible and disregarded now than when he'd been a living black man in the white man's world of the sixties and seventies. A ghost who can't make himself be seen most the time, one who gets weaker every time he tries. A ghost who can't even touch the people he wanted to help. A ghost who didn't know how to be a ghost.

*Yeah,* he thought, *that was smart. Tear me out of the damn grave and then leave me to figure this shit out on my own.*

"You want me to save these folks," he yelled, glaring up at heaven, "then you got to give me just a little help." But his voice was empty. Even the chirping birds failed to hear him. He closed his eyes and shook his head, cursing God and all his white-bread dumbass angels. "You can't be so damn cruel that you'd bring me back just to watch everyone I saved die, one by one." He shook his head. "Not even you're that cruel, Lord."

The silence all around him seemed to mock that claim.

### (6)

Val sat on the side of the bed and brushed a blond curl from her brow, but Connie did not even look at her. She just lay there, silent, lost inside of herself. "Sweetie? You okay?" Val said softly.

Connie said nothing. Did nothing. Val shifted her position carefully, hiding her own grimace of pain, trying to force some eye contact. Gently, but insistently, leaning over her, searching her sister-in-law's eyes for any kind of reaction, for even the slightest connection, but it was like looking at the glass eyes of a doll. "Come on, honey, you can talk to me." Nothing.

The nurse—Half-Pint Horror Williams—came in to do her routine with thermometer and blood-pressure cuff, and Val stood up and moved over to the guest chair, lowering herself carefully into it, favoring her bruised left shoulder. She watched as the nurse worked, saw that Connie allowed herself to be touched and moved and manipulated, that she never protested, never resisted, and never truly reacted. She just *was*.

Val knew that it was not catatonia, because Saul had related conversations he had had with Connie, as had the staff psychiatrist Dee Simonson, but this was the second time today Val had come into her room to speak with her, and both times Connie had shut down as soon as Val had walked through the door. The first time Val hadn't seen the change happen, but this second time she had. Connie had been reading *Ladies' Home Journal* and when Val had opened the door, Connie had just let the magazine spill out of her hand and slide to the floor. Then she turned her face away and when Val had walked around to look at her all she saw were empty doll's eyes. It was definitely deliberate. Inexplicable and weird, but deliberate. Still, Val did not give up on it, and she sat with Connie for ten more minutes, speaking softly to her for a while, and then just holding her hand. It was like sitting with the dead.

When Val had finally given her a final good-night kiss and had scuffed her way slowly out of the room, Connie closed her eyes for a full minute, feeling the tears that wanted to rise to her eyes, feeling the stitch in her chest that wanted to break free as a sob, feeling the deep and utter contempt—the burning, fiery red furnace of contempt that burned in her heart. For herself. When the nurse came in to give her a pill, Connie was curled into a fetal position, a pillow held tightly over her head, her body spasming and jerking as she wept.

## (7)

Terry Wolfe was only missing because he wanted to be. His cell phone was turned off, his house phones unplugged, and his wife Sarah was manning the fortress walls to make sure no one bothered him. He had not told Sarah everything that was going on, but she'd been there for enough. When he had come shambling in last night, she had held out her arms to him and he had clung to her, sinking to his knees, weeping against her breasts.

"I need to sleep," he whispered brokenly. "Please, God, let me sleep."

Sarah had led him upstairs, took him into the shower and soaped him from head to toe, then toweled him off and took him to bed. There in the silent darkness she had kissed him and loved him, and then held him while he drifted off.

He slept for twelve hours without dreaming and didn't even wake when Sarah slid out of the bed to go and take care of the kids. When he did wake, he didn't open his eyes, didn't even move for another few hours; he just lay there and thought about how the last month had been for him a slow descent into hell and since Ruger had come to town the pace was picking up. Even without the manhunt and all of the hurt to the people he cared about Terry was reasonably sure that he would be insane or dead by Halloween.

The whole thing had begun to spin around him when the crop blight started back in July as Pine Deep's first wave of corn crops came due for harvest. Hack Jeffers reported an outbreak of gray leaf blight on half his crop, and by the end of that week four other farmers had reported crop infestations. The following week it was eighteen, and from then on it was an accelerating downward spiral. Not just gray leaf, but a variety of blights ranging from Stewart's bacterial leaf blight to northern corn leaf blight, and in the following weeks there were reported cases of stalk rot, gibberella, fusarium, and diplodia ear rot diseases. By the first week of September there were widespread cases of maize dwarf mosaic and maize chlorotic mosaic, as well as armies of weevils, root worms, and stalk borers of all kinds. One of the farmers who had been hit the hardest, Jacob Troutman, had said to him, "If I was a superstitious man, Terry, I'd think this town was cursed. We have more plagues than Egypt ever saw during Moses' time."

Teams of specialists were brought in from private and government agencies to try and salvage some of this year's crop, or to prevent the diseases from returning next season, but the trend was downhill. As mayor of a town whose income is half based on farming, Terry knew that leaf blight diseases could be found in almost any field, but to have so many different kinds of diseases and so many aggressive species of crop-destroying insects present in one town was beyond his knowledge, and apparently beyond the experts that were brought in from all over the country. Nor was it just the corn crop that was dying—the pumpkins, peaches, apples, and tomatoes were equally spoiled. Only two major crops were untouched: garlic—which made up about 5 percent of the town's agriculture—and the holly farms north of town. In a season of strangeness there were things that stood out as stranger still, such as the fact that a handful of farms, including Henry Guthrie's place, showed no sign of the plague at all, and that made no sense; and if a solution could not be found, then most of the farms would fail. That meant bankruptcy and financial ruin for many of Terry's friends.

Every single farm in town was owned by a family that had worked the land for generations. No one was starting new farms in town, and the youngest farm in Pine Deep was over sixty years old. To destroy those farms would be to destroy the history of the town. To Terry it felt like murder.

As he was struggling with the blight on one hand he had to use the other to manage the town's other major industry, Halloween. October put the nonagricultural half of Pine Deep into the black. The better restaurants—meaning the ones that the owners claimed were haunted—were all booked through November 1. Craft stores, like the Crow's Nest, made a mint on costumes and spooky decorations. Terry himself owned the nation's largest Haunted Hayride attraction, into which he'd sunk a half million dollars of expansion money just before the blight hit.

As mayor, Terry also had to be Mr. Cheerful because of all the celebrities the town attracted throughout the season, and this year the festival would be bigger than ever. Terry had to speak with managers and publicity people to assure them that the stars would each receive the royal treatment. Ken Foree, star of the original *Dawn of the Dead,* was going to emcee a marathon of all of the Living Dead films; horror special effects wizard Tom Savini was judging a monster makeup competition on the campus; and scream queen Brinke Stevens was appearing at another film marathon— this one leading off with her classic *Sorority Babes in the Slimeball Bowl-O-Rama,* which would be shown in a gigantic tent on the Hayride grounds; and another scream queen, Debbie Rochon, was doing a signing in a tent at the Hayride. *Good Morning America* was going to do a Halloween morning broadcast from Town Hall, and Regis Philben was set to do a live presentation from the Hayride the Thursday before Halloween. Screenwriter Stephen Susco, whose latest film, *The Grudge 2,* was just about to be released, would be hosting a screening of both films in that series and giving a talk on American interpretations of Japanese horror films, and writer-director James Gunn was in town to promote the DVD release of his recent horror film, *Slither.* There were rumors some of the cast of that film might show up with him.

Plus this year there was going to be a Little Halloween celebration—a rare event for the town for years where there is a Friday the thirteenth in October. It allowed Pine Deep to have another day of celebration, parties, and events. All of these things meant tourist dollars, and they might have all gone off without a hitch except for the next nail that had been driven into Terry's peace of mind. Karl Ruger. Now Henry Guthrie was dead, Terry's best friend was in the hospital, and there were murderers loose in town.

Just at the point where a foolish man might have said "Well, at least nothing else can go wrong"—and Terry was far too superstitious to have even thought that—things continued to go wrong. The bad dreams Terry had been having for weeks had grown dramatically worse, so vividly real that Terry was in no way sure that they weren't real. Each night he had a variation of the same terrible dream in which he saw himself sleeping next to Sarah and while they slept he *changed.* The transformation began deep beneath the skin and the dream-observer part of Terry saw rather than felt the muscles and bones subtly begin to change, to transform, as some new organic pattern fought to emerge. This change was terrible. His legs and arms twisted into muscular parodies of animal limbs; the flesh of his face stretched tight and then tore apart in bloody rags to reveal the long snout and fiery red-gold eyes of a monster. Clawed hands reached for Sarah as she slept, trusting and defenseless beside him, and on the nights where luck spared him a fragment of grace he woke up before those claws touched his wife's naked skin. On other nights, it was like he was a passenger on some thrill ride in hell, strapped into the mind of the beast, looking out through the scarlet windows of its eyes, unable to intervene or even cry out as the monster rolled onto Sarah. On those nights he wanted to die.

His psychiatrist talked about stress, about overwork, about taking on too much responsibility, about the dangers of wearing his heart on his sleeve. Terry listened with diminishing patience, know that the man had no clue, no trace of insight into what was really happening. He waited, nodded, and thanked him, then hurried out to have the prescriptions filled. Antipsychotics, antianxiety drugs. They were slow to take effect, and what little good they did him just melted away two days ago when his little sister showed up. The fact that Mandy had been dead for thirty years did not deter her from appearing when only he could see her. She was still a child in her little dress, her red hair in tangles, her skin shredded. But her voice was old, weary and angry, as bitter as acid.

It was at that point that Terry realized that hope—real hope—was gone. It was only a matter of time, he knew, before he stroked out, or had a coronary. If he was lucky. If he was unlucky, and that seemed to be his pattern, then he would probably just crack and go howling into the night, running mad until they netted him and carted him off to Sicklerville State Hospital, where the men in the white coats would change his diapers and wipe his drool and let him rot.

Seeing Mandy might have been bearable—sort of—had she not been so adamant, so determined to get him to commit suicide, and in truth last night he was one heartbeat away from washing down a fistful of tranquilizer and antipsychotic meds with good whiskey; but then Sarah had called him. Fate, it seemed, was not a total coldhearted bitch. Standing there with his hand clenched around the pills, he listened to her voice on the phone, that soft and sweet voice that he loved so dearly, and she had asked him to come home. Home.

He stood on that knife-edge for a long time, and then he had washed the pills down the sink and gone home. To Sarah, to his kids, and to sleep. Now, as the day wore on he lay in bed and searched in his soul for one single reason to get up. He could find none except shame, and after a while that was enough. He let out the chestful of air that he'd been holding and slowly, cautiously, got out of bed, listening for sounds of Sarah and hearing her clattering pots downstairs. He tiptoed to the bathroom and closed the door before turning on the small light over the sink to search for signs of change in his face.

The face in the mirror had changed, that was sure enough—but not into the snarling mask of a monster. Instead Terry saw a face that looked forty years older than his thirty-nine years. Sunken cheeks, rheumy eyes with bruise-colored bags under them. Rubbery lips. Ashy skin. "Christ!" he breathed, and then stopped, aware that he had just uttered a profanity. Terry Wolfe never, ever cursed. He thought about it for a long time, examining his face and at the same time looking as far inward as he dared. "Shit on it," he concluded, and he liked the sound of it.

There was a pair of sweats and a T-shirt hanging on the back of the bathroom door and he pulled these on and went through the bathroom's connecting door into the twins' room, and then out and downstairs, through the quiet house, and into the garage through the kitchen door. He opened the passenger car door and sat down as he fished his cell phone out of the glove compartment and saw that he had missed seventy-one calls. "Holy shit!" He said and again stopped to listen to the mental echo of the obscenity, and again he liked the sound of the obscenity. It felt . . . liberating.

Terry scrolled through the missed numbers: Gus, Crow, Saul Weinstock, Harry LeBeau, and Frank Ferro, that cop from Philly. Seventy-one calls. What the hell had been happening while he was asleep? Setting the phone down on his thigh, he flipped down the visor and opened the little panel that hid the mirror. He turned on the dome light and stared into his reflected eyes, searching, searching, for the monster. If it was there, he couldn't see it.

"Thank God," he said, and then picked up his cell phone again and stepped back into the world.

# Chapter 6

## (1)

Late that afternoon Ferro advised Gus to impose a curfew on the town. The chief looked at him as if he's just suggested that they should all dance naked down Corn Hill. "With Boyd still out there it's the safest thing," Ferro insisted.

"The town selectmen will have my balls if I do that. This is October!"

LaMastra looked from him to his partner. "See, Frank, I told you he'd go all *Jaws* on us." In a mocking tone of voice he said, "We can't close the beaches . . . it's Fourth of July weekend!"

"Vince, please," Ferro said.

Gus went as red as a tomato, his body swelling as if it was about to burst. "This is hardly something to joke about—"

"We apologize, Chief," Ferro said, shooting a harsh look at LaMastra. "Vince and I are both tired and frustrated."

The chief grunted. They were sitting in Gus's office on Corn Hill. There was a lot of bustle as off-duty officers were coming in to replace the working shift. Everyone looked angry and there was a lot of harsh chatter about what they'd do if they found the bastard who had killed two of their own.

"But," Ferro pushed on, "a curfew does seem to be the best course of action. Boyd is still out there, and—"

"Don't patronize me, Frank. I'm not stupid. I know how dangerous the situation is, but you have to appreciate my position. Pine Deep is a tourist town and decisions that affect the tourism industry are not made by me. Terry makes the principal decisions—"

"The mayor's off the radar, Chief," LaMastra observed.

"Which means that Harry LeBeau has authority," Gus said stubbornly, "and even then he has to get a majority vote from the selectmen, even in a police emergency." When he saw the looks on their faces he added defensively, "I didn't set it up, but it's more than my job is worth to issue a curfew without permission." He paused, realizing how that sounded, and added, "Even if I do agree."

"Well, can you at least give LeBeau a call and set things in motion? The sun is already down."

Gus stared at him for a long five count, then abruptly stood up and walked into his private office and slammed the door. Through the glass Ferro could see him snatch up the phone. He turned to LaMastra, dropped his voice, and snapped, "Jesus, Vince, do you have to make smartass comments to everyone? What is it with you?"

Unmoved, LaMastra quietly said, "I guess my bullshit tolerance has bottomed out over the last couple of days. Working with that guy is maybe a short step up from working with a sock puppet."

"It's his town."

"Oh, screw that, Frank. People are dying—*cops* are dying. I just don't see why we should be even asking him. I thought the mayor put us in charge."

"Of the manhunt, yes, but this is a town policy issue. We push too hard on this and the mayor makes a call to our boss and we're both writing parking tickets in West Philly."

"Don't tell me you're going to play politics here."

Ferro shrugged. "The chief's making the call, isn't he?"

Through the glass they could see Gus, his face even redder, gesturing emphatically as he shouted into the phone. They shared a look, eyebrows raised, then settled down at desks to update their reports on their laptops. Ten minutes later Gus's door banged open and he stalked across the room toward them, face dark, a thick vein popping on his forehead. He stopped in front of Ferro's desk and glared down at him. "Well, I pitched the curfew idea to LeBeau and eight of the selectmen one at a time and got my ass handed to me by every single one of them."

Ferro flicked a warning look at LaMastra, who only mouthed the word "*Jaws*."

"Best I might get from them was permission to issue an advisory."

" 'An advisory,' " Ferro echoed.

"We can broadcast a suggestion that 'everyone stay indoors until the current criminal investigation is over.' " He said it with the intonation of someone repeating a quote. "Since almost every business in town subscribes to the township listserv, we can send out an e-mail with the same suggestion, and that is as far as they are going to budge until they hear from Terry."

Ferro stared up at the pocked surface of the drop-ceiling panels. "Okay, then that will have to do."

The e-mail was drafted and sent, with the request that each store owner forward it to his local client list—a suggestion Gus thought would be universally ignored—and a copy of it was faxed to the local radio station, WHWN, the "Voice of the Pennsylvania Pinelands," which was broadcast out of Pinelands College. Word had already spread about the murders that morning at Guthrie Farm, and the whisper-stream spread the news about the "advisory." The overwhelming reaction from both townsfolk and tourists was to pour into the streets. Within a couple of hours Pine Deep became one huge party, with impromptu bonfires flaring up in the farmers' fields closest to the town proper, and tailgate parties sparking to life in parking lots of a dozen stores. More than half of the shops on Main Street and Corn Hill decided to stay open past the usual closing hour, and all the bars and restaurants were packed with chattering crowds. When Ferro and LaMastra left the chief's office to walk back to the Harvestman to turn in, they encountered huge crowds of people, laughter, blaring music, and a pandemic of celebration. As they passed the open door of Jacko's Pub, a drunk girl in a very tight T-shirt staggered out of the door, her forehead painted with a lipstick jack-o'-lantern, a drink in either hand. "Here fellas, these'll just kill ya!" She tried to hand them the drinks, but Ferro gave her his stony face and pushed past. LaMastra paused for a moment, took the drink and downed it in a single gulp, winked at the girl, and then hurried to catch up with Ferro, his throat burning with whatever was in the drink.

## (2)

Val and Crow sat side by side on his cramped bed, Crow's good arm around her. Both of them were now free of the IV bottles and Weinstock had said that they would be released the following day. Polk sat by the door staring at the news, and Toombes was slumped in a chair by the window reading a Walter Mosley novel, but she also kept glancing up at the TV, which showed the burgeoning party in Pine Deep.

"Gotta love this town," Crow said, giving Val a gentle squeeze, mindful of her wrenched shoulder.

"This is crazy," Val said sourly. "People have no respect. No common sense, either. Don't they know what's out there?" Her voice was fierce enough to make both cops turn and look at her, but she was unabashed. "People can be so damn *stupid* sometimes."

"I heard that," Toombes murmured, and then bowed her head over her novel again.

Crow's cell rang and he disentangled himself from Val and reached for it, checked the display, and said to Val, "It's Terry!"

He flipped the phone open. "Hey, Wolfman . . . where the hell you been?"

"Hi, Crow. How are you? How's Val?"

"Able to sit up and take nourishment."

"Good, good," Terry said in a vague way that made Crow think he hadn't even registered the answer. "Look, I just got off the phone with Harry and he more or less brought me up to speed." He cleared his throat and when he spoke again his voice was a bit more human. "Jesus, I can't believe that Ruger actually attacked you at the hospital. I'm glad you killed the bastard." It took Crow a second to register what Terry had just said. Jesus? Bastard? *Wow,* Crow thought.

"I doubt anyone'll shed tears at his funeral," Crow muttered.

"And . . . I heard about Nels Cowan and Jimmy Castle. It's horrible but . . . I'm off-balance with the timetable here. Are they sure Ruger didn't do that?'

"Ruger was DOA when that went down. Apparently his buddy Boyd did it."

"Boyd? That doesn't make any sense. Those Philly cops told me he was harmless."

"I guess they were wrong."

"God*damn* it!" There it was again.

"Have you been watching the news?"

"I'm watching it now. Place is going to hell, and I've got to get back on top of this situation. I'm heading over to Gus's. Talk to you later."

"Hey, wait a min—" But Terry had hung up. Crow slowly closed his phone and turned to Val.

"What was that all about?" she asked. He told her, emphasizing the startling changes in Terry's vocabulary. She arched an eyebrow. "Terry? Cursing? Oh, come on. . . ."

"Hand to God, sweetie."

"Must be strain," she said.

"Must be something."

### (3)

Vic spun around, whipping a pistol out of his belt and dropping into a shooter's crouch as Kenneth Boyd stepped heavily out from between two maples. Vic's scowl melted away and he smiled as he straightened, easing the hammer down and shoving the gun back into the shoulder rig he wore under his windbreaker. He'd been waiting for over an hour, seated cross-legged on the tailgate of his pickup, chain-smoking and working things through in his head, waiting for Boyd, who took his sweet time getting there.

Boyd stood in the darkness under an elm, staring hungrily at him. The forest and the field were both cast in shadows thrown by the mountains, but Boyd stood in the heart of the darkness, shying away from even the wan daylight.

Vic stretched his legs and stood, affecting a yawn, then he turned and as he started walking toward the forest he slapped his thigh and whistled. "Here, boy!"

With red hatred in his eyes, Boyd followed, his lips curling back to reveal a row of jagged teeth that looked more like they should belong in the mouth of a barracuda rather than a man. Together they went deep into the woods.

Vic always kept a small canvas folding chair in a zippered vinyl bag stowed behind one of the rhododendrons by the edge of the swamp. He unzipped it casually, pointedly not looking at Boyd, showing both his lack of fear and total disregard for the creature, especially here in the presence of the Man. He took his time setting up the chair, pushing the legs down into the mossy earth until they held firm against roots or stones, and then he sat down, facing the muddy pool. Bubbles were constantly rising to the surface of the pool, popping with a mingled smell of sulfur, methane, and rotting meat. Vic had long since grown used to the smell, but he took a lucifer match from his shirt pocket, popped it alight with a thumbnail, and held the flame to a fresh cigarette, then flicked the still burning match at Boyd. It bounced off the creature's cheek and save for a tiny flaring of eyes and nostrils Boyd did not react. Those eyes never left Vic's throat, however, and after a few minutes, as Vic sat there and smoked—his own eyes fixed on the black pool—cold spittle gathered in Boyd's mouth and dripped in fat drops to his chest.

As he finished his cigarette, Vic said aloud, "Einstein over there nearly screwed the pooch, Boss." His words were directed to the rippling surface of the pool, and he cocked his head to one side as if listening to an answer. "Yeah, I think we can turn it around. Worst case is that everyone'll think Boyd here just went off his nut. I can make that work for us." He listened again. "Sure, but it's all based on whether Boyd will do what we say. He should have stayed out of town, should have gone to ground, but here he is, big as life and twice as ugly. If it was me, I'd cap him right now. Got those *special* rounds in your old Luger—they'd take Shitbag here down quick as you please, then I could leave him where he can be found and then let things go quiet for a while. Halloween's coming fast, and cops crawling up everyone's ass could slow things down." He listened again, sighed, and nodded reluctantly. "Okay, I can see that . . . but I still think we should dump this one and just work on the other one. Well . . . the other *three* now. Maybe they won't be brain damaged like this useless turd." Vic leaned forward, his face, his eyes, his entire being focused on the center of the swamp. "You know I will, Boss. One thing in all the world you never need to do is doubt that. But if Boyd here steps out of line one more time—if he endangers the *plan* one more time—useful or not I'm going to put him down like a broke-dick dog. I won't let anything stop the Red Wave. Not anything, and not anyone living or dead."

He listened again and his face slowly registered surprise, eyebrows arching, and he looked from the swamp to Boyd and back again. "You can do that? You can—what word am I looking for here, boss?—you can *dial up* the brainpower on this moron?" He grinned like a kid. "That's just too cool! But let's not overdo it. Just enough to make him toe the line and maybe help with some fetch-and-carry nigger work I got to get done."

Beside him, Boyd dropped down onto hands and knees and then leaned forward until he was able to dip his whole face into the swamp. He lay there for ten minutes, buried head and shoulders in the black bubbling ichor of Griswold's grave. When he eventually pulled back a green-black slime oozed from his ears and nose and mouth. Boyd got slowly to his feet and staggered back to the treeline, watching Vic with eyes that were a shade less milky and bland. Not intelligent eyes, but eyes that showed the dawning of an animal cunning that had not been there before.

Vic bent and ground out his cigarette, then slid off the chair onto his knees and also fell forward onto his palms, leaning out over the edge of the swamp and craning his neck out and down until his face was nearly touching the mud. He did not immerse his face in the mud, but instead closed his eyes and bent further still and kissed the roiling surface of the swamp. "With all my soul and all my hated, I am for thee," he said, and it was the closing line of a ritual that he had acted out many hundreds of times, and which others had acted out many tens of thousands of times before him. Boyd, watching, tried to understand and, just for a moment, felt a stab of jealousy spear him through the heart.

### (4)

Every reporter in the region had the story of the killing of Jimmy Castle and Nels Cowan, and it was front-page news from D.C. to Boston, riding as it was on the coattails of the hostage-murder drama at the Guthrie farm. Locally it was big enough to earn program interruptions for news bulletins. Nationally it was above the fold in the morning editions and below the fold by the evening press. By morning it would have faded into inside stories everywhere except in eastern Pennsylvania and parts of New Jersey. Then the October 2 morning edition of the *Black Marsh Sentinel* came out with an exclusive by reporter Willard Fowler Newton. The headline said it all:

CAPE MAY KILLER SLAIN IN PINE DEEP
AMERICA'S MOST WANTED MAN KILLS THREE,
DIES IN HAIL OF GUNFIRE
POLICE COVER-UP SUSPECTED

Newton's article had about the same effect as tossing a hand grenade into a crowded room—everyone was blown away.

The *Sentinel,* knowing it had one hell of a story, printed four times the usual number of copies and churned out special editions all through the day. By seven-thirty that morning, the radio stations had picked it up and were force-feeding it to the commuters in five counties; by nine it hit the bigger affiliates and the story again went national. TV reporters quoted it verbatim because their field reporters did not have a single fact aside from the regularly issued—and clearly evasive—press releases from the mayor's office and the chief's office. Not one of those press releases had so much as whispered "Cape May Killer," let alone suggest that the man responsible for the attack at Guthrie Farm was the same killer.

It was top Philadelphia *Daily News* columnist Nick Robertson who first linked the story to Pine Deep's haunted history with a story headlined SERIAL KILLER IN SPOOKTOWN. On CBS, Gail Harkins, her face frowning in concern, talked about how the "tragic events of last night were the latest chapter in a centuries-long history of menace, mystery, and murder in this quiet, upscale town." Mitzie Malone of New York's Channel 9, speaking in a hushed haunted-house voice, said that "in a town that boasts the country's greatest number of spooky stories and campfire tales you would think that one more monster on the loose would not be noticed—but this monster is not out of a fireside yarn. This monster *(dramatic pause)* is real." The evening commentator for Fox News called Karl Ruger the "ghostmaker," hoping it would stick. It didn't. Instead Ruger was simply labeled a "monster" and that was appropriate enough. None of the reporters seemed to be able to keep their stories free of clichés. The term "macabre" racked up a lot of mileage; every lurid adjective was dragged out and squeezed into the Who, What, Where, Why, When, and How of the story. For the first half of the day, though, the *Black Marsh Sentinel owned* the story. By ten that morning Dick Hangood was sitting at his desk with a smug grin on his face as he watched the way the story broke on the networks. Every time one of Newton's sentences was quoted, Hangood made a tick mark on a scratch pad. By noon the page was black with them.

Newton himself was in the middle of it, and the other reporters were elbowing each other out of the way to interview him. Fired up by his first major story, and by the celebrity that came with the exclusive of the year, if not the decade, he held court in front of the chief's office, which was thronged with scared and angry townsfolk and a swarm of reporters from all over the eastern seaboard.

One side effect of Newton's story was that angry attention was suddenly focused on local government, a furor deliberately fueled by the news media who, as one, cranked up their studied self-righteousness and demanded—ostensibly on behalf of *The Public,* but actually on behalf of their ratings—that the mayor's office and the police department respond to the allegations of a cover-up. Harry LeBeau responded by closing his shop and sneaking out the back way in order to head home and hide. Terry, for his part, was reading the papers and watching the news, and thinking it all through. This was becoming a make-or-break situation, and it had to be played just right. His nerves were beginning to grow taut again and he could feel the claws of the beast scratching at the inside of his brain.

So, the press descended on the police department. Gus Bernhardt, his face as red as a boiled lobster, hemmed and hawed as he tried to field eighty questions at once, most of them accusatory. Why had he not informed the public of the danger? Why was there a cover-up? How could the authorities let such a dangerous man walk around free? Sergeant Ferro was so tired and disgusted by all that had happened that he had the perverse urge to let the chief sink under the tide of questions, but a couple of the city journalists recognized him and immediately he was barraged. Unlike Bernhardt, Ferro was used to press conferences, and he had his own method for dealing with the pressure. He gave answers that were so dry and boring that most reporters found listening to him excruciating. Willard Fowler Newton was not so easily dissuaded; he grilled Ferro with questions like machine-gun fire and after a few minutes even Ferro found himself tripping over his words and casting around for an exit. Standing to one side, LaMastra fought valiantly not to crack a visible smile.

Then at the stroke of one, the back door to the chief's office banged open and through it walked Terry Wolfe. He wore a white shirt with the sleeves rolled up, a dark blue tie loosened at the throat, and he had unbuttoned the top two shirt buttons. His hair was just slightly tousled and his curly red beard looked a little wild. The effect was that of a man who has been seriously at work all night, a man who has been in the trenches. He walked right through the middle of the crowd, which yielded and parted for him (though they continued to babble questions at him), past a grateful Gus Bernhardt and a skeptical Ferro—who had become convinced the mayor had wigged out—and stopped in the precise center of the crowd. Everyone was speaking at once, yelling, demanding, imploring, reviling, questioning, accusing, but Terry said nothing, did nothing other than fix his blueberry eyes on the nearest reporter and then turn very slowly in a full circle, making deliberate eye contact with as many people as possible. His stare was as hard and unfaltering as a statue's, and from the subtle arch of one eyebrow and the set of his stern mouth it was clear that he was not going to speak until he had a more attentive and respectful audience. He did not say a word, but gradually every voice faltered and grew silent. By the time he completed the full turn the crowded office was totally quiet except for the rustling of clothes and a small, embarrassed cough here and there.

Ferro, watching, was impressed. He and LaMastra exchanged a brief look. "This should be good," LaMastra murmured.

Terry had prepared himself for this moment. Since calling Gus late yesterday he had spent hours getting himself calm, gathering all the details, mentally rehearsing his comments, and listening to all the updates from the news services. Terry felt like ten miles of poorly paved back road, but he had showered, and dressed in the kind of outfit that would project the image he wanted the people of his town to see: not a shifty politician dodging the situation, but a leader of the people who was there on the front lines with the troops. Not an Italian suit but rolled-up shirtsleeves and all of the long hours stamped on his face. He crammed the other things—the hallucinations, the monstrous mirror images he was seeing, and the fear—into a closet in the back of his mind and made himself be The Mayor. He was good at this sort of stuff, and he knew it; and it was not all artifice—he genuinely cared about his town, though he rarely had a chance to show it. Right now, though, he needed to show a lot of it. He needed to be The Man in Charge. He waited out the silence, standing nearly six-five and powerful in the center of the reporters, few of whom were anywhere near his height, and none of them his equal in gravitas.

"Ladies and gentlemen of the press," he began in the stentorian tones he had learned long ago in high school debating society, "and my fellow citizens of Pine Deep. For those that don't know me, my name is Terrance Wolfe, I am the mayor of Pine Deep." He paused for effect, gave a small self-effacing smile. "I am aware of the depth of concern you all must feel about what has happened, and I understand your confusion about the way in which this situation was handled by myself and the members of the interjurisdictional task force. If you will allow me, I will present all of the available facts to you. However, before we begin, I would like to say that out of respect for everyone's deadlines, I will first read a prepared statement and then I will field questions. I think it would help us all if there were no questions until I finish the statement, because the information I have is extensive and will probably provide you with most or all of what you need to tell your readers."

He paused again, smiling the kind of smile a high school principal would give when addressing a group of incoming freshmen. Terry knew how to project both his sincerity and his command so that few people ever felt compelled to interrupt him. He deliberately avoided the use of contractions so that he sounded formal, and yet pitched his voice to be on the corporate side of affable. The length of his pause, and the sweep of his dark, intense blue eyes, cemented his words into every crack and crevice of the silence. "Very well. I assume most of you have your tape recorders and cameras rolling? Good. Let me begin with the prepared statement."

He took a folded sheaf of papers from his shirt pocket, and after giving the crowd another brief pointed look, he began to read. It was long and involved. Terry was aware that there was going to be a lot of pressure to explain why the authorities had attempted to cover up the fact that the infamous and infinitely dangerous Cape May Killer had been running amok in Pine Deep and that one of his associates was apparently on a murder spree even now. Terry had decided not to try and weasel out of it, but to come right out and admit it, telling the straight truth: that they did not want to attract the attention of a lot of rubberneckers who might seriously compromise the effectiveness of the investigation. It was a crucial issue for Terry because his personal credibility as the mayor of the town was at stake, and elections were not all that far off.

Watching, Ferro had been curious to see how the mayor would handle it, and he found himself changing his opinion of Terry with each sentence. The mayor not only turned it around, but also made it seem that the cover-up actually aided in the early resolution of the Karl Ruger manhunt, more or less suggesting that it was part of a carefully crafted snare that had brought Ruger out of hiding so that he could be taken down.

Terry didn't actually lie, but he played fast and loose with the truth, sometimes using rather vague (though seemingly detailed) accounts of actions taken, plans drawn, and manpower employed to sell his version of it. He sold it beautifully. So beautifully, in fact, that Ferro could see just when it was that the gathered reporters took the bait and when Terry jerked the line to set the hook. By the time Terry was well into the third page of the statement, everyone watching was convinced that, working together in a high-security cabal of law enforcement teams, the Philadelphia narcotics task force and the Pine Deep Police Department had laid a cunning trap for the Cape May Killer, and had closed the trap around him with great courage and professional efficiency. Even the attack at the hospital was made to seem like a trap that had been set using Crow—and here the press was reminded that he had been reinstated as a police officer—as bait. Ferro felt himself believing what Terry was saying, and he couldn't help but smile as Terry worked the room like a top-grade grifter getting ready to sell five thousand acres of swampland as prime beachfront property.

LaMastra nudged him and leaned over to say, "Next time we're up for a pay raise, I want this guy as the point man for the union."

"Amen to that," agreed Ferro.

The statement was a long one, and that was also part of Terry's plan. He wanted to so thoroughly overwhelm the press with all the minutiae of detail that the very thought that there was some shifty reason for the previous cover-up would be dismissed as obviously foolish. Of course, there still was a minor cover-up underway in that some of the details from the autopsy of Tony Macchio were being withheld, as were some of the decisions made by the group of cops clustered behind him that, in hindsight, might not present the whole bunch of them (Terry included) in the best light. Leaving only two relatively inexperienced men alone at the Guthrie farm when it was clear that Boyd (and for a while, Ruger) was still on the loose, casually deputizing a shop-keeper and sending him off to the Haunted Hayride when a patrol car would have been more official and safer for the kids at the attraction, not being able to find Ruger after he'd been shot by Crow and possibly by Officer Jerry Head—things like that which could make all of the men involved look a little asinine, possibly criminally so in this litigious society. So, rather than present the whole truth, Terry pre-

sented a more acceptable edited version of it in such ex
hausting detail that the reporters began to fidget, which was
good. Terry knew that a fidgety reporter is less likely to want
to ask a thousand additional questions.

He concluded with a moving statement about the officer
who had been gunned down in Philadelphia, and the two officers killed the previous day, urging that the reporters ask
their readers and viewers to pray for the families and loved
ones left grieving by this senseless tragedy. It was great the-
ater and the reporters ate up every morsel he fed them.

When he finished, he gave the crowd another long silence,
forcing the eye contact again. "Now, ladies and gentlemen,
questions?" A lot of hands went up, but not as many as
would have stabbed the air had the prepared statement been
shorter or less packed with ad nauseum detail. The first hand
that rose belonged to Willard Fowler Newton. "Mr. Newton,
isn't it?" murmured Terry, recognizing him from other press
events and flashing him a warm and sober smile. "I believe it
was you who first broke the story. An excellent piece of journalism, you're to be commended."

Newton was tipped off balance by the praise. He cleared
his throat. "Yes, Mr. Mayor, er . . . thank you. Sir, can you
tell me the cause of Karl Ruger's death?"

"Of course. As I *mentioned* in the statement," he said,
scoring his point gently, "the suspect sustained injuries during a confrontation with the police. This took place at the
Guthrie farm. Later, still weakened by wounds received, he
was shot and killed by Mr. Crow, who is—I might remind
you again—a part-time officer who won several citations for
bravery over the years. I think everyone will agree that he
should receive another one for stopping this cold-blooded
and very dangerous killer."

"I see. And you say Mr. Ruger was shot several times?"

"The autopsy has not yet been performed, but the Bucks
County deputy chief coroner, Dr. Saul Weinstock, said that a
preliminary examination revealed what appears to be several
bullet wounds."

," said Newton in mildly mocking amaze-
with _several_ bullet wounds he survived a
d then was able to sneak into the hospital and
Crow?"

fixed a concerned frown on his face. "Obviously
the wounds were not all that serious, though collectively
they proved to be serious enough to have given Mr. Crow an
edge in their second encounter." Newton opened his mouth
to speak but Terry stepped in with: "This morning I spoke
briefly with Mayor Grayson of Philadelphia and also the
Philadelphia police commissioner, expressing my gratitude
for the exemplary work of Officer Jerome Head in the rescue
at the Guthrie farm. I expect that he, too, will receive a commendation."

"What about Rhoda Thomas?" asked a reporter from Trenton.

"Health-wise, she's doing well. She is a fit young lady
and a fine police officer, and I believe a commendation is in
order for her as well." Again Newton opened his mouth to
speak and Terry took control of the moment by saying, "The
police forces don't always get a lot of good press, especially
in these troubled and conflicted times, but I think we can all
agree that the spirit of cooperation and the level of profes-
sionalism demonstrated over the last few days by officers
from Philadelphia, Crestville, Black Marsh, and, of course,
Pine Deep, present a fairer picture of the strength, intelligence, and courage of the modern law enforcement officer. I
am proud to have played a part—a very small part, mind
you—in the operation, and to have seen a terrible threat to
society like Karl Ruger brought down."

LaMastra leaned close to Ferro again, whispering, "That's
laying it on a bit thick."

Ferro shook his head. "Look at them—they're eating this
up. Right now he could sell them subscriptions to their own
papers. This guy's incredible."

The questions kept coming in from the throng of reporters, but now none of them had barbs on them. Terry was

the story now and the reporters were hanging on his every word. Several times Newton tried to put some teeth back into the press conference but he was no match for Terry Wolfe, and in the end every time Newton asked a question the other reporters started giving him dirty looks.

"What's next, Mr. Mayor?" asked a Scranton reporter. "Are there any leads on the whereabouts of Kenneth Boyd?"

Terry dialed up a graver expression. "Kenneth Boyd is now being sought as the primary suspect in the murders of Officers Cowan and Castle. Police departments in Pennsylvania, New Jersey, and New York are working together to spread a net so finely meshed that I can guarantee you Boyd will not slip through."

Newton snuck another one in. "What if he's still here in Pine Deep?"

Terry's eyes drilled holes through the little man. "Then God help him, Mr. Newton, because here in Pine Deep we have no compassion at all for cop-killers."

Terry knew that he had just scored a classic sound-bite moment and he kept his grim game face on while the cameras rolled. A statement like that was a showstopper and from his body language alone he made it clear that this was the ball game. He held that face, forcing eye contact with Newton until the reporter dropped his own gaze, and then Terry turned to the general crowd. "Ladies and gentlemen, I want to thank you all for coming here today. Without the resources and guidance of the press things could get out of hand and you are all to be commended on the tasteful and considerate way with which you've handled this crisis. You have my thanks. Now, as I'm sure you'll understand, the law enforcement officers and I have some serious work to do and every minute counts. We want to wrap this thing up, so let us get to work."

He paused to shake hands with a few of the reporters, clapping some on the shoulders, and every once in a while taking a senior reporter's proffered hand in both of his and leaning close to share a private word, the content of which was meaningless, but the obviousness of the confidence making its mark on the younger journalists watching. The reporters thanked him and gave him their support in the way reporters sometimes do when a great statesman is bearing the burden of some national crisis. Watching, Ferro was so dazzled by the mayor's finesse that he had to restrain himself from applauding.

As the reporters shuffled out to file their stories, Gus turned a beaming face at Ferro and LaMastra. "That's why no one sane will run against him."

"Jeeez-us," breathed LaMastra.

When the press was gone, Terry settled a muscular haunch on a desk, folded his arms, cocked his head to one side, and looked at the gathered cops. "Well?" he said.

At that point the officers actually did applaud. Ferro stepped over and shook his hand. "That was pretty amazing, Your Honor. You should run for president."

Terry ignored the comment and turned to face Ferro. "You think you can catch this guy?" His voice was hard, his eyes harder.

Ferro meet Terry's stare. "I have as good a chance as anyone, sir."

Terry continued to stare at him for a moment. "Before I came here I called the Philadelphia chief of police. You are now officially detached to the Pine Deep Police Department as officer in charge of this investigation, effective immediately and for the duration of this investigation. Not the State Police, not the FBI, and not Gus. You are in charge, which means you are responsible. The entire manhunt is yours to run, and I expect you to get it resolved right away. Are we clear on that, Sergeant?"

Ferro nodded. "We are." He had been about to say more, but Terry abruptly turned away, effectively shutting him out, and spoke to Gus. "Gus, you are responsible for the town proper and tourist security. I expect you and Detective Sergeant Ferro to liaise and compare notes, and to do whatever is necessary to protect the citizens of Pine Deep and to ensure that the financial security of the town is not adversely affected by these events. I hope that is clear to you both."

"Terry, I—"

"Thank you gentlemen. I will expect regular reports." With that Terry turned and walked out of the office, got in his car, and drove away.

# Chapter 7

## (1)

"Lois, where are my goddamn keys?"

Vic stood at the foot of the stairs and his voice shook the whole house. He pounded his fist down on the newel post. A door opened upstairs and Lois stepped tentatively out into the hall. "Honey, I saw them on the stair post just a few minutes ago."

"I've only been home for half a goddamn hour. How the hell did they go missing in half a goddamn hour?"

"Maybe Mike—" Lois started and then clamped her hand over her mouth. She had been about to suggest that Mike had moved them when he come in from school, then realized that this was one of Vic's favorite traps and she had stuck her foot right into it. "I mean—maybe they fell down—" she finished lamely, but Vic was already smiling. He turned and vanished around the corner, heading to the kitchen.

Mike looked up from his history textbook, knowing what was coming. He had heard Vic yelling, had heard what his mother had said, and knew the routine by heart. He gripped the book tightly and waited for the first hit. Vic's hand swept out and backhanded him across the cheek. It was hard, but Mike had felt much worse from Vic. Even so, it rocked him and the force turned his whole body so hard that his chair legs scraped across the floor.

"Where are my keys?"

Mike blinked away the stars in his eyes. "I—I thought I saw them on the TV."

It was as if Vic and he were reading from a script they'd rehearsed to performance levels.

"Did I put them on the TV?"

"No."

A pause as Vic tilted his head as if listening.

"No, *sir,*" Mike amended.

"Where did I put them?"

"You put them on the newel post."

"How then did they get to the top of the TV?"

"I guess I put them there."

"You *guess*?"

"I put them there, sir."

"Did I ask you to move my keys?"

"No, sir?"

"Then why did you freaking *move* them?"

This was the point at which Mike either had to fake an explanation or give a sullen silence. He'd learned that sullen silences usually brought this part of the ritual to a quicker close. Explanations drew it out and gave Vic more time to get hot. It was better not to let Vic really get going. Mike said nothing, so Vic belted him. This time is was not a casual how-do-you-do backhand, but a real corker of a forehand slap with nice form as Vic put his hips and shoulders into it. Mike could almost appreciate the way in which Vic turned into it like a ballplayer knocking one up into centerfield.

Mike closed his eyes as the blow came in, having learned from experience that open eyes can catch part of a finger and that was worse, and he tried to move with the blow to take the edge off it. Not that it mattered much because Vic was a pro and a pro knew how to swing. Mike never actually felt the blow—he almost never did—all that he had was an awareness of the moment before it landed and the moment after it knocked his body into motion, as if the blow itself was too intense for his mind to process. There was a big white flash like a photo strobe and Mike was falling, one sneaker tangled in the bottom rungs of his chair, his hands still holding onto the history book, the floor rushing up toward him. His shoulder hit the linoleum and he slid at least a full foot. *Mom must have waxed the floor,* he thought with his connoisseur's appreciation of the minutiae of such moments. His head swung on his neck and tapped the floor once, twice, before he settled with his back against the dishwasher and his legs still tangled in the chair.

*Good one, Vic. Nice form and follow through. Let's see what score the judges give you. A seven-point-five. Ooooh, bad luck. No blood, no perfect score.* Mike's mind was handling the commentary, awarding tenths of points for aftershock and degree of pain. Vic had missed his ear, so there was another mandatory deduction there.

Vic crouched down, his face red and eyes intensely hot. He jabbed Mike's forehead with a stiffened index finger with each syllable. "Don't. Touch. My. Freaking. Keys."

There was a second part to this performance, but Mike wasn't in the mood to see how many of Vic's buttons could be pushed this early in the day. "I'm sorry, sir," he said in the most sheepish voice he could manage. "It won't happen again."

Vic glared at him, and his face showed the disappointment he must have felt for so easy a win. He snorted and stood. "See that it doesn't." Then he turned and left the kitchen. A moment later the front door slammed.

Mike lay there a moment longer, feeling the burn of pain on his cheek, assessing the kitchen from that perspective. It was immaculate, even the floor, and he appreciated that now that his cheek was resting against it, and even wondered if it actually was clean enough to eat off of. That was one of Vic's requirements. How many times had Mike heard Vic growl at his mom, "That floor had better be clean enough to eat off of, Lois, or you'll be pissing red for a week. Don't even *think*

I'm joking!" Mom never thought Vic was joking. Mike sure as hell never did.

A full minute passed and Mike wondered if Mom was going to come down to see if he was okay. She used to always do that, but lately . . . well, lately Mom tended not to hear much that she didn't want to hear, or see much that she didn't want to see. Nowadays she was almost always a little drunk, except when she was a lot drunk. He lay there and waited to hear her footsteps on the stairs. Nope. Nothing. Sighing, Mike rolled over onto his back, feeling the ache in his ribs flare along with his other bruises. He stared at the ceiling, enjoying the cool firmness of the waxed linoleum under him.

Slowly, with great care and no great hurry, he sat up. Then he stood up and righted his chair, sliding it back toward the table. He bent and picked up his textbook and set it on the table, then went over to the cupboard above the sink and got down the big bottle of Advil. Mom had bottles of it all over the house. He popped off the cap and shook six geltabs into his palm and popped them into his mouth, washing it down with two glasses of tap water. Then he went back to studying.

### (2)

Tow-Truck Eddie came in from his part-time job and threw his hat onto the chair by the door, unbuckled his equipment belt and hung it over the back of the chair, and walked across the living room to switch on the TV. It was tuned to a religious station, but he used the remote to prowl around until he found the local news station, broadcast from the student-run TV studio at Pinelands College. Mayor Terry Wolfe was speaking to a group of reporters. Flashes popped so fast it looked like Wolfe was standing in a strobe light. From what he could tell it looked like the press conference had just started and Eddie stood there, fascinated, hanging on every word. He had always respected the mayor. It always seemed to Eddie that Wolfe shone with a very bright, very pure inner light despite his being a Jew. Of course, he knew from town chatter that Wolfe hadn't seen the inside of a synagogue in years, so maybe the Light of Truth had broken through for him. Eddie hoped so. He liked the mayor and would hate to see him swept away when God cleansed the world.

Thinking that, Eddie glanced at the calendar thumbtacked to the wall by the kitchenette. Eddie had circled the 31st of October with many red rings that had gone round and round until they had cut through the glossy paper. He had torn off the pages for November and December because they wouldn't be happening now. The world was going to end on what the pagans called Halloween. That was what God had told him, speaking in his head day after day.

Into his mind flashed an image of the evil imp disguised as a boy on a bicycle that God in His glory had revealed to Eddie as the Antichrist. The Beast. All day yesterday Eddie had prowled the roads in his wrecker looking for the Beast, certain that he would find him, and he had found nothing. When he had come home late last night to change into his police uniform, he wondered if his belief that he would find the Beast was a prideful thing, and if so, maybe it was that sin that had resulted in his failure to do so. He prayed for forgiveness and for strength to aid him in his search.

He closed his eyes for a moment so that he could recall the passage from John 2:18, "Dear children, this is the last hour; and as you have heard that the antichrist is coming, even now many antichrists have come. This is how we know it is the last hour."

Every chance he could he took his wrecker out and prowled the roads looking for the Beast, and each time he found nothing. Not a single trace, and no hints or guidance from above. Why was it so hard? It had to be some kind of test, he was sure of it. Sitting there while the press conference rambled on, Eddie picked up one of his Bibles and searched for passages about arrogance and pride, trying to burn the words into his brain. He swore to his Father that he would never let pride overcome his judgment. Next time he would make *sure* the Beast was dead. Dead for good and all. Opening the way to God's promised thousand years of peace on Earth. He smiled.

Eddie turned back to the TV screen and continued to smile at Mayor Wolfe's face. Yes, here was one who could be saved, and he recited from Romans 13: "The hour has come for you to wake up from your slumber, because our salvation is nearer now than when we first believed. The night is nearly over; the day is almost here. So let us put aside the deeds of darkness and put on the armor of light."

Thinking this, he stripped off his clothes so that his own armor of light would glow from beneath his skin and shine throughout his house, and then he went upstairs to pray.

## (3)

When Terry left the press conference he had every intention of just driving home, popping a handful of Xanax, and climbing back into bed. He did get into his car and did drive away, but just as he braked at the stoplight a voice next to him said, "Everyone respects you, Terry. Everyone likes you."

He turned and looked at Mandy, who was sitting crosslegged in the passenger seat, her large green eyes filled with light, her pale heart-shaped face framed by masses of red curls—a brighter red than Terry's darker reddish brown. Terry gripped the steering wheel with both hands until the leather cover creaked within his fists. He squeezed his eyes shut for a moment, then popped them open, hoping that it would have cleared his vision of the sight of her. Mandy was twirling a strand of hair around one finger. The front of her green dress was slashed and hung in red tatters down her chest.

"You have to leave me alone," he said.

Mandy sighed. "Everyone in town loves you, Terry. They trust you."

"Go away."

"They rely on you to try and make things right. That's what you do." Her voice was Mandy's but the diction was that of the adult she had never lived to become. "If you keep doing this then you're going to let everyone down." She reached out with a blood-caked finger and touched his sleeve. Terry whimpered at the touch and jerked his arm away. The streetlight turned green and the car behind him tooted its horn. "If you keep doing this you're going to hurt everyone—"

"Stop this, goddamnit! You've got to stop saying this stuff—"

"Terry . . . if you keep trying to fight it, you're only going to lose. You know that. It's getting stronger, Terry. *He's* getting stronger. You're falling apart, and when you break down *it* will take over." Mandy leaned toward him and he cut a look at her face. There was nothing childlike in those green eyes, nothing innocent in the harsh curl of her lips as she said, "You're going to be just like him and you know it!"

Screaming in denial, Terry stamped down on the brakes and at the same time swept a backhand toward her. Not to hit her, but to drive her back, to drive away what she was saying. His hand met no resistance until it thumped against the backrest of the empty seat.

With trembling hands he dug in his pocket for his pill case, fumbled it open, and popped a blue 1-milligram Xanax tab into his mouth. There were only three more in the case, and only one of the 4-mg Risperdals—not that the antipsychotics were doing him any good. The Xanax was better because it just mellowed the edges of things. As soon as he could trust himself to operate the car, he drove straight to the pharmacy to get his prescription refilled.

### (4)

Mike Sweeney sat on the edge of his bed holding an ice pack to his face, wondering why he wasn't in as much pain as he should have been. Vic had hit him a good one and

Mike was an expert on bruising. He could always predict how big a bruise would follow a certain kind of hit, how much it would hurt, when it would fade. This one should have been a solid seven on his pain scale, and he should be feeling a dull ache at the base of his skull. Whiplash was another old comrade, but even though there was redness and swelling, it wasn't half of what he expected it to be. Maybe not a quarter as bad.

It was weird, and Mike knew that he should be alarmed—not that he wanted to feel worse, but what was happening wasn't normal. That was obvious, and he had sat there for half an hour just thinking about it—and then like a switch being thrown he *wasn't* thinking about it. Or about anything.

*Fugue.*

When he blinked his eyes clear, an hour was gone from the day and the ice bag was just slush, lying on the floor where it had fallen. Mike reached down and picked it up with no surface awareness, either of it having fallen or of now picking it up. The time and everything it had witnessed was gone. Just gone.

*In its fugue the chrysalis evolves.*

If he had looked in a mirror at that moment, he would have seen that the bruising on his face had diminished by almost 80 percent.

*In its chrysalis the imago undergoes a steady process of change.*

The TV was on, the sound low, and Mike started watching it, catching up to the flow of time without being aware of having stepped out of its stream, catching replays of the mayor's press conference. Mike sat there and watched until it was over and then turned and looked out of his bedroom window for a long time, his consciousness coming back on line one circuit at a time.

It was only the second of October and the leaves were already turning colors. They seemed pretty, but somehow Mike didn't like the look of them. It was like they were too bright, too flashy, like the shiny suit of one of those guys who hangs out by the schoolyard and tries to dazzle you with his clothes and his ride and all the time he just wants to sell you some weed.

He scratched his bruised cheek. It hurt, but not as much as it should have.

*Even when it slumbers the chrysalis continues to change.*

### (5)

Vic Wingate switched off the radio and stared through the windshield as his pickup rolled quietly down A-32 toward the canal bridge. He'd just heard the load of horseshit Terry Wolfe had foisted on the press. He snorted and slapped his jacket pockets until he found his cigarettes, shook one out of the pack, and punched in the dashboard lighter. That gullible bunch of dickheads had swallowed every scrap of nonsense Wolfe had tossed to them, and it was very convenient to Vic's plans to have such a master of spin control as Terry Wolfe. Quiet and calm was good for business. Well . . . for Vic's business at any rate. He lit his cigarette. Vic's and the Man's.

### (6)

Crow was back in Val's room, and Saul Weinstock was with them, all of them glued to the TV as Terry worked his magic with the press. Every time Terry made a particularly brilliant statement Crow and Weinstock yelled "Boorah!" at the screen. Val just rolled her eyes.

"Terry looks pretty sharp," Weinstock said. "Better than he has for days."

On the TV a pair of news commentators were dissecting every single word Terry had said. "I have to admit," Val said, "Terry was in rare form. He really owned that crowd of reporters."

"Except for that little guy," Weinstock said. "The one that looks like George from *Seinfeld*. I've seen him around. He's the one that broke the whole story. Willard Fowler Newton, from Black Marsh. Doesn't look like much but he must be a hell of a reporter if he was able to figure out everything that was going on."

Crow pursed his lips. "Well, the story is coast-to-coast now, so strap yourselves in, kiddies, I think we're about to have a helluva ride."

Totally without inflection, Val said, "Yippee."

Weinstock looked at his watch. "So . . . you two ready to check out of this hotel or what?"

## (7)

Terry and Sarah Wolfe arrived in late afternoon to take Crow and Val home from the hospital. Two armed police officers—Head and Golub—escorted them from their rooms, one leading the procession of two wheelchairs and the other bringing up the rear. Both of them carried shotguns at port arms. A half-dozen other officers had been brought in to create and enforce a cordon that kept the press back from the hospital entrance as the patients were carefully handed into Terry's Humvee and buckled in. Once everyone was in, Head and Golub lead the way in their unit, with the Humvee following, and another police car following, with Coralita Toombes behind the wheel. Police barricades were set up across the parking lot entrance, blocking the press vehicles in for ten minutes, allowing them all to make a clean getaway.

Val's farm was still a crime scene, so Crow and Val spent the night with Terry. Just the effort of leaving the hospital and getting in and out of cars exhausted them, and Sarah got them into bed and tucked in, bullying them into taking their pills. In ten minutes they were asleep, face-to-face, their foreheads touching. Terry headed back to the office, his artifice of calm slipping inch-by-inch.

Golub and Head stayed in their unit, parked in the driveway, eating turkey-and-cheese sandwiches Sarah made for them, sipping hot coffee, watching the flocks of tourists go by, listening to the frustrated reports of the officers engaged in the search. Between bites, Golub said, "You think this Boyd clown is still here in town?"

Head shook his head. "Nah. He's long gone by now. My guess, he's over in Jersey somewhere. Probably looking to boost a car and head north to Newark or the Apple."

"I hope you're wrong, man," Golub said, and took another bite. "I would love for us to catch this prick."

"Catch?" Head said with a cold smile that looked like a shooter's squint. "Nah, nobody I knows wants to catch him."

# Chapter 8

## (1)

"I saw you on the news," said Harry LeBeau as he barged into Terry's office in the municipal building, "and although you did a good job of handling the press, I have to say that I don't like being left holding the bag. Gus and everyone else was looking for you all day and—"

"Oh, shut up, Harry," Terry snapped, looking up from the stack of papers crowding his desk. "I'm not in the mood to listen to your whining." LeBeau skidded to a halt and he stood there, eyes bugged in surprise, mouth working like a fish. Not once, not even at the height of the blight, had Terry ever snapped at him, or even raised his voice. LeBeau stood there, unable to form words. Terry's blue eyes were hard as quartz. "You're the deputy mayor and there's more to that job than putting your title on business cards. Once in a while you have to step up and grow a set. If I was off the clock for five frigging minutes and you had to do some actual administrative work, then that's just too bad. Later I'll block out five minutes and have a good cry about it. Same with Gus Bernhardt. We've got killers running amok in this town at the start of our busiest season and all he seems capable of is sticking his thumb up his ass. What I don't need, from you or Gus, is any bullshit about how unfair life is, because I can say with no risk of contradiction that I've got more on my plate right now than you have on yours. So why don't you pirouette around and scamper back to your store and leave me alone? Close the door on your way out."

There was absolutely no opening to make any kind of response to that, so LeBeau backed out of the room and pulled the door shut. His eyes were burning with tears of shame and hurt as he retreated down the hall to his own office.

Terry sat there, staring at the closed door, his fingernails scratching the hardwood top of his desk. Over the last few days his nails had become gradually thicker and harder. No one had commented on it, except for Sarah, and he'd told her it was just a side effect of his meds. He knew different; he'd read each package insert for each drug, and none of them mentioned this. Nervously he scratched at his desktop. There were deep grooves worn in the polished oak. He heard the sound of slow, ironic applause and he turned to see Mandy standing in the corner by the window, her face half-obscured by the leaves of a potted ficus.

"You can shut up, too," Terry said to her and turned his face away. In his bloodstream a cocktail of Xanax, Risperdals, and Oxycontin was coming to a boil. He had the worst case of dry mouth he ever had, but at least his hands weren't shaking. "I don't have time for you, either."

Mandy looked at him for a long minute, but the next time Terry glanced over to the corner of the room, it was empty.

## (2)

Crow sat hunched forward, elbows on knees, pajama top pulled up as Saul Weinstock probed the bullet grazes on his sides and made hmm-ing sounds.

"So, how's it look?" They had been out of the hospital for only a few hours, fresh from their naps, when Weinstock breezed in to mother-hen them. He made it sound casual, just something to kill time while they repaired the plumbing at the morgue, but neither Crow nor Val were fooled and they appreciated the gesture. Val was in the rocking chair by the window with Party Cat curled on her lap; she scratched his throat and he purred like an air compressor.

Weinstock pursed his lips. "Sissy-boy little wounds. I'm really surprised you have the balls to pretend you're wounded in action."

"That joke's getting old, Saul."

"You want sparkling bedside banter, watch a rerun of *Scrubs.*" Weinstock shrugged. "I told you already, you just got shot through some fatty tissue. No muscles were nicked, and these are already starting to knit. Just keep it clean, try not to get shot again, and you'll be okay. The wrist will be tender for a while, though, so keep it wrapped. Next week you can go see Young Kim over at Fit & Able for some PT. Your face, though. . . ."

"What about my face?"

"You're still ugly as an ape. With any luck the bruises will hide that for a few days."

"You're not a very nice man," Crow said.

Weinstock grinned as he put fresh dressings on each wound and secured them with white tape, then he dragged over a chair and sat down. Peering at the items on Crow's bedside table, he selected an apple from a huge fruit basket that had just arrived from the Pine Deep Business Association and bit into it. Crow readjusted his clothes with some effort. "It's all right, Doc, I can do it all by myself."

"Okay," Weinstock said, not having moved a muscle.

Val said, "I called Mark just before you got here. He said that you were planning on keeping Connie another couple of days. Is she okay?"

Weinstock shrugged. "Physically she's just about fine, but psychologically—well . . ." He held his hand up and waggled it side to side.

"Mark's not much better," Crow said, and Val shot him a look. "Hey, sweetie, tell me I'm wrong. I've tried talking to him half a dozen times, and he just blows me off. That or he takes offense at anything I say. Thinks I'm blaming him for getting nailed by Ruger."

"He's ashamed," Val said, and Weinstock nodded agreement. "Dad was old and Mark was starting to consider himself the man of the family. I know it's juvenile, but in a lot of ways Mark's just a big kid, all his business acumen notwithstanding. He was never a physical person, even when we were little. Never liked roughhousing with the rest of us. Considered himself too cerebral for that sort of thing. Then when Ruger came along, he was overwhelmed by the man. We all were. He never had a chance against him."

"Few would," Weinstock said.

"Crow did."

"Hey, I had an edge," Crow said and made a karate-chopping motion with his hands. "I got the kung-fu grip."

"It doesn't matter how many black belts you have, honey," Val said, unsmiling. "Mark is measuring what he was unable to do against what you were able to do, and he doesn't like how that makes him feel. So he's taking it out on himself, and everyone around him."

Weinstock nodded. "He's clearly taking it out on Connie, too. Blaming her for nearly getting raped."

"Which is pretty stupid—" Crow began, but Val cut him off.

"No it isn't. Sad, but not stupid. Mark's frustrated and angry—I can sympathize. You think I don't blame myself for what happened to Daddy? And don't you dare tell me that's stupid, too, Malcolm Crow, or I'll toss you out of this window."

Crow mimed zipping his mouth shut.

"I've known guys like Mark," Weinstock said. "Both in college and in business. Guys who either come from money or who have made themselves into very successful businessmen, like my Uncle Stanley. When you get powerful enough in business, when people jump because you tell them to—not because they're physically afraid of you but because it's your name on their paycheck and they're living paycheck to paycheck—then you start equating that kind of power with physical prowess. The hype about 'captains of industry' and 'boardroom lions' is easy to swallow, and easy to equate with actually being a tough, powerful person. Then along comes a Karl Ruger who's right out of the jungle and suddenly it's all about real physical power—the power to hurt, to kill—and then all the illusions are just gone." He snapped his fingers. "Mark believed the hype that he was a corporate tough guy, and maybe in the boardroom he is formidable, but down on the level of the predators he's just somebody's lunch. Now who does he have to measure himself against? Malcolm Crow, who is a short half-step away from village idiot . . ."

"Gee, thanks, Doc."

"We're talking Mark's perception. You own a small shop in town—Mark owns half a dozen businesses and has interests in, what, ten more?"

"Over thirty more," Val corrected. "Plus he runs the financial aid department of the college and has oversight on scholarships."

"Right," said Weinstock. "That's power, as far his worldview goes. He has power over companies that make your little shop look like a street-corner pretzel stand. So, measuring himself against you on a daily basis he's the alpha and you're way in the back of the pack. Then what happens? Karl Ruger breaks in and roughs everyone up. Does what he pleases, touches what's not his to touch, *proves* to Mark that anything he wants is his for the taking. Mark suddenly sees that no amount of corporate muscle is going to mean a thing . . . and when Ruger goes after Connie, there is nothing Mark could do to stop him."

"In fairness, Saul, he was tied up!"

"You think that matters? Do you really think that Mark hasn't thought of what would have happened if he'd been untied when Ruger tried to rape Connie?"

Crow looked at his fingernails.

Val said, "Ruger would have beaten him up again, maybe crippled him, he would still have raped Connie, and would then have killed both of them."

"Right," Weinstock said emphatically. "He's probably mad at Val because she, at least, escaped from him out in the fields, and then was able to come back and attack Ruger in such a way as to save Connie."

"He'd have killed me if Crow hadn't gotten there. He was strangling me outside. I couldn't fight him any more than Mark could."

"Yeah, but Mark didn't see that. He was still inside tied up, and you were outside. By the time he'd been freed Crow had shown up and had done what Mark could never have done—he fought and defeated Ruger. Mark, being tied up, could not even so much as hold his wife to comfort her. He had to just lie there, helpless. Essentially impotent. And Connie—she shares the same kind of warped perceptions of the world as her husband. She saw her husband fail to protect her. That she wasn't actually raped doesn't much matter, because she knows—she *knows*—that Ruger would have done it and Mark would not have been able to stop him. Imagine that rattling around in your head."

"No White Knight anymore," Val agreed, nodding.

"Great," Crow said glumly.

Weinstock sighed and rubbed his eyes. "I'm keeping Connie in so my counseling staff can tag-team on her and try to break through at least the initial layers of the gunk that's formed over her perception of herself and of her husband."

Val looked skeptical. "You think you can do that in a couple of days?"

"Sadly, no. I think Connie's going to need a lot of therapy for a long time. As for Mark? In a way he's lucky he had some teeth knocked out because it gives me a tenuous medical reason for not kicking him loose. Between us, though, I'm keeping him in for 'observation' mainly because I'm hoping the therapists will help him realize that this was beyond his control—and that its okay because some things are beyond our control. All in the hopes that he and Connie will reconnect in a way that will rebond them and start some mutual healing."

"That's a lot to expect," Crow said. "You might have to knock a few more teeth out."

"Also, to send him home now, without Connie, would

mean that he would have no choice but to interact with you two. I don't know if he can handle it."

"Doesn't matter," Val said. "We're family.

Weinstock looked at Crow. "What about you, sport? You up for being there for Mark and Connie?"

Crow reached over and took Val's hand, lifted it to his lips, and kissed the engagement ring he had given her. "Like she said . . . they're family."

Weinstock cleared his throat, finished his apple, and walked into the adjoining bathroom to wash his hands. When he came out he pulled his chair over closer to Val, his face composed. "Your turn, missy." Val had a bandage wrapped around her head and a thick gauze pad covering her right eye. Weinstock removed the wrapping and examined the bruising. He shined a light in her eye and asked her to follow it as he moved it around. "Hmm," he said. "Some good news for a change. The eye is fine, no loss of motor function, pupils dilate correctly, visual acuity appears to be unimpaired, tear ducts seem to be functioning normally. As you know, there is a hairline crack of the orbit but that's not as bad as it could have been. What did he hit you with, anyway?"

"Just his hand," she said.

Weinstock whistled.

"You wouldn't believe how strong that son of a bitch was," Crow said.

"Overall," Weinstock said, "I'd say that you'll be fine and with no lasting ill effects. Headaches for a while, of course, and I'll leave you some stuff for that. Bruising looks bad, but that's in the nature of bruising—it looks bad and then it looks worse and then it goes away."

"Do I have to keep wearing that bandage over my eyes? My depth perception is so crappy I keep walking into walls."

"Nope, but just take it easy. Use ice a couple of times a day, and you might want to wear sunglasses when you go out—there may be some light sensitivity. As for your ribs— all those years totin' barges and liftin' bales has done you some good. You have hairline cracks of two ribs, but you're so darn fit that your obliques are acting like natural splints. I doubt you'll get more than a twinge out of them, and they'll heal fast."

"Okay. What about my shoulder?"

"Ah, that's kind of a metza-metz thing. Initially you had a sprain of the shoulder, but after that second attack . . . well, I had Billie Whitby take a look at the second set of MRIs and you have a minor partial thickness tear of the rotator. Very minor, luckily, but when things here settle down we can schedule you for an arthroscopy. You'll be playing tennis by the spring. In the meantime I'd leave that Viper of yours in the garage," he said. "Speed shifting is not going to feel very comfortable. And—"

"Can I shoot a gun?" she said, cutting him off.

"What?" Crow and Weinstock said it together, and both rather more loudly than they had intended.

Val's dark blue eyes were fierce and with the bruising around her face and her crooked nose and black hair, she looked absolutely ferocious. "Boyd is still out there. People keep dying on my farm. I have guns, and you know I can shoot . . . the question is, is it safe for me, for my shoulder, to shoot a gun?"

"Val," Crow began, "it's not going to come to that . . ."

"Hush," she snapped, and he did hush. She tapped Weinstock's chest with a stiff forefinger. "Tomorrow I'm moving back home. To *my* home. I can only do that, though, if I can safely carry and use a gun."

"Val, I don't think—"

"Yes or no, Saul?"

He folded his arms and sat back in his chair, glanced over at Crow, who held both hands up, palms out, and sighed. To Val he said, "Okay, here's the situation and you do with it as you please. *Can* you fire a gun without doing further damage to your shoulder? My answer—probably. A pistol, small caliber. Shotgun—out of the question. No big-caliber pistols, either. A .25 or even a .22."

"Sissy guns," she said, flicking her hand dismissively.

".22's are the weapon of choice of your professional hitman," Crow observed sagely, but they ignored him.

"Now," she said, "if I were to use a heavier caliber, say Dad's old .45, what would be the downside?"

"Well, two things . . . first, you might have trouble lifting it. The shoulder isn't bad, but it's not one hundred percent . . . and the recoil from something that heavy could—and probably *would*—exacerbate the injury to the rotator, in which case you're looking at a far more invasive and extensive surgery."

Val got up and walked across the room to the far window, and though her face was set and stern, she did trail her fingers lightly across Crow's shoulders as she passed him. She chewed her lip for a minute, looking out at the leaves blowing around in the backyard, pushed by the early evening breeze. Without turning, she said, "I'll risk it."

### (3)

Vic's pickup truck was dark blue and in the shadows cast by the east wing of the hospital it was invisible, snugged back as it was between the two massive air-conditioner fan units. The engine was idling quietly but the lights were off. Vic had picked up a pack of Tiparillos and had one of the cheap cigars, unlit, between his teeth. His tongue constantly flicked the open end of the plastic stem as he watched the part of the parking lot that he could see from where he had parked. The east wing was mostly labs, the morgue, maintenance, and storage. There were two truck bays for deliveries, closed and locked now. There was a wire fence with two gates, one for entry, the other for exits. The entry gate was closed and locked. The exit gate was still open and there was a single vehicle parked just inside of it. Hospital security staff in their little putt-putt golf cart. Two men in it. Denny Sturges and Al Antowiak. Vic knew them both. Couple of mouth-breathers who would never amount to anything more than night shift at the ass end of a hospital. Both of them wore guns, but Vic was sure neither had ever fired them, and if they ever tried they'd probably blow each other's dicks off. He smiled. Beyond the fence a Pine Deep police unit shot by, lights flashing but no siren. Vic didn't give it much thought. The whole bunch of them—local cops as well as the crews from other towns that had come in like gunslingers to help with the manhunt—were chasing their own asses. They'd never find Boyd, Vic was sure of that, and his smile thinned, went colder.

Behind him, in the bed of the truck, there was a soft, heavy sound as something turned over. He glanced in the utter blackness of the rearview and saw nothing but could imagine the heavy tarp tenting as something shifted under it. *Impatient asshole,* Vic thought. *Well, that's okay.* He pressed a stem on his watch and the time glowed in green LED digits: 10:58. If Polk's intel was correct, then the Two Stooges over there in the golf cart would lock up the parking lot in two minutes. After that they'd drive by once every half hour and check that the locks on both gates were still engaged. Half an hour was plenty of time. Vic figured it would take maybe half that time. Plenty of room for error.

He waited out the two minutes patiently. At the stroke of eleven the guards drove their cart outside the gate and Sturges hopped out, looped the chain through the poles, hung the big Yale in the links, clicked it, and climbed back into the cart. By 11:02 they were gone. Vic nodded, appreciating efficiency and good timing, even in wetbrains like those two. As soon as the golf cart vanished around the corner, he jerked open the door of his truck—no light came on, he'd taped the button down—got out and walked to the tailgate.

"Rise and shine, cupcake," he said, tapping the metal rim of the truck bed softly. By the time he'd lowered the tailgate, the thing under the tarp had crawled down from its nest behind the cab. Vic grabbed a corner of the tarp and whipped it back as Kenneth Boyd lumbered down off the bed, eyes glaring rat-red in the darkness. "Jeez, you stink!" Vic said, wincing and waving a hand in front of him. He pulled a small plastic tub of Vicks VapoRub from his pocket, unscrewed the cap, and daubed a little under his nose.

Boyd wrinkled his nose at the smell. Maggots wriggled in the deep cuts on his face and three layers of dried blood were caked around his mouth. He was as tall as Vic, and heavier, and could have ripped Vic's arm right out of his body, but when Vic took a single step toward him, Boyd recoiled. When Vic had returned the Vicks to his pocket with one hand he'd drawn his Luger with the other. He pointed it at Boyd's head. Boyd's eyes were feral and wary. Vic saw that Boyd recognized the danger in that gun, and nodded.

"I guess you really are getting smarter in your old age, Boyd ol' buddy, 'cause you're not giving me any of that snarl and hiss shit. Good, because now is not the time for me to be getting into a pissing contest with Night of the Living Dead, you dig? The Man's been in my head just like I'm sure he's been in your head—such as it is—and you know what we got to do. Clock's running, so get to it."

He lowered his pistol and stepped to the door that was set into the wall between the compressors. It should have been locked and it should have been attached to an alarm, but the knob turned without protest and the door opened with no sound at all except a faint creak of hinges.

"C'mon, boy," Vic said. "Fetch!"

With only a hungry growl Boyd shambled past him into the bowels of the hospital. Vic glanced at his watch, then settled back against the cold hospital wall to watch the gate.

### (4)

"So, what does that mean?" demanded Willard Fowler Newton. "How exactly am I overdoing it? This morning I was your ace reporter. Now I'm a leper?"

Dick Hangood chewed his cigar from one corner of his mouth to the other, and continued to stare silently at Newton. Noxious blue fumes from the cigar polluted the room, giving it a London fog appearance. "Newt, I don't know how to answer that question exactly," he said, "because it seems no matter what I say about that damned article of yours, you do a rewrite on it, add about ten column inches of editorial, and try to sell it back to me . . . and it's really starting to piss me off."

"Oh?"

"Do you want to know why?" Hangood tapped an inch of ash into a ceramic tray. "I'll tell you. You see, the way it works around here is that I am the editor and you are the reporter. With me so far? Good. My job, in case you never had a chance to review the office handbook, is to decide which reporter should be assigned to which story, and then make some informed decisions on what they should write about those stories. Still with me?"

"Well, I—"

"As editor, I have the additional responsibility of reading each and every story that crosses my desk and making decisions on the correctness of the grammar, the completeness of the information, and . . ."

"Yes, but—"

*"And* . . . to decide if anything should be added or cut." Hangood puffed blue smoke at him. "So if, just for the sake of argument, one of my reporters hands me an article that I think may be . . . shall we say . . . too biased, or too incendiary, or perhaps even a little unfair in certain regards, it is my job—my job, you understand—to either rewrite the piece, or ask the reporter to rewrite it. That's clear enough, isn't it?"

"Sure, but I—"

"However, there is another aspect to my job, one that I don't always relish, but one that I am bound by both because of my job description and my obligations to the publisher—who, need I remind you, owns this paper—and that sometimes requires me to order either a total rewrite of the piece, reassign it to another reporter, or, in the case of this particular article, shit-can it." With that he picked up Newton's article on the deception and political games playing in Pine Deep and dropped it with great precision into his wire-mesh wastebasket.

"You can't!" Newton cried, leaping to his feet.

"Ah, but I just explained that I, indeed, can."

"You . . . you . . ."

Hangood held up a warning finger. "Watch your adjectives, sonny-boy. What you say now can affect your next paycheck, meaning that it will affect whether you will be getting one."

Newton clamped his mouth shut but tried to telepathically project the long string of astonishingly descriptive vulgarisms that tingled like pins and needles on his tongue. Hangood smiled benignly around the stump of his cigar, then raised his hand again and stabbed the air with a thick finger, indicating Newton's vacant chair. *"Sit!"*

Newton sagged back into the chair, his lungs emptying the unspent words as a long sigh of defeat.

"Good. Now listen to me." Hangood leaned forward and rested his hairy elbows on the desk. "You are the golden boy of the moment, and I am fully aware of that. You've just given the *Sentinel* the biggest story we've ever had, and the sales have gone through the roof. The publisher and I are happy with you, and I think you'll see an expression of our pleasure come payday. But that, as the saying goes, is yesterday's news. Today you are sitting on the fence between continuing to be the golden boy and getting your ass bumped down to writing about dog shows and town fairs."

"What's going on, Dick? That article is—"

"Is what? Libelous? Incendiary? Needlessly provocative?"

"Isn't that what we're all about? Trying to expose the corrup—"

"No, it isn't. What do you think this is? The *Washington Post*? We're a small-town newspaper and that means we live and die on advertising dollars. The advertisers in small towns are almost exclusively local businesspeople, and in small towns the local businesspeople make up the entire body of local political power. Capiche? Not to mention the fact that our town, our sweet little burg of Black Marsh, can't even sustain us—we get eighty percent of our advertising from Pine Deep. Now, do you really think it is prudent to run an article that attacks, even condemns, the mayor of Pine Deep, as well as the police department and the whole town in general? Especially when said mayor is being quoted and sound-bited by every media on God's green Earth? Personally, I do not think that's such a keen idea, Newt. I think that is one of the stupidest ideas I've heard in a long time."

"But it's the truth!"

"So what? Since when did the truth matter in journalism? We write slanted and biased drivel so we can sell papers."

"We have a respon—"

"Oh, please! What are you, a Boy Scout? You working on your Walter Cronkite merit badge?" Hangood sighed and rubbed his eyes. "Newt, you are actually a pretty good reporter, better than the average hack working for our little rag, but you're only good when you stay the hell away from politics. You start writing about politics and suddenly you're Oliver Stone writing a movie script. Conspiracies, hidden meanings, secret arrangements, black ops, and shadow governments. Christ, Newton, has anyone ever told you that you live in a small town? The extent of corruption around here is that the more taxes you pay the less you have to worry about parking tickets. This is not D.C., this is not Philly or New York. This is Small Town, USA. In Small Town, USA, we do not try to sell papers by smashing down local government and—no, don't you dare try to give me your patented speech about the truth and the public's right to know! The public around here wants to know which antique dealer is having a sale on Shaker furniture and what the Corn Growers Commission is planning to do about the newest tax bill. Forget politics, Newton, you don't have the disposition for it, and I say that for your own good. I know you like to write about politics, and sometimes you are even *right* in what you say, but you get too worked up about it."

"This story is the natural extension of the feature on Ruger."

"I know it is, but it is injurious to the financial welfare of both Pine Deep and Black Marsh. That is a fact, and don't bother trying to make an argument for truth over money, because the publisher cares a lot more about how well this paper sells than what it says. Sad, maybe, but true, and he does sign our paychecks." Newton made a rude sound. He knew Hangood owned half of the paper himself. "Anyway,"

Hangood continued, "that article you wrote yesterday was a dandy, and it was quoted all across the country. You are the first writer on the *Sentinel* to have a piece picked up, word for word, by all the major wire services."

"So, doesn't that give me leverage to—"

"No, it doesn't, but it does give you some consideration. The article you wrote about the corruption in Pine Deep is dead, gone, never existed. It's not even a rumor in this office. Accept that or resign." Hangood waited, puffing blue clouds. Newton said nothing, his silence providing his grudging answer. "Okay. We're done with that. Let's start clean on the next issue."

"Pray, what is that?" There was enough frost in Newton's voice to lower the temperature of the room several degrees.

"I am going to offer you a very plum assignment. I talked it over with the publisher, and we've decided to assign you to writing a feature."

"Oh no! No you don't! Not another Daffodil Festival piece—"

"Shush! I am talking about a major feature, not some puff piece. A front-page feature with as many interior pages as you can fill."

"On what?" Newton asked bitterly. "The secrets of how to make corn dollies?"

"Actually, no. I want you to write an extensive feature on the haunted history of Pine Deep and surrounding towns." Newton stared at him, not believing what he was hearing. "Hear me out, Newton, hear me out. You've only lived here for about eight years, so you probably don't know much about the history of the area."

"Who *cares* about the history of the area?"

Hangood's flat stare silenced him. "If you would like to try and be a reporter for a moment, I'll explain. Good. Now, Pine Deep is the oldest town around here, much older than Black Marsh, Crestville, or any of the other burgs. It was settled way back in the Puritan days. Since it was settled there have been a series of weird and unexplainable events that have earned the town its reputation for being Spooksville, USA. Now, you may think that's just boring stuff, and normally you would be right, but I have a little fact that just might whet your appetite."

"Pray tell."

"I'll bet you didn't know that there was another series of brutal murders in Pine Deep, long before this one. The reports differ, but the general consensus is that there were seventeen or eighteen savage murders in and around Pine Deep."

"The Pine Deep Massacre, The Reaper Murders, the Black Harvest, whatever—I know this stuff already, Dick, the other papers have already played that card. Big deal. That was, what, thirty years ago?"

Hangood smiled. "There's more."

"More?"

"Oh yeah. Vigilantes, hidden bodies . . . that sort of thing. They even have a legend about the killer from those days."

"A legend?"

"Yeah. He's become the local bogeyman in Pine Deep. They use his name to scare little kids."

"The Bone Man!" Newton cried. "You're talking about the Bone Man. That's the other name they use for the Reaper."

"The Bone Man indeed. He was blamed for the murders and somehow accidentally got himself beaten to death. Some folks say his ghost still haunts the back roads of town, looking for the men who killed him. Some folks say that he was wrongly accused and is looking for the real killer, and can't rest until he finds him. Some say he *was* the Pine Deep Reaper. Lots of local legends, real juicy stuff. I'm thinking of getting Grace McCormick to illustrate it. She's the one does all those spooky calendars. My publisher wants me to try and sell it to *Parade*."

"*Parade?*" Newton asked. A sale to the color Sunday supplement was huge.

Seeing that Newton was swimming around the lure, Hangood jerked the line to set the hook. "Here's the kicker . . . among the families involved in that original massacre were the Guthries, the Wolfes, and the Crows."

Newton could only stare, though his mouth kept forming words that had no sound.

Hangood knocked more ash off his cigar, smiling blandly. "Interested?"

## (5)

He opened his eyes in the darkness, unsure for a moment where he was. It was cold and the darkness was total, without the slightest trace of light. There was no sound, either. He could have been adrift in the farthest reaches of space, or at the very bottom of the ocean. It took him a moment to realize where he was, and then another moment to realize that he had been asleep and dreaming. It surprised him. He didn't know he could sleep. Or dream. Somehow the thought that he could reassured him, made him feel stronger.

He lay there, reviewing his dreams, trying to remember the pieces and assemble them into something coherent, but the harder he tried, the more elusive the fragments became until they were all gone, leaving him with just the awareness of the cold and the dark.

Then there was a sound. It was the first he had heard in hours. Or was it days? A muffled sound, like a footfall, but then it was followed by a scraping sound. It came again. A muffled thud and then a scrape. Thud and scrape. Rhythmic, orderly, and getting gradually louder. Not very loud, but louder, or perhaps *closer*. Or, he wondered, was it that he was hearing it more clearly because he was trying to.

Thud . . . scrape. Thud . . . scrape.

Then silence. He lay there and tried to hold his breath, then realized that he was not breathing at all. He didn't do that anymore. Did not need to. He smiled, liking that.

Silence.

Suddenly his world was filled with light and noise. The light was muddy and indistinct, but it was there and he stared at it, wondering why it was so unfocused and just as he grasped why the light changed as the rubber sheet that covered him was pulled down and then he felt movement as the table he lay on rumbled out into brightness over well-oiled rollers. He blinked once, twice, then his eyes focused, adapting unnaturally fast from utter darkness to the harshness of fluorescents. He looked up and the first thing he saw were the banks of lights on the ceiling, and the second thing he saw was the face of the man who had pulled him out of darkness.

The face was horrible, bloody and cut and filthy, with eyes that burned like coals and torn lips that writhed and trembled around a mouthful of jagged teeth.

He saw that face, and he smiled his own saw-toothed grin. "Boyd," he whispered. He had to take a breath to speak the name.

The thing over him glared down at him, lips working, Adam's apple bobbing as it tried to speak. "Karl . . ." it said.

# Chapter 9

## (1)

That night Crow and Val had dinner with Terry and Sarah. While they were at the table none of them brought up anything related to Pine Deep's troubles, though their efforts to keep the conversation sanitized and light bordered on farce. The fact that Terry and Val cared little for one another even though she and Sarah were close did nothing to warm the room, even with a fire crackling in the living room and Ralph Vaughn Williams's *Pastoral Symphony* sweetening the air. By the time the dessert plates were cleared and Sarah was pouring second coffees, Terry was looking thin with strain. Sarah caught Crow's eye and, with the kind of telepathy old friends possess, with a flick of a glance toward the back door communicated a suggestion to Crow. He winked and said, "Terry, why don't we take our cups outside and catch some air. You gals don't mind, do you?" Normally a comment like that would have gotten him a sharp reply from Val—who never liked to be left with the dishes—but she had caught the look between Sarah and Crow, and read it right.

"Sounds like a good idea. Too cold out there for me," she said. "I'll help Sarah clear away."

Terry only grunted, picked up his cup, and shambled after Crow. Behind the house was a huge hardwood deck with two big glass-topped tables and a dozen chairs scattered around. Crow lowered himself carefully into a redwood chaise longue and Terry parked his rump on the rail. For a while all they did was look at the stars. Orion was magnificent, his jeweled belt glittering. The wind had died away in late afternoon and though it was cold, both men were comfortable, Terry in a wheat-colored cable-knit sweater over charcoal cords, and Crow in jeans and a red flannel shirt over a sweatshirt advertising the *Wild River Review*. Party Cat came darting out to join them, the little hinged door slapping behind him. He started to jump up on the rail to be near Terry, then appeared to change his mind and crawled onto Crow's lap. Terry didn't notice.

For a couple of minutes they discussed the manhunt, and Terry brought Crow up to speed on what Ferro and Gus were doing to find Boyd. "All they found the first day were some footprints, but that petered out to nothing. Yesterday they had twice as many men in the woods and still found nothing. Today, same thing, and Ferro even had some guys rappel down the pitch from the Passion Pit to Dark Hollow. Nothing. What's the line from *The Fugitive*? Where Tommy Lee Jones tells his guys he wants a hard-target search of any residence, gas station, farmhouse, henhouse, doghouse, and outhouse in the area? Well, that about sums it up, but no one's so much as found a whiff of Boyd. Nothing. Ferro's pain-in-the-butt partner, LaMastra, thinks Boyd left town, but since he did that before and then came back to kill those poor cops, I don't know how much I'm willing to believe it. Understand, I hope he has left," Terry concluded bitterly. "We need this to be *over*!"

"Christ, I hope so," Crow said, but he didn't think it was. Not with those enigmatic last words of Karl Ruger nibbling at him night and day, but he didn't want to tell Terry about that quite yet, especially with the look of strained exhaustion painted on Terry's face. He took a sip to let the moment pass before broaching a different subject. "So, tell me, bro, you still having those nightmares?"

Terry stiffened, but did not turn. "Did Sarah say something?"

"No, you did, you lunkhead. In my store, couple days ago, just before all the fun and games started."

Terry nodded. "Fair enough." But he didn't elaborate right away. Crow gave him a "go ahead" arch of the eyebrows but by the time Terry finally answered Crow's coffee had cooled by several degrees and Party Cat had fallen asleep, his head on Crow's crotch. The air was utterly still and off in the distance they could hear music from the bars on Corn Hill. Despite the ongoing manhunt, tourists were still pouring into the town and everywhere there was laughter and music. Even Crow thought that was weird.

When he spoke, Terry's voice was soft and Crow had to forcibly tune out the music to catch his words. "Crow, next to Sarah you're the one person I really trust." He turned to see if Crow was going to make one of his smartass comments, but Crow just raised his cup in silent acknowledgment of the trust, so Terry continued, "And I know that if anyone is going to have my back, and to not judge me based on what I'm about to say, it's going to be you."

"We've been each other's wingmen for a lot of years, Wolfman."

"And don't ever think I don't appreciate it. I know I'm sometime high maintenance." He sipped his coffee and set the cup down. "For the last month or so I've been having problems, and the nightmares are just part of it . . . but let's start there." He described one of the dreams to Crow, going into more detail than he had even shared with his psychiatrist, and once more he turned to see if there was any mockery or humor on Crow's face, but while Terry was talking, Crow had just leaned forward, listening, his face very serious, his cup forgotten in his hands.

When Terry finished, Crow asked, "And you say you're having some hallucinations where you think you see this monster face in mirrors and such?"

Terry nodded. "How crazy is that?"

Instead of answering, Crow asked, "What does the beast look like?"

It wasn't the question Terry was expecting and his surprise showed on his face. "What does it matter? A monster's a monster."

"When it comes to nightmares, I don't think so. Maybe if we understood the kind of critter you're seeing it might mean something, you know—the way one thing means something else in regular dreams. You dream of hotdogs flying through the Lincoln Tunnel and it means you need to get laid."

A crow flapped out of the east and landed in the tree above him, cawing softly. "It's a wolf," Terry said at last.

Crow nodded. "Well, that much makes sense."

"How?" Terry loaded that one word with a hundred questions.

"Well, last time I looked at the name on those checks you give me to manage the Hayride, your last name is 'Wolfe.' Not really much of a stretch. If you're dreaming about becoming a beast and fate conveniently gives you a last name like that, it's pretty much a gimme. Plus, we've all been calling you Wolfman since grade school. Look at me—Crow— if I dreamed about becoming a bird, what do you think would be first on the list?"

"No," Terry said with a vigorous shake of his head, "it can't be that simple."

"Not saying it is, brother," Crow said, "but it's at least part of the puzzle. What's your doc say about it?"

"He thinks it's stress."

"And you *don't*?" He waved his hands to indicate the town. "You're the mayor of Shitstorm, USA. Can we say 'blight'? Can we say 'township-wide financial crisis'? Not to mention Ruger and those other ass-clowns shooting up the place."

"This started before Ruger."

"Has it gotten worse since he's been here?"

A silence, then Terry nodded. Crow gave a "well, there you are" hand gesture.

"No," Terry said, "there's more."

## (2)

Vic always drove carefully. He'd never so much as logged a parking ticket, let alone a speeding ticket, so when he saw that there was a police unit behind him he didn't sweat being pulled over. On the other hand, he was less than half a mile from the hospital, heading away from it on the only major road that passed those gates. He stared at the headlights of the cruiser in his rearview mirror and his mind was working, working.

When the light ahead turned red, he made a decision and braked to a stop, pulling halfway onto the shoulder and waving his arm out the window. As the cruiser pulled up Vic could see that it was Dave Golub riding alone. He knew Golub through Polk. A big Jewish kid playing cop to pay his way through law school. Vic grinned. "Hey! Dave!"

Golub peered through his passenger window and saw who it was. He put his unit in park and hit the button to drop the window. "Vic?"

"Yeah, glad to see you," Vic said and jerked his door open. "You're a gift from God, let me tell you."

"Everything okay?"

"Oh, well it is and it ain't," Vic said, flashing his grin. "I hit a deer a couple miles back. Mashed the son of a bitch but good and slung him in the back." He jerked a thumb toward the truck bed. "But I just heard a thump and I think the poor bastard ain't dead after all. Mind taking a look?"

Without waiting for an answer he started walking back toward the tailgate, knowing that Golub would follow. He just hoped he wouldn't call it in, but didn't think he would. Vic was a townie and everybody knew Vic. Vic never got drunk, never got into trouble, and he was a buddy with Polk.

Golub said, "Sure, but I'm no vet," and got out.

As he crunched along the gravel on the shoulder, Vic waited, one hand inside the cab holding onto the corner of the tarp, sizing Golub up. The kid was huge, maybe six-five and beefy tending toward soft. Vic knew he could take him if he had to, but that wasn't on the menu.

"Let me see what you got," Golub said, putting one hand on the rim of the bed and using the other to shine his light at the tarp. "If it's still wounded I can call someone to bring out one of those humane-killer things, and—"

As he said this, Vic whipped back the tarp. There was nothing humane about what happened next.

## (3)

Val parted the curtains just slightly and peered out. The kitchen was dark and she could see Terry and Crow outside. "What do you think they're talking about?" she asked.

"Besides what's going on in town?" Sarah asked from the doorway. She had her arms folded and was leaning against the frame. "Probably talking about Terry's dreams."

Val let the curtains fall closed and turned to Sarah. "Dreams?"

"Come in to the parlor." When they were seated on opposite sides of the fireplace, Sarah leaned close, taking Val's hand. "I know you and Terry don't get along that well . . ."

"That's ancient history."

"No, it isn't," Sarah said, "but it's good of you to say it. The point is, Terry loves Crow like a brother, and if I had to guess what he's doing out there, he's opening up to him about some stuff he should have told him weeks ago. You see . . . Terry has been having some problems." She paused. "Psychological problems." Val squeezed Sarah's hand, and Sarah took a breath and plunged ahead. "Terry is telling Crow, and I need to tell someone, too, and I was going to call you a few days ago, and then all of this stuff happened with your dad, and the farm and all."

"It's been bad for all of us, honey, but if you need to get something off your chest don't worry about how I'm going to take it. Tell you the truth, right now I need to be somebody's rock, if you know what I'm saying. I'm not good at being vulnerable—I need to be the strong one. That make sense?"

Sarah smiled and there were tears in her eyes. "Of course

it does, Val. Sometimes I think you're the toughest one of all of us. I know Crow thinks that, too; and it may surprise you to know, but so does Terry." She dabbed at her eyes. "I don't know if he's ever managed to say it, but he's really sorry about what happened. He knows he betrayed you, he knows he broke your heart. It was a bad time for him and if he could take it back and make it right, he would, but sometimes Terry is wound so tight he doesn't know how to reach people. Sure, he's great at press conferences, but he's never been very good at getting to the heart of things. You know that as well as anyone."

Val nodded, and thinking about the grudge she'd been holding for almost sixteen years she felt suddenly ashamed. She sighed, and then gave Sarah a rueful smile. "Okay, sweetie, as far as I'm concerned that stuff is ancient history. I'm officially calling a truce."

"Thank God," Sarah said, and the relief was plain on her face, "because right now I need you to help me with what Terry's going through. If you want to . . . if you can."

"Sarah . . ." Val said, squeezing her hand again. "We're all in this together."

Sarah took another deep breath and let it out as a sigh, her eyes shifting from Val to the fire and then to her hands, which were wriggling and knotting in her lap. "It's . . . well . . . I think Terry is losing his mind," she said.

### (4)

"More . . . like what?" Crow asked slowly.

It took Terry a full minute to make his mouth form the words. "Crow . . . my dead sister, Mandy's been following me lately." When Crow's mouth dropped open, Terry added, "And she's been trying to get me to kill myself."

"Holy leaping ratshit!"

"How well you put it," Terry said with a weak smile, but his voice cracked. He looked at the coffee in his cup, sighed, and emptied the cup over the rail, stood up without a word, and went inside. When he came out he had a bottle of

Weyerbacher Imperial Pumpkin Ale. He unscrewed the cap, tossed it out into the shadows, and took a long pull.

Crow forced himself to say, "Why, Terry? Why would Mandy want you dead?"

Terry pulled a chair close to the chaise longue and sat down, leaning his big forearms on his thighs, his blue eyes crackling with tension and fear, the beer bottle swaying like a plumb bob from his laced fingers. "Mandy is afraid that the beast is going to take over and that I'm going to become . . ."

"Become what?" Crow whispered. Icy hands were clamped around his spine.

Tears filled Terry's eyes and for the first time Crow truly had a measure of the hell that his friend was in. "Crow . . . she thinks that if the beast takes over I'll become just like Ubel Griswold."

Each of those words hit Crow over the heart like punches, and each one was a harder blow than anything Ruger had thrown at him. *Ubel Griswold sends his regards.* "Oh my God!" he croaked, when he found his voice. He steeled himself to ask, "Terry . . . I've asked you a dozen times since we were kids and you always blow me off . . . but how much do you remember of what happened to you and Mandy that day?"

Which is when Terry's cell phone rang. The sound made Crow jump and spill his coffee all over Party Cat, who hissed and leapt up and ran out into the yard. As Crow jumped up to slap at the lukewarm stains spreading on his jeans, he heard one-half of the conversation. "Hello. Gus . . . yes, what's—? *What?* When? Jesus H. Christ, Gus . . . how did he get into the bloody *hospital*?" A pause. "Was anyone hurt? Well, thank God for that. No, I'm at home. I'll . . . be there in just a few minutes."

Terry snapped his phone shut and stood with his eyes closed and one hand clapped over his head, fingers knotted in his hair as if he wanted to rip a handful of it out. He took an awkward step backward and staggered, but Crow darted forward and caught him before he fell. He helped Terry to the rail and took the phone out of his hand.

"Terry, what's wrong?"

Terry Wolfe leaned on the rail, sucking in great lungfuls of air. "Is this never going to stop?" he asked the night. The crow in the tree cawed again, a little louder this time; then in a fractured voice he said, "Kenneth Boyd just broke into Pinelands Hospital and stole Karl Ruger's body."

Crow felt as if someone has just punched all of the air out of his lungs. He opened his mouth, but there was nothing in his vocabulary to respond to that, so he stared at Terry as around them both the moon opened its mocking white eye and the dark silence roared.

# Interlude

The Carby Place was one of those farms that would have been a delight for a wandering Tom Joad: ramshackle and down at the heels, but honest, and it grew crops that fed the family with just enough left over to bring in a few thousand a month. Every month it was a stretch to meet the bills, pay something on the mortgage, put clothes on the kids. There were only thirty such farms left in Pine Deep, and with inflation and the blight, soon there would be none. Gaither Carby knew that and still he managed to crawl out of bed every morning, pull on his work clothes, choke down a breakfast, and then lumber out to the fields to try and fight another battle in a lost war. He could sell out, and after the mortgage was settled there would be enough equity left to maybe buy a trailer home in Bensalem, and then maybe finish out life working some shit job until he was old enough to apply for social security. Either way he looked the road went nowhere.

Gaither Carby was the great-grandson of the Carby who had bought the land and built the farm. He was fifty-eight and looked seventy, with arthritis starting in his hands and steel pins in his left knee. He had the blocky build and thick,

callused fingers, and the bleak fatalism of the heavily mort-
gaged man who was seeing everything his family had ever
owned being gobbled up by the Pine Deep Farmer's Bank.
He knew it was an old story, repeated a thousand times a
week across the country, and he knew that there was nothing
unique or exceptional about him or his to elicit any kind of
help. No Farm Aid, no Willie Nelson and Neil Young. He
was going to lose the place within two or three years, and
that would simply be that.

When the workday was finished, Carby came in from the
fields, showered, ate dinner, and then went back outside for a
smoke. Lily didn't let him smoke in the house, and Jilly, his
sixteen-year-old, always complained it made her ill. His boy,
Tyler, never bitched about it, or about anything for that matter, but Carby seldom felt like fighting the same fight every
day, so he took his pipe and went outside to walk the fence
and think.

Tonight he wasn't thinking at all about his money troubles, or what it was going to cost him to replace the head
gasket on his battered Ford pickup. Tonight he couldn't have
cared less about the mortgage payment due on Wednesday or
the fact that the sprinkler system on the western ten acres
was older than he was and needed an overhaul. He didn't
care about the heating bill, the cost of day labor, or the fact
that he'd recently discovered that his sixteen-year-old daughter was taking the Pill. Tonight he was thinking about what
was going on in town. Yesterday he'd had lunch with Gus
and some of the boys from town, and even though everyone
was all laughs and buddy-buddy, he could see in their eyes
that they were scared. Even Gus was scared. Killers running
around, people dying. Carby was scared, too. So scared that
he had unlocked the gun cabinet and made Tyler clean, oil,
and load each rifle and shotgun, and then, with the whole
family trailing along, he'd taken one long gun to each bedroom in the house, wrapped it in a pillowcase, and put in between mattress and box spring.

"Any of those rat bastards break in here, I want everyone
to grab the closest gun. We ain't going to end up like Henry

Guthrie, God rest him." Carby had taught Tyler and Jilly how to shoot before they were out of single digits and by the time they were in their teens both of them could drop a pheasant at fifty yards. Lily? Well, she could fire a shotgun and anyone could hit something with a shotgun, especially an intruder in the close confines of a small farmhouse. Even so, Carby was scared for his family. He walked the fenceline with his pipe between his teeth and his own shotgun in the crook of his arm; the gun was broken open at the breech but loaded with buckshot. His dog, a big shepherd named Spooker, was back at the house with the girls and Tyler.

*Life's a bitch and then you die,* he thought as he walked. He'd always loved that expression. As close to Zen as he had ever seen, with the exception of *No Pain, No Gain,* which he had tattooed on his left shoulder back in his wrestling days. Not pro wrestling or any of that TV comedy, but Greco-Roman during his four years at Pinelands College. Carby had studied animal husbandry and agriculture, and for the most part he hadn't learned much beyond get your cows to screw and plant as many crops as you can.

"Yeah, life's a bitch and then you die," he said aloud, and that made him think of death. Not just the headline deaths out at the Guthrie place, but death closer to home. His buddy Bailey Frane had buried his mother yesterday morning. Passed in her sleep, even though she'd been healthy as a horse for all her eighty years. Carby had stood by Bailey during the funeral and had sipped kitchen whiskey with him all afternoon, the two of them growing more philosophic about life and death as the tide-line of the bottle receded.

There was a breeze coming out of the southwest and he stopped for a moment at the edge of a fallow field where he planned to grow blueberries next season. So far the blight hadn't touched the berry crops in the region, so he thought he'd try blueberries, strawberries, blackberries, and maybe some raspberries. The better berries sold pretty well in farmers' markets or to the buyers for the store chains; the second-best always sold to the jelly companies in New Jersey.

He sniffed the wind, searching for the scents he liked—

tilled earth, manure, sweetgrass—but then he frowned. There was an odd smell on the air; threaded through the earthy smell of churned soil, wood smoke, and dried corn, there were other scents, and Carby had a farmer's nose. There was some old skunk there, but that was from roadkill over on Seven Mile Road on the other side of the Pine River, less potent than it had been a few nights ago. A whiff of gasoline, too. And something else. Sweeter, but not sweet like fruit. More like the sugar-up-your-nose stink of something left out to rot. Sweet like that. Nasty sweet. He took his pipe out of his mouth and held it at arm's length, clearing his nose as much as possible. The breeze brought the olio of smells again, and there it was. The bad sweet smell. Only this time it was stronger. Fresher. Nearer, he thought.

*Dead deer out in the woods,* he thought, but the idea of something dead in the woods spooked him. What if it wasn't a dead deer out there? What if that Boyd fellow had killed someone else and what he smelled was a dead body out in the woods?

"Balls," he told himself and he screwed on a mocking smile. Even so, he reached over to the fence rail, tapped the coal out of his pipe, grinding it into the mud and put the warm pipe in his pocket so that he had both hands free. For a moment he stood there unconsciously holding the shotgun at port arms, sniffing the wind like Spooker. The dead-sweet smell was, if anything, stronger, and that wasn't right. The breeze was coming out of the west, blowing across Pine River. The state forestland was north and east of his place, and Pinelands College was south and east. There were no deer woods to the west. Just farm fields and the river, and on the other side of the river was a big auto junkyard that covered more than a square mile.

With the pipe gone his sense of smell began sharper with each breath, and now the dead-sweet smell was much stronger. Not distant at all and . . . not a dead scent, really. More like sick-sweet. Earthy and rotting and somehow—he fished for the word—*vital.*

"Balls," he said, and decided that he'd had enough of

moonlit strolls. He had walked the fenceline for half a mile and it ringed his property, but if he cut across the fallow field he could be home in just a couple of minutes. He looked due east to where the lighted windows of his home gave the house its own definition against the utter blackness of the fields and forest beyond. Those yellow rectangles had always looked homey to him, warm and inviting and—even he had to admit it—safe, but now those tiny dots of light seemed dwarfed by the immense darkness and as he looked at them he thought he had never seen anything look as lonely.

Carby started out across the field, looking down as he went to pick a path through the shadows on the ground. It wasn't until he was a third of the way across that he saw the mound, and it stopped him in his tracks. The hump of dirt wasn't big, no more than three feet high at the crest, but it was there and he sure as hell hadn't made it. He hadn't done any digging in this field all year.

"What the hell is this shit?" There was a small flashlight on his keychain for finding key slots on the fence locks, and he fished in his jeans for his keys and then flicked it on. It was so dark out that the tiny flash threw a pretty good beam and Carby played it over the mound. It was maybe eight feet long, but only a yard high in the middle and tapering off pretty quickly toward each end. The dirt was rough and chunky like it had been hand dug, not clean packed the way a shovel would have done. He shone the beam all along it and then swept the area around the mound. He saw two things that caused gooseflesh to pebble him from feet to hairline. All around the mound were footprints. Clear prints that went this way and that, sometimes standing alone, sometimes overlapping. City shoes with smooth soles, the complex tread-pattern of sneakers, and the rippled ridges of work boots. He counted five separate pairs. That was the first thing, and it froze him to the spot.

The second thing he saw made his pores open and burst with cold sweat. Just beyond the mound, maybe ten feet farther on into the darkness, was a second mound. He moved the light around and saw a third. And a fourth. All of them were about the same length, the same height. All made up of hand-churned clods of dirt. Then he saw the fifth mound. It was not as high as the others, nor as rounded on top. In fact the top of this mound was ragged and the sides had caved back from the crest. Carby swallowed a lump the size of a corncob. His flash beam played over the uneven dirt and even without drawing any closer to it he could see that this mound was *open.*

Open was a strange thought, and Carby took a step closer, examining the mound, trying to understand them all, but trying to understand this one more because this one bothered him more. This one looked even more like a . . .

*Grave?*

He didn't even want to think that word, but there it was. The thing looked like a grave. "Oh, shit," he said, and a thousand thoughts flew around in his head like hysterical crows in a lightning-struck tree. *Christ!* What if Boyd had killed someone else and had come out here to the ass-end of town to hide the body? No, *bodies!* Terror had him by the throat. What if Boyd had been killing folks all day and had buried them here on the farm. On *his farm!* Mary, Mother of God, that would be the end of things. No one would ever buy crops from a farm where bodies had been buried. This was the end of the farm, sure as cows shit brown. This was the end of *him.* Blinking sweat out of his eyes, Carby took a step closer, and then another, crouching to see along the beam of the flashlight, expecting to see a dead hand sticking up out of the earth like a stand of asparagus, hoping he wouldn't see that and yet weirdly fascinated. He was bent at the waist, head bowed, peering at the mound from four feet away when the earth *moved.*

Carby froze as if sprayed with liquid nitrogen, his eyes bugging wide. The shotgun was something stupid and forgotten in his hands as he stared at the movement, still locked in the awful fascination and at the same time not really understanding what he was seeing. The mound of dirt trembled— and Carby had the fleeting thought that it was loose fill stirred by the wind—but then the farmer in him realized that the wind was blowing the wrong way for dirt to fall toward him. He watched, wide-mouthed, as the dirt fluttered down, running in dry rivulets as the whole mound began to shudder. A large clod broke off and fell right by his toe. He picked it up. It was ordinary dirt, of course, loosely packed and cool. Another clod fell out of the mound, and another. Then one large clump, right near the top, seemed to lift. Carby stared at it, still unable to explain or understand what he was seeing. The heavier clump rose, standing almost on edge, and then broke under its own weight and the individual pieces toppled off in all directions.

Carby straightened and leaned over to try and see what had disturbed the dirt. Was it a gopher in there? A rabbit? He truly could not understand it. He leaned close and shined the flashlight into the hole created by the large clod. The weak yellow light of the flash illuminated the hole with a splash of light, glimmering on small pieces of smooth stone in the soil, glinting off a fragment of an old Coke bottle, reflected redly off the eyes of the face in the mound.

Carby let out a cry and jumped back. He backpedaled and fell down. It had been a face in there! The thought horrified him. Had someone . . . buried a body out here? The thought made him gag. Was that it? Boyd *had* murdered someone and carted their body out here, burying it in his fallow field. He looked around wildly and saw the other mounds.

"My God . . ." he whispered. Five of them. That cop-killing son of a bitch had come out here and buried five bodies in his field. "Jesus God Almighty." He reached for the fallen flashlight and wiped the dirt off the lens, then swung the beam back to the mound, and all thinking abruptly stopped. His heart nearly stopped as well. He was aware only of sensation: the constriction in his chest, another hard lump in his throat, an iciness sweeping down his legs. His skin crawled. Carby had always heard that expression, but until that moment he had never actually experienced the grisly sensation of the muscles under his skin knotting and writhing as his body chemistry misfired. His glands discharged microfluids into his system, his nerve endings sent out signals triggered by shock, and the adrenaline discharge made the hair on his scalp ripple like wheat in a cold wind.

The dead body in the mound was struggling to sit up. It pushed dirt away from its mouth, pushed at the heavy clods, clawed at the soft soil for purchase until it sat erect. Then it turned a dirt-smeared white face at Carby and smiled. Carby screamed once, a shrill, tearing scream of absolute horror, and ran.

He had no idea when he got up, or how. He had no thought at all. He just ran, the shotgun in his hands as forgotten and useless as the flashlight that now lay in the dirt behind him. A quarter of a mile away the lights of his house beckoned with welcome and safety. In the house there were door locks and a telephone. Inside the house were his son and daughter. Inside his house was his wife, Lily. They were all farm people, they all knew how to handle guns and every gun in the house was loaded. In the house was one big, mean sonovabitching German shepherd. In the yard beside the house there was a car. The walls of the house, even in shadows, looked tall and strong and safe. If he could only get there, get inside. Gaither Carby ran as fast as his thick legs could carry him. He never once looked back; he never paused, never slowed, even when his bladder released and warm piss ran down his legs. He ran until that seized-up heart in his chest began to hammer again and he ran until lights burst in his eyes like fireworks. He ran as if his life depended on it.

But he didn't run fast enough. A dark something came out of the shadows to his left and smashed into him, knocking him sideways with terrible force, tearing a strangled scream out of him before the weight of the thing slammed him down and drove all of the breath from his lungs. He hit hard and slid a few feet across the sandpaper roughness of the fallow field. He was blind from the shock but he could feel fingers bunching the cloth of his jacket, could feel the heat of breath on his cheek and something bent low over him. It was man-sized but it panted like a hungry dog and its weight was oppressive. Gasping a lungful of air, Carby swung a strong overhand right, aiming blindly, and he felt

his knuckles crash into something that crunched like cartilage. A nose? An ear? He shook his vision clear and pounded
his fists at the hands that held him down. Around him he
could hear the pounding of feet as someone else ran up to
join the fight. He heard other sounds, too.

He heard the low snigger of laughter. The figure on top of
him was a dark silhouette but Carby knew it was a man, and
he hooked punch after punch into the man's ribs. He heard
them go, felt them break under his punches, but the figure
just crouched there, holding him down, not even grunting
with the pain.

"Let me go, you shit-eating bastard!" he bellowed and
swung his biggest punch yet, cracking right across the point
of his attacker's jaw. The blow snapped the man's head
around and he toppled sideways as Carby kicked and scrabbled out from under. He spun around onto all fours as the
man that had brought him down rolled away. Carby looked
left and right. There were four other people there. Five in all.
Ringed around him. One on the ground, crouched like
Carby, was on all fours; four were standing. Two of them
were close enough for the starlight to cast their faces in cool
blue-white light.

One was a man that Carby had never seen, dressed in
khakis and what looked like a polo shirt. It was so weirdly
incongruous to the situation that Carby just stared. The man
was in his midthirties, with a handsome face and a trim little
mustache. Carby turned to his left and looked at the other
person whose face was starlit. A woman. A woman he knew.
Eighty years old, with a dowager's hump and a tangled mass
of gray hair, dressed in her best church clothes. Carby definitely knew her, had known her all his life. Just yesterday he
had sat drinking kitchen whiskey with her son, Bailey. Just
hours after six men lowered her coffin into the ground at
Pineview Cemetery. Andrea Frane.

Carby's mouth hung open to scream, but there was no
sound left in him. Andrea opened her mouth, too. More than
once Carby had seen her without her dentures, her toothless
mouth caved in on itself, but that mouth was not toothless

any longer. Now it had brand-new teeth that gleamed white and wet in the starlight. She opened her mouth to show all of her new teeth to Carby as the others stepped up and took him by the arms and shoulders. The man with the polo shirt grabbed Carby by the hair and wrenched his head to one side, exposing the vulnerable flesh of his neck and throat as Andrea Frane stepped closer and then bent toward him with her gaping, toothsome mouth.

PART TWO

# SEASON OF THE WOLF

*Early morning, October 3rd, to sunset, October 7th*

There is no hunting like the hunting of man,
and those who have hunted armed men long enough
and liked it,
never care for anything else thereafter.

—Ernest Hemingway,
"On the Blue Water"
*Esquire,* April 1935

Wolf comes hunting, pale moon overhead
Big gray wolf comes hunting, blood moon overhead
Better lock your doors, better say your prayers
'Cause the wolf's come hunting . . . hunting for your child.

—Oren Morse, *Bad Moon Blues*

# Chapter 10

## (1)

In his dreams he was usually Iron Mike Sweeney, the Enemy of Evil, a planet-hopping, dimension-crossing super-hero with high-tech weapons and vast powers that made him invulnerable to harm. In one of his favorite dreams Mike was the squad leader of a team of interstellar commandoes and in those dreams he moved with the ruthless efficiency and eyes-on-the-prize clarity of focus of Jack Bauer—if Jack Bauer had been a spaceman. Frequently the villains in his dreams looked like Vic—and even in the deepest of his dreams Mike realized what *that* was all about—and in each of those dreams the Enemy of Evil would kick the ass of alien invader-Vic, or demon-Vic, or monster-from-beyond-Vic. Those were pretty good dreams because it felt good to blast Vic with a laser or cut his head off with a two-handed broadsword.

Sometimes—rarely over the years and then almost exclusively over the last few months—Mike's dreams changed into very regular and specific nightmares. In those dreams he would be walking through a dark swampy hollow. The bushes and trees around him were on fire and there were people lying everywhere. Dead people, covered in blood, torn apart. In those dreams Mike always carried a samurai sword, a *katana*, in his hands, which was odd because in his adventure dreams Iron Mike Sweeney always used either a blaster or a big knight's sword, never one of the slender Japanese blades, but in these new dreams it was always a katana, and its blade was always smeared with bright blood.

In these dreams the dead people were people Mike knew. Crow was there a lot, and he almost always wore a big tank on his back of the kind that exterminators or lawn-care guys wore, and the hose was clutched in Crow's dead hand. The only part of him that wasn't covered in blood was the front of his T-shirt, which showed the logo for band called *Missing 84*, which Mike had never heard of. Crow's fiancée was usually alive, but she'd been beaten to her knees and was weeping over the body of her father, Henry Guthrie. There were other people: Dr. Weinstock from the hospital, sprawled with his throat torn out, and the chief of police sitting with his back propped against a tree and his legs spread, a piss stain spreading on his pants as he dribbled blood from his nose and mouth and ears. Others, too, like his mom. She wasn't dead, but stood naked and covered in blood—and when he was awake Mike wondered how sick it was that he dreamed of his mother naked and tried to imagine how much of his life would be spent in therapy because of that image—and his mom was laughing as the forest burned and people died. There was a dark man standing next to her, also laughing, but he was hazy like an out-of-focus photograph and Mike could discern no details.

Last night Mike had been through that dream again, all of the familiar images of pain and loss and horror, all the way up to the point where a shadow passed over Mike and he turned to see what had cast it. He turned and looked up . . . and up and *it* stood there: impossibly huge, monstrous, towering above the flames, laughing in a voice that rumbled like thunder. A vast creature like something out of horror movies, with hairy goatlike legs, the muscular torso of a man, a whipping tail with a barbed point, and vast black wings. A mouth that was filled with teeth the size of daggers and horns that were splashed with gore. A monster Mike had seen on TV and in films and that he'd read about in books, but though this was the form of the devil in every aspect, Mike knew that even its shape and appearance were a lie. A special effect, or at least *done* for effect. Not that it made the creature any less terrifying. If anything, the deliberate choosing of this image—an aspect intended to be reviled and feared on a primal level—showed the subtlety and mockery of the beast. In these dreams the monster would spread its great arms as if to encompass the burning hollow, the forests, the town, and the world, and he would hiss "Mine!" just before reaching for Mike.

This is how his dreams had started last night, and then at the moment those massive hands were closing around him the dream changed as abruptly as if someone had clicked a TV remote and immediately Mike was on his bicycle out on A-32, pedaling fit to burst his heart, his breath burning in his throat, as behind him the Wrecker barreled down on him, its horn blaring like the howl of a hellhound and the spiked bars of its chrome grille breaking apart in the middle to form two rows of jagged metal fangs. That dream also played itself out, all the way to the point where the wheels of the trucks rolled over him from the toes upward, pulverizing his bones and pulping his flesh while worlds of fire exploded in every cell and his mind absorbed all of it without escape.

Then last night, as this dream literally ground to a halt with his skull exploding into blackness, he should have awakened—as he had the night before, and the night before that—but again some perverse hand punched the Great Cosmic TV Remote and his consciousness was switched into a new dream. A brand-new dream, not a rerun. Mike was always aware that he was dreaming even when he was in the deepest part of his sleep. Part of him—he was never sure if it was his essential self or some alien part—was always watching as things happened. This had always been the case with him, even during the adventure dreams of Iron Mike Sweeney, the Enemy of Evil, and that part of him knew that it was not he who was controlling the Great Cosmic TV Remote. If it had been, he'd have channel surfed away from the burning forest and out from under the wheels of the Wrecker and back into an adventure dream in which he was the buff hero with a big sword rescuing a scantily clad heroine who would look suspiciously like Scarlett Johansson.

This new dream was, in its way, stranger than all the others, and in its way it was part of all the others. A blend. The burning forest was there, though instead of staggering through the forest looking at all the twisted dead, Mike rode down a long hill toward it. The hill started out as Route A-32, and the Wrecker was hot on his tail, the grille snapping at his back tire, but then Mike got a weird kind of second wind and it gave him the grit to amp it up. His legs became a blur and the thin rubber of his tires send up a high keening wail as he shot forward, moving faster and faster, pulling ahead of the Wrecker. Behind him the horn screamed in frustrated protest, but Mike was flying forward now, the wind moving across his cheeks so fast it felt like cold water. His red hair snapped behind his skull like the streamers of a torn flag.

The black flatness of A-32 changed under him and he looked down to see that asphalt had become hard-packed dirt and then a rutted road, but still he rode on. Several times he would surge his weight upward so high that the bike would lift under him and they would sail right over a deep pothole or a fallen branch. Nothing could stop him. As the tires thumped back down on the dirt the shock would go through him, but there was no pain in it. The jolt felt good because his muscles were hard and yet loose, tensed only where they needed to be, like a top athlete's would be in the heat of the championship race. His lungs worked, but there was no burn in his throat. This was a pace that would kill anyone else, but it couldn't kill him because it was *his* pace.

As the bike jolted back down he felt something bump hard against his back. Something long and comfortably heavy was slung across his back. He could not see it, but he knew what it was. His sword. His *katana*. A samurai sword with a wrought-iron hilt made to look like November trees whose branches were filled with crows. He knew the crows-in-the-trees pattern was painted on the black lacquered sheath.

His bike followed the path as it began to plunge down away from the highway, down into the shadows of Dark Hollow. The shadows cast by the mountains and the tall trees closed in around him, but Mike did not lose sight of the road. In this dream Mike could *see* in the dark. In this dream Mike understood the dark—though the part of him that was watching the dream did not understand what that meant. It was enough that the Mike in the dream understood it.

Down and down he rode, the path smoothing out as it neared the bottom. Ahead Mike could see the first of the burning trees and shrubs, and he knew he was reaching the place where the dead would be. Where the creature would be. Where the killing would be. The farther down he went the more of the forest was ablaze and he could feel the heat on his skin. It was leaning into a picture of hell, because the fire was filled with screams and bodies that twisted and writhed as they shrieked. Mike loved the fire, loved what it was doing, though he didn't understand why he loved it. The slope bottomed out and broadened into a clearing and this field was packed with hundreds of people—some burning, some not. Those that were not aflame spun toward him, hissing like snakes, glaring at him with crimson eyes, snarling with mouths filled with yellow fangs.

These monsters clustered around a small knot of people—Crow, Val, Dr. Weinstock, a few others he didn't know—and had been closing in on them as Mike swept down and skidded to a stop, swinging the back end of his bike around so that a plume of dust was kicked up into the air. Bits of twig and leaf in that plume caught fire, and for a second Mike was hidden behind a veil of that fire, then he leapt through the curtain, drawing his sword and howling with a bloodlust that was a match for any monster in any of his dreams. He felt older, bigger, powerful, insanely confident.

He laughed in triumph as his blade flicked out and cut one monster's head from its shoulders. The creature instantly turned to a pillar of flaming ash and then exploded into dust. Mike landed in front of the crowd of people—and even

Crow looked helpless and weak—and the creatures all hesitated. Mike's sword flashed through the air and then he swept it down and slashed a line in the ground in front of his feet. The line burned as if the tip of the sword was filled with kerosene.

"Let's do this!" he said aloud in a line cribbed from the movie *Blade*.

The monsters snarled and in a single mass of teeth and claws they closed in on Mike and his friends, but Mike's sword became a blur of bloodstained silver as he leapt to meet them, slashing and twisting, skewering and then whipping the sword free and using the same motion to kill a creature lunging at him from behind. The monsters died by the dozens, they died by the score. Flames ignited everywhere as they died, and Mike never stopped laughing as he whirled and lunged and killed and killed and—

The scream behind him made his freeze in place and when he snapped his head around he saw that indeed *all* of the monsters had closed in at once. Not one at a time the way they did in the movies, but all at once. More than a hundred of them. Maybe two or three hundred. All at once. Mike's flashing sword had killed fifty, sixty of them . . . and the rest had fallen on Crow and Val and Dr. Weinstock and the others and had torn them to bloody shreds. Mike stared as the last of his friends—Tyler Carby, from his homeroom class—was dropped to the ground, head lolling on a neck that was no more than raw meat and strings. Everyone was dead. Everyone. Crow and Val lay in a tangle of broken limbs and burst flesh and the only part of them that was not streaked with blood was her left hand where the diamond engagement ring glittered in the firelight, sparkling like an accusing eye.

"No . . ." Mike said—and the dreaming Mike and the watching Mike said it as one. One pale voice that caught fire and vanished into silent smoke. The ring of monsters all leered at him with looks that were almost comical what-did-you-expect looks. Mike tried to lift his sword, but it was too heavy for him. Around him the ring of monsters closed like a fist.

Mike Sweeney woke up with the sound of his own death scream in his mouth. He almost screamed out loud, but even in the worst moment of panic he still remembered Vic and so he snatched his pillow and pressed it to his face and screamed into that. It was three in the morning, and Mike did not go back to sleep at all that night. He didn't dare.

## (2)

On the pitched eave above Mike's window, the Bone Man sat cross-legged in the cold wind of 3:00 A.M., his guitar across his thighs and night birds perched on both shoulders. He heard Mike's scream as loudly as if the boy had shrieked it in his ear. He stared up at the moon, whose arc was cutting itself into the horizon over past the hospital.

"Damn, boy" he said to the wind, and shook his head. "Damn . . . you almost had it."

One of the night birds shifted and cawed softly. The Bone Man nodded, as if the bird had said something profound. The wind that blew through him was cold, and he could feel it. He always felt cold, and now he felt colder still.

"Damn," he said, and then he said, "*Dhampyr*." The night-bird cawed more loudly this time and the Bone Man started to play one of the old songs, trying to work what magic he could to soothe the mind and the soul of the thing below that was no longer exactly a human boy.

## (3)

In the basement two floors below, Vic lit a cigarette and settled back in his Barcalounger, drawing in a deep lungful as he scrutinized the face of his guest. The menthol felt good in his throat and chest. The chair was comfortable, too, a Frasier model—real leather in a nice chocolate brown. The other thing that felt good was the pistol laying on his thigh, the trigger guard resting on his crotch, the barrel more or less pointed in the other man's direction. Not an overt threat but more than a suggestion. Behind him were shelves of books, floor to ceiling, wall to wall, many of them stolen, some purchased through second, third, and fourth intermediaries. A lot of them banned by the church for hundreds of years. Nothing you could find on eBay.

Vic exhaled and the smoke joined the blue cloud that had formed over his head. He'd smoked a lot of cigarettes this evening. "You stink," he said, which was true enough. The other man smelled of dirt, old blood, shit, and Christ knew what else.

The man seated in the other chair—a straight-backed wooden chair with knobbed legs—just stared at him, his eyes flat and without expression, his face wax-white, the skin of his cheeks sucked in and moistureless, his mouth nothing more than a red slit.

"I feel . . . strange," Karl Ruger said, and his voice was a dry whisper in his throat.

"No kidding." Vic took another drag. "I'm curious . . . does any of this shit hurt?"

"Hurt?"

"Yeah. You're just about as jacked up as anyone I've ever seen, sport. You had the shit kicked out of you, you been shot more times than Bonnie and Clyde, and you slept in a refrigerator for a couple of nights. That can't feel good."

"No," said Ruger, looking down at his hands. They were as white as cream except for some streaks of dirt, though the fingernails had thickened and grown dark, almost black. Ruger flexed them. With the loss of so much fluid—almost all of his blood and water—his hands were unnaturally thin, almost delicate. Even all that he had taken from that cop, Golub, hadn't done much to flesh him out. "No—no pain."

"Sorry to hear that," Vic said with a nasty grin.

Ruger raised his eyes. They were no longer without expression. "Kiss my ass."

His gaze was hard on Vic for a while and then drifted sideways to scan the room. As that stare left him, Vic could feel a change in frequency or perhaps of vibration, and he noted it down in his mental filing cabinet. He watched as Ruger assessed the basement—Vic's domain. It was Vic's totally private space, hallowed ground where Lois and Mike were never allowed to set foot. The basement was partitioned in a mirror-image of the partitions in Vic's own mind, and he was aware of it—and was aware of what the basement and its contents were telling Ruger. There were gun racks heavy with rifles, shotguns, and pistols; along one wall there were stacks of unopened boxes of Panasonic DVD players, HD and plasma TVs, Black and Decker microwave ovens, and Craig CD players.

In the far corner was a computer workstation with a laser printer next to which stood a tall stack of yellow leaflets bearing a crudely drawn caricature of a Jewish man who looked shifty and avaricious, cringing beneath a bold, black swastika. In the opposite corner was a complex telephone rerouting and answering system that serviced several different lines: Vic Wingate's Gun Repair, White America, the Aryan Brotherhood, the National Socialist Party, and a pornography distributorship called V.W. Enterprises. At this end of the basement was a second computer workstation and a Mission table that was piled high with bundled stacks of money that were splotched with reddish-brown stains. Old blood. Ruger sniffed the air as he looked at the bills and Vic noted just the smallest lift of one of Ruger's eyebrows. He filed that away, too. Ruger turned to face Vic but let his gaze linger significantly on the money before shifting back to meet Vic's assessing stare. "That looks familiar," he said mildly.

"Finders keepers," Vic said. "Guess you're shit outta luck."

A shrug. "I can always get more." As he said this he flexed his thin white hands.

Vic said, "Tell me something else, sport . . . how's the old noggin' working? You know who you are?"

"I know."

"Can you tell me your name."

"Blow me."

"Fair enough." Vic thought for a moment. "The Man wants me to determine whether you're damaged goods or not. You understand what I mean by that?"

Ruger said nothing, but he smiled. A tiny lift of cold lips.

"He and I have gone to a lot of effort to bring you to this

moment, right here, right now. I want you to pay attention now 'cause this shit's important."

"I'm listening," Ruger said softly. His gray tongue flicked over his dry red lips.

In one smooth movement Vic picked up his pistol and pointed it at Ruger. "If it turns out that your brain's turned to mush just like your buddy's then I hate to break the news but it's beddy-bye time, you dig? And don't get any ideas about leaping over and trying to wrestle this away from ol' Vic. That would be the last stupid move you ever made, 'cause I made these loads myself and if you were to guess that they're *special* then you'd be right. Am I making myself clear?"

"As glass," Ruger said. He never even glanced at the gun. His black-within-red-within-black eyes were fixed on Vic's.

There was a sound above them—Lois's footfalls as she walked from the study to the kitchen. A pause, then a *thunk* as the refrigerator door closed, and her footfalls retreated back down the hall. Lois getting more ice for her drink. Vic and Ruger both stared at the ceiling and then lowered their eyes at the same time, reestablishing contact. "Just so we both understand who's in charge here."

"Your house, your rules," Ruger said.

"Just what I wanted to hear."

"What happened to Boyd? Why's he so messed up?"

Vic shrugged. "Not exactly sure. Theoretically he should have turned out like you, but for some reason his brain turned to mush. Basically he's cold cuts with teeth, and even though the Man was able to dial up his wits a notch or two he's as close to brain dead as one of you clowns can be and still walk around."

Ruger was still smiling. "Why?"

"Don't know. Not even sure if the Man knows."

"I thought *he* knew everything."

Vic's eyes became slits. "He knows everything that matters." He raised the barrel of the pistol until it pointed at Ruger's face. "And let's be clear on one more thing, sport—it'll help us get along. You don't make any wise-ass comments about the Man. Not ever, you read me loud and clear?"

Ruger's eyes glittered. "Griswold is my God," he said.

Vic looked at him for a long time, trying to read those eyes, looking for mockery, looking for a lie, but finding neither. He set the pistol down, stubbed out his cigarette, and then leaned forward, elbows on knees. "Then we have a lot to talk about."

# Chapter 11

## (1)

Terry arrived at the hospital at the same time as Gus, Saul Weinstock, and Frank Ferro, the four of them converging in the parking lot and then heading downstairs to where Jerry Head was standing vigil on one side of a streamer of yellow crime scene tape that was stretched across the doorway. Other cops thronged the hall, and from the inside of the room there were flashes as the criminalists took photos and documented the scene. "What the hell happened here?" Terry snapped before Ferro could open his mouth.

"Pretty much what I told you on the phone, sir." Head looked as tired as Terry felt. "The night patrol was making its regular sweep of the back lot, where deliveries and such are made. It was supposed to be closed and locked at eleven. They said that they noticed that the chain on one of the gates looked funny and—"

"Funny how?" asked Ferro.

"They said it wasn't hanging the same way that they had left it. They stopped to investigate and found that the chain had been cut, probably with bolt cutters, and that it was just looped through the bars. They called it into the head of security—"

"Brad Maynard," Weinstock provided.

"—and Mr. Maynard came out to investigate, verified

what the security guys said, and they did a full sweep of the parking lot. At first they didn't see anything out of place, then when they went around and tried every door they found that one of them was unlocked." He tilted his head toward the left end of the corridor. "That's the door right there. Where bodies are wheeled out by funeral directors and such."

"Was the door unlocked," asked Ferro, "or had it been forced?"

"Unlocked," Head said, and there was a moment of silence while everyone digested the implications of this. Terry rubbed his eyes and he suddenly looked about ten years older.

Weinstock was shaking his head. He was wearing sweats and sneakers—the easiest stuff to jump into after he'd gotten the call. "That door is always locked and there's a security alarm on it that goes off if it's opened without a key. There are only a few keys, and they're registered and numbered."

"That'll help," Ferro said. "Go ahead, Jerry."

"Well, as you know most of us out-of-town cops have been using the hospital cafeteria as a kind of mess hall during all this stuff, so when the break-in was noticed they sent someone to see if there were any of us there. I was just sitting down to eat but I came down here right away to check it out and secure the scene, which is when I called it in to Pine Deep PD. While I was waiting for them to show, I verified that the door was, in fact, unlocked, and from what I can tell there's no sign of forced entry. No scratches on the lock, nothing bent out of place. Door and lock are sound, just unlocked. I saw some footprints, kind of muddy, coming in from outside. They kind of fade out halfway down the hall, and I have them taped out and Dixie McVey's standing over them to make sure no one scuffs them up."

"Good job. What else?"

"By this time Jim Polk showed up and he and I began checking all of the rooms on this level. When we found that the morgue door was unlocked, we investigated and found that someone had definitely been in there. Like the exterior door, there were no signs of forced entry. We checked it out and saw that most of the doors to those drawers where the bodies are kept were standing open, and three of the drawers had been pulled out."

"Whose?" Weinstock demanded.

Head looked at him. "Well, Ruger's of course, and the two officers, Castle and Cowan."

"Son of a bitch!" Gus said. "Was Ruger's the only body missing?"

Head nodded. "The only way we even knew it was his was because of the toe tag. It had been ripped in half and the pieces were lying on top of the rubber sheet that I guess had been over the body."

"Isn't there supposed to be video surveillance of this room?" Ferro asked, turning to Weinstock.

"Yes, there is, but—"

Head cut him off. "Excuse me, sir, but Mr. Maynard went up to the security office and did a playback. He said that the camera does a slow pan back and forth every sixty seconds, so the picture changes and it's fixed focus so the resolution is crap, but even so we have pretty clear video images of what appears to be Kenneth Boyd opening the drawers and bending over all three bodies. Then the camera pans away and when it comes back Boyd's got Ruger slung over his shoulder like a sack of potatoes and he's limping out of the room."

"You're sure it's Boyd?" Terry and Gus asked at the same time.

"No question. I've got that asshole's face burned into my brain. Mind you, the guy looks really messed up, but it's him. He was all filthy, covered in mud and stuff like he's been hiding out in the woods, like we thought. Stringy hair, lot of visible cuts, and something's wrong with his right leg. It was all twisted and if he hadn't been carrying Ruger I'd had bet the leg was broken."

"Ruger told Val that Boyd's leg was broken," Terry observed.

"Apparently Ruger was not a doctor," Weinstock said. "You have a broken leg you don't carry a full-grown man around over your shoulder, and before you ask, being hyped on coke wouldn't make a difference, it's a matter of structural integrity."

"Point is," said Ferro, "he has some kind of injury to his leg—which our criminalists will be able to tell us more about once they've had a chance to look at the footprints in the hall—but it isn't serious enough to have prevented him from breaking in here and stealing Ruger's body."

"Didn't slow him up from attacking those cops either," Terry said bitterly.

"Or maybe it happened during that attack," Ferro said. "Anything else, Jerry?"

"No, once we determined that Boyd was not in the morgue, I sealed the scene and made some more calls. The rest you know."

Gus said, "What the Christ does he want with Ruger's body? I mean . . . Ruger *is* actually dead, right?" Weinstock just gave him a look. "They why risk breaking in here to steal a corpse?"

"Gus," Ferro said wearily, "I am so far beyond understanding what's going on in this psycho son of a bitch's head that I don't know what to think. First he leaves town, gets clean away, and then comes back to kill a couple of cops and steal his accomplice's body. If there is a logic to any of that, then it escapes me."

"I'm with you on that," Weinstock said.

"Jerry, I want to see the shift roster for tonight," Ferro said. "No one goes home before I get a chance to talk to them, and that means everybody had better be able to account for every second of their shift. Somebody unlocked that door, so maybe we can pin down who it was and find out why they'd be helping a meltdown like Boyd."

"Are you suggesting that someone in town has a connection with Ruger and Boyd?" Gus asked.

"I'm open to other suggestions if you have them, Chief." His eyes were hard. "Okay, let's go take a look."

The morgue was just as Head had described it, with many of the cold-storage drawers opened and three of the tables pulled out. The sheets that had been on Castle and Cowan were hanging off, the ends trailing to the floor, and the bodies of the officers left in horrid display, their torn and bloodless flesh wretchedly exposed. The eyes of the officers were partially open, lids uneven, dead stares empty and disturbing. Ruger's drawer was empty, the rubber sheet heaped on the floor. The two halves of the toe tag that Head had found on the sheet had been placed in plastic evidence bags, their locations noted with flagged markers. The lead criminalist, a state cop named Judy Sanchez, came over to greet Ferro and the others. She had worked the double murders at the Guthrie farm and already met everyone. She was about five-six, with kinky dark brown hair cut short and a spray of dark freckles across her nose that did nothing at all to make her look girlish. She had flat black eyes and a hard mouth and gave the men a curt nod as she stripped off a pair of latex gloves. "What do you have, Judy?" Ferro asked.

"Not a lot, Frank. The videotape is the real find. Pretty much tells us what we need to know. Brad Maynard is dubbing a copy right now. We'll leave the dub here and take the original and dump it to digital so we can use the filters on it to clean it up for court, in case it gets that far."

"Any doubt that it was Boyd?" Gus asked.

"Oh, hell, no," she said. "Regardless, I'd like Dr. Weinstock to look at it. There are some anomalies."

"I told them about the leg," Head told her.

"I watched that tape five times, and unless I'm beginning to lose it that leg definitely looks broken, though how in hell he's walking on it is beyond me. I'll let you form your own opinions, though. As for this," she jerked her chin toward the empty table. "This is kind of odd. Looks like Boyd started at one end and kept opening doors until he found Ruger, and he clearly pulled out the drawers of Castle and Cowan, pulled the sheets back, and there is some indication that he did some damage to each body."

"What?" all of the men said it in a shocked chorus, even Head, and she held up a hand.

"From what I can see—and Dr. Weinstock will have to

verify this in a postmortem—it looks like Boyd may have intentionally damaged the already torn flesh on the throats of both corpses."

Terry blanched. "But . . . *why*?"

Sanchez shrugged. "My guess? He may have been trying to disfigure the bodies to make identification of the murder weapon more difficult."

"You've lost me," Terry said.

Weinstock was nodding. "All weapons, even very sharp knives, leave trace elements in the wounds, and by manipulation of the wounds we can often get a fairly clear picture of the type of weapon used in the murder—smooth-edged knife, serrated knife, garden trowel, what have you. Microscopic traces will tell metal from plastic from wood, and so on."

"It helps in court," Ferro added. "If the suspect is found in possession of a weapon and that weapon can be matched to the wounds . . . well, there you go."

"Okay, I get it." Terry looked at Sanchez. "So you're saying that Boyd messed with the wounds to disguise the weapon he might have used? Wouldn't he just have tossed the weapon away by now if he was concerned with that sort of thing?"

"Mr. Mayor," Sanchez said, "I'm no forensic psychologist, but I don't think we're dealing with a rational mind here. There's also some indication of ritual, and we might need a psychologist to take a look at that."

"What do you mean by 'ritual'?" Terry asked.

"Boyd apparently dribbled blood onto the faces and throats of both corpses. There's no pattern I can see except that there are a few drops of blood on the lips of each and more on the throats of each."

"Holy Mother of God," Gus whispered and his face went gray.

Ferro grunted. "Sounds like Boyd's really lost it. Extreme violence, apparently senseless acts such as stealing Ruger's body, and now blood rituals."

"I'll back you up on that," Weinstock said. "In purely

clinical terms I think it's safe to say that this Boyd character is a total freak-job."

Sanchez nodded. "That part of it will be up to you to sort out, Doc. For my part, I also took some measurements of footprints and such."

"The ones in the hall?" Head asked doubtfully.

She shook her head. "No, there was some water on the floor and he walked through it. Clear limp evidenced by the gait and spacing, and a step-scuff pattern that suggests he was partially dragging his right leg."

"And yet he carried a two-hundred-pound man out of here over his shoulder?" Terry asked skeptically.

"If we hadn't had that tape, sir," Sanchez said, "I'd have argued pretty strongly for an accomplice, but the tape is the tape. You should watch it."

They did, crowding into the small morgue office. Brad Maynard came down with a copy and they played it half a dozen times. On the sixth replay Vince LaMastra joined them, his face still puffy from sleep, his square jaw rimed with yellow fuzz. He watched the tape over Ferro's shoulder and when Boyd, disheveled and very clearly limping on a twisted right leg, staggered out with Ruger's body slung over his shoulder, he said, "That's sick. He looks dead."

"He is dead," Terry snapped. "That's why he was in the damn morgue."

"No," LaMastra said, reaching out to tap the screen. "Him. Boyd. He looks dead. It's weird."

They watched the tape a seventh time, and Boyd looked dead that time, too. No one said anything for a while. Finally Gus murmured, "I wish to hell he *was* dead, the bastard."

Later three of them—Ferro, LaMastra, and Gus met in the doctors' lounge. Terry left for home, and Weinstock was overseeing the post-forensic restoration of his morgue. Gus made a pot of coffee and they settled down with cups, looking over the staff rosters for that evening. "Most of the staff don't have access to the door keys and security codes," Gus said. "That leaves the maintenance staff, the security people, a few of the top docs, and the officers eating in the cafeteria—Head and Chremos from Crestville. And Jim Polk, who was here visiting Rhoda Thomas." He consulted a chart. "Call it twelve people in all who were here at the time of the break-in."

"Okay, then we need to interview each one," Ferro said.

Each person with potential access was brought in separately and interviewed by the three of them, with Ferro taking point on most of the interrogations. No one admitted to having tampered with the codes, and when asked to turn out their pockets—a request that was met with flat hostility by almost everyone except Head, who understood the drill—no keys turned up that shouldn't be there. Each person was made to write out a detailed list of where they were all night and who they spoke with. "So where does that leave us?" LaMastra asked in disgust as the last of the interviewees left.

"Nowhere," Ferro said with a sigh.

"God," murmured LaMastra, "I love police work."

## (2)

When the car passed Vic rose up out of the tall weeds and continued moving down the bank to where the iron leg of the bridge was fitted into its massive concrete boot. He paused for a moment and took set down his backpack, unzipped it, and then removed first a pair of 12-power binoculars and then a high-resolution Nikon digital camera with a telephoto lens. He sat down with the weeds above shoulder height and put the binoculars to his eyes so he could study the old bridge that linked Pine Deep to Black Marsh. The bridge was a two-lane affair with close-fitted railroad ties stuffed between steel I-beams. It was sturdy enough, and though it rattled and shook, it would probably not even need rebuilding for another decade. That thought caused Vic to smile. He set the binoculars down and picked up the digital camera. It was very expensive, with a two-gigabyte memory card that took ten-megapixel images. Vic rested his elbows on his knees to study the camera and then took over fifty ultra-close-up photos of the bridge and each of its supports. The morning sun was clear and bright, perfect for high-res photography.

A farm truck came along the road and Vic just lay back in the weeds, invisible. His pickup was parked fifty yards up a curving access road that was almost never used. When the truck had passed, Vic sat up and then stowed his gear back in his bag. He rose, leaving the bag in the weeds, and moved farther down the bank to the closest iron leg, keeping a weather eye on the road. Confident that no one was coming, he pulled a Stanley tape measure off his belt and spent the next few minutes measuring both the concrete base and the steel leg of the bridge support, pausing to jot some numbers down in a notebook. The last measurement done, he pocketed the book, clipped the tape measure onto his belt, and climbed the hill to recover his bag. He checked the road carefully and then headed up the access lane to his truck.

Pine Deep was completely surrounded by water, with the Delaware on its eastern flank and the Pine River on the west; the Crescent Canal bordered it in the north, and a hooked arm of Pine River swooped down to meet the Delaware again in the south. In colonial days, before the town was officially organized it was generally called Pine Island on old maps. There were four bridges connecting the town to its neighbors: Crescent Bridge, Old Corn Bridge, Swallow Hill Bridge, and this one—the Black Marsh Bridge.

Vic glanced at his watch. It was just 7:00 A.M. He smiled. There was plenty of time to quietly measure all of them and still have most of the day left to do some other chores. At home he could download the digital pics onto his computer and make a closer study of stress points to pick just the right spots to plant the dynamite.

After that he could settle down and have a nice long conversation with his new houseguest. That should be enlightening. He was whistling a happy tune when he pulled his pickup off the access road and headed north up A-32.

## (3)

Karl Ruger sat in darkness while Vic was out. There were basement lights he could turn on, but he preferred the darkness. It was less dark to him, he knew, than to others, and that knowledge pleased him. It made him feel like a cat. Not a little housecat, but a big hunting cat. A leopard slinking through the jungles, eyes seeing all the way through the shadows. Like that.

Ruger used the time alone to prowl through Vic's library, and what he read was enlightening. Such as the fact that it didn't matter that it was bright sunshine outside. There were no windows in the cellar, and all he needed was to stay out of direct sunlight, out of the heavy UV. That was just one of the things he learned in his first hour of browsing, his searches through the pages nudged along by the voice in his head. The voice of his god; the same voice that had spoken in his thoughts moments before Tony had crashed their car the other night. Tony and Boyd hadn't heard anything—the message wasn't for them. *Ruger, you are my left hand.* While Griswold had whispered to him time had seemed to slow, to revolve around Ruger's need to hear the message of his god. *Vic Wingate has been my John the Baptist . . . he has paved the way; but you, Karl . . . you will be my Peter, my rock, and on this rock I will build my church.*

"Yeah, you're damn right," he said to the darkness, and there was great love in his voice. Dark and twisted, but as passionate as any monk who whipped himself by night in the darkness of his cell.

He wondered how much of the Plan Vic really knew. He knew a lot, sure, had laid the groundwork, and even Ruger had to admire the attention to detail as Vic had outlined it all a few hours ago. When the Red Wave hit the poor bastards in this town wouldn't have a chance. Not a prayer. Props to Vic on that. And Vic seemed to know a lot about what Ruger was, and what his limits were, pro and con. He kept that pistol with him all the time, with its *special* loads. Another point for Vic. Vic had even drawn up a list of the locals who were least likely to be missed while the Man's army grew—loners, families in isolated farms, unpopular assholes who wouldn't be missed under any circumstances. Vic called it his Greatest Hits, which Ruger found funny; it was the only time he and Vic had laughed together. Boyd had started the recruitment, but now that Ruger was in the game the whole process would accelerate so that they would be completely ready on Halloween.

For all that, it wasn't Vic who was seeing the most important part: Vic, blackhearted son of a bitch though he was, couldn't *turn* anyone, couldn't make more soldiers for the Red Wave. Vic could kill people, true enough, but only Ruger, and to a lesser degree Boyd and the ones that brainless jackass already recruited, could make a kill and then turn that kill into a *recruitment*. It didn't matter that there were already twenty soldiers out there like him because in truth *none* of them were quite like him. The Man had told him so. He was special. A general, a king among them, just as the Man was a god to their kind. This was the pecking order. Vic thought it was the Man then him and then everyone else on their bellies below him, but that was bullshit. Ruger knew different because the Man has whispered inside his head while Ruger was doing time in the morgue drawer. Ruger was key to the ongoing success of the Man's agenda. So, once the Red Wave hit, what good would Vic really be to the Man? Either he'd have to be made into a soldier himself, and Ruger didn't like that idea, or Vic would have to be someone's lunch.

That thought made Ruger smile in the darkness.

Vic must know that his usefulness was limited, too, otherwise he wouldn't be holding back so much information from him. He clearly knew more about what Ruger was than he let on. Maybe even more than was in the books. It didn't take a brain surgeon to figure out why. Vic wanted to have an edge over Ruger and his recruits even after the Wave came and passed, and Vic needed to be seen as a valuable resource just in case Ruger ever exceeded him in the estimation of the Man.

Ruger looked down at the clipboard that lay on his lap. Once Vic had gone out for the day Ruger had started making a list of things he did, and did not, know about who and what he was. He was wasting no time. When Vic came home Ruger would hide the list. There was almost a month to go before Halloween. Plenty of time to poke around, read a book or two, and maybe do some experimentation. It was always better to be more in the know that the mooks you had to deal with. Not that Vic was really a mook—he was smart and he was sharp, but he wasn't as smart or sharp as he thought he was, Ruger was sure about that.

He looked down at his list. The word "blood" was written near the top and he considered that point. Yeah, he could feel the urge, but it wasn't at all like he expected. It wasn't an ache in the stomach like a starving man would get, or even a burn in the veins like a junkie. This was way deeper than that—more like a stirring in the groin, something sexual. Ruger knew all about that and he knew that only a total idiot let his dick drive the bus. That kind of thing could be controlled. Maybe, he thought, even refined. That would take some thinking, maybe a little practice.

He heard muffled footsteps echoing from upstairs. Vic's wife, Lois. Ruger hadn't met her yet, but he could smell her, even all the way down here. Gin and perfume, nervous sweat and fear. A nice combination. She might be worth practicing on one of these days when Vic was out. He'd have to think about that.

Lower down on his list was the word "sunlight."

"Go outside and you'll burn, sport," is the way Vic put it. Ruger saw that a lot in the books, too, and he'd seen it in movies. The thing was, that it wasn't in all of the books. Not the older ones, anyway. He had to wonder about that and thought of ways to test it.

"No time like the present," he murmured as he got up. The back door was closed and locked and Vic had the key, but that didn't mean jack shit to Ruger. He took the doorknob in one hand and closed his left hand around the deadbolt assembly and pulled. It resisted his pull, but only for a second, and then the screws Vic had sunk into the oak just tore loose with a screech of protest and the door jerked inward.

"Well kiss my ass!" Ruger breathed, impressed. It was far easier than he had thought it would be. Good to know. Outside the sunlight filled the entire alleyway and by instinct Ruger lunged back away from its touch as it painted the door with clear light, but then he stopped, just on the safe side of the line of the glare, still in shadows. He licked his dry lips and stared at the light outside for a full minute, counting the seconds. Looking at it was no problem, and that was good. Then he raised his left hand and tentatively reached out, coming right up to the dividing line between shadow and sunlight, and then crossed it with just the tips of his fingers. His hand was shaking as he felt the warmth wrap itself around each black nail, around the paper-white skin.

It hurt. It hurt a lot, but he did not catch fire. His skin didn't blacken, didn't even turn red. Even when he leaned forward and let the golden morning light bathe his face and hair. Not a whiff of smoke. Only pain, and what was pain to him but an old friend?

Ruger closed the door and went back to his chair. It took over two hours for the pain to subside, and for a while he had to grit his teeth together to keep from yelling. Time passed slowly, and while it did Karl Ruger learned a lot about himself, and about what he was. It was stuff he was certain Vic would not want him to know.

While the pain was at its worst, Ruger used the agony to focus his mind, used it like a whip to keep his train of thought on its tracks. As he endured the misery of it, he thought of Malcolm Crow, and of all the things he would like to do to him. Crow, and that black-haired Guthrie bitch. Twice he had tried to kill them, and twice he'd had his ass handed to him. There would have to be a third time, and he didn't know if he could wait until the Red Wave to see it done. No, by the time the Wave hit he wanted them both broken and dead. Or better yet . . . recruited. *Yeah*, that had a nice feel to it.

A fresh wave of pain hit him and he kept the hiss of suffering inside as a plan began to form in his brain. *Yeah,* he mused, *maybe recruit Val Guthrie and then use her against Crow.* First break his heart, then break him down, and when he had nothing left, maybe Ruger would let Val send him on with a big, red kiss. He closed his eyes and with that thought in his mind the pain transformed from agony to true ecstasy, and he reveled in it, allowing the pain to be both his teacher and his mistress. There was a lot to learn from pain, and how one handled pain; Karl Ruger had learned a lot over the years, but right now he was learning its deeper secrets. Boy, would Vic be surprised.

### (4)

Three hours later Vic was in his lounger, his face showing more anger than he wanted as he watched Ruger continue to stare out the backdoor's peephole. His phone rang and when he saw it was Polk he flipped it open. "Make it brief," Vic snapped.

"Just got home from the hospital. I got grilled by that nigger cop, Ferro, but it's cool. After I let you in I went out a service entrance and came back and visited Rhoda, so I was in her room when everyone started making a fuss. I'm in the clear. All they know is that someone let Boyd in, but they don't know who. They just know it wasn't me."

"Good work, Jimmy boy." He closed his phone without saying good-bye and called to Ruger. "You thirsty?"

"Of course I am."

"You have any idea what to do about that?" Ruger was standing at Vic's cellar door, peering through the peephole at the empty street. He didn't answer the question, so Vic said, "You deaf?"

"I heard you," Ruger whispered. "If you're hoping to get some jollies by seeing me jones for some O-positive, then too bad. It's not like the movies, asshole. I can wait." He touched the wood of the door with the tips of his long white fingers and as he watched the street he drew his fingertips slowly down the length of the door, from head height to waist level. Each black fingernail left a visible groove in the oak and little curls of wood fluttered to the cement floor. "When I need to feed, I'll feed."

Vic heard the faint screech as the nails grooved the wood. There was no visible change in his face, but his hand moved with apparently casualness from the armrest to the butt of the pistol tucked down between thigh and cushion. "I just fixed that shit, so don't go messing with it." In truth he had been furious—and visibly shaken—when he'd come home and found that Ruger had torn the lock open. At the time he had wheeled on Ruger and had given him a searching, accusing glare. "Did you try to go out?"

Ruger kept his face bland while he said, "Do I look like a Crispy Critter? I'm not stupid, you know." Then because he knew more explanation would be needed, he contrived another lie. "I was getting antsy and wanted to take a look outside and just tore open the door, forgetting what time of day it was." He was pretty sure Vic bought that, and thereafter Ruger changed the subject.

Vic lit a cigarette. "You know, sport, everyone in town is talking about how Malcolm Crow and Val Guthrie bitch-slapped you. Twice. That cockup at the hospital was a real mess." Ruger answered with silence. "What am I supposed to think about that, sport? What's the *Man* supposed to think about that?"

That far end of the cellar was mostly in shadows and Vic's face was a pale vagueness in the gloom. Even so, Vic could see—or thought he saw—the red burn of Ruger's eyes.

"News flash, asshole—when you come back from the dead there's no how-to manual. I was barely turned when I hit the hospital." He licked his lips. "Times are changing, though. Every minute I keep learning more about what I am. I'll bet I know some shit that you don't know."

Vic snorted. "Don't put too much down on that bet, sport, and don't try and pussy out of this. Own it like a man. You screwed up."

"If you think I'm a screwup, then cap me, Wingate," Ruger said quietly. "Otherwise go stick it up your ass."

Vic picked up the pistol. "You think I won't?"

Ruger smiled and Vic could definitely see that. Rows of jagged white teeth. Crow had kicked his front teeth out, but already they were starting to grow back—though they were keeping their jagged ridges. It made Ruger look like a cannibal. "If the Man wanted me dead he could reach out and snuff me out just like that. You know it and I know it." Now it was Vic's turn to be silent. "So, if I'm still alive—and if he sent you and my ol' buddy Boyd to go and hijack me from the hospital—then I'm thinking the Man doesn't think I'm all that much of a screwup."

"Maybe," Vic said grudgingly, "but it sure doesn't mean that you're employee of the month, either. To me you're as useful as Gertie here." He waggled the pistol. "And I think we can get along fine without you."

Ruger gave a short, cold bark of a laugh. "You think you're king shit, but you're no more on the policy level than I am. We're all fingers on the Man's hand, and we should bow down and kiss the ground every time we even *think* of his name. Instead you're second-guessing him. I find that very interesting."

"Smooth talk for a screwup, sport." But Vic shifted in his seat as he said that.

"By dawn tomorrow I'll have done more for the Man than you've managed in thirty years, so the next time you want to blow smoke about something, just blow it up your own ass." He took a small step forward. "Remember—there's a lot more of *us* now than there are of *you*." He jerked his chin toward the pistol. "I'll bet you don't even take a shit without that next to you these days. Getting scary out there, isn't it?"

"Don't try that Bela Lugosi crap on me, sport. I was running with the Man before you figured out which hand to use to jerk off with." He sat back against the leather cushions. "I'm still waiting to hear this grand plan of yours for Crow and that Guthrie bitch. You pretty much blew your chance to make it look like an act of vengeance from a man on the run—which was the plan as I recall—so you'd better not be planning something too crazy. We want tourists in town, not more cops, you dig?"

"I have something low key in mind for them. Y'see, I planted a *seed*."

"What's that supposed to mean?"

"At the hospital, I put a worm in Crow's brain and I think the little bastard is going to come to us. Well . . . he's going to come to the Man." Ruger's smile faded but there was still laughter in his red eyes. He turned away and bent to the peephole again. "And that should be a real treat." He grinned at Vic. "Something the Man suggested. You don't need to worry about it. The thing you got to do is figure a good way for us to introduce Val Guthrie to my ol' buddy, Boyd."

"Boyd? Why, you afraid to do it yourself?"

"Time's not right for me to risk being seen around the Guthrie place, or don't you agree? I mean, hell, you went to such great pains to get me out of the hospital—made sure Boyd was seen hauling my ass out of there. Everyone *knows* I'm dead, but Boyd's in the catbird seat right now. He's the man of the hour. I think we need to have him pay the Guthrie slut a visit, maybe give her the standard *recruitment* speech."

Vic thought about it, then gave Ruger a grudging nod. "You want to fry Crow's grits for him. Make him hurt first, am I right?"

"That's exactly what I want. Nice to be on the same page."

"It's nasty and devious—much as I hate to say it, I like it. Be careful, though. Boyd going after those cops wasn't any part of the Plan. He was supposed to get lost until those Philly cops left town, and I even drove his ass out of town, but he went off the reservation and came back to where he last saw you. Who the hell knows why. Guy's brains are mush, so, even though the man gave him a tune-up, I think you'd better have a talk with him, too, just to be sure he follows the playbook. You want to *turn* Guthrie, not have Boyd scatter her pieces all over the county. That's no good to us.

That's shock, not hurt, and if you want to hurt Crow that won't get you the best bang for the buck."

"I'll handle Boyd."

"Point is, because of Boyd's screwup the Plan is starting to change. We have more police attention than we need, and we have the wrong kind of media buzz. We need to do everything on the sly now, especially as far as Crow goes. Now we have to be more careful about how and when we take him off the board. He's one of the only two people who can keep all the big Halloween celebrations going at full tilt. Him and Terry Wolfe. Wolfe's looking pretty shaky lately—and we both know what *that's* about—so if he has a breakdown, or *turns*, then Crow will have to stay alive and in play. So . . . hands off him until we know what's happening with Wolfe."

"What about Guthrie?"

"It's a good plan, but let it wait a couple days. Maybe save it for Little Halloween. Hurrying's not going to help us right now. Besides, you've got plenty of other work to do."

Ruger looked at the wall clock and his body shuddered as if in climax. "Sundown. Time to go out and play."

# Chapter 12

## (1)

The shades were up and the curtains pulled back to allow as much morning light as possible to wash over them. Both of them were propped up on pillows with coffee cups steaming on the bedside tables. Crow had his arm around Val and she was resting the unbruised side of her face against his chest. They had learned the routines of cuddling while avoiding bruises and stitches and sore places. Across the room the TV was on with the sound muted as a petite blond read the weather on Channel 6. Sarah had brought them coffee a few minutes ago, told them Terry was still out at the hospital, and then left them to deal with the day that lay ahead of them.

"You can still back out," Crow said softly, stroking Val's shoulder. "Terry and Sarah would let us stay here. Or we could just shack up at my place. The cats would love to have you visit."

"No," she said firmly, then smiled a bit. "Thanks, honey, but . . . no."

Crow let it go. Last night, as they were climbing into bed, Val had told him that she wanted to go home, but Crow had wondered what kind of ghosts would be there. Would they be able to feel Ruger's toxicity? Certainly they would feel the utter loss of the presence of Henry Guthrie. If it was up to Crow, he would have her sell the damn place and they could buy a town house somewhere on Corn Hill, but Val wouldn't even listen to that kind of talk. Guthries had always lived there and by God Guthries always would. "I won't be chased out of my own house," she said. "I won't be chased out of my own life. Besides, Ruger's already taken enough away from me."

He kissed her hair as they sat in the window bay watching geese mill around in the yard.

Val said, "Crow?"

"Yeah, baby?"

"About our getting married?" He tensed. "Are you sure?"

Crow laughed. "No, it was just a whim."

She smacked his chest lightly. "You know what I mean."

"I'm not sure I do," he admitted.

"When you proposed at the hospital . . . you knew I needed something real to anchor myself to. It was so wonderful, so sweet of you, but I don't want to think that you did it just to make me feel better. Like some kind of distraction therapy."

He laughed again, harder. "Yeah, you found me out. You see, I found it pretty useful carrying around a two-carat Asscher-cut engagement ring just in case some random woman needs a little emotional pick-me-up. It's worked dozens of times."

Val raised her head and studied him with her dark blue eyes. "I'm not joking, Crow."

His eyes still twinkled with humor. "You are possibly the dumbest smart woman in the world if you don't know how much I love you. I love you more than anything else in the universe, Valerie Guthrie, and I've been planning to pop the ol' question for some time now but couldn't find just the right moment. Though in retrospect proposing while I was whacked out on morphine may be a questionable interpretation of 'the right moment,' it seemed to work out okay."

Val kissed him, sweetly and softly, careful of the stitches in his lips and mouth. "My God! It was *so* much the right time. But tell me—tell me right now, right here, looking me in the eyes—are you *sure?*"

Crow pulled her closer and kissed her lips and her eyes and buried his face in the fragrant softness of the side of her throat. "My sweet love, I am more sure of that than anything else in my life. I have to be with you, now and forever. I love so much that if I even think about living a second without you I think I'd go nuts. I'm babbling, I know . . . but I don't know how else to say it. I want to be with you, I want to marry you, and I want to have everything with you. Life, house, two-point-five kids, dog, station wagon, PTA, crab-grass, and middle-age spread—the whole enchilada." Her eyes closed and a single tear leaked out of her bruised eye. He didn't see it, but when it fell on his chest, he pushed her gently back so that he could see her face. "Hey . . . are you crying?"

"Of course I'm crying, you idiot."

"Val, I—"

"Crow . . . I have to tell you something and if you want to take back your ring, if you want to back off, I will under-stand, but I *have* to tell you."

Crow's heart turned to a block of ice. "You are scaring the shit out of me here."

"God, I hope not." Her face was serious, but there was a bright light there, sparkling in her eyes like spring sunlight on late winter snow.

"Then tell me," he said, and braced himself.

"Crow . . . my love . . . I'm pregnant."

Crow could actually feel his mouth drop open like a trap-door. If he was still breathing, he wasn't aware of it, though he knew that his heart was still beating—it was right there in his throat. He saw the look of desperate hopefulness in her eyes begin to change into a look of broken-hearted fear . . . and he wanted to say something smart, something pithy.

Instead he just yelled. A great big whooping bellow of pure joy.

Val felt herself yanked forward and Crow crushed her to his chest. They both howled in pain and then they both laughed, and a moment later they were both crying and kiss-ing each other. Crow kept saying: "Babybabybabybaby . . ."

but Val didn't know if he was using an endearment for her or just trying out the new implications of the word. Either way, she felt the knot that had been wrapped around her heart split apart and her whole chest seemed to be filled with warm helium. She wanted to leap into the air with him, and she was sure that they would both float.

Feet pounded on the steps and Val turned her head—which made Crow miss her face and land a big noisy kiss on her ear, which hurt, but who cared?—and the door burst open and Sarah Wolfe was there, looking shocked and desperate. "Oh my God," Sarah yelled, fear in her eyes, "what's going on, who's hurt, did you fall . . . ?"

Val wrapped her arms around Crow's neck and pulled his face to her chest and spoke over his tousled hair, pitching her voice high over Crow's constant *Yee-haws*. "We're having a baby!"

Sarah stopped, mouth in a perfect O, her inability to process this registering on her face. "A . . . baby?" And then she was hugging them both.

### (2)

Frank Ferro sat at the head of the conference table with Vince LaMastra to his right. At the far end sat Terry Wolfe and to his left was Gus Bernhardt. Filling out the rest of the big oak town council table were two FBI agents—Agent Henckhauser and Special Agent in Charge Spinlicker, from the Philadelphia Field Office—and three state troopers—Sutter, Wimmer, and Yablonski. Everyone had coffee cups in front of them except SAC Spinlicker, who had a Diet Pepsi in a can. This was the first meeting with the FBI and was intended as a preliminary assessment to see if the Bureau felt it was necessary and appropriate to take over the case. The room looked like what it now was: a war room. Maps of Pine Deep were tacked to the walls, notes and photos were taped haphazardly on every available surface, dry-erase boards stood on easels, and reams of computer printouts were stacked on the floor.

The SAC leaned forward and steepled his fingers, fixing Ferro with a steely and openly accusatory look. "You checked *everywhere?*"

Ferro's reaction was to lean back in his chair and smile at Spinlicker. "Well, Agent Spinlicker, clearly if we had searched *everywhere* we'd have found him."

"You implied—"

"What I *said* was that one hundred and sixty-three men, six teams of dogs, and two spotter airplanes have spent the last several days combing every inch of the Guthrie farm and much of the surrounding woods. We've broadened the search to include ninety other farms, the grounds of the Haunted Hayride, the campus of Pinelands College, a large portion of Pinelands State Forest, and the canals. My assessment, Agent Spinlicker, is that Kenneth Boyd is not in any of the areas we're searched."

"And found jack shit," LaMastra summed up.

Spinlicker shared a glance with his partner, and smiled ever so faintly. To Ferro he said, "And Kenneth Boyd has managed to elude all of your efforts." There was just the slightest emphasis on the word "your."

In the stiff silence that followed Bernhardt cleared his throat. "In all fairness, sir, the area they searched is pretty dense."

"It also comprises less than an eighth of the entire borough," said Trooper Yablonski. "The village itself may be small, but the borough of Pine Deep is pretty damn big. There are a lot of places for one man to hide."

The SAC let silence be his comment on that, and on the handling of the operation as a whole. He picked up a folder from the table, opened it, and riffled through the papers, occasionally making a small and dismissive "hmm" sound. "Quite frankly, Sergeant Ferro, it makes me wonder how well you—"

Then there was a sound like a gunshot and everyone jumped in their seats and spun toward Terry, who had just slammed his palm down hard and flat against the table.

"Agent Spinlicker," he snapped, "if you think there is a problem in the way things have been handled then come out and say it." He glared at the SAC and at that moment Terry Wolfe seemed to fill the room.

Spinlicker hedged. "I didn't say that, sir."

"I know. You're pussyfooting around it. If you have a problem with the way Sergeant Ferro's handled things come out and say it right now."

The air between them crackled like the charge between two poles. Spinlicker said, "No, sir."

Terry's face remained hard as a fist. "Then sit there and shut the fuck up."

Henckhauser gasped audibly and the Staties exchanged startled looks. Gus was shocked at the language he was hearing from Terry; Ferro was staring at the mayor, and LaMastra was grinning. Terry saw the smile and wheeled on him. "And you can wipe that shit-eating grin off your face, Detective. I'm not saying that you guys have done such a great job either."

That wiped LaMastra's face clean.

Addressing the whole table, Terry said, "This is my town, gentlemen, but this is *not* my mess. It's yours. Now clean it up!" Again his palm came down on the table hard enough to make everyone jump. "One of my closest friends is dead. My *best* friend just got out of the hospital along with his fiancée, whom I've known since kindergarten. One of my cops is dead, and so is an officer loaned to me from a neighboring town. I have a hospital worker in intensive care with a split skull, a woman who was nearly raped, her husband who had his face kicked in, shots fired in my hospital, two other cops down with injuries, and now a body stolen from the morgue. Every reporter in the world is here and according to the news stories I'm starting to see, this town—*my* town—is becoming a joke in terms of safety. I heard this town mentioned on the *Daily Show* last night, and on Leno. As a goddamn *punchline*. So, when I tell you that I am one hundred percent fed up with this bullshit you had best believe I'm serious. About the last thing I want to hear or see is you lot getting into a jurisdictional pissing contest. Am I getting through to you on this?"

"Loud and clear, sir," Ferro said. Spinlicker and the others just nodded. Gus was staring at Terry with a look of fascinated awe.

"Then let me make something else clear. October is the biggest income month for this town. We're already reeling from the crop blight and a lot of local farmers are likely to lose their farms. If you—" he fished for an appropriately savage word but only came up with an acid-laced version of "*officers of the law*, working together, cannot find one man—one injured man, mind you—then we are likely to lose the entire tourist season. That means Pine Deep is going to go into the tank." He leaned forward, his blues eyes as hard as gunmetal. "If, on the other hand, you can manage to find this guy, then there is still a chance we can pull off enough of a season to stay afloat. That, gentlemen, is a very real concern and I want to know right now that this is going to happen." He made eye contact, brief but penetrating, with each man at the table, one after the other. "Make me believe that this is going to happen."

### (3)

Ferro and LaMastra lingered with Gus after Terry and the others left. They stood at a window that looked down at the parking lot, watching SAC Spinlicker and Agent Henckhauser get into their car. Even through the soundproof glass the watching officers could feel the vibration as the FBI agents slammed their doors. Their car laid an eight-foot patch of burned rubber across the asphalt.

"So," Gus said dryly, "I guess we won't be sharing the case with the feds."

"So it seems," Ferro agreed. His face still wore its funeral director moroseness, but there was a drop of humor in his voice. "Nice that they said they would keep in touch and advise. Very helpful of them."

"Funny thing is," LaMastra said, "that if you told me that a small-town mayor could bitch-slap a couple of feds like that I'd have called you a liar." Ferro just nodded at that.

"So we're on our own again," Gus said.

"Once this thing starts winding down," LaMastra said, "I expect we'll see those two again. Right around the time when someone gets to take credit."

"Mmm-hm," Ferro said, smiling faintly.

## (4)

After a long and rather giggly breakfast with Sarah and Val, Crow showered and dressed and began packing the few belongings he'd brought from the hospital. In ten minutes Sarah was going to drive them out to the farm and he knew that would pretty much be the end of the incredible feeling of joy that was still bubbling inside of him.

A baby. *His* baby. His and Val's, which was even better. Son of Crow—he'd already decided that it was going to be a boy for no reason more mature than hoping that the kid would like science fiction, blues, jujutsu, and gory horror flicks. He couldn't quite see "Daughter of Val" grooving on any Rob Zombie films side-by-side with ol' dad. On the other hand, Daughter of Val would probably be smarter and better looking than Son of Crow, so there was that. On the *other* other hand, the kid could be Grandson of Henry, in which case he'd be smart, good-looking, tough as nails, and a lot taller than Son of Crow.

*Crow . . . my love . . . I'm going to have a baby.* If there had ever been a more beautiful set of—and here Crow had to count on his fingers—nine words, he had never heard them and could not imagine them. Son of Crow. Sounded great. Very heroic, very comic book superhero. "Wait till I tell . . . *everyone!*" he said aloud. As he packed he started singing, "I am a daddy," to the tune of "I'm in the Money."

Crow sat down on the edge of the bed and pulled his cell phone out. There were only two bars so he got up and moved around the room until he got four of them. Getting a clear cell phone signal in Pine Deep was always a crapshoot. He had to sit in the window seat and wedge his shoulder into the corner to get enough bars to make his calls.

The first person he called was Terry Wolfe. Terry answered on the second ring with a terse, "Go."

"Terry . . . it's me."

"Crow? What's up, everything okay there?"

"Yeah, man. You in the middle of something?"

"Not really. I just wrapped up a meeting with the cops."

"Are they anywhere with this?"

"No," Terry said, and his voice sounded like all the weariness in the world. "And no one has floated a useful theory as to why Boyd would risk breaking into the morgue just to steal Ruger's corpse."

"Sounds like Boyd is off the rails," Crow offered. "Maybe there's no one in the driver's seat anymore."

"Who knows. There's another wrinkle in this, too."

"Jeez, Wolfman, I'm not sure how many more wrinkles this town can take."

"Now you're singing my song. Keep this between us, okay?"

"Lips are sealed, bro."

"We think Boyd has at least one more accomplice." Terry told him about the hospital door being opened and the alarm disabled. "He had to have inside help."

Crow chewed on that for a minute. "I find that hard to buy. If there was an inside man, why didn't he just dump Ruger onto a gurney and wheel his ugly ass to the back door? That way Boyd would never have been spotted at all."

"Saul Weinstock raised the same concern, but Ferro said that the inside man may have known about the security camera. The hallway surveillance camera has been broken since the middle of September, so anyone who went into the hall to unlock the doors would not have been spotted. Only if he'd actually entered the morgue would the tape have picked him up."

"Okay . . . I can see that, but that means that this inside

guy had to know all of this. The broken camera, the morgue camera, everything, and he'd need access to the keys."

"Right. They checked out everyone who was on duty last night and got nowhere. Just dead ends and no leads."

"This doesn't make me feel too good, Terry."

"Me, neither, but at least you're out of it."

"And I'm happy as hell about that, too. So's Val." Then he slapped his forehead—and winced all the way down to his toes. "Geez, Terry, I am the world's biggest idiot."

"Not a news flash there."

"No, I mean I forgot to tell you why I called."

"If this is more bad news I'm going to go lay down in traffic."

"Terry . . . Val and I are going to have a baby!"

There was a silence followed by a sound that Crow was absolutely sure was a sob. Just the one, and then more silence. Finally, in a strange, choked whisper Terry said, "Thank God." And then without warning he hung up.

Crow looked at the phone in his palm. That was certainly not the kind of answer he expected to get. "Weird," he said, and then punched in a new number.

### (5)

Saul Weinstock stood in the small morgue office, watching the cleaning staff put the finishing touches on the room. The forensics teams had finally left and the last streamers of crime scene tape had been torn down and stuffed into trash cans. Ferro had given him an all clear to reopen for business, and with three autopsies still pending, it was going to be a long day. All of this should have been done ages ago, and Weinstock didn't like how much the delay made him look like the top idiot at Dumbass Rural Hospital. His cell phone rang; he saw it was Crow and answered, "Hey, buddy."

"You sound chipper," Crow said,

"I'm not, but thanks for your lack of perception," Weinstock said with a grin. "How are you doing? How's Val?"

"That's what I was calling about," Crow said and went

into a two-minute rant about impending fatherhood. By the time he reached the point where he was planning to coach Little League, Weinstock was laughing.

"I know already, you chucklehead. Oh, don't act so surprised—she's my patient, I'm her doctor, remember? Confidences become fast and loose in such circumstances. You don't want to know the details—they're so sordid."

"How long have you known?"

Weinstock paused a bit before answering that one. "Since, um, last Saturday. When you guys were brought in after all that happened. She asked me not to say anything until she had a chance to tell you first, for reasons that should be obvious even to someone of limited intelligence, such as yourself."

"Thanks, bro."

"Got your back, man. In any case, when you guys were brought in Val told me that she'd taken an EPT that morning and came up positive. She said that she was going to tell you that night, but then Ruger showed up and everything went to hell in a handbasket. Now that she has, and having heard your plans to be the most annoying parent in history, can I assume that you're happy about this? You didn't ask for your ring back, did you?"

"Geez, Saul, what kind of a dork do you think I am?"

"Should I answer that or would you prefer a long awkward pause?"

"Bite me."

"Anyway . . . I do want to congratulate you, Crow, and to tell you, all kidding aside, how happy I am for you and Val. With all the crap that's been happening around here it's sure as hell nice to have something really good happen. Mazel tov!"

"Thanks, and corny as it sounds, it's like a fresh start. Shame Henry's not here to see his grandkid. Or his daughter get married."

Weinstock moved across the room to allow the cleaners to mop where he was standing, and he lowered his voice to a confidential whisper. "Remember yesterday when I said that

I wanted to keep Mark and Connie here for a bit longer? Well, between you and me, I think Connie is in some deep shit. This morning I talked with the staff psychologist and the news just isn't encouraging. Long story short, Connie is exhibiting all of the symptoms of post-traumatic stress disorder consistent with having been the victim of a completed rape, which we both know was not the case. If I were a superstitious man I'd say that Ruger put some kind of hex on her, but since I'm not a superstitious man, I'm going on the assumption that Connie may have had some preexisting psychological problems. Point is, she's not responding to the treatments—and even this short-term there's always some kind of forward movement, at least to the professional eye, but my people say no—and the meds we're giving her to ease her stress are just making her retreat into sleep. She goes hours and hours without talking, and then she'll break down into hysterical tears for no visible reason."

"I tried calling Mark again today. He blew me off like he's been doing."

"He's been a real bear to the nursing staff, too. Bites the head off anyone who comes in the room. He had one nurse in tears and another who wanted to strap him to a wheelchair and shove him down the fire stairs. I can hold on to them maybe—and I mean *maybe*—another couple of days and then I have to kick them both out of here." He considered. "Or . . . I think I'll decide that I don't like the way the reseating of his teeth is going. I mean he does have the blue lip-tinting you can expect from ecchimosis, so I guess I can use that to keep him in a little longer, at least until we take the gum sutures out."

"That's a hell of a risk, Saul. I didn't know you liked Connie and Mark that much."

"I don't. This is for Henry. For Val, too, I guess."

"You're the best, Saul."

"Yeah, well don't spread it around. Anyway, go celebrate being a responsible adult with at least an adequate sperm count. Congrats and give Val my love." Crow clicked off and Weinstock closed his phone and dropped it in his lab coat.

The cleaners finished, packed up their mops and spray bottles, and left, both of them giving the room a spooked glance, their eyes darting toward the polished steel doors behind which lay three corpses. No—four bodies, because what was left of Tony Macchio was still behind Door #2. Three murder victims and one murderer who had been slaughtered by the Cape May Killer. He couldn't blame the cleaners for being spooked, even with the lights on and the cold-room doors firmly shut, and he knew that it wasn't just the fact that it was the morgue that was giving them the jitters—it was the fact that someone had broken in and stolen— actually *stolen*—a dead body. It was all very creepy, and Weinstock had to agree with their reactions. This whole thing was giving him an increasingly bad feeling. Not just the grief over Henry's death and the deaths of the two cops, and not just the proprietary sense of violation he had about the violence and theft here in *his* hospital. It was just a general case of the heebie-jeebies. One of Crow's words, and nothing Weinstock could think of described more aptly what he was feeling.

A really big case of the heebie-jeebies.

## (6)

Newton came back to his desk with another cup of coffee, sat down, set the cup on a little electric hotplate, and frowned at the screen. All afternoon he had been busy making notes for his feature article, planning his research, surfing the Net to see what data were available, checking the *Sentinel*'s microfilm records of thirty years ago, and outlining his plan of attack. Most of the town's folklore was easy enough to find—there were literally thousands of articles and over a dozen books written about Pine Deep, recent and long past. What was missing from all of this, however, were detailed and accurate records of the Pine Deep Massacre of 1976. That it had happened was certain, because there were secondary references to it, and he was able to cobble together a list of the victims by burrowing through public death notices, both in the paper's records and at Pine Deep's Town Hall. But there was no reliable account of the actual events, and none of the issues of the *Black Marsh Sentinel* for that year had been committed to microfilm. He found that really odd, since there were microfilm records of papers from 1960 through 1975; and from 1977 to 1998, when the paper began storing issues on disk and in Web site archives. But 1976 was missing. The whole calendar year.

Newton called one of his friends at the *Pine Deep Evening Standard and Times*, which was owned by a chain that published papers in most of Bucks County's towns. "Toby?"

"Hey, my man Newt. They offer you the anchor of the *CNN Evening Report* yet?" Toby Gomm edited the op-ed page and was usually good for an info swap.

"Not yet. I'm holding out for *Nightline.* Hey, Toby, listen, Dick's got me doing a feature piece on P.D.'s haunted history, you know the kind of thing."

"Yeah, we've done a million of them. Bo-o-o-oring."

"No kidding. Look, I wanted to go a little further, maybe flesh out the backstory by including some stuff from the Massacre of Seventy-six. You got anything on that?"

"Before my time, but I heard about it. Haven't run anything on it lately, for the obvious reasons."

Bad for tourism, Newton thought, but asked, "You got anything in the archives from September, October of that year?"

He expected Toby to have to look into it, but he said, "Nope."

"Nothing? You mean you didn't cover it?"

"Nope, I mean that our microfilm records from the mid-seventies through about eighty-two got melted in a fire. Some asshole maintenance guy tossed a lit cigarette into a trash can and burned half the records room down. You have to remember that—it was when we moved to the new building. Late 1990."

"No, I was still in college."

"Didn't miss much. Trash fire is no news even when it's old news that's on fire. No biggie, though, we're a corporate rag . . . we leave hardcore journalism to our colleagues in Black Marsh."

"Very funny."

"On the other hand . . ." Toby said. "I do know a guy who knows everything about what went on there. His family got caught up in it. Brother even got killed."

"Are you talking about Malcolm Crow? The guy who shot Ruger?"

"Yep. He's always being used as a source for haunted history stories."

"I know. Dick told me that his family was involved, but I just haven't seen anything about the Massacre that he's quoted in."

"You won't, either, but I talked about it once with him. Kind of. Was back when he was on the cops, and he was walking a line between being a real hotshot cop and a total screwup."

"Oh?"

"He drank," Toby said in a way that said it all. "He was at a bar once when I was there waiting for a friend. Crow was there, totally bug-eyed. This was just about the time that Terry Wolfe was about to open the Hayride. Anyway, because of the Hayride and the tourist bucks that it would draw, the haunted history of the town came up and Crow started holding court, telling these crazy stories about ghosts and stuff. Most of the folks in the bar that night were regulars and had heard this shit and they started slipping off to take a leak but never came back, but I kind of felt sorry for the guy and hung out with him for a bit. Somewhere around the fifth or sixth round of boilermakers, Crow leans over to me and says, 'But none of that shit is the real shit, you know?' I didn't know, and I asked him, and he told me some of what had happened back in seventy-six. And let me tell you—it *was* the shit. Total *bull*shit. I mean, it was clear that he believed what he was saying, but I thought it was the drink talking and pretty much let it go in one ear and out the other."

"So . . . how's this helping me?"

"Because he's off the sauce now, and he's the hero *du jour*, so go ask him."

"That's great, Toby, thanks for the lead," Newton said, though he didn't feel any thrills of expectation dancing through him. "I owe you one."

"Just share the scoop next time."

"Will do," Newton lied, and rang off. He pulled the County Yellow Pages down and looked up the number for Crow's store but it rang through to the answering machine. Same result for the Guthrie farm. He called the Haunted Hayride but it was closed. Finally he swallowed his pride and called Mayor Wolfe's office.

After listening patiently, the mayor asked, "Is this the same Newton who broke the Ruger story? The fellow I met at the press conference?"

"Why, yes, sir, it is, and I—"

The mayor said, "Go shit in your hat," and hung up. Which only made Newton more determined to get the story. He was starting to get the first faint whiffs of another cover-up, and that made him tingle all over.

### (7)

"How's it going, Iron Mike?"

"Crow?" Mike's heart jumped into his throat and he nearly dropped the phone. "Oh my God! I heard about you on the news! Did Ruger really break into the hospital? Did you really kill him? Did Miss Guthrie really shoot him, too? Did—"

"Whoa! Slow down . . . only forty questions at a time," Crow said but he was laughing. "Yeah, things got pretty hairy the other night. You probably saw most of it on the news. I'll fill you in on the rest later. By the way, it's Val, not Miss Guthrie, and yes, she'll be okay."

"Jeez . . . it was bad enough losing her dad and all. Now this." Mike was sitting on his bed amid a sprawl of comic books, mostly *Hellboy* and *Ghost Rider*. He shot a quick glance at the closed door—he knew Vic wasn't home—and said, "Tell . . . um, 'Val' . . . that I'm sorry about her dad. I know how she feels. Kinda."

"Yeah, kid, I know you do, and I'll tell Val. It'll mean a lot to her."

"Thanks." Mike cleared his throat. "How are you?"

"Like Superman if he'd been beaten with a Kryptonite tire iron."

"Ugh. You gonna be in the hospital long?" His tone was uncertain, but his face looked hopeful. The day after the violence at Val's farm, when Mike had gone to visit Crow at the hospital, Crow had offered Mike a job at his store, the Crow's Nest, and the store was the closest thing to a real safe haven Mike had ever known. He couldn't wait to get started with his new job.

"Actually, we're out already. We left yesterday and stayed over at a friend's house. Val and I are heading out now to go back to her place," Crow said. "Which is why I called. I can't afford to have the shop closed down for too long, not this time of the year. I won't be at the store today, but tomorrow bright and early I want to meet you there to show you how to run things. In the meantime if you can swing it today I'd like you to feed my cats. My guinea pig, too. There's a key hidden under a flagstone in the back. It's the second from the left-hand side of the step and there's a chip out of one corner. Lift the opposite corner and you'll see the key in one of those plastic thingees."

"Okay, I can do that, but when you said 'run things' I—"

"I may be staying at Val's for a couple of days."

"Wait . . . you want *me* to run the store by *myself*?"

"Yeah."

Mike sat there, too stunned to even feel pain. "Alone?"

"Yeah . . . good with that?" Crow paused. "Mike—I'm counting on you here."

"Crow, I don't know if I—"

"Yes, you can. Jeez, kid, you know the layout of that store better than I do. The register is a snap, and you can open up right after school each day. Mornings and early afternoon are never my best times anyway, so you working afternoons and evenings will keep me out of the poorhouse. Besides, let's face it, isn't the store a better place to spend your days than hanging around the house?"

That said it all. Mike could not talk about Vic with anyone, not even Crow, but he knew that Crow understood. He felt tears stinging in the corners of his eyes. "Crow . . . I . . ."

"Dude," Crow cut him off, "if you are planning to make some kind of 'I won't let you down' speech, then save it. Both of us hurt too much for that and besides it's way too After-School Special for either of us. Just say, 'Thanks, Crow, you're one helluva guy.'"

Mike laughed. "Thanks, Crow, you're one helluva guy."

"This I know. Now, I called Judy from the yarn place across the street, and she'll keep her eye on you if I'm not there. She has the same kind of register if you have questions."

"Wow," Mike said. "Okay . . . this sounds great."

### (8)

Saul Weinstock said, "Turn him over," and watched as his nurse tugged the cold, limp body of Nels Cowan on its side. Bending close, Weinstock examined the buttocks, the backs of the thighs. He frowned and reached for a scalpel. "Hold him steady," he said and plunged the razor sharp blade into the corpse's white left buttock, then drew a long line down toward the top of the thigh. He removed the scalpel and stared at the black mouth of the wound. "That's weird," he said.

The male nurse, still supporting the ponderous weight of the corpse, peered over its shoulder. "What's weird?"

"Well, as you know, when the heart stops pumping, all of the blood settles down to the lowest points on the body, it gathers in the buttocks, the backs of the thighs, the back, so the procedure to drain the blood is to open those areas and let the blood drain out."

"Uh huh," said the nurse, who did know this and wondered why he was getting a lecture.

"So, tell me, Barney," said Weinstock, "what's wrong with this picture?"

The nurse looked again. "Oh," he said after a handful of seconds.

"Yes indeed," agreed Weinstock. "Oh."

"There's no—"

"Not a drop."

"None?"

"None," said Weinstock flatly.

Barney lowered the body back onto the stainless steel table. "Well, doctor, look at all the massive trauma to the neck and chest. Surely with all that flesh torn away the blood would have drained out."

Weinstock shook his head. "Doesn't work that way. No matter how traumatic a wound, there is pretty much no way to completely exsanguinate a body short of hanging it upside down after decapitation. This body is completely drained. Look at the face, at the arms. The veins are collapsed, the body is shrunken."

"He was lying out there in the mud," Barney said. "Maybe the blood just drained into the mud."

Weinstock thought about that, then shook his head. "Nope. I saw the crime scene photos. I read Dr. Colbert's report. There was some blood, true enough, but not nearly enough."

"Then . . . what?"

"Hell if I know," Weinstock said, and then shrugged. "Okay, now I want to take a look at the other guy. Castle. Wheel him out here. Let's look at him right now."

Barney gave his own shrug and went into the cold room. While he wrestled with the body of Jimmy Castle, Weinstock glanced over at the tape recorder that he'd started running at the beginning of the autopsy. The counter was ticking along steadily, having recorded all of his remarks to Barney. Frowning, he did a few more tests to Cowan, piercing the lower back, upper back, calves, thighs: trying to find blood. His frown deepened as he examined the ragged wounds at the throat. Strange wounds, not like knife wounds, not like any kind of wounds he had ever seen outside of a textbook.

He bent close, gingerly pressing the flaps of skin back into place like puzzle pieces, reconstructing the throat as accurately as possible. The loose strips of skin added up to most of the throat, though some small sections were missing. Probably lost in the mud or destroyed when Boyd did whatever it was he did to the corpse the night he broke into the morgue to steal Ruger's body. Even so, there was enough to piece together most of the throat. Weinstock used his fingers to hold the patchwork in place, and stared at what the marks on the flesh told him.

"Oh my . . . *God*!" he breathed softly, and he could feel sweat popping on his forehead and spreading under his arms. He looked up quickly as the nurse came crashing through the double doors, pushing a gurney. The naked body of Jimmy Castle lay on the steel surface, his white face wiped clean of all its former easy smiles, his body robbed of animation, dignity, and humanity.

Barney barely glanced at the doctor, didn't see the brightness of his eyes or the sweat that ran in trails down the sides of his face. "You okay, Doc?"

Weinstock grunted something and reached out to pull the second gurney closer. Together, Weinstock and the nurse hoisted him onto the second of the steel surgical tables. Weinstock said, "Help me get him on his side. Good. Hand me that scalpel. Thanks." Weinstock repeated the same cuts he made on Cowan's body.

Barney looked at the incisions and then at Weinstock. "No blood."

"No blood," Weinstock agreed slowly, his voice soft, thoughtful. He set the scalpel down and eased the body onto its back. He shifted position, standing near to Castle's head, his body blocking the view from the nurse as he poked and probed at the dead officer's throat.

"What's it mean?"

Weinstock turned toward him, and now Barney could see that sweat was pouring down the doctor's face. Weinstock folded his hairy arms and leaned a hip against Cowan's table, looking slowly from one body to the other and back again. He was trying to look casual, but his face was hard and his eyes almost glassy. Then he reached over and punched the Off button on the tape recorder and looked up at the nurse, who was beginning to fidget. "Let me ask you something, Barney," he said slowly, his voice as taut as violin strings. "How much do you like this job?"

"Huh?"

"Your job, being a nurse here at the hospital, how much do you like it?"

"Uh . . . well, I like it just fine, Doc."

"Means a lot to you, this job?"

"Yes sir."

"Got a wife? Kids?"

"Sure, Jenny and I have just the one. She'll be ten months on Monday."

"Ten months? My oh my. Babies are expensive, aren't they?"

"You said it."

"So, I guess it would be a safe assumption that you really need this job?"

"Sir?" Barney was frowning, beginning to feel really nervous.

"I mean, with a wife and a new baby, you need to keep this job, am I right?"

Carefully, afraid to commit himself, Barney said, "Ye-e-es."

"Uh huh." Weinstock rubbed at the corner of his mouth with the back of his bent wrist, his eyes fixed piercingly on the nurse. "Well, let me just say this, then. Right now there are just two people who know about the condition of these two bodies. Correct?"

"Um . . . yeah, I guess so."

"Just the two of us. Now, I am going to write a very confidential report on the condition of these bodies. I will only be sharing that report with Mayor Wolfe, and perhaps with the chief—and *no one else*. I can reasonably expect those two gentlemen to keep this confidential, you understand?" He paused. "You know about it as well."

"Well sure, but I—"

"And you need to keep this job."

Barney said nothing.

"So I can also expect that you won't tell anyone, either."

After a long pause, Barney said, "Yes, sir."

Weinstock nodded. "Understand me here, Barney—I like you and we've known each other for a long time, so I'm not threatening you. Don't take it that way, please, but something is very, very wrong here and I need to know with absolute confidence that you are going to maintain the confidentiality of this at all costs."

Barney's face was flushed with anger, but he took a couple of breaths and nodded. "Whatever you need, Dr. Weinstock."

They looked at each other for a long moment, then Weinstock gave a single curt nod. "Okay, I am going to do the autopsies on these officers, and you are going to assist me, correct?"

"Yes, sir."

"However, once you leave this room, you are going to forget everything that happened here, understand? Everything you see. Everything I say when I make my notes." He paused. "Everything."

"Yes, Dr. Weinstock. Absolutely clear. You can count on me."

Weinstock wiped sweat from his face with a paper towel. "Good," he said softly. "Good man."

"Dr. Weinstock . . . what's going on? What's happening?"

Weinstock looked at him for a very long time, his dark eyes intense, bright, but also watery. "What's happening?" he murmured. He gave a short, harsh bark of a laugh. "What's happening is something that can't be happening."

Barney frowned at him and felt very afraid.

# Chapter 13

## (1)

When Jim Polk's cell phone rang he nearly pissed on his shoes. He jiggled and finished as fast as he could and was zipping up with one hand while digging his phone out of his pocket with the other. He flipped it open, saw Vic's name on the caller ID and almost—almost—didn't answer. Instead he flicked a glance at the police cruiser parked at an angle to the entrance to the Guthrie farm, where he could see his partner, Dixie McVey, reading a copy of *Celebrity Skin* magazine. Oblivious. Polk shifted out of sight behind a big oak and punched the RECEIVE button. "Yeah," he said.

"You alone?" Vic asked.

"Yeah. Me and Dix are doing some bullshit shift, sitting on our thumbs outside of the Guthrie place. Waste of fu—"

"Are you alone?" Vic repeated, adding some edge to it. "Can McVey hear you?"

"No, I stepped out to take a whiz."

"Well, put your pecker back in your drawers and listen up."

"Okay, okay . . . go ahead," Polk said neutrally, absolutely sure he didn't want to hear whatever it was Vic was going to say.

"What's the scoop on this manhunt bullshit?"

"They're still looking for Boyd. Nobody's found shit."

Vic chuckled. "They will. I just made sure Boyd would be spotted far away from here."

"You tried that shit before and the dumb son of a bitch came back."

"Ancient history, it's all been sorted out now. I can guarantee that he'll do what we want from now on."

Polk felt sick. "About that, Vic . . . why'd he have to let Boyd kill Nels Cowan? Nels was okay."

"Well, life's a bitch sometimes, but trust me when I tell you it wasn't part of the Plan. Boyd screwed up but now he's more or less on a leash. Either way, these things have a way of working out, so I'm looking at it less as a killing and more as a recruitment."

"What's that supposed to mean?"

"Exactly what you think it means, Jimmy."

The sickness in Polk's stomach turned to greasy slush. "Oh, Jesus . . ."

"That ain't why I called, though. Your cousin Kenny still work at the quarry? Still the shift foreman?"

"Nah, he got promoted two years ago. He's assistant manager now."

"Even better. You tight with him?"

"Sure, why?"

"Good. 'Cause I want you to get him to buy you some dynamite. I'll e-mail you the specs on how much I need."

"What the hell do you need dynamite for?" Polk said, his voice jumping an octave, and he looked around as if he expected Dixie McVey to be standing right there taking notes.

Vic's voice was chilly. "You don't need to know that, Polk."

"Bullshit, Vic, I—"

"Let me rephrase that, dickhead . . . you don't *want* to know. Am I being real clear here? If not I can swing by your place and explain it to you in person."

Polk closed his eyes and leaned back against the tree.

"I'm pretty sure I remember giving you a shitload of cash the other day, Polkie," Vic said. "And I'm pretty sure you didn't give it to charity. From what I heard you bought a bottle and a piece of ass the second you were off the clock. That means you spent my money, Polk. That means you spent *his* money. So far I ain't asked you for much—least not anything big. Now's the time to earn your dime."

"Vic . . . I mean . . . dynamite? For God's sake!"

The laugh that came through the cell phone was filled with delight. "God don't got nothing to do with this, Jimmy-boy."

There was a silence while Vic gave Polk the time to think about his life choices. "Damn," Polk breathed.

"That's my boy," Vic said. "Check your e-mail when you get home, then I'm going to give you two weeks to get what I wanted. Two weeks don't mean two weeks and one minute. Let's both be clear on that. Let me down on this, Polk, and I'll send over one of my new friends to have a chat with you. Believe me when I tell you that you'd rather I kick a two-by-four up your ass than letting, say, Boyd dance you around a bit."

"Jesus Christ, don't even joke like that," Polk said.

"Who's joking?" Vic said and Polk felt his bladder tighten. If he hadn't just taken a leak he would have pissed himself right there. "And there are worse than him working for the Man. Oh *hell* yes."

Polk actually gagged and he pressed his eyes shut and leaned back against a tree, banging the back of his head against the gnarled bark once, twice.

"You still with me, sweet-cheeks?" Vic asked.

"Jesus . . ."

"You knew these days were coming. We both knew. You got a choice here. Be strong and stand with us, and you're going to come out of this like a king—or, as rich as one, any-way—but," and he lowered his voice to a silken whisper, "you cross us . . . you cross the *Man* . . . we'll eat your heart, and that, Jimmy-boy, is not a joke. *We will eat your heart.* Tell me you're hearing me loud and clear."

"Yes," Polk said, his own voice shocked and shamed down to a whisper. Vic was laughing when he hung up. Polk pressed his head back against the tree and kept his eyes squeezed shut, trying to squeeze Vic's words—and all of the terrible truth in them—out of his mind.

### (2)

Barney was gone now and Saul Weinstock sat in his office listening to the playback of the autopsy tape, hearing his own words as he described what he and Barney had discovered as they cut open first one corpse and then the other. The loss of blood. The shape and orientation of the wounds on their throats—wounds Boyd had broken into the morgue to try and disguise. That he had made a piss-poor job of it was no consolation. The tape reached the point where he had described the wounds, and he punched STOP and then rewound it to hear it again. He did that half a dozen times. The report he had to fill out lay on his desk and he had to tell the authorities something. It was already well past the point where he should have turned in his findings. To delay even five minutes would be to hinder the police operations, but to include these observations in what would become crucial documents would mean that everyone from the FBI on down to Gus Bernhardt would think that he was either a loony or a damn poor ME.

He sat back in his chair and rubbed his tired eyes. Castle and Cowan had been dead for three days now. Crime scene investigation had kept their bodies at the farm for some hours, then the flood in the morgue had delayed the autopsies for a day, and then Boyd's break-in had delayed things even further. Why? What was the purpose of stealing Ruger's body?

Then there was the next anomaly to consider: The bodies of both officers had been exsanguinated, the veins totally collapsed as if some kind of suction pump had been used. The same bizarre bite patterns had appeared on both men. Not just throats torn out, but throats that had clearly been punctured first before the flesh was ripped away. The punctures on Cowan were right over the jugular; Castle's punctures were over the left carotid. What kind of pump would have a clamp or fitting that would leave such marks? Add to that the fact that premortem bruising of Castle's wrist clearly indicated that a human hand had gripped Castle's wrist hard enough to burst the flesh and rupture the capillaries before— impossibly—ripping the arm from the socket. Not even a man hyped up on unlimited amounts of cocaine could muster that kind of strength, Weinstock knew that much. Which left him with a number of inexplicable or downright impossible pieces of evidence. To present these findings would be a total disaster. His competence would be called into question and that would taint all of the evidence should there ever be a trial. He put the cap of his pen in his mouth and chewed it as he thought.

The questions had to be answered. Why had Boyd attacked those two cops? Why and by what means was Boyd physically strong enough to tear a grown man's arm out of the socket? How had he then exsanguinated them? *Why* had he done that? What had he done with the blood? Why had he broken into the morgue? Why steal Ruger's body? Why disfigure the cops? On the videotape it had clearly shown Boyd limping on what appeared to be a badly broken leg. If his leg *was* broken, how had he carried Ruger—the man weighed two hundred pounds—and if his leg was *not* broken, why fake it? Then there was the matter of the broken pipes in the morgue. It was also very odd that they had taken that moment to disconnect, just in time to prevent the autopsy of Karl Ruger and to delay the autopsies of Castle and Cowan. Was that coincidence? That had happened when Crow and Val were still there at the hospital, which meant that there were plenty of police all over the building. It seemed unlikely that anyone could have slipped past all that security and gone down to the morgue to kick loose some pipes. He'd brought the matter up to Ferro, but the detective hadn't seemed convinced that it was anything suspicious, especially since the morgue door had been locked. Odd, though. Far too many odd things.

Weinstock was a practical physician, and in his years as a doctor he had seen very little to support a belief in coincidence. Everything was cause and effect. If you don't know the cause, look at the effect and backtrack in the same way you look at the symptoms to diagnose the disease. He told his residents that all the time. So, if the effect of this is two corpses drained of all blood, visible bite marks on the body, and two clearly visible puncture wounds on each throat, then what is the cause?

He shook his head and sat back in his chair. "You're a goddamned idiot," he told himself, saying it out loud, putting as much mockery as he could into it, trying to shame himself out of that kind of fanciful stupidity. Then in a quieter voice, he said, "You're crazy."

## (3)

Coming home to the farm was the hardest thing Val Guthrie had ever done, and Crow knew it. The place wasn't hers anymore—Ruger had made it his that night—and now she would have to reclaim it.

When Sarah's Humvee crunched to a slow stop on the gravel in the half-circle drive in front of the big porch, Val's hand closed around Crow's thigh and squeezed. It wasn't tight at first, but by the time the engine stopped and the silence of the late October morning settled over them, it felt to him as if she had diamond-tipped drills on the end of each fingertip. He didn't let on, though, either in expression or word; if it would help her deal with the moment, Crow would have given her a saw and let her cut the damn leg off. Sarah seemed to sense it, too, and sat there behind the wheel, door closed, hands resting quietly in her lap.

Eventually Val's grip eased and Crow took her hand in his. "Whenever you're ready, baby. No rush."

The house was huge, gabled, recently painted white with dark green window trimming and shutters. Gigantic oaks stood like brooding sentinels on either corner of the house, and smaller arborvitae flanked the broad front stairs. The porch was also painted green and there was a porch swing that Henry had made by hand for his wife fifteen years ago.

Crow saw that all of the crime scene tape had been removed. Score one for Diego.

"I guess I can't sit out here forever," Val said.

Sarah turned in her seat. "Honey, you can sit there until the cows come home and the national budget is balanced. In fact, I can turn this puppy around and you guys can come back home with me, which would make a lot more sense." It was the third time Sarah had made the suggestion.

Val reached out and gave Sarah's forearm a squeeze. "Thanks, sweetie," Val said, "I'll be fine." She absently touched her silver cross, tracing the shape of it over her heart.

"We could do a hotel," Crow said.

She shook her head, took a breath, jerked the handle up and, with slow care for her aches, got out. Crow got out on his side and walked around to stand beside her. Above them the house was immense and filled with ghosts.

"Damn," she breathed, and then walked toward the front door, chin down, jaw set, as if she were wading through waist-deep water. When they got to the front door, though, Val stopped. The door was new and still smelled of fresh paint. Val reached out to touch the new door, then turned to Crow. "You?"

"Diego. I called him, asked if he would tidy things up a bit."

Val kissed him and there was a single glittering tear in her left eye. "Thank you," she said. Taking a long, deep breath, she reached out and opened the door, hesitated one last moment, and went inside. Crow glanced at Sarah, eyebrows raised, and followed.

That was just before noon. Now it was midafternoon, and Val was asleep on her father's bed. She had gone in there to be among his things, not even wanting Crow's company. He heard her crying a few minutes later and every atom in him burned to go in and hold her, but he knew that it was the wrong thing to do. Sometimes grief should be private.

The interior of the house was spotless. Diego, as usual,

had been better than his word and his promise to "tidy up a bit" had resulted in a house that fairly gleamed from polish and soap. There was no trace of the violence of that night, and none of the leavings of the army of cops that had passed through since. Sarah and Crow had a quick lunch and then she left, and ten minutes later Val drifted downstairs and silently came to sit on Crow's lap at the kitchen table. Her eyes were puffy from crying, and when he wrapped his arms around her and held her close, she started crying again. Not the heavy sobs of earlier, but softer tears. He stroked her hair and held his tongue.

### (4)

The lab work from the autopsies had come back and was spread across his desk, but Saul Weinstock was staring through it as if he couldn't see it. He held a tumbler of Glenfiddich in his hands, the level having dropped over the last half hour from six fingers to two. Weinstock's eyes were red-rimmed and bright, as if he had a fever. The flush in his cheeks supported that look, but Weinstock was not sick, nor was he drunk. What he felt was a shock so profound that it reverberated through his chest like the echo of a gunshot.

He was mortally afraid; and the thing that had really driven a wire right into Weinstock's brain—and that had moved him from coffee to Scotch—was the lab report on the scrapings taken from beneath Nels Cowan's fingernails. Apparently the officer had fought back pretty hard, and during that struggle he'd raked his fingernails across his attacker's exposed skin. Weinstock had gotten good scrapings, more than enough for lab purposes. The report on them had come back with a handwritten note from Dr. Ito, the senior technician, paperclipped to it:

Saul
   Not sure how these samples got contaminated, but the tissue scrapings you sent me are probably not from the crime scene, as you'll see in my report. It's that or

someone's playing a pretty sick joke. Personally I find
this kind of joke fairly inappropriate considering the
circumstances. When you find the prankster, kick his
ass for me.

Don

There hadn't been any prankster. Weinstock had taken
those samples himself, and had personally dropped them off
at Ito's lab. He sipped his Scotch and picked up the lab report on the skin samples, reading and rereading the line that
was already burned into his eyes. "The tissue samples are in
an advanced state of necrosis consistent with decomposition
of 48 to 72 hours duration." Nineteen little words that had
hammered a crack in Saul Weinstock's version of the world.
It made LaMastra's comment about how Boyd looked on the
video echo like thunder in his head.

Weinstock went back to the morgue and took a fresh set of
samples from under each man's fingernails, and walked them
again to Ito's office. Ito was out, but his assistant promised to
have the new set of labs back tomorrow. Until then, Saul Weinstock could do nothing, so he walked thoughtfully back to
his office. He closed the door and walked to the window. It was
already dark and he felt a cold itch at the base of his spine.

"You're being childish," he told himself, saying it out
loud in hopes it sounded better. It didn't. He looked down at
the parking lot, at the long shadows cast by cars and SUVs,
calculating how long it would take him to get from the
lighted entrance of the hospital to his car. How long it would
take him to unlock the doors, get in, reset the locks, start up,
and get the hell out of the shadowy lot. "Now that's just
silly," he breathed. His workday was over, he should be
heading home to Rachel and the kids.

Instead he drew the blinds, turned on the desk lamp as
well to add more light to his already bright office, and then
took the Scotch bottle from his desk drawer and poured two
fingers into his coffee cup. He wondered how much Scotch
he'd have to drink before he felt brave enough to simply

walk out of the hospital and get into his car. He hated himself for his cowardice because none of what he was thinking about the physical evidence of the case could be right. He had to be reading it wrong. Too much work, not enough sleep, and the stress of so much violence in town. Just a stress thing, that's all.

Weinstock sipped his Scotch and in his mind the seeds of some very dreadful thoughts were beginning to take root.

### (5)

Through the window they could see the stars shimmering like embers. The fingers of an old tree scratched the attic shingles. Pale clouds drifted like faint ghosts across the sky, sometimes covering everything with darkness, sometimes invisible, always riding the easterly wind. It was October 5 and midnight was newly laid to rest. Everything looked and felt the way it should in October—blustery and mysterious. With the storm shutters thrown wide and the curtains pegged back, Crow and Val could see the night sky from her bed. She lay with her head on his chest, and he had his arms around her, and around them both was a thick patchwork quilt her mother had made years ago.

"You sure everything's locked up?" she asked, and Crow nodded.

"Did I hear you on the phone when I was downstairs?"

"Uh-huh. I called Connie."

"Ah. How'd that go? How is she?"

"She's still mostly out of it, but at least she's talking now. Just a bit. Girl stuff, mostly. And about Mark." She sighed. "Mark's still being so mean to her."

"I know."

"He's not like Dad at all. I mean . . . there is a good heart there, but he's always so afraid of things. Never takes risks, never looks outside the box. Right now he could make a hero out of himself if he just stopped trying to lay blame on Connie. Or on himself. It solves nothing. It's stupid for him to feel bad because he couldn't stop Ruger."

She snuggled against him. "I wonder what makes a man like Ruger tick. What makes him so . . . *evil*."

Crow just shook his head, not wanting to share his thoughts. *Ubel Griswold sends his regards.* He hadn't told Val about that yet—neither those words nor the change he had seen come over Ruger at the hospital—and wasn't sure he ever would. Those red eyes. Those teeth. If Val hadn't found Shank's pistol—if they both hadn't managed to empty two guns into Ruger—would that change have continued? Would Ruger have become the same kind of monster as Griswold? He didn't think so—and what he had seen in the hospital argued against it—but if not the same kind of thing, then what was Ruger becoming? What would he have become if they hadn't killed him? Crow thought he knew; there was a word for it, but he resisted any attempt by his conscious mind to acknowledge that word. He shoved it away, terrified of its implications.

"Baby," he said gently, "I don't know about you, but this is not a conversation I want to have before going to bed."

She smiled, kissing him again. "Yes, doctor."

Outside the wind was blowing the trees and the bushes and whistling through the ironwork of the weathervane.


Twice that night Crow tried to initiate lovemaking with her, and twice he failed. Both times it started well, with tenderness and slowness and care, not just for their mutual injuries, but for the hurts inside; but each time as Crow had moved to be on top of her, as he nestled down between her warm, soft thighs, for just a moment Crow's face had been replaced in Val's mind by the grinning face of Karl Ruger. The first time she had yelped—nearly a scream—and Crow had moved off her, confused and hurt, instantly embarrassed by his nakedness, wondering what he had done wrong, if he had moved the wrong way. It had taken a long time for her to articulate enough of what she was feeling for him to get it, and the process had to work its way through the thicket of insecurity and rejection that such a reaction had inspired in him.

The second time was over an hour later, after they had talked about it and then lapsed into quiet they began light touching, gentle kissing, and ultimately circled back to the same moment. She didn't yelp this time; she didn't scream— instead Val's entire body went tight and rigid and the sweet kisses turned to sourness on her lips. Crow's caresses changed from sensual to harsh. It was as if she could actually feel the calluses of Ruger's brutal hands on her thighs and breasts, and Crow could see the revulsion ripple in waves across her face.

There were a number of ways Crow could have handled it. Frustration, cajoling, anger, peevishness, but Crow understood what it felt like to be invaded by darkness, to be polluted by it. The abuse he had suffered from his own father had been comprehensive. To have done anything forceful or insistent at that moment would have been the same as doing actual harm, so instead Crow settled himself gingerly down onto his back, curled his arm around her with just the barest hint of pressure. Not a trap, but an open door. He said nothing, did nothing. When she finally settled against him, stiff as wood, he kissed her hair and stroked her arm, letting stillness settle over them. For a long time Val's muscles were as unyielding as rock, her lips compressed in a tight line against her teeth. One of the candles guttered out and Crow made no move to relight it. When she still held rigid, he said, very softly, "It's okay. It's too soon."

She could not even speak past the stricture in her throat and Crow didn't try to urge her because he knew that to try would be to force her to rasp out something harsh. Silence was good. After a while Crow leaned his head against hers, smelling perfume and shampoo and wood smoke in her hair. Long minutes later Val found his hand in the dark and closed her fingers around it with all her strength. "I'm sorry!" she whispered desperately.

"No," he murmured, "no, sweetheart . . . there's nothing

for you to ever be sorry about. This is all *his* fault." He couldn't say Ruger's name in that sacred space. "Let's just lie here and listen to the wind over the corn. Hear it? It sounds like the ocean."

He held her close, not daring to make a single move except to kiss her hair and hold her hand. It took her hours to relax, to completely settle back against him. They spoke little, and only at first; after a while it was the silence between them and the wind over the stiff corn that wrapped her fears back in their box and shoved them out of sight. In the end, somewhere well after midnight, it was she who rekindled it between them. The last candle had guttered out and he was on the soft edge of sleep when her fingers relaxed their hold on his. They drifted across to his chest and he held his breath for a moment as she pressed her hand flat as if trying to feel his heartbeat through her palm. Then he heard her release a pent-up breath, which at first he thought was another sigh of sadness and frustration, then she shifted and turned more toward him in the dark, bending to kiss him. First his chest, right over his heart, then in a slow line up his chest to his throat and over his chin to his mouth. The kiss was so soft that it was like a warm vapor on his lips.

Crow did not move. He sensed that if he moved, if he did anything to exert any control over the moment, even something as simple as acknowledging it with words or a murmur, she would flee back down into her personal darkness. All he did was to respond to her kisses, letting her set the level of intensity, to decide how much or how little they kissed. After a long time she propped herself on her good hand and swung one thigh over him; he still did not move to help her. She reached down and took him in her hands and guided his hardness into her and she was wet and hot— feverishly hot—and as she sat down on him he filled her. He heard her hiss but he made no sound. Not even when a single scalding tear dropped from her cheek and burned onto his chest.

Her thighs hurt him, brushing the bandages over his injuries, but he didn't care, didn't dare let it show, forced himself not to flinch, and accepted what was happening with careful joy. His heart was hammering so forcefully that he thought she must hear it. Val sat astride him, her palms flat on his hard stomach, and for a while she was motionless, though he could feel her trembling; then slowly, tentatively, she began moving her hips. He wanted to cry out, to express what he was feeling, but hc forced himself to be silent, to merely accept this gift, this sharing, knowing how difficult it was for her to open herself in all these different ways. She did not come quickly, and almost didn't come at all. Crow's mind was in such a different frame than simple physical need that he also kept on this side of that precipice for longer than he ever had before with her. Then with a gasp and a small cry the orgasm blossomed inside her like a white starburst; it flooded him with heat and need and he came with her, and at that moment he, too, cried out.

Val collapsed down on him, weeping, kissing him with a hundred quick kisses. Crow wrapped his arms around her to hold her close, and the night and the darkness went away.

# Chapter 14

## (1)

He sat cross-legged on the roof of the farmhouse, his bony knees jutting out on each side of the corner. Above him the moon was a swollen pustule on the face of the bruise-black sky, and the stars with their cleaner light seemed to shrink back from it as it hung in bloated display above the swaying corn. Below him was an attic filled with old memories and dead spiders, and below that was Val's room where she and Crow lay asleep. For hours both of them had been dreaming, and for hours the Bone Man had sat there playing the blues, doing what he could to chase away the monsters in their minds.

## (2)

In his dream Little Scarecrow fled through a distorted landscape, running as hard as nine-year-old legs could run, his heart hammering in his chest, his mind numb with fear. Behind him *it* pursued. Little Scarecrow could not see what it was; he almost never saw it until the very last moment, but he knew it was there, could hear its shambling bulk as it smashed through the weirdly twisted hedges, could hear the click and scratch of its claws on the pavement as it chased him down the length of Corn Hill. The street was impossibly long and oddly narrow, all the buildings loomed tall and crooked above him as he ran. The ground glistened with rain that smelled of diesel oil and rotten eggs; the clouds above were backlit with odd purple-red lights as if the whole town was inside a swollen body and Little Scarecrow was seeing the light of the world outside through veins, blood, and muscle tissue.

The beast followed him, its claws tearing chunks out of the street as it ran, its breath like the cough of a steam engine. Little Scarecrow wanted to turn, to see it, to know the shape and form of the monster. Maybe that would help contain it, maybe that would dwindle it down to something that could be identified and understood instead of a formless, measureless, dark malevolence. He wanted to look, but he did not dare. He tried to dodge in and out of alleyways and other people's front yards, and sometimes he thought he'd lost the thing, that he was safe, then he would hear the gruff snarl of its voice, hear the clickety-clack of its nails, feel the trembling echoes of its vast bulk as it ran after him. He thought he could feel the heat of its stare on his back, and sometimes he staggered under the weight of its hate and hunger.

In his dreams, even though it was always the same dream, he felt confused about which way to go, which direction to take. He wasted precious seconds in indecision at every turn, and each time the beast gained on him. Finally, inevitably, he would choose the back streets that led in a circuitous route toward his own yard. He would scamper through the hedges into the half-lighted quarter-acre behind his house, race past the long rows of unkempt rosebushes, weave in and out of the scattered lawn tools that his father had left to rust, past the lawn chair where his father sat and drank beer and watched with cold, drunken eyes as his youngest son fled for his life and the only thing he would do was lift the sweating can to his lips and drink. Little Scarecrow ignored his father, making sure even in his panic to steer out of the reach of any casual swipe or kick. He tore along toward the rickety old set of swings. As always his brother, Boppin' Billy, would be there, and as always Little Scarecrow's heart would leap in his chest. Billy was older, tougher, smarter. Billy knew how to wrestle and he could thread a needle with a football pass, and Billy knew everything that was important to know. With the last bits of his failing strength, Little Scarecrow ran toward Billy, calling his brother's name, confident that if anyone in the world could save him, then Billy certainly would.

Billy turned, smiling, confident. His grin was lopsided, but his eyes were sharp and as hard as baseballs. Little Scarecrow ran to him and skidded to a stop, aware that the beast was dangerously close, that it was coming closer with horrible speed.

"Billy! He'll get me!" Little Scarecrow wailed.

Billy gave him a confident wink and opened his mouth to say something, but from his mouth spewed a torrent of dark blood that was as black as oil in the moonlight. The blood splashed Little Scarecrow's face and chest and hands.

"NOOOOO!" he screamed as Billy's eyes rolled high and white and he sagged backward. His head lolled on a loose neck and then the flesh tore completely and fell away from his body before Billy's corpse fell forward in a limp sprawl.

Little Scarecrow screamed and screamed. He felt the claws of the beast as it seized the shoulder of his jacket and spun him around. Little Scarecrow stared up in terror at the face—at that horrible, impossible face! Red eyes flared at him, eyes filled with hate, with hunger, and with triumph. A long muzzle wrinkled back to reveal rows of dripping teeth like racks of knives. Little Scarecrow stared into the black depths of the mouth, he felt the heat of its breath, smelled the carrion stink as the muscles of the beast bunched, tensed—and then it lunged at him . . .

. . . And he woke up, as he always did, just as he felt the claws tear through his flesh. Even a marginally kinder universe would have let him wake up a moment sooner.

Crow sat up in bed, clamping a hand over his mouth to stifle the scream that was bubbling there behind his tongue. He turned and shot a worried, desperate glance at Val, but she was still deep in sleep, her face slack and painted blue-white by the starlight.

He closed his eyes and exhaled through his nose, deflating the scream and calming the spasms in his chest. His heart was fluttering inside him like a baseball card stuck in bicycle spokes. Then with the soothing clarity of a breeze blowing over hot skin he heard another sound. It may have been another dream, or it might have been a peculiarity of the wind as it whistled through the drains and pipes that clung to the side of the hospital walls, but as he lay there Crow thought he heard—faintly, just a whisper—the sound of a guitar played far away. Soft, sad music. Mississippi blues played by a deft hand—one that knew how make the strings weep and moan. Like the way the Bone Man played all those years ago. The sound could not be there on the wind, it was so ghostly and thin that it was probably not there, even though when Crow strained to hear it he believed he actually did. The music—sad as it was—was a comfort to him. Listening to it, Crow drifted back into sleep. This time he didn't dream at all, which was a blessing.

### (3)

It was the dream about the Change. Terry lay there, aware that he was dreaming, which made it worse, because Sarah was really there beside him just as she was in the dream. In both worlds her warm reality was pressed up against him, back and buttocks and feet all snugged in, her breathing steady and deep, her vulnerability absolute.

He could feel her heat, smell the fragrance of her shampoo and the faintest traces of fabric softener from the pillow under her head. Terry drew in those smells and found that he was becoming aware of other smells, smaller ones, subtler ones. Smells he would never have noticed before or perhaps never have been able to detect before, but that were now distinct and unique. Perfumes in their bottles on the bureau across the room. He'd never noticed those before. Dust bunnies under the bed. A whiff of cedar from the closet. The Desenex in his gym shoes. Potpourri in a bowl in the hallway. The lingering smell of the salmon they'd had for dinner. The detergent from the dishwasher downstairs. He could smell everything, and not just smell it—he knew what each smell *was*. Each one was separate, distinct; he could catalog them all.

It was the same with sounds. Party Cat's breathing was as loud as if he'd fallen asleep in front of a microphone, but he was in the twins' room all the way down the hall, and though Terry's own bedroom door was closed he could hear the kids breathing as they slept. He could hear dry leaves skittering along the shingles on the roof, and he could hear when the sound changed as the leaves fell into the rain gutter and slithered along the metal. He could hear cars on Corn Hill, but he could also hear the growl of a truck way out on A-32. Somewhere way out on the breeze he could hear the sound of someone playing blues on an acoustic guitar—something sad and sweet. He could hear the blood racing through the big veins in Sarah's sweet, soft throat. Terry could hear all of these things, just as he could hear the slow grinding mumble of his bones as they began to shift and change under his skin. His skin moved with a sound like someone stretching wet leather. Why could Sarah not hear that? It was so loud.

Then the pain started. First it was a dull ache in his bones, an almost indefinable throb of the kind his Gram used to call growing pains. An ache that seemed to hover around each bone rather than actually be a part of them, a throbbing that made him want to move, to shift, to find a new position in which to lie, but he knew that he couldn't shift away from what was happening in his bones and cartilage. Then his skin began to hurt as it stretched over the new bone-shapes. He'd felt an ache like that once before when he'd broken his ankle while hiking and the whole joint had swelled inside his boots, and then continued to swell when he'd managed to pull the boot off, swelling until it seemed like the skin itself would have to split. Back then the skin hadn't split—though Terry had gone through long hours where he perversely wanted to take a pin and pop the swelling to see if his ankle would explode. Now that same feeling of swelling-to-bursting was blossoming in every joint, not just his ankles but his knees and hips, his elbows and wrists, each separate joint of his fingers. It was like someone was pouring gallons of hot blood into him, pumping it under his skin.

He wanted to scream, needed to scream, *had* to scream, but he bit it back—literally bit down, plunging his teeth into his lips, aware that the skin was tearing, aware—oh God how aware—of the delicious salty blood that was filling his mouth. His teeth, those biting teeth, felt huge and so, so *wrong*. He clenched his hands—swollen and misshapen as they had become—and dug his nails into his palms until there, too, blood welled hot and sweet-smelling.

Beside him Sarah stirred in her sleep and wriggled tighter against him. He almost did it then. Right then. He almost reached for her with hands and with mouth, with hunger and with *teeth*. Almost. After a moment Sarah drifted back into her dreams, sliding deeper beneath the surface and was unaware of anything but his warmth and nearness while Terry ate his screams.

The night boiled around him and gradually, with infinite and perverse slowness, the urge retreated, leaving Terry sweating and trembling, lips and palms slick red, breath hissing in and out of his flaring nostrils. Again the awareness of every sound, every smell came flooding back and Terry's senses filled him with an animal keenness. He lay awake, terrified of that dream, of the nightmare he had just escaped, dreading the thought of going back to sleep for fear that the dream would start again and that this time he would not be able to shake himself awake from it.

Terry was very much mistaken about that. He had not been asleep for hours. He had not been dreaming at all.

### (4)

Barney caught Weinstock just as the doctor was about to open his office door. "This just came," he said and handed over a large envelope.

Weinstock looked at the label. The second set of lab reports on Cowan and Castle. Barney was still standing there, visibly fidgeting. "Is there a problem, Barney?"

"This is more about those cops," the nurse said quietly, glancing around to make sure no one else was in earshot. "Isn't it?"

Weinstock gave him a long, steady look. "I thought we had an agreement about this, Barney," he said.

"I . . ."

"I'm doing some follow-up work," Weinstock said evenly. "Do you feel that you need to say something about this matter?"

Barney stiffened. "No, Dr. Weinstock." He opened his mouth to add something, thought better of it, and clamped his jaw shut.

"Have a good evening, Barney," Weinstock said, and he kept his gaze steady as the nurse turned walked down the hall, back rigid. When Barney turned the corner, Weinstock quickly opened his office door, hurried inside, locked it, and began tearing at the envelope. His fingers trembled and fumbled as he tore it open and pulled out the sheaf of papers from the lab. For a slow five-count he closed his eyes, not wanting to see what was written there and bracing himself for the worst. If they matched the first report he didn't know what he would do. Weinstock had checked the staff schedule to make sure that his request for new labs would not go to Don Ito—Ito had the day off and another and more junior tech had processed the samples. That was good because until he was sure what was going on he wanted to keep the whole thing off the radar. He opened his eyes and began to read, first the reports on Cowan's blood and tissue work, and then Castle's; then he read through them both again.

"Almighty God . . ." he breathed. The shadows in his office suddenly seemed to loom up around him and never in his life had Saul Weinstock been as deeply terrified as he was at that moment.

**(5)**

Mike Sweeney drifted between three dreams. First it was the nightmare of the burning town and the death of everyone he knew and that melted into the dream where the Wrecker chased him and ran him down, grinding him to red paste on the black highway. The third dream—the *new* one—that was the worst by far. It always started out okay, with him feeling immensely powerful, pedaling his bike faster than the wind, swooping down the long hill to the Hollow at the base of the mountains, skidding to a stop amid the flame and the hordes of murdering monsters. He would leap off, dragging his sword out of its sheath, the blade bright with mirrored flame, launching himself into a murderous attack. It was the kill that thrilled him most, and he was good at it. Naturally, easily, gleefully good at it. His sword would flick and dance, seeding the air with scarlet droplets of blood. He would dodge and twist, too fast to catch, too strong to overwhelm, too powerful to be stopped. His enemies would fall around him, unable to stand before his fury.

And yet still his friends would die. He would kill the monsters until they were stacked like cordwood ten deep around him. Or he would cut them, watching as they burst into flame. But always, always, always there were too many, and they would overwhelm his friends. Even while he survived. Even if he went on to kill every last one of the monsters, his friends—Crow, Val, Tyler—all of them would die.

Then he would hear the voice of the Beast—this time a beast he could see, and he would turn and there it was. Fifteen feet tall, with great bat wings spread wide and gnarled goat legs with hooves that split stones when he stamped. Curling horns arched up from his head and in his mouth his teeth were like daggers. A devil in flesh, the demon god of some new hell.

*"LOOK AT ME!"* it would roar in a voice that shook the world. Mike would begin to scream then. Even with all of the other monsters dead around him and his sword still in his hands, he would begin to scream. It was not an inarticulate

howl of rage or pain or even terror. It was a word that he
would scream, and the screaming of that single word would
tear blood from his throat and rip him raw. The sound of it
would shatter the cold steel of his sword and shatter the
bones in his own legs, dropping him down onto his knees as
agony exploded upward through his thighs and into his
groin. He would scream that one word over and over again
until the screaming of it burst him apart more surely than the
wheels of the Wrecker, and in his dreams Mike would feel
himself dying, would actually feel his skull splitting and his
throat rupturing as his blood fought to escape his veins.

He would scream the word, "Father!" And then he would
die.

Mike cried as he was wrenched out of the dream into the
darkness of his room and the temporary shelter of the waking world. Misery stitched itself through every inch of his
body and burst into his brain like a white-hot light. Fireflies
seemed to dance in the shadows of his room. Mike's heart
was a creature scrambling to escape the trap of his chest; his
lungs sought to breathe in an airless void. In his darkness he
imagined he could still hear the sound of his own voice
screaming, and the absurdity of what he was screaming did
nothing to ameliorate the terror that it engendered. Mike
clutched his blanket to his thin body, trying not to scream
here in his room, afraid of what word would come out. Even
so, as overwhelming as his terror was, it should have been
worse, but Mike was too young, yet, to perceive the difference between nightmare and prophecy.

**(6)**

Weinstock pushed the morgue door open slowly and
stood there for a long time, just looking into the room. There
were just two small lights on and the place was filled with
cold shadows. Weinstock shivered and almost—almost—
turned to leave. Had there been the slightest distraction, just

the ding of an elevator bell down the hall or the buzz of his pager, he would have seized the moment and gone to do anything but what he was planning to do. He waited . . . and waited . . . and all was silent, the shadows without an uninterrupted challenge. A thick bead of sweat was plowing a channel through the hair on his back and he kept licking his lips.

"God," he murmured, "what am I doing?" He went inside. He didn't want to do this in the dark and so he swiped a hand upward to turn on all the ceiling lights and then went around and switched on every table lamp, and even switched on the big examination lamp in its metal hood so that harsh white light bathed the empty stainless-steel dissecting table. Everything was clean and light sparkled from metal fittings and instruments. The brightness helped. It made what he was thinking seem even more absurd, and he needed it to be absurd. Saul Weinstock needed to be proven one hundred percent wrong.

Normally he would have turned on the microphone that hung down above the steel dissecting table so he could create an official record, but there was nothing normal about this. The autopsy had already been performed. What he was doing now was as far from standard hospital protocol as it was from the protocols of the county coroner's office.

Instead he set up his own tape recorder and inserted a one-hundred-minute cassette. Next to this he set a good quality Sanyo Tapeless CameraCorder that could record everything he did with DVD quality. He was off the reservation with this, so if he got caught he wanted proof. If proof was to be had.

Next he wheeled over a metal cart on which were a complete set of tools, including a dissecting knife with a retractable four-inch blade, a foot-long brain knife, long-handled scissors, forceps, and other items. He switched on both machines, introduced himself, gave the date and time, and then pulled Jimmy Castle's body out of its drawer. He took in a deep breath and let it out before slowly pulling back the sheet to reveal the body.

Castle's skin should have been gray-white and flaccid, the tissues deflated by the loss of fluids, with cheeks and eye sockets sunken in. During the first autopsy he had attempted to take the standard 20-ml blood sample for testing but couldn't find any, even in the lowest tissue areas where blood usually settles after the heart stops. He was able to take samples of urine and cerebrospinal fluid, but as far as blood went there was barely a drop to be found. That had been the beginning of this problem. During that autopsy Weinstock had made a big Y-incision starting at Castle's neck and running down to the thighs, cutting in an arc around the navel, exposing the internal organs and then removing them for weighing and testing. After the autopsy the organs were placed in a large plastic bag, set into the empty stomach cavity, and the big incision sewed up. The samples were sent to the lab and the bodies returned to cold storage. The Castle and Cowan murders were still open cases, and their bodies might remain in the Pinelands morgue for weeks. Which gave Weinstock a chance to do what he had to do.

He looked at the Y-incision he had made, started to turn away to pick up a knife and then stopped, turned, and reached up to angle the overhead light differently, bending closer to peer at the incision. He blinked, bent closer still.

"No . . ." he said and reached for his dissecting knife. Steeling himself he drew it quickly along the line of sutures that held the flaps of the moistureless dead skin together, the steel edge cutting evenly through the surgical nylon. He finished his cut just at the navel and with nothing to hold them in place the flaps of skin should have sagged away. They did not. The long jagged line he'd cut in Jimmy Castle's chest and stomach—which he had used to open him up and remove all of his internal organs—was stuck fast. Almost as if it had begun to heal. Which was, of course, quite impossible.

**(7)**

Across his thighs, the Bone Man's guitar was laid strings-up; he was strumming it like a Dobro, sliding along the frets with the cut and sanded neck of an old Coke bottle. The music he played was so quiet that it might not have been there at all, and as he played, he could feel Crow and Val relax within the knotted fists of their dreams, could feel Griswold's grip slacken on them, at least a bit. Mike, too. The music, the *blues,* could do that much at least. It wasn't much, but he smiled, taking his victories where he could find them.

Midnight was poised to strike and the Bone Man kept playing as the darkness hammered the town. Stretching out with his awareness, using what he had, the Bone Man could feel each of the hearts in the town beating with the pulse of night. He heard whispers and cries, felt warm hearts and cold. It was hard for him to care about this town. About most of it, anyway. This town had hated him. Hell, this town had *killed* him. Beaten him, broken him, and hung him on a scarecrow's cross like some mockery of Jesus. Worse even than that, these people had hung the reputation on him of killer, called him a monster, blamed him for the murders he had helped stop while at the same time whitewashing Griswold's name. They had taken that nickname some kids had given him—the Bone Man, 'cause he was so skinny—and used it to build a nightmare boogeyman legend. Now he was the Bone Man to everyone here, and the Bone Man was a monster, a bad man. Something evil.

The Bone Man stared out from his rooftop perch, sneering at the town of Pine Deep as it slept its troubled sleep. "You don't know what evil is," he said aloud, aiming his words at the town like a gun, but his voice was a whisper more silent than the wind. For two pins he'd let Griswold, or the Devil Himself, take the whole damned town.

Except for a few.

He strummed his guitar as the wind blew past him and thought about those people, the ones who had liked him, who had cared about him. They were the only ones from Pine Deep he could remember without anger. Henry Guthrie and his wife, Henry's brother and his cousin. His daughter, little Valerie, Li'l Bosslady. Boppin' Billy Crow and his brother, Malcolm—Little Scarecrow. Terry "Wolfman" Wolfe and his little sister, Mandy. Big John Sweeney. Just a handful. Henry was dead now, his body on a cold slab in the bowels of the hospital. Henry's wife was two years in her grave, and his cousin Roger had been killed during that slaughter thirty years ago. John Sweeney had gone off Shandy's Curve in his Malibu. Everyone thought he'd fallen asleep at the wheel, but the Bone Man knew different. He knew that Vic Wingate had rigged that car. Done something to the steering. Vic had wanted John dead so he could get next to Lois Sweeney, and he'd managed it; and John Sweeney wasn't dead a week before Vic had pumped Lois full of Ecstasy and Mescal and had fed her to Griswold. Not as a blood sacrifice like he'd done with so many others, but as something else; and that was nearly sixteen years ago, during one full moon when Griswold's spirit had hijacked another man's body so he could live for just a few days. He'd *lived* all right. He'd done things to Lois that had driven her into the bottle and she'd never dared peek out of it since, not even when she found out she was pregnant. Vic had stepped in and married her before the baby was born, grinning all the time at what he had stage-managed. That left Big John Sweeney's boy, Mike, at the mercy of Vic Wingate—only Mike wasn't Sweeney's son. Anyone who really looked at the boy could see that. Big John had been black Irish, with brown eyes and black hair, but Mike had red hair and blue eyes. In another couple of years, if he lived long enough for that, Mike would look like his real father—the man whose body Griswold had hijacked for one ugly night—and then everyone would know for sure. But even that was complicated, because Mike actually had *two* fathers. Three if you count Big John. There was the father of his flesh, and the father of his spirit. Or, maybe that second one was the father of his *nature*. Mike Sweeney was one who would bear watching—and watching over. There was trouble there, sure enough, and no way in the world to know how those cards would fall.

The Bone Man strummed his guitar, seeding the air with sweetness while all around him the darkness twisted and writhed.

# Chapter 15

## (1)

LaMastra burst into the conference room with a walkie-talkie in one hand. "Frank! Boyd's been spotted." He hurried over to hand off the unit. "It's Jim Polk"

Ferro grabbed the walkie-talkie. "Polk, Ferro here. Tell me."

"Sir," Polk's voice said with a crackle, "We got a call from Gaither Carby, he's a local farmer who was driving back to Pine Deep across the Black Marsh Bridge when a guy cuts across his path. Carby damn near runs him down 'cause the guy was limping pretty bad. Carby slows down to see if maybe the guy's hurt and the guy takes a couple of shots at him. Carby floors it and gets out of there. He called it in and from his description it seems pretty likely that it was your boy."

"How long ago was this?"

"Fifteen minutes. Carby doesn't have a cell phone, so he had to drive to a neighbor's house and use their phone. I took the call here and rolled some units."

"Good work," Ferro snapped. "I'll head out there right now."

Ferro tossed the walkie-talkie to LaMastra as they raced to the door. "'bout goddamn time we caught a break," he growled.

* * *

Jim Polk switched off the walkie-talkie and motioned for Ginny to cover the phones while he went out back for a smoke. As soon as he shut the alley door he pulled out his cell and punched in a number that was answered on the first ring.

"How'd it go?" Vic asked.

"Like you said. Carby has his story straight. The jerkoffs from Philly are heading out to the bridge now. How is it at your end?"

"Neat and tidy. Boyd tramped footprints all over the bridge and they should be able to find his shell-casings, too."

"That's great. Is he really gone this time?"

"He's as gone as I need him to be," Vic said. "He'll be seen at least three times over the next week, and each time he'll be farther from here. By the time they lose his trail completely he'll have been spotted up in Trenton. After that, nobody's going to see him again until trick or treat night. At that point—well, it won't matter who sees him." Vic was laughing as he disconnected.

Polk leaned back against the door. "God save my soul . . ." he breathed, but his Catholic rituals were thirty years out of practice and as dry as his mouth.

### (2)

"Excuse me . . . are you Malcolm Crow?"

Crow's hand was just getting ready to fit his key into the door lock of his store when he heard the voice and it startled him enough to make him drop his keyring. Crow turned and saw a dumpy little man with a diffident smile standing by the open door of a battered old Honda Civic, a folded leather notebook in one hand.

"Who's asking?" Crow asked as he carefully squatted down to retrieve his keys, though he thought he already knew who this guy was. His face had been all over the TV.

"Willard Fowler Newton, *Black Marsh Sentinel*."

"Nice to meet you," Crow said. "Now get lost."

"What?"

"No interview, no questions, no answers, no nothing. Go before I set the hounds on you."

"I haven't even asked yet."

Crow unlocked the door but didn't pull it open. "No, but you were gonna, and the answer would have been no." He jangled the keys in his hand and instead of making eye contact with the stranger he looked up and down the street for some sign of Mike.

"It would just be a few questions?"

"Nope."

"It won't take long. Just a few—"

"No squared. No to the fifth power." Crow reached for the handle.

"I could beg."

Crow blinked. "What?"

"I'd be happy to beg," Newton said. "Or grovel. I grovel nicely." Newton got down on his knees and clasped his hands in front of him. "How's this?"

"Impressive," Crow said, laughing quietly. "Now get the hell up, Newbury."

"Newton."

"Whatever. Get up, you look like an idiot." As Newton rose, Crow cocked his head to one side and thought for a moment, then snapped his fingers. "I know you . . . you're the joker who broke the story about Ruger. You look taller on TV."

Newton's throat went red. "I stood on a box."

Crow cracked up, then immediately pressed a hand quickly to his side. "Ow!"

"Are you all right?"

"No I'm not all right, you friggin' cheesehead. I got shot the other day, or don't you read the papers?" His love handles burned under the bandages, but the pain passed quickly. Crow blew out cooked air through pursed lips and cocked an eye at Newton. "You're still here?"

"I'd like to ask you a few questions . . . and just so you know, it's not about the Karl Ruger thing." Crow opened his mouth but before he could say anything Newton plowed ahead. "I've been assigned to write a feature on the haunted history of Pine Deep. It's for the Sunday edition that'll be out the week before Halloween. I'm researching the whole thing, starting way back and going up to the Pine Deep Massacre of thirty years ago."

Crow narrowed his eyes suspiciously. "Yeah? Just what do you think you know about that?"

"Not enough," Newton said honestly. "Mostly just what everyone seems to know, which is more urban legend than historical fact. Apparently, thirty years ago some guy named Oren Morse killed a bunch of people and—"

"Well, there's where you're wrong, Mr. Newton," Crow snapped, jabbing the air with a stiffened finger. "The Bone Man never killed any of those people. He was not the Reaper, and anyone who says different is a frigging liar!" His face went scarlet as he took a threatening step forward.

"Whoa, Mr. Crow, I didn't mean to offend—"

Crow glared at him, but the moment passed and he backed up a step. "Look," he said with less venom, "I know a lot of people think the Bone Man was the Reaper, but I know for a fact that he wasn't."

"What makes you so sure?"

"Because I was *there* when it all happened."

"But that was thirty years ago. You couldn't have been more than—"

"I was nine, but I remember it all. Every charming detail like it was yesterday, so don't go telling me who killed who."

"Mr. Crow," Newton said, holding his hands up, palms out. "Look, I'm just trying to find out what happened, okay? I'm not the one who's saying Oren Morse did the killings. That's the local legend. To me it's just a starting point, but I wanted to interview you so I could get your take on it. The people I asked so far say you're an expert on local folklore. I can't count the number of articles I saw on the Net that quote you about one ghost story or another. So don't get me wrong—if I don't have the full story it's only because I haven't *gotten* the full story yet."

Crow chewed on that for a moment and saw, far up the hill, a tiny figure on a bike. Mike heading to the shop to start his first day. "Look, tell you what, Newt—can I call you Newt?"

"If it gets me an interview you can call me Kermit the Frog."

"Fine. If you want to interview me, Kermit, then meet me at the Guthrie farm tomorrow afternoon. You know where that is, I'm sure. Be there at four. No other reporters, no cameras, just you. Bring a tape recorder if you want, but I get to decide what gets said and what gets printed. That's the deal I always make with reporters, and I won't say word one without an agreement. Don't worry, you'll get better value for your time if you play it my way than if you don't."

"Okay then. But, tell me something, Mr. Crow . . ."

"Just call me Crow."

"Okay. Tell me, Crow, why is it you're so sure that Oren Morse didn't commit all those murders."

Crow's eyes drilled holes through Newt. "Because the Bone Man saved my life, that's why." He paused. "Come around four tomorrow and I'll tell you all about it."

He ambled away into his store as Newton stared after him. "Goddamned *right* I'll be there," he said to himself.

### (3)

Ferro and LaMastra arrived at the crime scene in less than ten minutes. The bridge was blocked off on both sides of the river by cruisers with their lights flashing. They had to wait for a criminalist, but that was routine because a blind man could read the scene, even with the dense cloud cover that cast the whole landscape in a false twilight gloom.

"Boyd must have been trying to cross the river," LaMastra said, working it out as they carefully picked their way up the slope to the bridge, careful not to smudge any of Boyd's muddy footprints. "You can see where he approached from upstream keeping down at the bank so as not to be seen from the road." He pointed. "Prints come up here and he must have been trying to make a dash for the Jersey side when that farmer—what's his name?"

Ferro looked at his notepad. "Carby. Gaither Carby."

"When Carby comes over and nearly hits him. Boyd takes some potshots at him and then hauls ass across the bridge."

Ferro nodded and they walked the length of the bridge, watching as step-by-step the muddy prints faded to nothingness as Boyd's shoes were scraped clean by the rough timbers. Even with the trail gone the evidence was clear enough.

"I got brass!" called Coralita Toombes, who was squatting by the steelwork on the left side of the bridge. She set up a few little markers that looked like tiny sandwich signs, each one sequentially numbered. "Three of 'em."

As other officers arrived Ferro had them fan out and search on both sides of the river, and a BOLO was issued for all adjoining New Jersey jurisdictions. Ferro chewed a stick of gum and looked slowly back and forth from one side of the bridge to the other, frowning. LaMastra saw the look and came over. "Problem?"

"No . . . not really. Just, doesn't this all seem like a bit of a rerun?"

"Yeah, but let's face it, the guy absolutely had to get out of town. With any luck the next time we hear from him he'll be getting picked up at either the Canadian or Mexican border."

Ferro nodded, but he didn't look convinced. Yet after three more hours of searching they found nothing to contradict the indications that Kenneth Boyd had left Pine Deep.

### (4)

Crow had time to get inside, switch on the lights, and slide a Coldplay CD into the box before the little bell above the door jangled and Mike Sweeney came in. Crow had been smiling while he waited for Mike to show up their first workday together, but his smile dimmed when he saw the vicious bruises that darkened the boy's face. By main force of will he dialed his smile back up to an acceptable brightness and said, "Welcome to the dungeon, Igor."

Mike grinned back, and though his smile looked happy there was just a trace of a wince there. Crow thought about he'd like to take a quick road trip over to Vic Wingate's place and beat him to within an inch of his miserable life. *No jury would touch me*, he thought.

"How are you feelin', Crow?" Mike asked, taking Crow's proffered hand.

"Like dookey. How 'bout you?"

"Good." It had been pretty clear to Crow that even walking across the floor had caused Mike some pain. Riding that bike must have been a bitch.

"Which falls under my personal definition of 'bullshit,'" he said.

"No, really."

"Bing! Bing! Bing! We're hitting a solid eight on the bullshit meter."

"Crow . . . don't, okay?" Mike eyes slid away from Crow's and his smile leaked away. In profile and with the bruises, Mike looked like an old man instead of a kid. Old and sick. Crow leaned on the counter that separated them and forced eye contact with the boy. "Look, kid, I'm not hideously stupid. If you're in pain, you're allowed to say, 'Gosh, Crow, I hurt like a complete sumbitch.' This is an acceptable response to inquiries about your current state of well-being."

It was clear that Mike couldn't decide whether to laugh or flee. His eyes had a shifty, uncertain look. Even so, he said, "Gosh, Crow, I hurt like a complete son of a bitch."

"'Sumbitch,' son. This is a hick town, the correct term is 'sumbitch.'"

"I hurt like a complete sumbitch."

"Good. Now watch your language, you juvenile delinquent."

This time Mike did laugh. A bit. "How's your . . . uh, I mean, Val?"

"My 'uh, I mean Val' is doing pretty good; and fiancée is the word you're fumbling for. She's home sleeping right now, and Sarah Wolfe is keeping her company. You know her? The mayor's wife?"

"I deliver their paper," Mike said, nodding. "Well . . . did. I guess I'm going to quit now that I'm working here."

"Val sends her best, by the way. She said that you're a sweetheart for helping me out here."

Mike flushed red.

"But enough of this banter, today we're going to explore the exciting world of retail sales. First step—inventory." He gave a stage wink. "Takes your breath away, doesn't it?"

"Yeah. I'm like . . . tingling."

For the next two hours Crow took Mike through the steps of checking the shelves against what was stored in the tiny stockroom and then filling out order sheets. Crow let Mike make the next ten calls while Crow tried not to backseat drive; by the fifth call it was easier to block the urge. They worked together to stock the shelves—a job Crow had left half finished when Terry Wolfe had talked him into going out to shut down the Haunted Hayride a few days ago, though it seemed like months to Crow. As they worked, Crow saw the boy try to disguise his many winces as he bent and stretched to fill the bins of costumes, baskets of rubber severed hands and other body parts, trays of goggly eyeballs, racks of Gummi centipedes and faux Cockroach Clusters, and tables filled with everything from smoking cauldrons to marked-down Freddy Krueger gloves (because, as Crow explained it Mike, *Nightmare on Elm Street* was soooo five minutes ago). At one point Mike was stretching his arm up to hang a half dozen Aslan the Lion costumes on a high peg when he gave a small sudden cry and dropped them. He pressed a hand to his ribs for a moment and stood there, wincing and making hissing-pipe noises.

"How's that rib treatin' you?" Crow asked with fake disaffection.

"Hurts," Mike said tightly, then added, "like a sumbitch."

"All of this happened when you fell off your bike, right? That your story?"

The pain gradually left his face, and Mike took in a

breath and slowly exhaled. He did not face Crow but instead appeared to be looking for an answer in the foamy packing materials of a box of plastic cockroaches. "Yeah. Bike."

"If I keep asking, am I always going to get the same story?"

"Probably," Mike said, fiddling with the label on the carton, peeling it with a thumbnail.

"Mike?" The boy did not look up.

"Mike," Crow said more firmly, "look at me for a sec." After a moment's hesitation, Mike did. His eyes rose to meet Crow's, fell away self-consciously, and then rose again. "Mike," Crow said softly, "I won't ask again. It's up to you to decide if you want to talk about it."

"I don't *want* to talk about it. I fell off my bike."

"Uh huh. Well, do me this favor, will you? Instead of feeding me a line of bullshit, just tell me to mind my own business. I'd rather you trusted me enough to just tell me to shut up than feel you have to lie to me." It took Mike quite a while to think that through, but eventually he nodded. Crow smiled. "Good," he said, then decided to step a little further out onto the limb. "Besides . . . you're not the only one who's ever been knocked around by an asshole of a parent. Not even the only one in this room."

This time Mike did look at him, and though his eyes glistened wetly and his face burned a furious red, he kept that eye contact for a long thirty seconds in which volumes were spoken. Crow broke the silence by saying, "Let's finish up this stuff and then I'm heading back to the farm. For the rest of the day you'll be on your own. Think you can handle it without pieces of rib puncturing your lung? 'Cause you're not on the health plan yet and the paperwork would be a bitch."

"I guess."

Crow started to turn away, stopped. "Listen, kiddo, whether you want to talk about it or not, I pretty much know the score. I know about Vic and how he treats you. Maybe not the specifics, but in general because it's probably pretty damn close to what I went through when I was a kid. My dad was a hitter and I was always getting my ass kicked and spent half my life making excuses for why I limped or why I had a black eye. Vic's not all that different from my dad—both of them are world-class assholes." He paused. "Am I right?" The kid shrugged. "So, starting today we're going to have a set of rules that we're both going to work with. Call 'em Crow's Rules for a Better Life, and Rule Number One is we don't let the assholes win."

Mike said nothing, but he was clearly listening.

"The assholes might score some hard points, but the rule is that we don't let the assholes win. You want to repeat that?"

Nothing.

"Sorry, didn't catch that."

Mike mumbled something.

"Kid, you're pissing me off. What is the number-one rule?"

"We don't let the assholes win, okay?" Mike snapped angrily, his fists balled at his sides.

Crow grinned at him. "Spoken like a champ. Which reminds me—aside from the low pay and nonexistent benefits package, there's another incentive to work here. I'm going to teach you to fight."

"You already showed me some stuff last spring. Me and Tyler Carby."

"That was just horsing-around stuff, I wasn't being serious and neither were you. You guys ever practice the stuff?"

"We goofed around in the schoolyard. Tyler wasn't interested, and it's no fun practicing alone." What he didn't tell Crow was that everyone in school thought Mike was still practicing martial arts, a lie he encouraged because it always gave him a reason to explain away the bruises. "What's it matter anyway? A few jujutsu moves ain't going to change things."

"That depends on the moves, and how you use them." He folded his arms. "When I offered you this job it was more than just because I needed an Igor to do the heavy lifting. I wasn't going to tell you this because I was going to be real subtle like and kind of sneak it on you from left field—but here's the bottom line, Mike. I respect you too much to blindside you, even if it's something that's for your own good."

"What are you talking about?"

Crow pulled a stool over and sat down so that Mike, still standing, was taller. He wanted to give the kid at least the subjective advantage of the dominant physical position. "I'm talking about getting *tough*."

"Tough enough to do what?"

"Tough enough so that you don't spend your whole life as somebody's punching bag."

"Look . . . I appreciate what you're trying to do, man, but I—"

Crow cut him off. "Don't, okay? I'm not trying to get all Mr. Miyagi on you, but I want to make a difference here."

"Who asked you to?" Mike shoved away the box he'd been playing with and it slid to the edge of a display case, tottered and fell, spilling white foam popcorn and six dozen plastic cockroaches all across the floor. "Ahhh . . . shit!" He made to bend down, but Crow touched his shoulder. Just a touch and then withdrew his hand.

"Leave it. Look, kid, I'm trying to say something here and you're not making it easy."

"I'm not *trying* to make it easy," Mike snapped.

"Will you listen?" Crow snapped back. "Okay? Just for a second?" Mike flinched back from that, but then held his ground. Crow took that as a good sign and plowed ahead, his voice softer. "Okay, I offered you this job partly because, as I said, I needed an Igor while I was healing from the ass-kicking *I* took, but the main reason is that I see a lot of myself in you. No, don't give me that look. You're smart, you're a comic book geek, you're mostly a loner, and you're getting your ass handed to you every time you come home. I know that territory too well to stand back and do nothing."

"This is not your business, Crow."

"No? Well tough, I'm *making* it my business. I gave you a job so I could keep an eye on you, and so I could teach you some back-alley moves, just like I learned when I was about your age. And, no, it's not going to be like a movie where we do a training montage while the soundtrack plays some motivational power chords. It'll take you months to get adequate and years to get really good, but if you don't start now you'll never get tough enough to finally stand on your own."

"Against Vic?" The kid's face was a study in disbelief.

"Eventually."

Mike snorted. "Eventually? That's just great. Does me a lot of good right now. You don't even know what you're talking about. You don't know Vic. You don't know what it's like living with him."

"I've known Vic a lot longer than you have, Mike, and though I don't know what goes on inside your house I know enough and can guess the rest. Am I saying this is going to be easy? No. Am I saying that you won't get your ass kicked some more? No—you will until the point where you're tough enough and then you won't. That could be months, it could be years, but it *will* happen, and all along the way, even while he's still the big dog around the house, you'll know that you're getting stronger, bigger, and tougher every day. *Every day*, Mike. You'll outlast the son of a bitch and *eventually* you really will be tough enough to kick his ass."

"Bullshit," Mike said under his breath, but there was a look in his eye and Crow knew that something in what he had just said had scored a point. Or touched on something Mike was already thinking.

Crow said, "I used to think that my dad would just beat me to death one day. I used to piss blood, I used to have double vision from getting stomped, and I had a thousand and one excuses I used on people to explain why my eye was black or why there were punch bruises on my back. At the time, when it was at its worst, I guess I never thought that it would end, that it would just go on and on and then I'd die. But I didn't. I outlasted my dad, and jujutsu helped. Understand, I wasn't one of those kids who took to martial arts like it was a religion or something. It was an *out*, you know? A way to outlast my dad. That's all it was, but, Mike . . . it was enough, you dig?"

Mike said nothing but there were gears turning in his head, Crow could see that much from the way his pale blue eyes were not fixed on him but locked on something unseeable in the middle distance. Very quietly he pressed his point. "I'm telling you that I'm going to teach you some self-defense, whether you like it or not." Crow put his hand on Mike's shoulder and this time left it there.

"You can't make me learn anything," Mike said, but still his eyes were staring at the screen displays in his head; even his voice was a little dreamy.

"You're right, I can't. You have a choice. Either you agree to let me teach you some moves, or you go back to delivering newspapers and we'll just call it a day."

That jolted the focus right back into Mike's eyes and he stared hard at Crow, shocked disbelief crackling there. "You'd really fire me . . . ?"

Crow held his face hard for a few seconds, and then he laughed. "Oh, hell no, you lunkhead. I'm talking outta my ass here, Mike. Truth is, I don't really know how to do what I'm trying to do. I want to do for you what someone once did for me, and I'm making a piss-poor job of it." He shook his head. "Help me out here, kid."

The moment stretched, and just about the time Crow was thinking *I lost him,* Mike said, "Let's just say I did stick around . . . how would it go? I mean, do I have to wear some kind of uniform and bow and stuff?"

Crow shook his head. "Nope. No uniforms, no bowing, none of that shit. Mind you, I'd really like to teach you ju-jutsu the old-fashioned way, be kind of an Obi-wan Kenobi sort of role model, but we don't have that kind of time. Ju-jutsu takes years, and we don't *have* years. So, instead I'm going to teach you how to fight. Quick and dirty, no pretty moves—just old-fashioned bust-up-the-bad-guys stuff. You with me?"

It took Mike a while and Crow gave him the time. Mike got up and went into the storeroom to fetch a dustpan and brush to clean up the mess, his blue eyes thoughtful, his freckled cheeks flushed with the aftereffects of their conversation. It wasn't until all of the popcorn had been swept up and tossed back into the box, and all of the plastic roaches tagged and set on a shelf that he stopped, turning around to face Crow. Mike was fourteen years old—fifteen on December 28—but when he looked at Crow his face was ten years older. Crow could see the man that Mike would become. In a weird aside inside his own head, Crow tried to superimpose Mike's face over that of Big John Sweeney, but it didn't fit. Not at all. The mouth and the nose were Lois's, yet those cold eyes, the red hair, the square jaw all made him look, strangely, like a young Terry Wolfe. But that was stupid. Crow shook the thought away so he could focus on what he was seeing *in* those eyes. Mike Sweeney, at that moment, had a look in his eyes as old as all of the pain in the world. Crow had been hoping to see a spark, a flicker of damn-the-torpedoes there, but all he saw was a young man with ancient eyes staring at him with no trace of hope, no fear of death. They were dead eyes.

"Sure," Mike said, "what have I got to lose?"

### (5)

Vic chain-lit another cigarette and tossed the old butt out the window. The inside of the pickup's cab was nearly opaque with smoke but Vic didn't care. His truck was parked on a side street near Corn Hill, engine off, all of the windows except one rolled up, and the driver's window was only cracked three inches. His cell phone lay on the dash where he'd placed it after he'd hung up on Lois, his brain churning over the conversation he'd just had. "Vic," she had said with placating brightness in her voice, "you'll be happy to know that Michael has gotten a new job. It pays better and he'll have regular hours so he'll always be home on time." She said that as if it was what Vic wanted to hear. "In a store. He's going to be a sales assistant in a store on Corn Hill."

"What store?"

"Why, the craft store owned by Malcolm Crow. You remember him? He's been in the papers . . ."

If she had said anything else of importance, Vic had not paid attention to it. He'd mumbled something about it being a good thing and had hung up, tossed the cell phone on the dash, and started smoking his way through a pack of Camels.

The fact that Mike was no longer delivering papers was a problem, that much at least was clear. Vic had pressured him into taking that job in the first place because it was the best way to steer him into the path of Tow-Truck Eddie. Now that was going to be harder—and it was hard enough because apparently Eddie couldn't find his own dick with both hands and a road map. He knew the Man needed Eddie to do the kid, but as far as Vic was concerned that whole scheme was a waste of effort. Mike should have been dead meat days ago, weeks ago, and instead he'd had one near miss and caught some bruises and since then all Eddie had managed was the occasional glimpse. It was already the sixth and Halloween was just twenty-five days away. Mike needed to be dead long before then, and certainly he needed to be dead *by* then.

*It doesn't matter.*

The voice echoed in his head, not his own thoughts but as familiar as his own.

"Your boy Eddie should have killed that little faggot by now, boss. What's the problem?"

*It isn't Eddie Oswald's failure. It's mine. I cannot touch the boy . . . sometimes I cannot see him. Much of the time I am blind to him.*

"Oh," Vic said, surprised, and for a long time he processed that. It was the first time the Man had ever admitted a weakness—ever—and Vic didn't like the feel of it. He said, "And that's why Eddie hasn't been able to find him? You can't—what—*steer* him in the right direction?" There was a profound silence and Vic knew that the Man would never respond to a question like that. He cleared his throat and said, "Boss, you should have told me you were having troubles seeing him. I'd have cooked up something, found some way to get the word out to Eddie. I know where the kid's going to be every day in the afternoons. You can steer Eddie there."

There was no answer, but Vic could sense a shift, as if the Man was somehow making himself more comfortable after sitting tensely for a while. It was an illusion, but the image worked for Vic. "Besides, Boss, we always have a fallback plan for the kid if it gets down to the wire and he's still alive. If he's still walking by Halloween morning then I'll take a baseball bat to his knees. He can't do us any harm with his legs broken in a dozen places." Vic grinned. "And boy would that be fun."

*Yessss,* the voice hissed in his head.

"It'll keep you safe, too, because as long as I don't kill him myself then what he is won't spread to the whole town. I know the risks, Boss. Stop fussing with Eddie Oswald—leave it me and I'll see that it gets done right."

*Not yet,* whispered the voice in his mind. *Eddie is still a useful tool.*

"Okay," Vic said, but a cloud of uncertainty was beginning to darken his heart.

# Chapter 16

## (1)

Tow-Truck Eddie was tired and he knew that weariness would make him inattentive. For three days now he had worked shifts as a part-time police officer, first guarding Malcolm Crow at the hospital and then patrolling the roads looking for the godless cop-killer Kenneth Boyd, and each afternoon he had gone home to pray and then take his wrecker out looking for the Beast. So far all he had gotten was one fleeting maddening glimpse of a boy on a bike turning a corner, and even then it may or not have been the Beast. Even the bike looked like a hundred other bikes in town. Patience, God had said . . . patience.

But how much patience? He prayed and prayed for guidance, and sometimes God spoke to him and sometimes there was nothing but an aching silence in his head. God always told him to be strong, to stay true, to have patience . . . and each day he rose from his prayers and went out with renewed hope that today—*today!*—he would find the Beast . . . and each time after driving for hours upon hours through roads clogged with tourists he came home with nothing more than his grief at failure.

"God! Sweet Lord of Hosts, grant me strength!" he cried aloud, kneeling before his altar, naked, humble, abased. He bent down and beat his forehead against the floor once, twice . . . seven times, harder with each blow until the floor-boards rattled and blood sang like angels' voices in his ears. He pounded his fists against his temples and his thighs and then against the floor and his tears fell like rain. "What must I *do*?" he begged.

Then the voice of God whispered a single word in his mind, the whisper of it as soothing as Gilead's balm. *Now*, it said. After such a long silence the voice caught him off guard and for a moment—just a moment—he knelt there and listened to it echo there in the vastness of his celestial thoughts. Then Tow-Truck Eddie leapt to his feet, his heart hammering with joy, and raced to get his clothes.

*Now! Now . . . now . . . now! He* was out there now!

Without bothering to pull on underwear Eddie dragged on a pair of workpants, pulled a sweatshirt over his head, and ran down the stairs, taking them three at a time and then leaping the last five. His shoes were by the door and he jumped into them without socks, without tying the laces, and he grabbed for the doorknob with one hand and his keys with the other. He slammed the door behind him hard enough to knock a cross from its nail on the wall and mere seconds after its plaster arms broke off on the floor the engine of the wrecker howled to life.

*Now . . . now . . . now . . . now . . .*

(2)

LaMastra held the door for him and gave him a nod as he entered the conference room. Detective Sergeant Ferro was seated in what had become his regular seat at the head of the table. Terry glanced at him and saw on the detective's face a look of quirky amusement.

"What's this I hear about Boyd taking a shot at Gaither Carby?" Terry asked sharply, his face cast into a harsh scowl.

Gesturing to a chair, Ferro said, "Make yourself comfortable, Mr. Mayor, I have a very strange story to tell you."

Terry looked down at him with an angry, weary face.

"Detective, I'm not really in the mood for any kind of story. Just tell me what's going on and cut the crap, okay?"

"Fair enough," Ferro said stiffly, but again he indicated the chair. With poor grace Terry sat down. LaMastra came over and parked one muscular haunch on the corner of a smaller nearby table; he sat there, casually swinging his leg.

"You know," said Terry, looking at his watch, "I'm supposed to be outside helping my town get ready for its busy season. I'm supposed to be shaking hands and talking to the press and generating business. I'm supposed to be meeting with horologists and other specialists to work on the blight program. I'm supposed to be trying to keep half of the farms in this borough from going under. Ever since your three bad boys came here—gee, was that only Thursday night? Feels like a frigging month ago!—ever since then, my quiet, artsy-fartsy little town has gone to hell in a handbasket."

"Sir, let me—"

"And now the big, bad Cape May Killer—who was brought to ground by a man *I* reinstated as a police officer and not by your storm troopers—has gone missing from the morgue, and his psycho cohort is shooting at my constituents. Is this some plot to make my life a personal hell? Doesn't the world of law enforcement *like* small tourist towns? Tell me, Sergeant Ferro, just what is it that we did to deserve all this crap?"

Ferro said nothing, allowing a little time for the words to cease their emotional echoes. Before he could speak, LaMastra said, "There now, do you feel better?"

Terry wheeled on him. "You know, I'm beginning to get a little weary of your smart-ass remarks."

Holding up his hands, LaMastra said, "Whoa! Sorry, Mr. Mayor, I was just trying to lighten the mood."

Terry rubbed his palms over his face as he sank back into his chair, and his hands somewhat muffled his voice. "About the only thing that could even begin to lighten my mood, Detective, would be the news this insanity is over."

"Well, sir," said Ferro after clearing his throat. "It appears that you are going to get your wish."

It took Terry three or four seconds to absorb that and for a moment he looked almost comical as he peered at them from between his opened palms. "What?"

Nodding, Ferro said, "We are going to be pulling out very soon, possibly as early as tomorrow."

"But . . . but . . ."

"Let me explain, sir," said Ferro. "While it's true that Boyd took a couple of shots at Mr. Carby, we have been able to gather reliable evidence to suggest that Boyd has since left town. Since this afternoon he has been spotted by three different eyewitness—in Black Marsh."

If he was expecting the mayor to jump for joy, Ferro was disappointed. Terry sucked his teeth for a moment as he sat with his head cocked. "Big deal. You told me the other day, too. Same thing, eyewitnesses and all. Didn't amount to much, though, did it? Boyd came *back* to Pine Deep, slaughtered two police officers, and stole a body from the morgue. Maybe you haven't checked a map lately, Detective Ferro, but Black Marsh is only right across a short bridge. People go back and forth across it every goddamn day!"

Ferro flinched as Terry hammered home the last few words. He gave himself a moment, and then said, "Yes, sir, that's very true. However, the three reports were all by reliable witnesses, so we know that—for better or worse—he *is* there. Since those reports we've had roadblocks at every bridge. We've already sent the bulk of the task force over to New Jersey and they are following several promising leads. Boyd was last seen climbing into the back of a pickup truck that was pulling out of a diner on A-32 near Wilson Mills Road south of Lambertville. We ran the plates and the truck was eventually located in a Pep Boys parking lot in Trenton. Driver said that he had no idea anyone had climbed into the back of his truck—he was playing his radio loud and didn't hear anything. He checks out, and we believe him. Boyd left dirty fingerprints all over the truck bed. Unfortunately, Boyd was no longer in the truck when it was located, so we have no way of knowing how far he traveled before climbing out again, but it's clear he's heading away from here."

"Best guess," LaMastra said, "is that Boyd's trying to make it to New York. We know from his jacket that he's well connected there."

"Still, no matter what his destination," said Ferro, "the bottom line is that there are no bad guys in your town anymore. Two are dead, one is elsewhere, and therefore, Mr. Mayor, this ball game is about over. Chief Bernhardt will be following up on the investigation of who might have let Boyd into the hospital, but that's far less important at this point."

Terry stared at them both for a long time, hardly breathing, processing what he had just heard, then he exhaled so long and thoroughly that he seemed to deflate. He leaned his head back and stared upward at the ceiling for nearly thirty seconds. Ferro and LaMastra exchanged a look; LaMastra shrugged.

"What about Ruger's body?" Terry asked.

"I doubt he took it with him, so we can only assume he wanted to bury it for some reason known only to himself. One theory is that Ruger may have hidden the money and cocaine and Boyd thought he could find some record of it on Ruger's person, a note or a lockbox key. Another theory is that he may have thought Ruger might have had some useful papers on him."

"Or, Boyd could just be a total nutcase," LaMastra said.

Ferro nodded. "From his recent actions it seems clear that Boyd is mentally unstable, so I don't really want to speculate on why he would want to do this, but there was no evidence that he took the body with him when he left Pine Deep. He just left."

"Well," Terry said, "then that means you guys really are done here. What else remains to be done?"

LaMastra shrugged. "We have to tidy up all the jurisdictional paperwork, check to make sure we have all the physical evidence we need, call in the troops, that sort of thing."

"What about the missing money and cocaine?"

Ferro spread his hands. "Chief Bernhardt will conduct a search and contact us if he finds anything. If he needs backup he can contact the state police. Ruger and Boyd must had hidden the stuff somewhere near the Guthrie farm, or maybe in the state forest, so it'll probably turn up sooner or later. Since your busy season is here, the chief's going to keep the reactivated officers on for now, so there will still be extra eyes open until the money and drugs are found, and until the media circus hauls down its tents and leaves town, which I assume will be in waves. The Cape May story is still newsworthy so some reporters will linger until they've interviewed everyone even remotely associated with the incidents here. Eventually they'll all be gone to cover other stuff and you'll have your town all to yourself. Despite everything, Mr. Mayor, all of this hullabaloo may actually help bring in tourist dollars, now that the real danger is over."

The mayor sat there and steepled his fingers. A number of expressions came and went across his haggard face, but he said nothing for such a long time that LaMastra started fidgeting. Abruptly Terry slapped his thighs with both hands, stood up quickly, and said, "Gentlemen, I can't say it has been a pleasure, but I do thank you for all you've done. Please feel free to visit again anytime you want to buy some pumpkins, watch a Halloween parade, or take a trip on the Haunted Hayride. Just don't bring any more serial killers to my town, okay?"

Rising, Ferro gave him a wan smile. "We'll keep that in mind, Mr. Mayor."

They shook hands, but there was no warmth in it.

### (3)

Tow-Truck Eddie's wrecker glided along in the line of cars waiting to make the turn at the stop sign. He was three cars away from rolling right abreast of the big display window of the Crow's Nest, and within his mind the voice of God did not speak in words but instead *pulsed* with an almost sexual rhythm, though Eddie did not relate the sensation to anything sexual. Instead he felt that incessant pounding in his brain and took it for the heartbeat of his own godly inner self, his Christ self, as it rose in a different kind of ec-stasy—as it prepared for the slaughter of the Beast. The Christ about to confront and conquer the Antichrist.

Another car turned and he moved forward. He could see the window clearly enough, filled with tombstones and sev-ered limbs, draped with cobwebs and hung with bats and spiders. Eddie's lip curled in disgust at the pagan display. Such things will fall and the sinners be brought to under-standing through blood and the Sword of the Lamb. Soon enough. A pickup truck made the turn and Eddie was now almost abreast of the store. He could see two figures moving around but there was sun glare on the glass and he couldn't make out the features. Then the last car in line made the turn and Eddie moved forward again and turned full in his seat to stare. The angle was better and there was no glare so he could see that the figure on the left was definitely Malcolm Crow. He flicked his eyes to the other, certain that it had to the Beast in his disguise as a human boy. He squinted, pick-ing out details. He could see that the figure wore jeans and a hooded sweatshirt. That it was not a large figure—about Crow's size, who was short—but the face was indistinct. He shielded his eyes, leaned forward, even cupped his hands around his eyes to shield them from any sun glare. The clothes were clear enough but the face remained blurred, like a photograph when someone has turned their head at just the wrong moment. Eddie stared and stared and then be-hind him a whole row of cars began nailing their horns. Eddie jumped, frustrated and angry, and took his foot off the gas, but even as the truck moved forward and again the angle of light on the glass changed to an even clearer view, the face of the second figure in the store remained blurred.

Doubt sewed threads through his heart and he turned and drove away. In his head the urgent guttural chant had stopped completely and when he spoke to God, there was no answer. Frowning, Tow-Truck Eddie made the turn and headed out of town.

\* \* \*

When the wrecker was gone, the Bone Man stepped from in front of the window and nearly collapsed, his hands falling away from the strings of his guitar. Perhaps if he had more substance, gravity would have grabbed him and dragged him down against the ground outside the Crow's Nest. Even so, a wave of sick exhaustion flooded through him. He tried to throw up, but he was empty, just a shell, and he didn't even have the benefit of that release. He was thoroughly drained. Since last night, when he had played his guitar in the night to try and soothe the terrible dreams that were spreading like a plague throughout the town, he had been weak. That alone had cost him, and all day he had tried to husband what little strength was left to him, to conserve what few powers he possessed. This last act of standing between the boy and the eye of the killer in the truck made him feel as if there was nothing left. He felt less substantial than a fleeting hope.

Yet there was still a faintness of a smile on his gray lips. The wrecker had moved on. The driver had *not* seen the boy. Somehow the act of playing his songs while standing in the way—in harm's way for sure—had turned the killer's eye. Maybe turned Griswold's eye as well. *God,* he thought, *please let it be so. Please throw me at least that much of a bone.*

Weary and sick as he was, his smile blossomed and he looked down at the lovely curves of his guitar and knew something he hadn't known before. *Is this why I'm here?* He wondered. *Is this why the grave vomited me back into this damn town? To save this boy?*

The Bone Man raised his guitar to his lips and kissed it, his eyelids fluttering closed.

*Let it be so,* he prayed. *God . . . have at least that much mercy.*

### (4)

LaMastra stayed in the car while Ferro went in to the hospital to say good-bye to Saul Weinstock.

"Real sorry to see you go, Frank," Weinstock said, and meant it.

The doctor was freshly dressed and neatly shaved, but Ferro thought he looked careworn. It was understandable. He said, "You're about the only one who is. From your esteemed mayor's reaction I was waiting for villagers with torches to drive us out of town."

Weinstock's left eye twitched, but he kept smiling. "Terry's under a lot of pressure. We all are. The blight and all, and the stuff out at the Guthrie's farm. He used to date Val, you know. Fifteen years ago or so. He liked Henry, and he's taking his death pretty hard. I guess we're all taking this . . . hard." Weinstock cleared his throat. "I personally would like to see you stay, Frank."

"Vince is glad to be leaving," Ferro said. "This place has gotten to him."

"And it hasn't gotten to you?"

"Well, it is a fairly creepy town, you have to admit. Says so on all the billboards."

"Yeah," Weinstock said, drawing out the word. For a minute it looked like he was going to add something, then just shook his head.

"Something up, Saul?"

The doctor took a second with that. He said, "Frank . . . if anything else weird turns up . . . ? I mean, anything associated with the case . . . can I call you?"

"Well—Chief Bernhardt is handling—"

"No, Frank . . . can I call *you*?" He paused. "If it's something I don't think Gus can handle."

Ferro studied him, then shrugged. "Sure. Why not? If it's associated with the case, you can always give me a call."

"What if it's somewhat tangential to the case?"

"You've lost me."

Weinstock started to say something, then smiled and shook his head. "I'm tired and I'm babbling. Have a good trip back, Frank. Come out sometime and we can play some golf. You play golf?"

"Badly."

"Good, 'cause I like to win." They stood and shook hands and Weinstock held on for just a second too long and squeezed just a bit too hard, then he let go and sank back down into his chair. Ferro gave him a last puzzled smile, a nod, and then left.

In the empty elevator he said to himself, "Vince was right. This town is screwy."

Twenty minutes later the phone on Weinstock's desk buzzed and he pushed the button. "The courier's here, doctor," said his secretary.

"Send him right in."

Weinstock was fitting the hard plastic cover over the cooler as his door opened and a young man entered, eyebrows raised expectantly. He wore a uniform and cap with the DHL logo on it. "Pickup?" the man asked.

"Right here." Weinstock sealed the dry-ice-packed cooler with orange tape. A second identical cooler sat on one corner of his desk. "Labels are ready. The labs are expecting these."

If the driver found anything unusual in a hospital's administrator personally sending samples to separate laboratories in Manhattan and Philadelphia, he didn't let it show. It probably never occurred to him, just another pickup. DHL handled tens of thousands of medical courier jobs every day. Weinstock signed on the electronic clipboard and the courier took one cooler in each hand, wished the doctor a "Nice day," and left.

When he was gone, Weinstock sank down in his seat and leaned back in his chair, closed his eyes, and tried to still the hammering of his heart. That took awhile. When he finally opened his eyes, the quality of sunlight in the room had changed and there were slanting shadows angled across his office, and he realized that he must have fallen asleep. Darting a look at the clock he was shocked to see that over two hours had passed. The sun was already behind the far mountains and night was coming on fast. "Shit!" he hissed as he jumped up and headed for the door. He wanted to be home before dark.

Once he was in his car, Weinstock punched Crow's number into his cell and listened to it ring five times before a voice answered: "Crow's Nest."

"Who's this?" Weinstock barked.

"Mike Sweeney, how may I help you?"

"Is Crow there?"

"He's with a customer, sir, may I—"

Weinstock punched the disconnect button. "Damn," he said as he drove through the gathering gloom.

# Chapter 17

## (1)

"They want to keep us one more day," Mark said, his frustration and tension clear all the way down the phone lines. "Seems they wanted to have another counseling session with Weeping Beauty."

"Mark! Do you have to be like that?"

Silence for a few heartbeats. "It's not like I said it in front of her."

"You shouldn't have said it all." She expected him to say something else, peevish or defensive, but there was nothing. She said, "What time tomorrow should we pick you up?"

"You don't need to bother," he snapped. "Buck Franklin from the Rotary is coming by."

"I'd like to be there anyway," Val said, "for Connie."

"Don't bother," Mark said, and hung up.

She set down the phone and looked at it thoughtfully for a while, lips pursed, twin vertical frown lines between her brows. Crow would have had something witty and biting and funny to say, even to the silent phone, but he wasn't here and the best Val could manage was, "ass," which was appropriate enough.

Around her the house was huge and silent, filled with brown shadows. She knew that every door was locked and every window shut and pinned. Crow had seen to that before he had left for town to put in some hours at the store. He wouldn't be back until the middle of the afternoon, and then at four a reporter was coming over to interview Crow about the events of thirty years ago. *That should be loads of fun*, she thought.

She went downstairs to her father's room, hesitated in the doorway for a while, steeled herself, and went into the room, past the bed that was now empty of both her mother and father, to the big oak wardrobe. The doors swung open quietly. She knelt down and dug around until she found a old shoebox tied with a piece of hairy twine. Val brought this over to the desk by the window and sat down. Though her left arm still ached it was better each day. She untied the twine, set the lid aside, and removed a bundle wrapped in an oil-stained cloth. Val unwrapped it and stared at the contents for a long while, frowning.

There was a small cleaning kit in the box, which she opened to the smell of gun oil. Val slowly and methodically stripped and cleaned the .45 Colt Commander. When she was finished, she loaded the magazine and slapped it into place. These motions hurt her shoulder, but not that much, and even if the pain had been intense Val would not have cared. When she closed her eyes she saw the dead face of Karl Ruger—but with his eyes open and his wet lips curled into a leering grin. Now, with the pistol, when she saw that face in her mind it would be at the far end of a steel gun sight. And if Boyd came calling, well . . . that would be too bad for him.

### (2)

Three times yesterday and twice today Tow-Truck Eddie drove past the Crow's Nest and slowed to peer in the window. After that first try, when all he could see was a blurred face, he'd circled back an hour later, but this time all he saw was Crow moving around the store. No one else. He tried it late in the day, near closing, and again all he saw was Crow. No sign of the Beast. Doubt chewed at him. This morning he parked his wrecker in a side street and walked past the store as surreptitiously as he could, pausing to peer inside. Again, just Crow, though this time he was with customers, all of who were adults. No sign of a teenage boy anywhere.

Could he have changed his appearance? This thought wormed its way into his thoughts and wouldn't go away, even though the great booming voice of his Father told him that the Beast in boy skin was there. Right there. Right now.

Eddie could not see him at all. Not even the blurred outline of him. Nothing.

He would keep coming back, though, he promised his Father that. Nothing on earth would stop him. Yet deep inside him, far down in the soil of his heart, the first real seeds of doubt were beginning to take root.

The Bone Man felt desperately weak, but even though he kept having to dip into the shallow well of his strength to hide the boy from those penetrating blue eyes he did not feel any weaker than he had earlier. Perhaps he had bottomed out somehow, had dropped as far as he could drop. Well, he thought, if that was so then it was so, and it was something he could—well live with was not quite right, and for once he smiled ruefully at the perversity of his condition—even so it was something he could endure.

The crucial thing for him was that this was something he was actually able to accomplish, and for once he truly felt that he understood why he had been brought back. If he could save the boy, at least until Halloween, then his life and death and whatever the hell this was would all be important. It would matter . . . and more important to him, it would make sense. He stood there invisible in the sunlight and watched the wrecker drive away, and despite the agonizing weariness the Bone Man felt *good*.

### (3)

"I'm going to throw some punches at you," Crow said, raising his hands and settling his body into a boxing posture—knees flexed, chin tucked into his right shoulder, hands high, fists tight. "What I want you to do is block anything you see." Mike's eyes were a little glassy, and Crow thought he saw the beginnings of tears forming. The kid's bruises looked a lot better today, but his eyes were still spooked. "You ready?" Crow asked, though it was clear the only thing Mike was ready for was a mad dash down the alley.

"Um . . . yeah. Sure."

Crow nodded and threw a light jab with his good arm, aiming four or five inches to the right of the kid's face and stopping three inches short. Throwing the punch hurt, but Crow kept it off his face. Mike made a clumsy swipe at it that missed and jerked back so fast it looked like somebody had pulled him with a rope. Crow took a shuffle step in and looped a big, wide roundhouse right that had no chance at all of making contact. Mike squeezed his eyes shut and wrapped his arms around his eyes.

"Okay," Crow said, lowering his hands, "that lets me know you're not ready for Golden Gloves." Throwing the punch without power only tugged at his stitches. It didn't really hurt, and he was glad about that. He'd had a good night's sleep last night, curled up in Val's arms, the both of them sleeping long and without dreams. Over breakfast Val had remarked on it.

"I feel almost human today." Her black hair was glossy and damp from the shower and there was the first trace of a sparkle in her eyes, something he hadn't seen in days. It had lifted Crow's heart and made him feel better, too.

Now, scuffling around the backyard with Mike, Crow felt ever closer to his old self—though he still didn't throw any punches with the arm Ruger had squeezed.

Mike, on the other hand, looked sheepish and ashamed, blossoms of red flaring in his cheeks as he continued to back away from Crow's approach. Finally, raising his hands palms outward, Crow said, "What was Crow's Rule Number One?"

The kid shrugged. He was still covered in bruises on every visible inch of his skin. By comparison he made Crow look uninjured and whole.

"Sorry, kid, that was my I-didn't-hear-shit ear."

"Never let the assholes win," Mike snapped irritably.

"Damn right." They were in the small yard behind Crow's shop and apartment. The yard was walled in by other stores except in the back and had a fine view of the hills, the distant farms, and the long snaking line of A-32. "Come on now, let's work on some moves."

Mike flapped a hand. "It's just that I hate that I have to learn this stuff."

"Would you rather just be Vic's punching bag forever?"

Mike gave him a nasty look. "Just get on with it."

"Okay, lesson one is going to be about how to evade and parry. The best block is to not be there. You follow me?"

"Yeah," Mike said. "Yeah, I do."

### (4)

Crow's phone rang just after they were back in the store and he snatched it off the wall. "Crow's Nest."

"Crow? It's Saul—are you alone?"

"I can talk. Mike's with a customer. What's up?"

"Crow, look, I don't want to sound paranoid, but ever since the other night there have been some pretty strange things happening here in town."

"You mean besides insane serial killers and body-snatchers?"

"I'm not joking around, Crow. I did the autopsies on—"

The bells above the door jangled and five people came in, laughing and chattering. Tourists. "More customers. Let me take care of them and call you right back."

"No, look . . . I'll talk to you tomorrow at the funeral. This will be better in person."

"Um, okay. See you then."

### (5)

Clouds had come up suddenly from the southwest and in the course of half an hour the sky went from a hard clear blue to a nearly featureless gray that was beginning to swell to a threatening purple. Val Guthrie was deep in the corn-fields on the east side of her property, her father's big .45 tucked into the waistband of her jeans, snug against the small of her back, hidden by a red-checked thermal jacket. She was walking the fields with Diego, a short, barrel-chested East Texan who had worked for her father for almost twenty years, doing spot tests of the soil pH. It was still a clean 6.54, far above the range of any of the surrounding farms, whereas most of the other farms had shown pH drops well below 5.0 and even lower. Val's soil remained solidly in the 6.0 to 7.0 range, even in the places where all that separated her fields from her neighbors was a wood-railed fence. Her closest neighbor, Charlie Kendall, had shown her the analysis of his samples and the levels of soil phosphorus, nitrogen, potas-sium, sulfur, magnesium, and calcium had all dropped, even when a sample was taken five inches from a healthy sample taken along Val's property line. "I don't get it," Val said. "It doesn't make any kind of sense. It's too weird to be an acci-dent of nature, and if there is something in our soil that's making a difference, then it has to be something that was de-liberately put here."

"Like reverse ecoterrorism," Diego said, trying for a joke.

"If it was something different in our soil it would *show*," she said, shaking her head in frustration, "but it doesn't."

"Nope," Diego agreed. After twenty years he still had that East Texas drawl. "I was talking to Spence the other day," he said, referring to Todd Spencer, his counterpart on the Kendall farm, "and he was saying that there was not one single stalk that didn't show signs of root worm. Not one. They're going to have to burn the whole crop, and this is weird because as you know they're growing that Mon 863, that insect-resistant corn from Canada. Shouldn't be even a small percentage of root worm over there."

"And we have no traces at all of them." Val shivered in the freshening breeze. "That's really weird, Dee."

"No joke," Diego agreed. There was a rustle behind them and they turned to see the stalks snapping back over the pas-sage of something that moved quickly through the rows.

"Deer," he said, shrugging it away. He went back to collecting soil samples, but Val continued to stare at the spot where they'd heard the rustle, frowning. Then she took a deep breath, held it for a moment, and let it out through he nose as if to cleanse herself of her jumpiness. Her cell phone rang, startling her.

"Hey, baby," Crow said and the day seemed to brighten for her.

"Hey yourself. I was going to call you soon. I need an insanity break."

"You mean a sanity—"

"You heard me."

"Nice to be appreciated for one's talents. Anyway, honeychile, I just called to check in. Mike and I finished his first lesson in Kickass 101."

"How'd he do?"

"Metza-metz. Started off by fighting me tooth and nail about even discussing it, let alone giving it a try, but he came around. Kid is seriously spooked, though. Vic Wingate has really done a number on him."

"Uh-oh, I'm hearing that Captain Avenger tone in your voice," she warned.

"Me? I wouldn't lay a finger on him," Crow said, then in a stage whisper added, "the slimy shit-eating bastard."

"Tch-tch," Val said, but in her heart she agreed with Crow. "Well, maybe one of these days karma will drop a transmission on him at the shop."

"From your lips to Kali's ears. On the upside, we did have a good session after he got into gear. Kid has some good reflexes. Really good, actually."

"Honey . . . do you think you can teach him enough to do any good?"

Crow made a noncommittal noise. "Time will tell," he said, and then changed tack. "So, how are you doing?"

"Okay, I guess. I'm out in the fields with Dee. Taking samples and such." She sighed. "And this afternoon I'll be setting up for the funeral tomorrow. God, this is so weird.

I'm doing ordinary farm stuff one minute and the next I'm planning how to memorialize my dad."

"I'm meeting that reporter out there at four. You want me to be there earlier?"

"No. I've got Diego and the guys." She told him about the plans, finding a strange sort of calm in the mundane details.

"Well, if you need me there today, sweetie, I'm there. You sound pretty wired."

"Thanks, but it's just that I . . . I keep seeing him everywhere."

"I understand, baby. Your dad's spirit is all over that—"

"No," she interrupted. "Not daddy . . . I keep seeing *him* everywhere."

"Oh," he said after a moment.

"No matter what I'm doing I always get the feeling he's right there, watching me from around a corner or peeking through the blinds, or following me through the corn. I can't seem to shake it. I mean . . . just now there was a deer walking through the corn and my first thought was *him*."

"Val . . . this is all still pretty raw. It's just been a week, it's going to take some time."

She made an ambiguous noise. Crow said, sounding startled, "Heck with the store. Let me tidy up a few things around here and then I'll be over. Want me to pick up some Chinese?"

"That sounds good."

"See you soon, my love."

"Crow . . . ?"

"Yeah, baby."

"I really do love you with all my heart."

"Me too, Val. See you soon."

She punched the OFF button and snugged the phone back down into her jeans, waved good-bye to Diego, and strolled back toward the house. As if in reflection of her mood, the sky was a weary gray with a sadness of clouds drooping low over the distant trees and a sigh of a cold breeze. A few birds flew overhead but they were hungry and lonely birds, flying fast to find other places where warmth and hope still prospered. Far above the clouds an invisible plane flew from some distant somewhere to another place, whisking by over the grayness of Pine Deep, the intermittent drone of its engine sounding like the moan of some sleeping person dreaming of pain.

As she walked, she came to the spot where her father had died and stopped. There was no sign of it now except for tattered streamers of yellow police tape tied to the fence posts. She climbed onto the fence and sat there in the cold, her short hair snapping in the wind, her dark eyes filling with tears, her mouth tight with cold anger, trying to grasp the impossibility of it all. Her father had *died* there. Right there, on that tiny stretch of earth that looked no different than any other soil anywhere in the world, and yet it was there, right there, that he had bled to death alone in the rainy darkness on that terrible night last week. The thought that his blood was still trapped within the soil made her feel at once totally repulsed and yet at the same time oddly comforted. It was a stupid thought, she told herself, but somehow she felt as though it meant that something of her father's spirit remained here, too, as if some trick of geomancy had allowed him to linger. With a certainty as if of ancient ritual Val knew that day after day, probably for the rest of her life, she would come out here and feel for her father's spirit in the air and in the soil. The thought that such a spirit, such a person who had been filled with so much vitality, so much love and gentle strength could simply *end* was just too horrible, and it made her feel terribly mortal. If Henry Guthrie could be snuffed out with no more than the flex of a finger on a trigger, then her own life, Crow's life, and the life of their baby were all equally transient.

She thought also of another Guthrie who had died there, just a few feet from where Daddy had been killed. Young Roger Guthrie, on leave from the Air Force, Val's handsome cousin who looked more like Henry than Mark did. Rog had been home just a week, but had picked a bad time for it. That was the year of the Black Harvest, three decades ago. A lot of folks had died that year, some from diseases born of the blight—but Rog had not caught any disease. He had been one of the victims of the Pine Deep Reaper. Right here, right at this spot. This place was awash in Guthrie blood, and the thought of it fueled Val's rage.

Val wiped her eyes, feeling the wind back and freshen. There was a hint of moisture in the air, and the tang of ozone; it smelled like snow but was too early in the year for that. A storm smell, she judged. *Another storm. God.* The last storm had come on like this, growing in the afternoon, building all through the evening and then exploding in the deep of night with a force that had shattered her life. If there could be a worse storm—or a storm whose power could do more damage—than the one that had blown Karl Ruger into Pine Deep, Val hoped that she would never live to see it. The very thought of it made her stomach take a sickening lurch.

Or was that morning sickness? She tugged her right hand out of her pocket and placed her palm and spread fingers over her stomach. She was forty and had never been pregnant before. When Ruger had broken into the house he'd punched her in the stomach and Val had been terrified that her baby—her *baby*, she was not used to even thinking that word—had been harmed. But Weinstock had examined her. She hadn't miscarried. Her baby was one thing about her life that Ruger hadn't been able to lay his hard hands upon.

Val stopped and turned, looking up at the clouds. They were not yet so dense as to be featureless and while she stared at them, at the shapes and shadows formed by the slowly changing billows, she imagined that she saw a face up there. *His* face. Just for a moment—a pale face with flashing dark eyes and heavy features. It was there for just a moment, for a heartbeat, and then it was gone, blown by cold winds into some other disguise and then to nothing as the skies darkened. Shivering with the cold, Val turned and headed home while above and around her the storm drew back its fist.

# Chapter 18

## (1)

When Newton parked in the turnaround, Crow was standing on the top step of the porch, a bottle of Yoo-Hoo in one hand, a Phillies ball cap pushed back on his head and a smile on his face. As Newton got out and approached, he saw that Val Guthrie was seated on a porch swing. He recognized her from the stock photos his paper had run after the shooting. Unlike Crow, she was not smiling, and her eyes were even colder and less welcoming than the cop's had been.

"Welcome aboard," Crow said and took one step down as he extended his hand. "This is my fiancée, Val Guthrie."

He nodded to Val. "Good afternoon, Ms. Guthrie. Please accept my condolences. And . . . thanks for taking some time out to chat with me. I can't even imagine how tough things must be for you both right now." He offered his hand to her and her grip was stronger than his by a long way.

"Glad to have you, Mr. Newton," Val said. "I read your articles. I appreciate the things you said about my father." Her eyes were a hard, dark blue and though there was obvious sadness in them, they were not weak eyes in any way. Her gaze was level, direct, and unwavering. "I've read other pieces about what happened, and some writers have used some pretty unfair descriptions, calling Dad 'an old man' and insinuating that he was too old to outrun the bullet that killed him. What do you think about that?"

Newton felt his neck get hot. He was never good around women at the best of times, and Val Guthrie made him immeasurably uncomfortable. A dozen different replies flitted through his head, but he liked the strength he saw in her eyes, and all thoughts of dissembling—or of defending his fellow journalists—melted away. "Quite frankly, Ms. Guthrie, even if your father had been a twenty-year-old Olympic track star he couldn't have outrun a bullet. No one can. That's why cowards like Karl Ruger use guns." Out of the corner of his eye he saw Crow give him a tiny nod of approval. Newton plowed on. "Since the other day I've been asking around about your father and the picture I got was that, despite his age, he was one tough son of a bitch, if you don't mind me being frank. So, if I interpret the facts right, I believe he died to save your life, which qualifies him in my book as a hero. I wish I'd had the chance to know him."

Val looked up at him for a moment. Her eyes didn't soften, but she did give him a small smile. "Thank you, Mr. Newton."

"Please, just call me Newton . . . or Newt. Everyone does."

"Val," she said, nodding. She was a very pretty woman, a few years older than Newton, and with the kind of intensity that had always frightened him. She wore a thin silver chain around her neck on which was a cross—surprisingly delicate for so strong a woman—that hung just above the vee of her blouse. He noticed that her only concession to apparent vulnerability was that she absently touched the cross from time to time, as if drawing comfort from it.

To Crow, she said, "I like this one. He can stay."

"You want something to drink, Newt?" Crow asked. "Ice tea? Something?"

"If you have another one of those," he said gesturing with his chin toward Crow's Yoo-Hoo, "then I'll have one."

"Good man." Crow went into the house and came back out with two cold bottles for them, and a cup of coffee for Val. To Newton he said, "Pull up a pew." They sat down, shook their bottles, opened them, and exchanged a nod as they took their first sips. "Where do we start?" Crow asked, wiping his mouth with the back of his hand.

"Well," Newton said, removing a small tape recorder from his briefcase, "first I want to know if it's okay if I tape this."

Crow nodded. "Sure, but I do have a couple of conditions before we start. I'm willing to tell you the whole story of the Pine Deep Massacre, and everything I know about the Bone Man, but only on two conditions."

Newton hedged. "What conditions?"

"First," said Crow, "you don't print any part of it I tell you not to print."

"I don't know if I can agree to that."

Crow spread his hands. "Have a nice trip back. Watch out for potholes."

"No! No, I mean, how can I—"

"Newt, listen to me, I'm going to give you a hell of a story. I'm not joking here, and it's as intense a story as you're ever likely to write. If I want something kept out of it, then you have to trust that I have a good reason, but you also have to trust that what I will let you write about will be well worth any small concessions. So . . . ?"

The reporter gave it some thought, but in the end his curiosity won out over any objections he might have otherwise raised. "Okay. I agree. What's the second condition?"

Crow smiled faintly. "That if you don't believe me, at least do me the courtesy of not laughing in my face."

"Of course not—"

"Good, 'cause some of what I have to tell you is going to be pretty hard to swallow. I haven't told this story to too many people—actually I've only told it to Val, and she was there for most of it—and I don't feel like being ridiculed for it."

From that Newton supposed that Crow had been too drunk to remember telling the story to Toby, but he decided not to mention it. "I can promise you that I won't laugh or mock or anything. Just tell me, and I'll listen."

"Okay," Crow said, nodding. "I'm taking you on faith, Newt. Don't make me sorry about that. You can turn your recorder on." He paused and closed his eyes, collecting scraps of old memories from a closet deep within his mind. He began speaking before he opened his eyes. "If you can believe it, except for Val's dad being killed, the stuff that happened here these last few days were nothing compared to what happened thirty years ago. I mean, Karl Ruger and his cronies were bad enough, but back then we had someone as close to the devil as anyone I ever hope to meet. And like I told you yesterday it wasn't the Bone Man . . . he wasn't the one the papers nicknamed 'the Reaper.' I'd bet my life on that right now, and I can say that because I did stake my life on it back then."

"Then, who . . . ?"

Crow glanced left and right as if looking to see who was listening and then leaned close and in a hushed voice said, "Ubel Griswold."

"I know that name . . ." Newton flipped through the pages of his notebook. "Griswold– yeah, he was the last of the victims, right? A local farmer?"

Crow shook his head. "I figured you'd have that wrong. I mean, yeah, Griswold was a farmer, but he wasn't one of the victims." He glanced at Val. "You know, baby, I don't think I've even said that name out loud in . . . what? Twenty years? Whew!" He turned back to Newton. "It's not a name one says lightly, no sirree. At least not me. Folks around here openly blame the Bone Man for what happened, but it was Ubel Griswold. He was an evil, evil man."

"You're confusing me here, Crow. Who was he?"

"*What* was he is a better way to put it." Crow considered. "First let me put things into perspective for you, so let's jump back thirty-six years ago to when Griswold first moved to Pine Deep, supposedly from Germany, and bought an old stone farmhouse in one of the more remote sections of town, way off of A-32 and nearly impossible to reach except by some obscure back road that's no longer even there. This was before A-32 was expanded and paved, you understand. Back then it was called the Pinelands Highway, which was a joke because it was just dirt and gravel. When they built A-32 twenty-six years ago, a lot of the smaller roads became officially abandoned since many of them were cut into the state forest. That's why they built the road in the first place, to keep traffic out of the forest. Anyway, Griswold settled himself down to raise cattle and generally kept to himself. His farm was small but he had a fair-sized herd for the available room. There are, however, no records of him ever selling a single one. Odd, don't you think?"

Newton shrugged. Even after eight years in Black Marsh, what he knew about cattle farming would barely fill the back of an index card. Other than the fact that they were big, smelly, and went "Moo!" he didn't know from cattle beyond medium rare at Outback Steakhouse. "Private sales?"

Crow shook his head and continued, "Griswold ran his farm more or less by himself. Sometimes he'd turn a couple of acres over to crops like pumpkins and corn and gourds, and then he'd hire day labor, always hiring drifters as his day labor. Not regular migrant workers, mind you, but hoboes, bums, guys like that. Never any local people."

"So what? Cheap labor is cheap labor, and, who knows, maybe he felt sorry for them."

Val said dryly, "I don't think that was it."

"No," Crow agreed, "I think he just liked the fact that these were people no one would ever care about."

"How do you mean?"

"If they went missing, I mean. No one would ever know if they went missing—no one would care."

Newton laughed. "What are you saying? That he was doing . . . what? Feeding them to his cows?"

"I think he was killing them, is what I'm saying."

"*Killing* them?" That knocked the smile from Newton's face.

"It lays out like this. For four years Griswold ran his farm with the drifters acting as day labor, and no one ever noticed a damn thing. Then the fifth year was the Golden Harvest."

"What's that?"

"Local farmer's legend," Val said. "The Golden Harvest was the year we had the best crop that was ever reaped in these parts. Who knows why, but the crops went absolutely wild. Understand—when you plant, the birds get about half the seed and of the rest only a fraction actually produces a harvestable crop. That's why farmers sow so many seeds, far in excess of expectations, so that the resulting crop will be enough. Well, that year it seemed like every seed that was sown took root and bore fruit."

Crow nodded. "And what a crop! Jesus God! Ears of corn so big that they actually made it into textbooks as agricultural oddities. Tomatoes bigger than softballs and sweet as sugar, and apples that would make any teacher cry. Newt, this was like farmer's heaven."

"What does it have to do with Griswold?"

"Don't rush me, son," Crow said with a crooked grin. "It actually has more to do with the drifters than with Griswold per se. The crop yield was so big that farmers just couldn't keep up, so they had to fish around for extra hands. A lot of them took on busloads of migrants from the ghettos in Philly and Trenton, and some of the others snagged up anybody who had two hands and needed a buck. A few farmers took on the drifters who usually worked for Griswold. As it chanced, that was one of the years that Griswold was not growing crops in his fields, he was just raising cattle."

"The cattle he never sold," said Newton.

Crow nodded. "The cattle he never sold, right. Henry Guthrie took on four or five of the drifters who had done field work before for Griswold and who were scouting around town for some shifts. Oren Morse was one of them. Now Morse—the Bone Man, as I prefer to call him—was a genuine cultural dropout. Young black guy, about twenty-five or -six. A blues-playing ex-hippie who quoted Santayana and Charles Bukowski and John Lennon. My brother Billy and I thought he was coolest thing going. We used to work side by side with him. We had lunch with him, listened to his stories about being on the dharma road like Kerouac. Even at eight I knew he was a good guy. Maybe not a pillar of any community, but he was a decent person—just a dropout from a world that he wasn't suited for. He'd dodged the draft in 1969 and then just kept on running. This was long before the amnesty thing. He wasn't running 'cause he was scared but because he actually thought the peace movement meant something and he didn't want anyone to put a gun in his hand. Does that sound like a killer to you? Anyway, all through that season, through the Golden Harvest, we worked and talked and we learned a lot about dreaming and thinking from him. We all wanted to be just like him, to be that free. Then the year of the Golden Harvest came to an end and the year that followed changed everything."

"Why? What happened?"

"Well, I suppose when you get a year like the Golden Harvest you can become soft really quickly. Everyone came out on top that year, from the farmers to the merchants to the everyday folk; that year was incredible. We all made money, we all had more than enough to eat, and I guess in some ways we all got complacent. Then the following year we had a different kind of harvest."

"Nothing like the Golden Harvest?" asked Newton.

Crow snorted. "No sir. What came that next year was a Black Harvest."

"A . . . Black Harvest? That sounds ominous. What was it?"

"Figure it out," Crow said. "We went from one extreme to the other. Where the year before every damn seed was taking root and producing stalks and vines heavy with succulent fruit, the year of the Black Harvest was a year of blight and sickness. It started at the end of June, which is when the first wave of crops are generally harvested, and the crops that grew were thin and sparse, or swollen with disease. You'd break open a big juicy watermelon and the meat inside would be spoiled and black and crawling with maggots. The corn was so harsh and foul that even pigs wouldn't eat it. Any person dumb enough or unlucky enough to eat the vegetables and fruits harvested that year fell sick, and soon we found that the diseases and decaying vegetation had bred some kind of virus or bacteria, or something like that—I don't know the biology of it, all I know is that a lot of people died that year. Highest mortality rate in the history of Pine Deep, highest per capita in the state for any one town, at least in this century. It was like a plague, and it swept right through the town, from mid-July until the middle of September, and it chopped down old folks and kids, and left a lot of the adults weak and broken. Forget the farm animals—those that didn't just drop dead in their tracks had to be slaughtered to try and keep the infection from spreading to Crestville and Black Marsh."

Newton held up his palm. "Wait a minute . . . you're describing what's happening this year."

Crow nodded, eyebrows arched significantly. "You should get out and meet the people, Newton. Everyone over thirty-five is talking about this being another Black Harvest year."

"It *can't* be that bad. There hasn't been a significant increase in deaths."

"No, not like before, and that's a plus," Val said. "Maybe it's because we have a hospital here now, or maybe the antibiotics and drugs are better now. Who knows? Some older folks and some kids have gotten sick, but we haven't had a real killer plague this year, thank God." Crow reached out and gave her thigh a small squeeze.

Newton said, "Did the blight spread to other towns?"

Crow shook his head. "No, and that's pretty weird, don't you think? Some folks said that it was because Pine Deep is surrounded by water on all sides, it's kind of like a little island. They said that the water boundary stopped whatever infection was in the actual soil. Of course that wouldn't stop an airborne virus, nor would it stop much of anything else with all the traffic that goes back and forth between Pine Deep, Crestville, and Black Marsh, but none of the surrounding towns experienced any increase in sickness or mortality and none of the crops of the other towns was in any way affected."

"Jeez, that *is* weird."

"On the other hand," Val said, "it's different from the current blight. This time there are cases of crop disease as far away as Lambertville, Stockton, and Frenchtown in New Jersey, and all through this part of Bucks County. New Hope, Upper Black Eddy, Doylestown, New Britain. Understand, it's not as bad anywhere else as it is here in Pine Deep . . . but it's spreading this time. No doubt about it."

Newton looked at her, then at Crow. "I have to say, folks, that this is making me feel a little sick myself."

"Buckle up, Newt, 'cause it gets worse," Crow said drily. "Folks who got sick back then, but who went to hospitals outside of town, or who went to stay with relatives in other towns, got better quickly and never had any lingering symptoms. Not one sick person who left town to recuperate died as a result of the disease."

"Oh, come on—"

"It's a matter of public record," Val said quietly. "Look it up."

"Yeah," Crow agreed. "That was a terrible year. I got sick, too, but not bad. My brother Billy never got sick, so he was okay. A couple of my friends from school died, though."

Val said, "Eventually the blight and the epidemic ended. Slowly, but it ground to a halt. There were fewer new cases of the sickness, and fewer deaths as the weeks passed and it got closer to October. Of course by then most of the crops had been chopped down and burned, so perhaps that halted the spread of the infection."

"I know you're going to think that this is romantic or morbid or something," Crow said, "but it was as if the souls of the people of Pine Deep were being harvested that year, instead of the crops." The reporter said nothing to that, nor did Val add anything to it. After a moment, Crow said, "Okay, so that sounded stupid."

" 'Sounded'?" Val said with a wicked little smile pulling at one corner of her mouth.

Crow motored on. "Obviously I didn't work at the farm that year, but the bunch of us hung out there all the time. Morse was there sometimes, too, but not to work. My brother Billy said that Morse was working out at Griswold's farm that season."

"Griswold's farm wasn't hit?"

"Oh, his farm was all but smashed flat. Nearly all of his cattle died in the first few weeks, and the meat must have been spoiled because Morse worked his ass off hauling off dead cattle and trying to keep alive all the new ones Griswold would import, but they all died, too. It must have been some nasty, disgusting work—but it was work. Drifters can't be all that picky, you know. So the weeks passed and Morse kept at it, and at the same time the town kept going to shit. Finally, by the middle of September the plague and the blight were over, probably because every harvestable crop was already dead. The crop that year was a complete and total loss. Just a year after the Golden Harvest, that year turned out to be a financial disaster. Whole families went down the drain, people lost their homes, their farms, and, as you can imagine when things go really bad really fast, there was a lot of anger and frustration. Even some violence. Fights broke out, people started getting hurt." He paused and looked up at the ceiling. "My dad was one of the ones who took his frustrations out with his fists." That statement hung there, and Newton was sharp enough to read into it what was meant.

Into the silence, Val said, "For some reason my family's farm wasn't hit by the blight . . . just like it hasn't been hit by this current blight. We were actually having a pretty good year, good crops. My dad took on more help than he really needed, hiring as many of the locals as wanted to work here, adults and kids. He hired Billy and Crow to be gofers on the farm, and, I think, to keep me company. Crow and Billy became friends with me and Terry Wolfe, who was my best friend at the time. That whole season we were always together." She paused. "Terry's little sister used to tag along with us. Terry and I were ten, Crow was nine, and Billy was twelve. It was fun having my own little 'gang.'"

"Her dad also hired Oren Morse when there was no more work at Griswold's."

Val nodded and sipped her coffee. "Dad had heard him play his guitar a bunch of times the year before, and the two of them had talked quite a bit. Politics mostly, and books. Dad liked him, and maybe felt sorry for him, thought that Morse could have been someone. So, when Griswold cut him loose from the cattle job, Dad hired him. Dad was like that."

"No one better," Crow said, almost to himself and he toasted himself on the sentiment and sipped his drink. "As for Morse, we were the ones who gave him his nickname. The Bone Man."

"You never met him," she said, leaning forward to make better eye contact, "and probably the only things you've heard about him are the rumors and local legends, making him out to be something between Jack the Ripper and the Boogeyman, but that wasn't who he was. He really was a good man. My dad was almost never wrong about people. He was a very good judge of character, which is one of the reasons he was so good in business."

"She's right," Crow said. "Henry'd look you right in the eye and he'd know right away if you were going to deal straight or if you were a shifty bastard. As I recall," he added with a smile, "he didn't much care for me when he met me."

"He liked you when you were a kid, honey," Val said. "He just had some issues with you when you were . . ." She trailed off, realizing that she was talking in front of a reporter.

"It's okay, baby, you can say it," Crow said, then he looked at Newton. "I used to be a drunk. Or . . . I am a drunk, though I haven't had a drink in years. What they call a sober drunk. I go to meetings. Val and I had kind of drifted apart as friends for a while there and when we met up again I was hitting the sauce pretty hard. That didn't wash too well with Henry and he told me in no uncertain terms to dry out or buzz off."

"He didn't phrase it that way," Val said.

"The hell he didn't. You weren't there, sweetie. Your dad looked me right in the eye and he was about fifteen feet tall and he told me to stay the hell away from his daughter until I had some self-respect."

"Jeez," Newton said, grinning.

"I tell you this, Newt," Crow said, "because I want you to understand Henry Guthrie. If he thought Oren Morse was a bad man he'd have never let him near his farm, let alone near his daughter, and yet we worked side by side with the man, and almost every night Henry'd have us all on the porch—us kids, a few of the regular farm staff, and the Bone Man— and we'd hang out and drink ice tea Val's mom made, with mint and lemon slices, and we'd listen to the Bone Man tell stories and sing the blues. We *knew* that man."

Newton considered this for a moment, and then nodded. "Okay, you sold me. If Henry Guthrie gave him the seal of approval then he's okay with me."

Val chuckled. "You kiss up very well."

"Part of the job," he said, and they all laughed.

Crow nodded to Newton. "You can leave all that shit about me being a drunk out of the article, okay?"

"Sure," Newton said a little too quickly, but then he caught the look in Val's eyes, which were as uncompromising as a fist. *Yeah*, he thought, *Henry Guthrie's daughter right enough. Screw with her, Newt ol' boy and she'll rip you a new one.* "Sure," he repeated with emphasis, giving Val a brief nod. She returned the nod and sat back in her chair.

"Okay, so where were we? Oh yeah," said Crow, "the summer was coming to an end and fall was coming on."

"And that," Val said, "was when people started getting killed."

"The Massacre?"

"Right," Crow said. "That's when it started. The first to die was one of the drifters. An old wino who'd been doing day labor with Morse, but who doesn't show up for work one day near the end of September. The Bone Man and another guy go looking for him after work, thinking maybe he's sick or something. The guy usually slept in a ragged bedroll under that old covered bridge near the reservoir and, he was there all right, but . . . well, I never saw it firsthand, but years later, when I worked as a town cop I looked at the case file, read the description, and saw the crime scene photos. The poor old bastard had literally been torn to pieces. *Pieces*, mind you—his throat was ripped out and his head was found thirty feet from his body, and the body had been partially devoured. No one knew what to make of it. Naturally, starving dogs were blamed. Seemed like a logical choice."

"Sure."

"Then it happens again. Same thing—another drifter. Guy never shows up for work, and when they find him he's in his bedroll, torn to pieces and partly eaten. Two kills on two consecutive nights just rocks the whole town. They formed groups, loaded their guns, and killed damn near every dog in and around Pine Deep."

"The killings didn't stop?" Newton prodded.

"Of course not. Wasn't any damn dog doing it, and the killings kept up, nearly every night. Third vic was another drifter, but the fourth wasn't any drifter."

"Who was it?"

Crow's eyes were as dark and intense as those of a real crow. "The fourth body they found that year, the body they found without its head and with its heart torn out of its chest was . . . my brother Billy."

Newton felt as if someone had just punched him in the stomach. "Oh . . . my God . . ."

Crow eyes glistened with unshed tears. "I thank God I never saw the body, and I never had the nerve to look at those photos in the file. They had a closed coffin, of course. Cremated him and spread his ashes over the baseball diamond. He had always wanted to play pro ball when he grew up." Crow wiped at a tear and gave a small laugh. "Man did he love baseball. Bone Man called him Boppin' Billy."

"Damn, Crow," said Newton, "I'm really sorry. I should never have—"

Crow waved it away. "No, it's okay. I'd actually want the story to be told."

"Yeah . . . I can see that. But why? I mean . . . why now?"

Crow looked at him over the mouth of the bottle, but Val

answered the question, her fingers lightly touching her silver cross. "Because he doesn't think it's over yet."

## (2)

"You'll have to sign for these, doctor."

Weinstock nodded, took the pen from the assistant security supervisor and signed his name on the clipboard.

"Doctor . . . you do know these are tapes from the interior cameras, not the ones in the hall? When the night guard told me that you wanted the interior cameras left on all night, I thought he was mistaken."

Weinstock's face showed no emotion, but in a cool authoritarian voice he said, "Is there a *problem*, Gary?"

"Uh, no, sir. It's just a little strange."

"Is it?" Weinstock said in a way that did not invite any further comment. "Can we assume that as the hospital administrator I have the authority to have a camera running when and where I please?"

The assistant supervisor stiffened. "Sir, don't get me wrong, I wasn't . . ."

"Then what were you going to say?"

"Well, it's just that the security assistant hasn't had a chance to review those tapes. We don't know what's on them, yet."

"Gary, if there is anything of note on these tapes, I'll bring it to the attention of your supervisor. Now, any further questions?"

Gary, seated behind his desk, had stiffened so much as to give the appearance of having snapped to attention. Weinstock took the tapes, turned without a further word, and walked away.

Back in his office he locked his door and popped the tape into the deck, sat down in his swivel chair and hit PLAY. For a long while he saw the morgue room, empty and badly lit. He hit FAST-FORWARD and the time code in the lower left speeded up. There was a blur of movement and he stopped, rewound the tape, and played it forward at normal speed. It took him nearly ten seconds to understand what he was seeing. It would take him the rest of his life to fully accept that what he was seeing was real. Numb, staring, immovable except for his thumb on the remote he sat there for over an hour, pressing STOP, REWIND, PLAY. Over and over again as icy tears streamed down his cheeks.

### (3)

Newton looked at Val and then swiveled his head toward Crow. "What do you mean about it not being over?"

"I'll get to that in a sec." Crow said. "So, with Billy dead, the people in town started to really get up in arms. Drifters getting hacked up they could more or less accept—you're a drifter, shit happens—but a popular town kid like Billy getting killed, well that was something different. Cops and men from town started scouring the brush, checking the forest, poking in every swamp and hollow around town. I don't think they had any kind of a clear idea what they were looking for—they were just looking. They needed to find something, and in a way it brought the town together. Instead of fighting each other, they were unified in searching out what had done this thing to Billy.

"Two days later I was in my backyard, just sitting on a swing and thinking about Billy. It was just around sundown, and I wasn't allowed to go anywhere out of sight of the house, of course, but I couldn't stand to be inside. I guess if my dad had actually cared about me he'd have had me inside with every door and window locked shut, but he was too busy drinking and he figured if I was in the yard what could happen? Ah well. Anyway, I was sitting there and trying to wrap my head around the idea that Boppin' Billy was dead. I was still all screwed up by the deaths of my friends, but that was from sickness, and I could half-assed understand sickness leading to death, but to die by violence, that was something totally outside of my experience, and it was hurting me. I felt lost and stupid, and somehow I even felt as if I was to blame. No, don't ask me how, it was just the sort of stupid thing a confused kid feels. Something about feeling like I was being punished for being a brat by having Billy taken away. Stupid shit.

"So, I just sat there and watched the sun go down, trying to understand the enormity of the fact that Billy was dead and was going to be dead forever, and that I would never, ever see him again. I kept wanting to, you understand. I think I even wished on the first star that came out just to be able to see him one more time. Maybe I was half asleep, or maybe I was so wrapped up in thinking about it that I had sort of hypnotized myself. Either way, just as the sun was dipping down over the treeline I heard something crunch down on a branch behind me. I actually believed it was Billy. Boppin' Billy come back to be with me, smiling that cocky smile of his. I remember that I was actually smiling when I turned my swing around to face him, grinning the way I always did when Billy came home from school. I swung myself around and I think I even said his name.

"But . . . it wasn't Billy, of course. That was stupid. It was—someone else. He grabs me by the front of my shirt and throws me—actually throws me—across the yard. I go flying, screaming, terrified, and crash right into a big azalea bush, land upside down, still screaming, hurt, confused . . . nothing making sense. I can hear whomever it is running at me, grunting and wheezing with effort. Sounds like a bear with all the noise he's making. I get only one brief glance at the man's face, and even then it isn't a good clear look. I have leaves and stuff in my face and fireworks going off in my head. When he grabs me again I try to hold onto the branches, try to keep from being picked up again. I never made the connection that this might be the same guy who killed Billy, dumb as that sounds. For a minute there I actually thought it was . . . my father."

"Your father?"

"Sure. He was always kicking the shit out of me. Sometimes it was as bad as what was happening that night in the yard. Sometimes he'd beat me so bad I'd be out of school for a week, two weeks."

"Jesus . . ."

"And you can leave that part out of the article, too."

"Uh, sure, man. Don't worry. "

"Good," Crow said firmly. "Anyway . . . the guy starts grabbing at me and I'm thrashing around, trying to hold onto the bush, trying to kick him, and this time I get a real good look at his face, which is when I really start screaming my head off. He suddenly lets go, and I fall and whack my head against the trunk of a pine tree. I'm lying there, stars in my eyes, and I hear the sounds of a scuffle and some screams and even something that sounds like a roar. The next thing I know, someone is grabbing at me again, but this time it's different, gentler. I stop fighting back and let myself be picked up. Once the fireworks in my head settle down I can see that the man holding me is Oren Morse, and the other guy—the real attacker—is running away down the alley."

"Damn," Newton said, scribbling furiously in his notebook.

"Then there were lights on in all the houses around, people are coming from everywhere. My father comes hustling out of the house carrying a big son of a bitch of a shotgun. Everyone swarms around me and Morse, and my father literally tears me out of the Bone Man's hands."

"Is that when they got the idea he did it?"

"No, not then. Too many people had looked out of their windows and backdoors and saw him fighting with some other guy—something they all conveniently forgot later when the Bone Man got blamed for everything. Right then they saw some other guy hotfoot it out of there and Morse helping me up."

"Morse chased him off, then?"

"Well, if no one else had showed up, I think both Morse and I would have been killed, but the Bone Man slowed the killer down long enough for the commotion to get the neighborhood up in arms. With all that had been going on in town, everyone was trigger-happy and came running with plenty of artillery. Typical of these things, nobody got a good look at the attacker. At least none of the neighbors, but Morse must have, though, 'cause later he knew where to go looking for the guy. But, I'm getting ahead of the story. I don't want to tell it out of sequence. Morse was kind of out of it right then. The other guy had smacked him around pretty badly, his nose was bleeding and all."

"The attacker got away clean?"

With a sigh, Crow sipped his Yoo-Hoo and then said, "The guy ran, all right, but he didn't give up. He went all the way over to the far side of town, the upscale part of Pine Deep. Mind you, at the time, the town was not as rich as it is now. Back then only Corn Hill was ritzy. Well, this sonov-abitch went over to Corn Hill and found another yard with another kid. Actually, two kids. He scaled this big wooden security fence and there was a little girl playing in the yard, right in sight of the kitchen window, and her older brother in his tree house reading *Fantastic Four* comics by the light of a Coleman lantern. He didn't waste any time throwing her around—he just pounced on her, tore her throat out, and hacked her body up pretty bad. They said it looked like a bear had mauled her."

"Good God. What happened to the boy?"

"No one has ever been able to put that together clearly. The popular version of the story has it that the boy jumped out of the tree to try and save his sister, and the killer gave him a couple of pretty bad slashes across the chest and left him dazed and bleeding. By that time their mother was running out of the house with a .22 caliber rifle. She found the boy sitting on the ground holding his sister's body. He was in a kind of coma, but he was alive. The little girl, of course, was dead."

"Jesus . . . that's horrible. It's so . . . sad!"

"Yeah." Crow wiped his mouth. "The boy was in the hospital for over a month, and when he snapped out of the coma, he couldn't remember a single thing."

"Maybe it's better for him that way," suggested Newton.

"Maybe. Who's to say?"

"Did you know those kids? I mean, did you go to school with them or anything?"

Crow looked at him, eyes steady and glittering. He said, "The little girl's name was Amanda. The boy is Terrance."

Newton made a note in his notebook. "Last name."

"Wolfe," Crow said simply.

Newton's pen froze halfway through writing the W. He looked up. "Wolfe? Terrance . . . *Terry Wolfe?*"

"Yeah."

"Then the little girl was—"

"Amanda Wolfe," Crow said. "Mandy, to us."

"Good God!" Newton chewed his lip for a long minute, then he gave a flustered series of blinks and looked at his notes. "Okay, now, from what I've read about the Massacre there were sixteen murders. Mandy Wolfe was number five."

"Right, but after that the killings stopped. Not completely, mind—just for a while. For twenty-eight days, actually. During that time whole town went absolutely crazy. There were carloads of guys with guns riding around, shooting at anything that moved. I think they managed to bag one mangy German shepherd that had escaped the original dog slaughter, three cows, and a guy getting a blow job from his neighbor's wife in the hedges behind his house."

"They kill him?"

"No, but she got so scared she nearly bit his pecker off."

"Resulting in nineteen stitches," Val said, "and two divorces. But they never bagged the killer, and by the end of those twenty-eight days, everyone had figured that the killer had skipped out and was terrorizing the citizenry of some other town. He'd had a couple of near misses that last night. Seems reasonable that he'd take off before his luck completely ran out, but on the twenty-eighth day the killings began again. Just like the first ones. People were attacked and savagely murdered. One of them was a cop."

Crow nodded. "The bastard hit him so fast that he never had the chance to draw his gun. Maybe he knew him, let him get close. Hard to say. Next victim was the cousin of a local farmer. His name was Roger Guthrie."

"Guthrie!" Newton looked sharply at Val, who nodded.

"He was my second cousin. Staying with us while on

leave from the Air Force. Rog was strolling through the cornfields out behind the house, smoking a cigar and just relaxing. We all heard him scream and when Dad and his brother, Uncle George, came running up with rifles, Roger was dead."

"That's incredible! Two murders in the same family, thirty years apart."

"In the same field, too," observed Crow hoarsely, "almost the same spot where Henry was gunned down."

That fact seemed nailed to the air in front of Newton and he sat there, staring for a while. Then he shook his head and his eyes refocused, and he rifled through his notebook. "How many deaths is that?"

"Actually Rog was the sixteenth. I skipped some of the others. You can look up the names, but we didn't know any of them. Just names and pictures in the newspapers. Roger, though, he was the last one killed during the massacre."

"But," Val said significantly, "there were two more killings."

Crow nodded. "Oren Morse . . . and Ubel Griswold. And"—he held up a finger—"this is where I go into the area of conjecture. What I think happened was this—Oren Morse tracked Griswold down, chased him into the woods, and murdered him somewhere out beyond the Guthrie Farm, somewhere in or around Dark Hollow."

"So . . . what? He thought Griswold was the killer because he'd seen him when he attacked you in your yard?"

"Sure," Crow said, setting his bottle down. "That *has* to be it. I mean, I saw Griswold's face, too, but since I'd only seen him once before in town I didn't recognize him at first. It wasn't until things had settled down that night and I was about to go to bed that I realized that I had seen my attacker's face before. Morse had *worked* for him, of course, and he knew him very well."

"Didn't he make a police report?"

Val said, "My dad told me some years later that Morse had told him that he'd tried to make a police report and the officer at the desk had laughed him out of the office. Nobody believed him."

"Did your father?"

"I don't know, but I think so. I asked him a few times, but he never really answered me. He'd just spread his hands and say something like 'World's a funny place, Val . . . who knows what people will do,' which is no answer at all."

"Even after his nephew was killed?"

"I think Val's dad was planning to go after Griswold himself," Crow said. "He never said as much, and I don't have anything but a gut feeling about it, but that's what I believe."

Val sipped her coffee, said nothing.

"So," Newton said in a summing-up tone of voice, "the Bone Man sees and recognizes the killer as the guy he used to work for, is rebuffed by the local cops when he tried to make a police report, and probably got a noncommittal answer from your dad, Val, when he shared his suspicions with him. Okay, so then what? He goes out as some kind of vigilante? I'm not feeling it. A guy who ran from the draft because he didn't want to carry a gun? That's a bit of a stretch, don't you think? I mean, do people change their character just like that?"

"Some people do. Sometimes an event can change a person's entire nature and personality," Val said, sharing a significant look with Crow. Newton had the impression, though, that she was referring to something else as well, but he let it go.

He said, "Crow, didn't you tell your father that you'd seen Griswold's face, and that you could identify him?"

Crow's face darkened a little. "Sure, I told my father. I told him everything I saw, and once I remembered whose face it was I'd seen I told him that, too. He beat the shit out of me for lying. Laid into me so hard I was sick for three days. People just assumed I was shaken up by the attack, but it was because of my father, and he told me to keep my mouth shut, to never say anything about it to anyone. Ever."

"Why? I would have thought he'd have wanted some kind of payback for what happened to his sons."

"The matter is a little more complex than that. You see, if

I'd named just about anyone else in town as the guy who'd attacked me, then my dad would have rounded up some of his redneck cronies and gone out and killed the guy. No question. But when it came to Griswold all bets were off because dear old dad all but worshipped Griswold. There were a handful of guys who used to hang out at Griswold's place. Young turks, mostly—high school age all the way to early thirties. My dad would have been the oldest, probably, at thirty-two. Youngest would have been Vic Wingate who works at Shanahan's. Also around the same age you have Stosh Pulaski, Phil Teague, and then a little bit older was Jim Polk, who's a local cop now, and our esteemed chief of police, Gus Bernhardt," Crow said, "who was ten years younger than my dad but already a cop, and maybe one or two others that I didn't know at the time. All of them were either closet-Klansmen or something like it. Don't forget, Newt, that we have more KKK members here in Pennsylvania than in any other state."

"I'd heard. Something to be proud of."

"You Jewish, by the way?" Crow asked.

"Only my mother's side, which I guess makes it official."

"So you probably have the same opinion of these boneheads as I do. So, then we have Griswold who was very probably of age to have been a soldier in World War Two—and who is German—and you have an interesting little clubhouse out in the woods where these redneck mouth-breathers can drink and raise whatever brand of hell they thought was fun. No way any of them would turn on Griswold, even if they believe he was guilty, which most of them probably did not."

Newton was shaking his head. "This must have traumatized you."

Val nodded and reached out to touch Crow's shoulder. "It did."

"More than I can express," Crow agreed. "Every part of that autumn traumatized me, and it took me a long time to get over it. It's one of several reasons why I had such a long love affair with the bottle. When you drink, you always have something to blame for your nightmares. And the booze hides them."

"But you don't drink anymore," Newton said, "so what about the nightmares?"

Crow glanced at Val again, and then shrugged. "They're back, and I have to face them without the support of my old friends Jim Beam and Jack Daniels. That's one of the reasons I'm being so candid with you, Newt. I guess it's a kind of therapy for me. What's the word? Cathartic?" He shrugged again. "I'm doing it to myself, and, I guess, *for* myself, I want to get it all out. Now, where were we? Oh, yeah. I had come out to the farm here for the memorial service for Roger Guthrie. Afterward I talked to Morse for a bit, and I told him that I thought the man who had attacked me was my dad's friend, Mr. Griswold, but the Bone Man told me to just forget I saw anything. He told me to make sure I stayed indoors at night, and made me promise to tell Val the same. Then he smiled, gave me a kind of pat on the head, and took off." Crow paused. "I never saw him again. Well . . . not alive anyway."

"What happened?"

"I don't know the details, you understand, because I wasn't there, but from what I've been able to figure out is that the Bone Man must have gone and confronted Griswold. They must have fought, and I think the Bone Man killed him. How he managed it, I don't know. Morse really was just a skinny bag of bones, and Griswold was this big tough son of a bitch, but Morse must have done it. Killed him and buried him God only knows where. No trace was ever found of Griswold's body. Not a single trace."

"What about the Bone Man? What happened to him?"

"They killed him," Val said simply, and when Newton looked at her she spread her hands in a gesture of disgust. "Beat him to death and then tied him to the scarecrow post that marks the boundary line between my property and the section of state forest over by Dark Hollow Road. Which is another tie-in to the present . . . *events*. That was the same spot where those two poor officers were killed."

Newton licked his lips. "I'm glad you're telling me this while it's bright daylight."

Val grunted, then picked up the thread of the story. "Crow and I were the ones who found him next morning. I screamed so loud my dad heard me all the way from the barn and he came pelting out with a pitchfork in his hands and ten of the field hands at his heels. I've never seen anyone look so scared and so furious!"

"He thought someone was attacking you," Newton said, and she nodded. "So . . . if the Bone Man really did kill Griswold, then who killed him? You think it was the crowd that hung out on Griswold's property?"

"Who else *could* it have been? I mean, what else would make sense?"

"Maybe Griswold killed him. Killed him, strung him up, and then took off for parts unknown."

"That's one of the popular theories," Crow said. "Though I've heard some talk that the town fathers did him in as a way of protecting the community, which paints them as heroes and the Bone Man as the villain."

"Which you think is horseshit?" Newton asked.

"Yep. I think that bunch of redneck assholes lynched him, either on Griswold's orders or as a revenge killing after their friend Griswold had been killed."

Newton sipped his Yoo-Hoo; Val sipped the last of her coffee. Crow blew across the neck of his bottle, making a mournful wail.

"Would you . . . um . . . know the names of any of these guys? Not just the ones who hung around Griswold's but the ones who may actually have had a hand in murdering Morse?"

Crow reached over and punched the OFF button on the tape recorder. "You didn't hear me say this, and if you print it I'll call you a liar. Are we clear?"

"We're clear."

"Okay. Gus Bernhardt let something spill once, years ago, back during that short—and I mean very short—period where he and I were kind of chummy. My first days on the job as a cop. We were both off duty and had been drinking and he let it slip that he was there when the Bone Man was killed, and then he clammed right up. Never said another word again but it was enough. No way on earth are you going to get that into print without poking a stick in the beehive."

"I guess not. Well, can you tell me—off the record—who else was there?"

"I never did put names to all of them, but from what I've been able to pick up here and there over the years, I can say for sure that Jim Polk was one of them. He and Gus were always thick as thieves. Maybe my dad, too. And Vic Wingate, and he is one mean bastard. If I had to pick someone as the ringleader at that lynching, it'd be Vic."

"He was just a teenager, Crow," Val said. "Just a kid."

"That bastard was never a kid," Crow snapped, his voice suddenly bitter and harsh. "He was born old, mean, and twisted. He was over my house enough when my dad was still alive, and from my earliest memory Vic was always very controlled, very focused, and as evil as the day is long."

"Evil is a pretty strong word, Crow," Newton said, but Crow only shrugged. "Okay, I won't print the names of the men you suspect. Can I turn my recorder back on?" Crow nodded and Newton hit the button. "So, what happened to Morse's body? Where is he buried?"

"In your hometown actually, Newt—Black Marsh. The people in Pine Deep nearly threw a fit when they learned that Morse's body was going to be buried in our local cemetery. There were threats and some of them were nasty, so Henry somehow managed to have the body shipped to Black Marsh and had it buried there. He put up a stone and even bought a suit for Morse to be buried in."

"So it was all swept under the carpet?"

"Sure. It wasn't long after that that the town started building up, going upscale. The Massacre was pushed back out of sight and no one really ever talks about it. We have too many fun ghost stories to keep us in business, no real-life tragedies need apply." He gave an ironic laugh. "In all the official reports Griswold was counted as murder victim number seventeen. Problem was that Griswold was local money who left no heirs, no will, no papers of any kind, so it was a bitch of a legal tangle to decide what to do with his property. It's still there. Fields and gardens all gone back to forestland now, I expect, but the big old stone farmhouse would still there, back past Dark Hollow. I think the property reverted back to the state, or something like that. I don't know how the law works on something like that. I would imagine the place is overgrown, and the local folklore insists the place is haunted."

"Sounds appropriately spooky. Ever go there?"

"No!" Crow said abruptly, startling Newton, but the look of alarm that had appeared on Crow's face passed quickly. He tried a dismissive laugh, but it sounded flat. "Uh . . . no, man, I don't think I would *ever* go there."

"Why not? Surely you aren't scared of ghosts! Not you, of all people."

"Ghosts? No . . . no, I don't think I'm afraid of any ghosts."

"Then what?"

"It's just . . . ah, man, it's really hard to say without sounding like I'm off my nut."

"Too late for that, sweetie," Val said softly. Crow gave her leg a little pinch and she slapped his hand.

"Why . . . what is it you're afraid of?"

Crow looked at him strangely. "Why, him, of course."

"Who?"

"Griswold."

"I thought you said the man was dead."

Crow shook his head vigorously. "You see, that's just it. He wasn't."

"Wasn't—what? Wasn't killed."

"No, wasn't a man," Crow said. "I don't think Ubel Griswold was a man." Before Newton could reply, Crow explained. "You see, when I looked into his face back then, even though it was just a brief look, and even though I could still recognize him somehow as Griswold, the face I saw wasn't a human face. So, I don't think he *was* a man." His eyes were intense, haunted. "I think Ubel Griswold was a monster."

## (4)

In the silent wormy darkness, he waits; beneath tons of muddy dirt, he waits. He is not lost in the utter blackness of his forgotten grave in Dark Hollow; he is not dwarfed by the immensity of it, but the lightless vastness of it. When he trembles and the ripples of each shudder rolls out through the roots of the mountain, he is not trembling with fear, or loneliness, or despair. He is shuddering with a darkly sensual delight that undulates outward and upward toward the town, throughout the farms, into wells and beneath cultivated fields until it laps against the rushing waters of the canals and rivers that ring all of Pine Deep. Beneath those millions of pounds of bubbling muck he is the poison in the earth, the author of blight and sickness, the soulless heart of corruption. As each new tourist car rumbles over the bridges and rolls along the black arm of A-32, as hotels fill and fill, as everyone in town turns blindly away from manhunt toward holiday, as hearts quicken with excitement at the coming of Halloween, he—down deep in his grave—laughs with a ravenous and expectant delight.

# Interlude

## (1)

Dad opened the door to the den and leaned his head into the room, saw Adrian and Darien in front of the big plasma TV, controllers in their hands, a continuous electronic gun battle rattling onscreen. "Look, boys, keep it down to a low scream and it'll be fine."

The twins turned and gave him identical stares with their big green eyes. They showed him identical smiles. Adrian said, "Sure, Dad. Sorry if it got too loud."

"We'll turn it down," agreed Darien.

"Thanks, guys." Dad gave them a warm chuckle and a wink and closed the door.

Adrian and Darien looked at the door their dad had closed behind him. Both of them wore their thin cat-smiles. Darien turned to his twin, his smile not reaching his eyes, and gave a slow shake of his head. "What an asshole."

Adrian nodded, turning the volume down only one notch. "No shit."

They turned back to the PS2, pressed the restart button. They had reached the thirty-second level, where Lord Vega and his Scarlet Assassins were laying in wait for Simon Dart and his companions when there was a sound at the window. The twins ignored it, focusing on the game. Then it came again. A tapping. Louder, more insistent, breaking through the game's hip-hop soundtrack. Adrian looked up. "What's that?"

"What?"

"That." The tapping repeated itself and Adrian jerked his head toward the window.

"Just a bird," Darien said, turning back to study the screen, which the pause button had frozen on an image of Simon Dart drawing his stun gun as two Scarlet Assassins were leaping down from a shadowy walkway. "Come on . . ."

"No, listen . . ." The sound came again. "There's someone at the window."

"Well, go look, for Christ's sake," said Darien. "Maybe it's Dylan with the stuff."

Darien smiled. "Cool!"

The "stuff" in question was stack of porn videos that Dylan's older brother had downloaded and burned to disk; Dylan had promised to swipe them and bring the stash by to share with the twins. Dylan was a bit of an asshole, but he was good for stuff like that, and the twins had no other source for that kind of thing. Dad, asshole that he was, had put parental controls on the home computer. Already Dylan had brought over some copies of *Hustler* and well-thumbed paperbacks about girls who liked to tie each other up and use whips and stuff. Adrian and Darien loved all of it, craved it, demanded as much of it as Dylan could appropriate. This latest batch was to be the real bonanza because one of the disks had a bunch of sex scenes from movies and there was one that showed Kate Beckinsale and you could see her tits. Adrian hadn't believed him at first, but Dylan had sworn on it, and the twins had half-bribed, half-intimidated Dylan into bringing over the disks. Dylan always hesitated, because if his older brother ever found out he would skin Dylan alive and hang his carcass out for the crows, but Dylan needed the approval of Adrian and Darien far more than he needed a whole skin. He had promised.

Adrian went quickly to the window, parted the drapes, and cupped his hands around his eyes so he could peer out into the shadows. Darien restarted the game and made Simon

Dart draw his gun and blow bloody holes in both assassins. He smiled wolfishly as their blood splattered on the walls. Adrian pressed his face to the glass. It was pitch dark outside and he couldn't see a thing, and then something loomed up right in his face and he let out a small startled cry. Dylan's pale face suddenly filled the lower pane of glass.

"Shit!" gasped Adrian.

"What?" called Darien distractedly.

"Little dickhead nearly scared the shit out of me."

"Is he out there?"

"Yeah." Dylan's face looked milk-white in the spill of light from the house, but his eyes were in shadows as he bent toward the glass. He reached out and touched the pane, tapping it with a fingernail. Adrian made a gesture that asked if Dylan had the goods, and the pale-faced twelve-year-old held up a vinyl CD wallet and waggled it. "Oh, yeah!" said Adrian.

"Go let him in," called Darien. "Hurry up."

Adrian jerked his thumb to indicate the door and Dylan faded back into the shadows. "Be right back," he said to his brother, and hustled out of the room to the entrance foyer. If Dylan truly had the promised goods, then the three of them would whisk away to the third floor, which was the sole domain of the twins. Their PS2 could play any kind of CD-ROM, and this was going to be jerkoff heaven.

Smiling in anticipation, Adrian stepped into the foyer, twisted the door handle, and jerked open the heavy oak door. "Come in, come in!" he was saying even as he swung the door wide to reveal Dylan Jamison standing in the doorway. Dylan was only five-three and thin but he had a huge smile on his wide, wet mouth. It was not a nice smile, not a pleasant smile, and the second he saw it Adrian, who had also been smiling, felt the grin drain from his face, leaking like liquid from a broken glass. He stared at Dylan, not understanding at first what he was seeing, and then he slowly, very, very slowly, began backing away from the door. Accepting the invitation to enter, Dylan stepped over the threshold, his smile stretching wider, seeming to tear his cheeks as he grinned, his pale lips pulling tightly back from his teeth. Behind him, other shapes moved, detaching themselves from the shadows, becoming figures that also moved and smiled.

Adrian tried to scream, but his throat had locked shut with the shock of what he was seeing. With a soundless cry of terror, he spun and tried to run, tried to race up the hallway to the family room, but Dylan caught him before he had taken five steps. He caught him by the hair and jerked him back so hard that Adrian's heels kicked up into the air and something in his neck went *Pop!* Adrian fell so hard on his ass that a white-hot firebolt of pain shot from his tailbone all the way to the top of his head. Dylan jerked Adrian's head back and whatever had popped before now went *Crack!* Lights exploded in Adrian's eyes and he felt himself being bent savagely backward, his spine arching too far too fast as all of the vertebra in his back popped loudly like a string of firecrackers. With tiny white hands Dylan pushed Adrian's shoulder and head apart to expose his neck, doing this with such force that the skin on Adrian's neck stretched and suddenly split, splattering Dylan's face with bright red dots. Growling low in his chest, Dylan bent close, his smiling lips brushing the soft skin, but then he paused and looked up quickly as a shadow fell over him. The man who stood over him smiled coldly, and in a voice that was no more than a graveyard whisper, he said, "Do it."

Dylan's eyes blazed as red as coals as he plunged his head downward, driving the long spikes of his teeth into Adrian's throat. Blood geysered past Dylan's face with tremendous hydrostatic pressure, spraying the wall and scattering ruby-red droplets on the sleeve of the man's coat.

Karl Ruger raised his sleeve and licked the droplets off with a long, sharp tongue. The taste was *exquisite*. Behind him, the two other shapes were becoming agitated, incensed by the sharp, sweet smell of blood. Ruger gave a slow, grand gesture, indicating the whole of the house with his bone-white fingers.

"Do 'em all," he whispered.

Gaither Carby and Dave Golub rushed past him, howling with red delight.

## (2)

Vic Wingate sat on the tailgate of his truck smoking a cigarette and watching the stars wheel overhead, listening distractedly to the screams coming from the nearby house. He knew he shouldn't be smoking this close to the two drums of paraffin in the bed of the truck, but he figured screw it.

The screaming only lasted a few minutes. He cut a look at the only other house within sight of this one, but it was four hundred yards away and no extra lights had come one, there were no yells, no inquiring calls. With this many trees around even screams didn't carry well. Vic knew that from long experience. He took a last drag, then ground out the coal on the heel of his shoe, put the butt in his shirt pocket, and stood up. It was a pretty night.

Turning, he reached into the bed and took hold of the corner of the topmost of the stacked body bags, braced his feet against the weight, and pulled. Though the carcass inside was two months dead it still had some weight, so he was careful of his lower back as he pulled it off the truck. He took his time hauling the others down, too, and laid them in a row. One for each of them, stolen from cemeteries around the county. A little bit of selective grave robbing. One here, a couple there, and some caretakers' palms greased along the way so no police reports ever got filed, no relatives notified. Some quick excavation with a backhoe, and then the empty coffin reburied with all of the sod neatly put back afterward. All told Vic had close to a hundred bags like these, piled like cordwood in a refrigerated storage unit he rented out on Route 202. The manager there has been receiving five large a week in cash since the first week of September, and was an old friend of Vic's. It wasn't the first time Vic had used the place to keep something fresh, and he'd swung by there tonight to get what he needed so there would be bones found in the ashes once this place was torched. The proper amount of bones. Residential fire like this, there was little chance of anyone ordering a DNA analysis of the remains. Or, what was the word? Cremains? Yeah, that was it, and Vic liked the word. Cremains.

He pulled down the last two—kid-sized bags. Just about the size of Adrian and Darien. The devil was in the details.

# PART THREE

# LITTLE HALLOWEEN

*October 10th to October 13th*

"There was about him a suggestion of lurking ferocity, as though the Wild still lingered in him and the wolf in him merely slept."

—Jack London, *White Fang*

I went Trick-or-Treating in a suburb once.
One lady gave me *The Look*;
One old cuss gave me a hard time;
One beautiful girl gave me the cold shoulder,
And one son of a bitch gave me the willies.

—Indigo Heart, "Monolog on Halloween"

# Chapter 19

## (1)

In movies it always rains at funerals. The crowds all stand around dressed in black, their umbrellas forming a ceiling above them. Maybe the hero stands hatless in the rain, too tough to need any umbrella. Either way, the skies weep at death and the hiss of rain is like the white noise that will be the only sound at the end of the universe. Crow thought about this as he stood holding hands with Val under a brilliant blue sky in the big field behind the Guthrie house. The sunshine was rich and warm and the shadows cast by the line of towering elms was soft and cool. Birds sang in the trees whose tops were riffled by a gentle easterly breeze. Crow thought that it should rain, that the heavens should indeed weep literally as well as symbolically when someone like Henry Guthrie passes out of the world, but there wasn't a speck of a cloud in the vast blue sky.

In accordance with his wishes, Henry had been cremated. There would be no tombstone, no marker, no specific anchor for his body; his ashes would be spread over the farm and that would create the link he wanted between his soul and the land he had loved so dearly. The ashes currently rested in a large silver urn that stood on a long table draped with white and crowded with flower arrangements sent by friends and family and business associates; scalloped along the edge of the table was the Guthrie family tartan, the greens and reds bright in the sunshine. Around the table were concentric circles of folding chairs and behind the table stood Rev. Donald MacTeague, who had gone to high school with Henry, had performed the wedding service for Henry and his wife, Bess, had baptized Val, and who had presided over the funeral of Roger Guthrie back in 1976, over Henry's brother George eight years ago, over Bess two years ago, and now over Henry. Mac, as he was called by everyone in town, looked very old to Crow, and he could see that Henry's death had taken a lot out of him.

As Mac slowly went through his homily, Crow surreptitiously looked around at the crowd. Nearly five hundred people had showed up for the service, a hundred of them standing after all the chairs were taken. Beyond the rings of guests there was a second ring of less formally dressed spectators made up of reporters from all over the county. Crow figured that no one beyond the fifth or sixth row could hear a word that Mac was saying, but no one had thought to bring a microphone for him, and when one of the press reps had asked if they could hang a lavaliere mike on him Val had withered him with a look that would have turned a stallion into a gelding.

Scanning the crowd though the opaque barrier of his sunglasses, Crow could see that anyone of any importance in town was there, from the selectmen and grower's commission chair to the owner of the tractor dealership on Harvest Hill Road near the Crescent Bridge. Gus Bernhardt was there, sweating in his ill-fitting uniform, and next to him were the four Philadelphia cops, Ferro, LaMastra, Jerry Head, and Coralita Toombes, who had carpooled out for the occasion. It was the first of three funerals they'd be attending this month, he knew, with burials for Nels Cowan and Jimmy Castle pending the release of their bodies from the morgue. Crow thought it very decent of them to show up here, since none of them had actually known Henry. When Ferro saw Crow looking in his direction he gave a small, curt nod. There were a few other officers present, but they were mostly local blues working security.

Mac concluded his remarks and indicated that everyone should sit down. While they were sitting, Crow leaned close to Val and whispered. "You okay, baby?"

She just squeezed his hand, keeping her eyes fixed on the urn and her mouth locked in a hard straight line. A soprano from First Methodist stood up and began to sing "Amazing Grace" while a bagpiper played along. When that was done they segued into another hymn that Crow didn't know. He lost interest in it and went back to checking out the crowd. Near the front, Terry and Sarah Wolfe sat next to Saul Weinstock and his wife, Rachel. At one point Mark, who was only one day home from the hospital and seated in front of them, began to cry quietly, and Terry reached out and massaged his shoulders briefly and then leaned close and said something in his ear. Mark nodded, sniffed, wiped his eyes, and let out a deep breath. When Terry sat back, Crow could see Sarah lean over and kiss his cheek.

What held his interest, however, was not this simple kindness, or Mark showing some emotion other than bullish hostility, but the haggard look on Terry's face and the shell-shocked expression Weinstock wore. If there was a competition for the most demonstrably stressed-out man in Pine Deep, Crow wouldn't have known who to bet on. Crow could understand Terry's stress, but why Weinstock looked so battered was an unknown. He tried to catch his friend's eye, but Weinstock just stared at the soprano with utter rigid indifference.

A flash of light caught his eye and he looked past the crowd and the press to the winding path that led past the field and back onto the road. He could see a kid standing there, with one sneakered foot on the gravel of the road and the other on the pedal of his bicycle, a hand raised to shade his eyes from the intense sun glare, light sparking off of the bike's reflectors. Mike. Good kid, nice of him to show up, even at a distance.

The soprano concluded her song and sat down while Mac stood up again, holding his hands wide as he blessed the crowd and then invited everyone to come up and file past the urn to pay their last respects. As soon as the service was concluded, Val turned to Crow and he took her in his arms and held her while she wept. He fumbled for a pack of Kleenex, peeled one out for each of them; she dabbed at her eyes and blew her nose. Crow got to his feet and took Val's arm, leading her over to where Connie and Mark stood. Crow shook Mark's hand and kissed Connie, whose eyes were nearly vacant. Crow wondered what pill she had popped before the service, but he was sure that if he knocked nobody would be home.

The four of them stood to one side of the table, and Mac came to stand with them as the tide of mourners funneled into a single file and came past, paused briefly before the urn, and then came down the line to say a word to Val or Mark, shake Crow's hand, and shuffle off. Terry and Sarah were the first ones there, and as Sarah leaned in to hug Val, she said, "Look, honey, the caterers have probably already set up by now, so if you don't mind I'm going to take over and run things up there. I don't want you to have to be bothered with nonsense like how many canapés are left. You just stick close to Crow and every else will be taken care of."

"You're a doll, Sarah. I appreciate it," Val said, looking greatly relieved, and kissed her.

Terry shook Mark's hand and then Crow's. "You holding up okay?" he asked.

"Yeah," Crow said, "I'm good. You?"

Terry made a ghastly attempt at a lighthearted smile. "Life's a real peach. See you up at the house."

Saul Weinstock appeared next, smiling a tight and humorless smile that made him look pained. Unlike Terry, Weinstock's grip was desperately strong and he gave Crow a quick hard pump, then used the grip to lean in close as he said, very quietly, "Let's find a place later to have a word. Okay?" He moved on before Crow could answer.

The rest of the crowd was like a blur of handshakes and

careful smiles. When it was over Val looked exhausted, and Crow wrapped his arm around her as they walked slowly up to the house.

### (2)

It was a typical post-funeral affair, with small conversational groups forming, breaking, reforming. Crow wandered through, shaking hands, exchanging bits and pieces of conversation with some of the distant Guthrie relatives and the general Who's Who of Pine Deep. The Philly cops were clustered together in a corner looking out of place; Crow saw Saul Weinstock come up and lead Ferro away for a private chat. They stood with their heads bowed together for five minutes.

While he was watching the crowds a couple of folks asked him for drinks and Crow realized that he had been standing by the small wet bar. Usually he avoided getting within sniffing distance of it, but he mixed and poured and tried not to remember their old familiar tastes.

"Can I put my order in?" Crow looked up from the Manhattan he was mixing and saw Ferro looking wry and amused, LaMastra flanking him. "You have time for a quick word?" Ferro asked.

"Sure," Crow said.

Ferro turned to LaMastra, put one hand on his shoulder, and nudged him toward the drinks table. "Presto change-o! You're now a bartender." Then to Crow, "Let's step over out of the line of fire."

Crow let himself be led far away from the bottles. "Thanks," he said.

"Hope you don't think I was overstepping—"

"Hell, no. My AA sponsor would throw a conniption if he heard I was mixing drinks."

Ferro gave him a dour nod. "I just had a brief chat with your friend, Saul Weinstock. He said that there have been some unusual things happening in town. Would . . . you know anything about that?"

"This is Pine—" Crow began but Ferro held up a hand to stop him.

"Please, Crow, if I hear that 'this is Pine Deep, things are always unusual' line one more time I think I'm going to go a bit postal. I _know_ things are unusual around here. I _know_ this is America's 'haunted holidayland,' yada yada yada. What I'm asking you, given the normal flow of odd happenings in Pine Deep, have you noticed anything outside of what you people _here_ would consider odd."

"Hmm," Crow said, "that makes me wonder what Saul told you."

Ferro's face had a thoughtful, almost calculating look. "Would you mind just making a comment first?"

Crow shrugged. "Well . . . I read the papers, I talk to people who come into the store. It's been a rough season. We had the blight—still _have_ the blight—and that means that there's a lot of tension and stress. There have been some fights. Probably people blowing off steam. You work your ass off all your life to try and make it work and then a bad season comes along and wipes you out, that's gonna hurt. People get frightened, they get angry, and they start swinging. Is that what you're talking about?"

"Anything _else_ unusual?"

Crow thought about it. "Well, we had a pretty bad fire last night. A whole family was killed."

"What do you think it was?"

"I'm not a cop anymore, Frank, and I'm not a fire inspector."

"A cop's always a cop," Ferro countered.

"Maybe, but I'm also out of the loop. Terry was my conduit into the department, and he's been wired ever since the Ruger thing."

Ferro nodded. "What about other things in town? Unexplained deaths, anything like that?"

"Not that I've heard of. Saul would be the one to talk to about . . ." his voice trailed away and he studied Ferro's eyes. "What exactly did Saul tell you?"

"Hasn't he spoken to you about his suspicions?"

"What suspicions? What are you talking about?"

Ferro's eyes were hard for a moment, but then his expression softened and he shook his head. "That's just it, Crow—I don't really know what I'm asking. I had a short talk with Saul and all he did was make extremely vague hints and when pressed wouldn't actually get to any point. If it was anyone else I would have thought he'd been hitting the sauce too hard and was just talking shit, but Saul Weinstock impressed me as one of the more level-headed men in this town, so I'm having a harder time walking away than I otherwise would have."

"Any idea what he was hinting at?"

"No. You?"

"No. He was pretty vague with me the last couple of times we spoke. Said he wanted to talk to me today, though."

Ferro grunted. "Interesting." He took a business card from his inside jacket pocket. "If there's anything in what he says, would you be willing to give me a call? One cop to an—"

"Dude, if you don't want me to play the 'this town is weird' card then don't play the 'brothers behind the badge' card on me. Saul's one of my closest friends. If there is something he needs and if that something is best handled by you, or if it involves the Boyd case, then yeah, I'll give you a call." With a smile he plucked the card from between Ferro's fingers and tucked it in his pants pocket. "Speaking of which . . . what about Boyd? Anything new?"

Ferro shook his head. "No one's had a whiff of him since he fled this jurisdiction. After the first few sightings in Trenton and Newark he's dropped off the radar, so the general feeling is that he's either gone to ground somewhere—a safe house—or he's out of the country."

"Gut?"

"I think he's dead."

Crow pretended to toast him. "Here's hoping."

"Mmm. It'd be nice if this case just quietly wound down and blew away. It's been a major pain in my ass for too long. Yours, too, I imagine. Speaking of which, how's your lady?"

They lapsed into a more genteel conversation and after a while Ferro shook Crow's hand and excused himself, and Crow watched as he and the other officers headed out of the house and, Crow thought, out of their lives.

He was looking around for Val when he felt a hand close around his elbow and turned to see Saul Weinstock standing at his side. "Word with you, Crow?" Weinstock's face had looked pinched earlier, and up close it showed even more signs of stress. "Listen . . . have you noticed anything, um, 'funny' going on around town lately?"

Crow suppressed a smile. "Everyone's asking me that."

"I know, I saw you talking to Frank. What did he say? He tell you what we were talking about?" Weinstock's questions came out so fast it was like they were wired together.

"He said you were bugged about something. What's up?"

"I told him that there have been some bad things happening around here."

"You said as much on the phone yesterday?"

"Yeah, yeah," he mumbled while fishing a tin of Altoids out of his pocket; he opened it, looked inside, closed the tin, and put it back without having taken one. Crow had the impression that Weinstock had not even registered doing any of that.

"You need to lay off the microbrews, kemosabe," he said.

Weinstock frowned. "Haven't had a drink yet today," he said, "but it's a good idea."

He started to move away but Crow caught his arm. "Dude . . . what the hell's with you? You're acting fruitier than a nutcake."

Weinstock smiled faintly. "It's . . . nothing. I'm just being paranoid."

"Saul," Crow moved closer, "don't give me that bullshit. Something's frying your grits and it's not the corn blight."

"I'm not sure I want to go into it right now," he said, and then seemed to remember that it was he who had brought it up. He took a breath, blinked a few moments, and then met Crow's gaze. "Look, some funky stuff has been happening at the hospital. I shouldn't go into it right now. Hell, I shouldn't even be talking to you about this."

"Too late."

"Crow . . . this is going to sound really crazy, but I want a straight answer."

"Ooo-kay."

"Do you believe in ghosts?"

Crow smiled. "Are you freakin' kidding me here? You're asking the biggest horror geek in Bucks County if he believes in ghosts?"

Weinstock touched Crow's arm. "I'm being serious here. Not Halloween stuff, either. Just answer me straight. Do you believe in ghosts?"

"Sure I do, Saul, but you don't, so why are you asking me?"

The doctor looked around at the other people milling in the kitchen, some of them smiling as they chatted and ate and drank. He licked his lips and then looked back at Crow.

"You're right. Forget I said anything." He went to move away.

"Whoa! Slow down, Saul . . . I didn't mean to insult you here . . ."

"You didn't. Forget I said anything." He clapped Crow on the shoulder, gave him an enigmatic smile, and then melted into the crowd, leaving Crow feeling completely at sea.

"What was that all about?" The voice came from behind him and Crow jumped a foot. He spun around and Val was standing there holding a paper plate piled high with salad. "What are you so jumpy about?"

"I just had the weirdest conversation with Saul," he said, and told her about it.

Val nodded. "I saw that he was looking stressed and asked Rachel about it, but she said that Saul's been overworked lately. He's been pulling a lot of long days at the hospital and is always exhausted, and yet she said—tired as he is—he can't sleep at nights. He usually sits up on the Internet or locked in his office at home and then falls asleep around dawn."

"Maybe whatever's eating Terry is catching," Crow said.

"I don't think so," Val said, and ate a forkful of spinach.

"Terry's been coming apart at the seams for weeks now. No, whatever's going on with Saul is something new. It's just been the last couple of days, Rachel said. Since those police officers were killed."

"That can't be it. Saul wasn't close with either of them."

"Then what's your suggestion?"

"I don't know. I'll call him tomorrow. Maybe take him out to lunch, see what's up." At that point Val's cousin Andrea and her fiancé came over to give her hugs and kisses and the tide of conversation turned back to the immediate. By the time the long day ended and Rachel and Sarah had helped Val and Crow clean up, Crow had completely forgotten about his conversation with Weinstock.

### (3)

Mike cycled back toward town, climbing the long hills, gliding down the other side, eyes always flicking left and right down side roads, expecting to see the grille of the big wrecker. Nothing. As the days passed he was becoming more and more convinced that the incident on the road had been different than he remembered it. Sure it was a near thing, and sure it was scary as hell, and sure it hurt a lot— but whether it was intentional or not was something he was less sure about. He was also certain that if it had been Vic driving the wrecker then that prick would have found some way to taunt him with the information. Vic would have used the threat of it to hurt him.

But who else in town had access to a wrecker? From what little he could see that night on the road, it looked like a big tow truck and that told him nothing. Shanahan's garage had a couple of them, and there had to be other garages with tow trucks in the area. He thought about the guys who worked at Shanahan's with Vic. None of them ever came over to the house; none of them were friends with Vic. There was Buddy Tobin, Josh Adams, and that big guy everyone called Tow-Truck Eddie. Mike thought about that as he swooped down another hill. Crow had said that Eddie was a part-time cop, and Mike had seen him that first day Crow was in the hospital. They'd passed each other by the front doors.

Then something occurred to Mike, and it seemed like a really good idea. If Eddie worked with Vic, and drove a tow truck, *and* was a cop, then he'd be the perfect person to ask about who might have been driving that wrecker out here that night. He was nodding emphatically to himself as he pedaled along. It was a great idea. He chewed on it, working it out. He could say that he heard from some kid in school that a wrecker had almost run some other kid down. Make it sound like something he just heard around school; he could ask the cop to see if he'd heard anything. Would the guy tell him if he had? Mike wasn't sure, but this was one area where his being Vic's stepson might be an advantage. All Mike had to do was drop Vic's name to remind him of that connection, and then idly ask the question. Yeah, that would work. He'd ask Tow-Truck Eddie.

He headed into town with the wind behind him while deep within his soul, far beneath his consciousness, the chrysalis within him screamed.

# Chapter 20

## (1)

Two days earlier, on October 7, Willard Fowler Newton had gone out to the Guthrie farm to interview Malcolm Crow and Val Guthrie. The interview had been going really well until Crow had said something that had caused Newton to break one of his promises. After that, things had gone very badly indeed.

Crow had said, "I think Ubel Griswold was a monster."

It sounded so silly. It was a nonsensical thing to say, and Newton had actually laughed out loud when Crow had said it, taking it as one of Crow's many jokes. Crow was not joking. Instead his face had gone dark and he had said, "Remember our agreement, Newt."

One of the terms of that agreement had been that Newton had to promise not to laugh in Crow's face—and he had done just that. He had laughed out loud and jabbed Crow in the shoulder in a *that's a good one* gesture, but Crow had slapped his hand away and then that small, affable guy, Crow the jokester, Crow the town chucklehead, had vanished and Newt was staring into the eyes of Crow the man who had faced down the Cape May Killer—*twice!*—and had beaten him. Had, in fact, killed him. The change was that abrupt. One minute Crow looked like a sawed-off Greg Kinnear with vulnerable eyes and an easy grin, and the next second—the next *split fragment* of a second—he was a cold-eyed stranger with no trace of humor at all in his face, and Newton could actually feel all of the warmth leak out of the moment like water from a cracked jug. Newton's laughter had died in his throat and he looked away from those eyes over to Val, and saw the coldest blue eyes in town staring back at him.

Newton said, "Oh, come *on*!"

"Perhaps you'd better leave," Val said, setting her cold coffee cup down. "I think we're done here."

"Jesus, Crow . . . Val . . . I'm sorry, I didn't mean. . . ."

Crow just waved it off. "Thought I could trust you, Newt. Sorry I was wrong."

Crow got up from where he'd been sitting on the step and went inside the house. After a full minute—an unending minute while Newton stood there and endured Val's coldly disappointed stare—it became clear that Crow was not coming back out.

He tried to explain to Val, to apologize, but she just stood up and regarded him coolly for a moment. "Go on," she said, "get out." Then she followed Crow into the house and closed the screen and storm doors both. The sound of the lock clicking was huge in his ears.

Newton had gone home, too. Halfway home he had used his cell to call Crow, but there was no answer. Caller ID was a bitch. The following day was the funeral for Val's father and Newton almost went out there, hoping to apologize, but he just couldn't make himself intrude into Val's grief, not even to get himself off the hook.

Newton had been dismissed before. He was a reporter and that meant he was used to slammed doors and closed mouths—and certainly he'd made no friends with Terry Wolfe after breaking the cover-up story—but somehow this felt worse, and it was more than losing a major source for the feature he was researching. He had *liked* Crow, and there had been a look of hurt in the man's eyes that was damn near unbearable.

When the phone rang at quarter to five in the morning of October 10, it startled him and he cried out before snatching at the bedside phone. "Hello?"

He expected it to be Dick Hangood, but it wasn't. "Okay, Kermit, here's the deal."

Newton paused. "Crow?"

"No, it's Tickle Me Elmo—now, you listening?"

He sat up, kicking the blankets to the floor. "Yes!"

"Val thinks I should kick your nuts up into your chest cavity, but I'm willing to give this a second chance."

"Um . . . okay . . . Thanks?"

"So, if you still want that story—and if you can keep your reactions on a short leash—"

"Yes! Crow, I'm sorry. You just caught me off guard."

"We'll kiss and make up later. For now I have a new condition to add to our arrangement."

"Sure! Anything!" He said, meaning it.

"Here's the deal, on Friday morning I'm going to go on a little field trip, and I want you to go with me. I'm going to go out to Ubel Griswold's old farm, and I want you to go with me."

"Sure," Newton said at once, and then what Crow said caught up with him. "Did you say—?"

"Yeah. Sound like fun to you? Me neither, but you meet me outside my store at seven-thirty Friday morning. Dress for the woods and pack a lunch. We're going to have to hike in. See you then," he concluded and then hung up before Newton could reply.

Newton lay in bed and stared up at the shadows on the ceiling and wondered just what the hell he had agreed to.

### (2)

"But he hasn't been home for three days!"

Officer Jim Polk spread his hands, sighed and said, "Look, Andy, there's not much we can do. Ritchie is over eighteen and you yourself said he took a lot of his stuff with him. Clothes and such."

"Which means he's run away!" stressed Andy McClintock, tapping his thick index finger firmly on Polk's desk.

"But at eighteen he's allowed to run away," Polk said. "According to the law, at eighteen he's old enough to leave home without parental permission, so there's really nothing we can do. Hell, at eighteen I was in the Corps and carrying a gun. Eighteen is a lot different from fifteen, and that's what you're not seeing."

"He didn't even leave a note. Nothing, not a damned word. Just up and goes one night." Andy McClintock was a big bear of a man, tall and stocky, tending toward fat but still strong from long hours working his dairy farm. He had callused hands and a permanently sunburned face. His eyes were filled with worry and it bubbled out of him as anger.

"I'm sure you're scared, and pissed off, but listen to me, Andy, 'cause I don't know how many more times I can say this—there isn't anything I can do. If he was sixteen I'd have his name and description sent out to every agency in the tristate area, but I'm not even *allowed* to do that with an eighteen-year-old."

Andy McClintock straightened himself to his full height of six feet and glared at the seated Polk. He opened his mouth to say something very biting, and Polk could all but smell the acid forming on Andy's tongue, but the moment of anger passed and Andy's shoulders sagged, his face looking both confused and helpless. "Jim . . . he's my only kid. . . ."

Polk rose, came around the desk, and put his hand on Andy's beefy shoulder. "Look, I'll ask around anyway, okay? Let a few of the other guys know, too, talk to some of my buddies in Black Marsh and Crestville. Unofficial. Maybe we'll hear something from someone. If we do, I'll let you know first thing."

"You promise?"

"Absolutely. First thing. But," he said as they stood in the open doorway, "just give the kid a little time. Let him blow off some steam, get laid, get drunk. He'll get it out of his system and come crawling home. Hell, we all did that at least once."

Andy nodded and shook Polk's hand and left. Polk watched him get in his car and drive out of the lot, then he turned and pulled the door shut behind him. The office was empty except for Ginny, who dozed at her desk, a Danielle Steele novel open and resting against her bosom. Quietly, unhurriedly, Polk walked over to the farthest desk and lifted the handset of the phone. He punched in a number and waited until someone picked up.

"Shanahan's Garage."

"Let me speak to Vic," Polk said. "Tell him it's Jim Polk."

"Minute."

Polk waited for nearly three minutes, then a voice at the other end said, "What do you want? I'm in the middle of a valve job."

"I just had Andy McClintock in my office, came to report him missing."

There was a brief silence. "Yeah? And?"

"I told him what I told all the others."

"How many's that? How many have actually been into the office to make reports?"

"Six, so far. That's a lot for just a few days, Vic."

"How many of them does Gus know about?"

"Maybe two. I've been doing the day work, so I've been taking almost all of the reports, and the ones I don't take usually come across my desk at some point. The only two I couldn't intercept were filed with someone else when I was off shift, but I can get into the computer and fix those."

"Has Gus said anything?"

"Nope. Far as he knows, it's just a couple missing persons. I've been inputting vacation notices for some of them, too. That way our guys are even doing drive-bys to make sure no one breaks in while the residents are away. I got all of this nailed down. Gus never checks, and I mean never. It's why he made me sergeant in the first place, because he knows I like to handle all the reports and shit. We're building a nice smokescreen, and public panic is helping. At least a dozen families have left town anyway because of the manhunt, and a lot of people have pulled their kids out of school. That's

stuff that happened without us doing anything, so it's working as a nice cover. We're covered here, Vic, but if this thing
goes on longer than a couple more weeks then it's going to
get hard to fudge it. For right now, though, no one knows shit
and that goes double for Gus."

"You'd better make sure you keep it that way, 'cause I
don't want him even getting so much as a whiff of this. Not
until the Man says so."

"No sweat. Gus ain't exactly the sharpest knife in the
drawer." He cleared his throat. "Even so, Vic, I think it
would be a good idea to have Ritchie call his dad, maybe say
that he's down in Atlantic City, or up in New York. Someplace he'd go with his buddies. Better for Andy to hear from
him than to start a fuss."

There was a short silence before Vic said, "That's a pretty
smart idea, Jimmy-boy."

"We should have some of, um, *them*, make some calls to
relatives or friends—and especially to their jobs. Call in sick,
or say they have to go out of town for some reason. Have
Carby and the other parents write notes to the schools saying
the family's going to visit relatives somewhere. Y'know, settle things down, make it look normal, otherwise people are
going to start talking, and then they'll starting wondering . . ."

"I get it," Vic said. "And you're right, that's a good plan.
I'll get some of the others to make calls, or send some e-mails.
Good friggin' call."

"Great, that'll help calm things down. Otherwise who knows
who might start putting two and two together." Polk paused
and braced himself before heading off onto a new tack. "Look,
Vic . . . this stuff you got me doing is pretty risky. . . ."

"And you're getting paid, so what's your point?"

"That's just it . . . I'm not sure I got paid enough for this
sort of thing. This stuff can get me a federal rap, let alone
state time. You have no idea the kind of risks I'm taking. I
just think what you're asking me to do is worth more than
you've given me so far."

Vic's voice was soft and wintry. "Am I hearing this right?
Are you putting the squeeze on me? Is that what I'm hear-

ing? Maybe you'd like me to come over and deliver it personally. Kiss your ass, too, to show my respect since you're doing such a stellar job."

"Vic, I—"

"Maybe you want to bang my wife, too? Would you like that? A little roll in the hay with Lois just to show my appreciation for all your hard work? Maybe a tidy little thank you blow job. How 'bout that? Just my way of saying thanks for being supercop."

"C'mon, Vic, I was just—"

"Or maybe," Vic said, his voice becoming even colder, "maybe you'd like one of *them* to deliver it? How 'bout that? Would you like that? Hey . . . I can have Ritchie himself bring you your cash. Bring you your reward."

Polk's throat seized shut. Blood roared in his ears and he could feel his gut knotting like a fist.

"Maybe even Karl himself? How would that be? Would you like Karl to hand deliver your blood money? That way you could explain to Karl how valuable you've been to us. I'm sure he'd be very impressed. You know how much Karl likes cops anyway. I'll bet he'd think you were the cat's ass, Jim. Yeah, maybe that'd be good. You and Karl. I could have him drop by tonight. Bring you a token of our esteem."

Only strangled sounds wormed their way out of Polk's throat.

Vic snorted with disgust. "Listen to me, asshole—you got your money, and you'll get more—but I'll be the one to decide what you get and when you get it. Do you understand me?" Polk gurgled something and Vic snapped, "I didn't quite hear that, Jim."

"Y . . . yes . . . !" Polk gasped.

"Good. Now you go and you do your frigging job and don't you ever dare try and put the squeeze on me again. Don't even dream about it. You just do your job and you'd better do it right, or so help me God I'll arrange a whole party at your place. Karl and Ritchie and all of *them*. I'll bet they could make it last a long time for you, and you really wouldn't like that, Jim, no by God you would not."

Vic disconnected abruptly at the other end. For a horrible frozen span of seconds Polk stood there, clutching the phone to his head, eyes bulging with terror, heart hammering in his chest. Then he slammed the phone down and made it into the bathroom at a dead run, just barely slamming his way into a stall before he vomited.

### (3)

"I know it's cool and all that," Mike said, "but why do I have to learn how to use a sword? How is that going to help me in a fight? I mean . . . I can't exactly pull out a samurai sword next time Vic gets in one of his moods."

Crow grinned. "Though that would be kind of cool . . . take a sword and cut a few pounds of ugly off that son of a bitch." He held a sheathed sword in his hands, admiring it fondly. The scabbard was finished in a matte black, rough and cool to the touch, and the knuckle guard, or *tsuba*, was a round plate of wrought iron in the pattern of a small flock of crows flying from tree to tree. By contrast, the sword Mike held was carved from a single piece of oak, with only a line cut like a channel running around the shaft to indicate the break between handle and blade. "I told you I was going to shortcut the process for you," Crow said, "but at the same time I need you to have some idea for where it comes from and how it works. Jujutsu is science and art kind of blended together."

In a fair approximation of Obi Wan Kenobi, Mike said, "A lightsaber is the weapon of a Jedi—not as clumsy or random as a blaster." He slashed it back and forth and made electrical humming noises on each pass.

Crow grinned at that. "I'll give you some books on the samurai, Mike . . . and you can look up some stuff on the Net. They were among the greatest warriors in history, and to them the sword was emblematic of their soul. In fact they believed that their sword was a physical manifestation of their soul."

Mike looked at his wooden sword and then at Crow's beautiful weapon and then cocked an eyebrow. "So . . . my soul is a beat-up piece of wood and yours is a work of art?"

"Well, of course, that's obvious," Crow said straight-faced, then smiled and shook his head. "No, the difference between the two weapons is like the difference between what you are and what you can become." When he saw that Mike wasn't following him, he tried it another way. "You look at the two swords and see the difference between us, or at least what you perceive is the difference between us, but in fact the difference is that your sword is blunt. Just like you right now. Now, consider Vic for a moment . . . he's dangerous, but he isn't sharp. He isn't refined. He's the perfect definition of blunt force." He saw Mike glance suddenly down at the wooden sword as if he wanted to spit on it and throw it away. "Whereas you may be starting blunt and unrefined you are not going to stay that way. Are you?"

Mike hefted the wooden sword and considered its weight, and then glanced at Crow's sword. He shook his head.

"So, I'm going to show you some things to do with the sword because the sword teaches us so much."

"Like what?"

"Glad you asked," said Crow, and winked. "Kenjutsu, the Japanese art of swordplay, may not be practical on the streets of the twenty-first century, that I'll grant you, but the process of learning the sword *is*. Very much so, because it teaches focus, balance, precision, timing, control. You see, there's a paradox in swordplay that is at the heart of its appeal. You know what a paradox is?"

"Dude, how many science fiction novels have I read? Of course I know what a paradox is."

"I stand corrected. Well, the paradox at the heart of kenjutsu is that there is no way to achieve perfection in swordsmanship. No matter how good you are, there is always a level of skill beyond where you are."

"So . . . what's that mean? That it doesn't matter how good you are?"

"Not exactly. What it means is that it only matters that you are striving to be better than you are." Crow let Mike chew on that for a moment.

Mike rolled his eyes. "Is this one of those 'the journey *is* the destination' things?"

"Yep, and if you're about to dismiss that concept just because you've heard it before—don't. In this case it's especially important because in learning the sword we aren't just learn to be good at it . . . we're discovering that each time we train we're better at it, and that the more we concentrate on it and the harder we train, the more subtle and deft we become. You see, when the samurai trained all those thousands of hours in swordplay, only part of it was to sharpen their skills in case they had to fight. What they were really doing was sharpening their souls." He paused. "They were refining who they were. Cutting away at the elements of their personalities that did not advance them forward in spirit."

"You're starting to go all Yoda on me here."

"Yeah, I guess." Crow sucked his teeth for a minute, assessing his own words. "Tell you what . . . let's just do some training with the sword and then we'll see if you're getting anything out of it. Is that simple enough?"

Mike shrugged. "I guess."

Crow walked over and flipped open the top of the plastic cooler that was set on the back step of his building, fished around in it, and then brought out an apple. "I'm going to throw this at your head," he said casually. "Try to knock it out of the way with your sword."

"You kidding me here?" Mike said.

"Nope," said Crow and tossed the apple. He threw it underhanded and without much speed or force, but it bumped Mike in the forehead despite the wild swings of the wooden *bokken*.

"Ow!"

"Sorry. Now, pick it up and throw it back."

Looking angry, Mike picked up the apple and threw it. Harder than he intended and much faster, right at Crow's face. There was a rasping sound, a glitter of sunlight on steel, and the two halves of the apple hit the back wall of the building on either side of where Crow stood. He held the sword in one hand, the scabbard in the other, and he was smiling. With a snap of his wrist he pointed the sword down at the floor and droplets of moisture from the apple flew from the oiled blade and patterned the flagstones; then with a flash that was too fast for Mike to follow, Crow swung the sword around and returned it to its scabbard.

"Holy shit!" Mike cried.

"Watch your language, you juvenile delinquent," Crow said, feeling pleased with himself—especially since he sometimes bungled that particular trick and screwing it up right now would have really sucked. That it had worked so well just then he counted as a nice gesture on the part of the universe—not for himself, but for Mike, whose eyes were sparkling with excitement. "So . . . you wanna learn how to be a samurai?" Crow asked.

Mike looked at the two pieces of apple, then at Crow's sword, and then at his own.

"Yeah," he said softly and when he looked up, Crow could see that something had ignited in the boy's eyes.

But Crow read it wrong. Mike was not standing there dazzled by what Crow had just done—he was impressed, sure—but seeing the sweet elegance of that cut had done something else to Mike and he was teetering on the edge of understanding it. He was also dangerously close to lapsing into another fugue state, but that part of his mind was closed to introspection. No, the realization that was slowly catching fire in his mind was how close all of this—Crow, the sword, the skill of the cut—was to the stuff of his recent dreams. Even the sword Crow held looked the same. Mike was almost positive it *was* the same, though he knew it couldn't be. As Crow's sword flashed through the air Mike felt as if somehow lightning had danced from the edge of that blade right into his chest. He felt supercharged and while he stood there listening to Crow speak and not taking in a single word, Mike's grip on the sword *changed*. It was a subtle thing, but as he held the sword in his hand his fingers flexed to let the handle rest more comfortably against his palm, his elbow bent a bit more to allow his forearm to counterbalance the weight of the long wooden blade, and he raised the tip of the sword so that it would not touch the ground.

He was aware of none of this. The changes were small, the corrections subtle, but thereafter he never picked up the *bokken* and held it incorrectly again. Weeks later, when he held a real sword in his hands, all of this would matter.

Worlds turn on such moments.

### (4)

Newton set his coffee cup down, rubbed his tired eyes, and turned back to his monitor screen. He had four Explorer browser screens open and he was nearly fried from surfing the Net all day, getting as much backstory as he could on the information Crow and Val had given him. He did background searches on every name Crow had given him—Vic Wingate, Polk, Bernhardt, half a dozen others—working to get inside of the story, to try and see it from the point of view of a nine-year-old Malcolm Crow. He also searched for any scrap of information he could find on Ubel Griswold. If he was going to go with Crow into the forest to find Griswold's old farm—thirty years overgrown—he wanted to know the man, perhaps to demystify him as a protection against what Crow believed of him.

The research, though, was hampered by too much information. Not specifically about Griswold, but about the haunted history of the town. Since 1957 there had been fifty-six separate university studies by paranormal researchers on the hauntings in Pine Deep. The Sci-Fi Channel had run a whole season of one of its ghost hunter shows in town in 2004. The Discovery Channel had done a special last Halloween on the remarkable number of graveyards in Pine Deep (eleven), and on how many of the graves were disturbed each year with no forensic evidence left revealing who had dug them up. When Newton had done a Google search on the keywords "Pine Deep" and "haunted," he got fourteen thousand hits. Granted a lot of them were repeats of stories about the town's yearly Halloween celebrations, and movie listings from the film *Ghostwalk* that Dimension Films had set in the town, but that still left thousands of references to strange happenings in the town. Malcolm Crow's name appeared as an information source on 1,944 sites.

"The man gets around," Newton said.

As Newton went through his notes, he cut and pasted any unique keyword into the search engine, usually getting some kind of hit, useful or not. When he reached the name Ubel Griswold, he put it into the search screen, hit the button and waited, expecting little. When he switched from using the local catchphrase "Pine Deep Massacre" to "Pine Deep" and "killings" he got more useful hits than he had gotten prior to interviewing Crow, including a list of all sixteen of the official victims, and then a university site that had seventeen names on the list, with Griswold's filling in the last spot. Then he hit one Web site reference to Griswold that was completely different from all the others:

. . . 1589: Peter Stubb (aka Peter Stube, Peeter Stubbe, or Peter Stumpf; aka Ubel Griswold, Abel Greenwyck, or Abel Griswald) is the subject of one of the most famous werewolf trials in history. After being tortured on the rack Stubb confesses to having practiced black magic since he was twelve years old. He claims the devil had given him a magical belt which enabled him to metamorphose into "the likeness of a greedy devouring Woolf, strong and mighty, with eyes great and large, which in the night sparkeled like vnto brandes of fire, a mouth great and wide, with most sharpe and cruell teeth, A huge body, and mightye pawes." He also claims to have killed and eaten animals and humans for twenty-five years. The court, appalled by these crimes sentences him to having his skin torn off by red-hot pincers before being beheaded.

—www.werewolfparadigm.upenn.edu/JonathaN

He looked at it for a while, grunted, and made a note next to Griswold's name on his notepad. The notation he made was "Ancestor?" That done, he moved on. It was an interesting coincidence of name, nothing more. He hit the back button to go to the Google screen again and kept working.

**(5)**

Terry Wolfe knocked on the door of the Crow's Nest despite the "Back in Twenty Minutes" sign. When he got no answer he pulled his Razor from his pocket, flipped it open, and punched in Crow's number. Crow answered on the fifth ring.

"Your door's locked," Terry barked.

"We're around back."

"I don't want to walk around the block. Go open the front door." He flipped his phone shut and waited with bad grace for Crow to unlock. Terry rubbed his eyes and sighed. He sighed a lot these days, and was even aware of it. He tried not to, but he kept doing it, only catching it on the exhale. He tried to work out every day, but lately he couldn't face the gym, couldn't even face his own Nordic-Trak. Though he didn't look it he felt soft and heavy, and his posture was bad. For days now he had been wearing his steel-rimmed glasses because he couldn't keep his hands steady enough to put in his contacts. His fingers shook so bad he was afraid of putting out an eye. Yesterday he had gotten his short hair and beard trimmed, but he hadn't shaved since then and above and below the neat beard there was an unkempt red-gold five o'clock shadow.

When Crow unlocked the door, Terry brushed past him, accidentally clipping Crow's shoulder. Crow grunted at the impact, but Terry just let it go; it wasn't worth the effort to apologize. "Jesus, Terry, you look like shit," Crow said.

"I feel like shit," Terry said as he lumbered through the store, pausing only a half-step when he saw that Mike Sweeney—looking sweaty and shifty—had come in from out back and had slid surreptitiously behind the counter. The kid waved and may have said something, but Terry didn't want to waste effort on pleasantries, either. Silently he walked through the shop and jerked open the door to Crow's apartment toward the kitchen, and went inside with Crow following along. Terry went right to the kitchen and opened the refrigerator door and looked bleakly inside, poked listlessly at the swollen and vaguely threatening packages of forgotten food, gave a disgusted shrug, and slammed the door. "Make some tea, will you? You got anything herbal?"

"Just peppermint and chamomile."

"Chamomile." Terry rubbed his callused palms over his face.

Crow filled the Wile E. Coyote kettle with water and set it on the burner.

"Why's that kid running the store? Since when does he work here?" Terry asked.

"Since the other day . . . like I *told* you the other day."

"I probably wasn't listening," Terry said.

"I've seen you look better." Crow cleared his throat. "Still having those dreams?"

"Every time I close my eyes."

"And, um, Mandy. You still seeing her?"

Terry grunted and nodded.

"Damn, brother. You talk to your shrink about all this?"

Terry pulled a big pillbox out of his pocket and rattled it. "All he knows how to do is prescribe drugs." Terry began opening cabinets, shoving boxes of Fruit Loops and Count Chocula back and forth in search of nothing in particular. He took a box of Wheat Thins from one cabinet, fished inside, stared at the cracker as if it was something totally alien to this planet, and then ate it without tasting it. He slammed the box back into the cabinet. Gloomily, he stalked back into the living room and threw himself into an overstuffed chair. In silence Crow finished making the tea and handed a mug to Terry, who took it with and a grunt. Terry said, "Crow, for God's sake, stop looking at me like I have two heads. If I'm going crazy, then I'm going crazy. Don't worry, once Halloween is over I'm planning on checking myself into a hospital for a nice long stay, and when I get out—providing they don't throw away the key—I'm taking Sarah and the kids to Jamaica for the rest of the winter. No crops, blighted or otherwise. And no Halloween."

"Sounds like a plan." Crow cleared his throat again.

"And stop clearing your goddamn throat."

"Well, dude, cut me a break. My best friend is going crackers on me and I have no freaking clue about what to say or what to do."

Terry looked at him and for a moment a smile softened the worry lines on his face. "Being my best friend is doing a lot, believe me."

"Pardon me while I say nothing during the awkward pause that has to follow that kind of statement."

Terry threw a small pillow at him; Crow ducked. "I really didn't come here to discuss my lost marbles," he said. "I think there's something wrong with Saul."

"*You* think there's something wrong with someone else?" Which made Terry grin again. Crow liked to see it. "But I know what you mean. Coupla times we *almost* had a conversation about something, but each time we get right up to it he gets spooked and bugs out."

"Saul's gotten really withdrawn the last couple of days. Skipped dinner last night, and those plans were made weeks ago, and blew me off again for lunch today. I talked to Rachel and she says he's acting weird at home, too. He's all paranoid, jumps at his own shadow. I just think something's wrong with him."

"You think he's sick?"

"If I had to guess, I'd say he was more scared than sick, and believe I know the signs and symptoms."

"Scared? Of what?"

"I don't know."

"Maybe he's seeing ghosts, too," Crow said.

Terry shot him a look. "That a joke?"

"No—hard as it is to believe. At Henry's funeral Saul asked me if I believed in ghosts."

"What'd you tell him?"

"Just what you'd expect me to tell him, that of course I believed in ghosts. Let's face it, big mon, I kind of believe in everything."

"All this seems to have started around the time the whole Ruger-Boyd thing got going. Did he say why he was asking about ghosts?"

"No. Not yet, anyway. Maybe this is not about ghosts, bro. Maybe this is like some kind of mass hysteria. Like a town wide case of post-traumatic stress disorder. With the blight, the Ruger thing . . . everyone's genuinely freaked, and for good reason. Happy suburbia doesn't really prepare folks for this kind of stuff."

"No kidding. Really?"

Crow grinned. He sipped his tea and said, "Terry . . . there's something else I want to talk to you about. You know that reporter, Newton from Black Marsh? The one you hate?"

"How could I forget?"

"Well, he's working on a feature piece about the town's haunted history, hoping to sell it to one of the Sunday color supplements like *Parade*. Anyway, he came out to the farm the other day and interviewed me and Val, and . . . well, I decided to tell him all about the summer of '76. Everything . . . including about Griswold."

Terry dropped his teacup and it shattered on the floor, spattering his trouser cuffs.

### (6)

"How'd he take it?" Val asked.

Crow was stretched out on his couch, alone in his apartment. Through the door he could hear Mike talking to a customer, but inside the room was quiet. Muddy Whiskers was curled into a warm ball against his hip. "It could have gone better. First he just sat there in stunned silence for like a minute, minute and a half—and then he started yelling. Called me stupid, called me an insensitive asshole, called me a few other words that a week ago I would have bet a thousand dollars that he didn't even *know*, and then he stormed out."

"Smooth," she said. "They should send you to the Middle East to see if you can work your magic there. Is he even speaking to you?"

"He'll get over it."

"I guess. Before that happened, he was opening up about his dreams and all that. He's a mess, Val, but at least he's seeing a doc, and he's able to discuss it with me. He said that when the season is over he's going to take Sarah and the kids to the islands for a long vacation."

"At least that sounds hopeful rather than crazy." She sighed. "Everyone's under a lot of pressure right now. Mark is still acting like a jerk and Connie spends half the day crying. I'm embarrassed to say it, but they're both starting to get on my nerves. I'd rather be alone here than have to babysit them. I do have my own stuff to deal with right now."

"I know you do, babe. Which is why I have something planned for tonight."

"Tonight? I told you that I had a Growers Association meeting tonight. I won't be getting home until after eight."

"Eight's good."

"What's the plan? And don't tell me there's a *Twilight Zone* marathon on—"

"Nope, but it is a secret. You go to your meeting and I'll see you at home."

After she'd hung up, Crow folded his phone and laid it on his chest as he stared at the ceiling, thinking about Terry and Weinstock, Mark and Connie. And Val. Always about Val.

*Ubel Griswold sends his regards.* It popped into his head like a firecracker and he jumped, sitting up so fast that his cat tumbled to the floor and howled in surprise and fury and his cell phone bounced off the floor and then skittered under the couch. All at once the immense reality of what he was planning to do on Friday hit him like a fist. Friday morning—just three days from now—he was going to be going down the long slope from the Passion Pit, deep into the darkness of Dark Hollow, and through the woods to try and find the house of Ubel Griswold. On Friday the 13th.

"Jesus Christ," he said.

# Chapter 21

## (1)

Crow went back in to the store and worked for a few hours while Mike sat behind the counter and finished his homework, a paper on Ray Bradbury's *Fahrenheit 451*. Crow used the time to make a battery of phone calls related to the big Halloween celebration. He called the Dead In Drive-in to make sure all of the films had been ordered, and then called Ken Foree, the star of the original *Dawn of the Dead*, and went over the itinerary for the presentation he'd be giving. Then he called Brinke Stevens and chatted amiably with the "scream queen" about the talk she would be giving after the screening of a couple of her films. Then he made a conference call to his two webmasters, David Kramer and Geoff Strauss, to remind them to post only PG-13 versions of Brinke Stevens's publicity shots on the Hayride's Web site—not the versions the two of them had downloaded and e-mailed to him. They were crushed, but Crow reminded them that the Hayride was a family attraction, after all.

He made a call to Pittsburgh and talked with Tom Savini, and went over the budget for the makeup effects workshop he was giving at the college. Savini was going to have the workshop students do full-on monster makeup so that the whole class would look like flesh-eating zombies. The materials were expensive, but every seat had already been booked and he asked Savini to consider doing a second workshop the following day. Pine Deep was going to *own* Halloween, no doubt of that.

When he was done with his calls, he ordered pizza delivery and when it arrived, Mike saved his file, shut down his laptop, and the two of them taunted each other with science fiction trivia while they plowed through double-pepperoni, onion rings, and large Cokes. Customers came and went, waited on by both of them, their mouths puffed out like chipmunks around big bites of pizza.

Munching the last onion ring, Crow strolled outside for some air. Corn Hill was crammed with cars as Tuesday afternoon faded into evening and the after-work crowd mingled with a fresh tide of tourists. There was laughter everywhere and music coming from at least three bars, the happy sounds spilling out into the street. It was dark, but the street was alight with neon and the glow from hundreds of store windows. Crow leaned against the wall by his door and watched the crowd as he chewed. He took his cell phone out of his pocket and punched in the number for Saul Weinstock. It was answered on the third ring.

"Crow! I'm so glad you finally called."

"I tried earlier but you were in a meeting, and then I got busy at the store. So, what's the big thing you want to tell me? You're acting very weird these days."

"A lot of things are very weird these days," Weinstock said softly.

"Oh good, you're being even more cryptic."

"Look, I need to run a few things by you. Can you come over tomorrow?"

"Can't . . . I'm taking a reporter down into Dark Hollow tomorrow. He's doing a story on the Reaper Murders and I—"

"You're *what*?"

Crow explained, but Weinstock replied with a huge sigh. "You're a moron sometimes, Crow. Jesus H. Christ. Look, I need to see you. Soon."

"Okay. How about tomorrow night?"

"'Night'?" Weinstock echoed. "No, I don't think that would be good. Can you meet me at my office Saturday morning? Say, nine?"

"Sure."

"Good. And, Crow . . . be careful down there. I mean it . . . really careful." With that he hung up.

Crow looked at his phone "Everyone in this town is freaking nuts!"

He went back inside. The store was empty of customers and Mike was perched on the stool behind the counter just staring off into space, his eyes half-closed like a mystic in a trance, and Crow had to snap his fingers a couple of times to shake the kid out of it.

"You're not getting weird on me, too, are you?" he said with a smile, and though Mike smiled back and shook his head, there was an odd distant and dreamy quality about him that dissipated slowly over the next hour. Crow didn't like that, either.

At five-thirty Crow pulled on his jacket and fished for his car keys from under the counter, shooting Mike a quick glance. The kid seemed to be back to his own self again, with no trace of the odd distance in his eyes. Even so, Crow lingered at the door and said, "I'm heading out to Val's. You going to be okay closing up tonight?"

"Sure," Mike said brightly. "I'm on it."

"You're sure?"

"Yeah?" Mike asked, surprised. "Why ask?"

Crow smiled and shook his head. "Just making sure I didn't work you too hard earlier. I threw a lot of stuff at you today. Maybe we worked out too hard . . . ?"

"No, I'm cool. It was fun." His smile began a little lop-sided. "Kind of."

"Okay. But if you feel tired or sick or anything, give me a call."

"Yesss, massster," Mike said in his best Igor lisp.

(2)

When Terry left Crow's apartment he had not gone directly back to his office. Instead he turned and headed the opposite way up Corn Hill, needing the simple mechanical exertion of walking to calm his nerves. Talking with Crow had neither calmed him down nor amused him as it often did. Crow was too deeply situated in what was going on—and what had gone on in 1976—to be of use as a diversion. Damn him.

It was late afternoon and the sky was thickening from pale blue to a darker purple and there was a promise of frost in the air. The Growers Association meeting was starting in a few minutes, and Terry had to be there, though God only knew what good it would do. What could *he* tell them that they didn't already know? The blight was slackening, sure, but that was only because it had already done just about as much damage as it could. There was very little left to destroy. Why in hell they needed him to tell them that they were all going down the crapper was beyond him. Damn them, too.

Damn all of them.

He quickened his pace despite the heavy crowds of tourists and there was such a look on his face that the seas of people parted before him. Even so there were too many people for his needs, so he veered sharply to the right and went down Steadman's Alley, which only had one store, and that only sold furniture, so the crowds were gone. Just a few stragglers looking for the main drag and a car or two looking for parking. At the first corner he turned again and was now walking behind the fenced yards of the stores and houses on Corn Hill. He passed Crow's yard and saw that Crow had hung his heavy bag out there. Tough-guy Crow with all his jujutsu nonsense. Damn and blast him.

At the end of Crow's yard he stopped, and turned and looked away from the line of fences up toward the fields beyond and the mountains that rose so powerfully to the southeast. Three tall tree-covered peaks—not tall enough to be snowcapped except in winter—but impressive and lovely against the darkening sky. Lovely to most, but not to him. Terry found them loathsome. Hateful. He stretched out his hand and the magicians of distance and perspective made his hand as great as the hand of God and the mountains were tiny mounds of dirt that he could just gather together in his fist and crush into dust. If only he could do that for real; if only it was within his power to take those mountains and what lay at their feet and crush it all to nothingness. With that one act he could, he was certain, wipe away thirty years of nightmares and pain. Of course, with godlike powers he could just roll back those thirty years and have kept the terror from ever coming near his family. If only. Terry lowered his arm and bowed his head and tried to fit his mind around the idea that Crow was really going to go out there in a couple of days. Out *there*. To where *he* used to live.

"Insane," he murmured and his voice broke on the word and he had to clamp a hand to his mouth to keep from screaming. He had tried to reason with Crow, had argued, had even yelled, but the idiot wouldn't budge from his plan.

"I need to do this," Crow had said over and over again.

"What do you hope to accomplish by going out there? He's dead!"

"I *need* to do this."

"Damn it, Crow—Griswold's dead!" Terry had roared and had then gasped and actually staggered as if saying that name was a punch to his own head. When had he spoken that name before? How long had it been? The name burned his throat like bile. He felt like his lips and tongue should have been blistered for having said it.

Now, half an hour later, he stood with his back to Crow's yard and stared at the mountains that loomed up like evil djinn above the shadowy corruption of Dark Hollow, and as he stood there he said it again. Not in anger this time, but to himself, and in a pleading tone intended to convince a disbelieving jury.

"Griswold's dead." Thirty years dead, and damn him to hell.

"No," she said, "he's not dead."

The voice came from behind him, but he didn't turn; instead Terry buried his face in his hands, not wanting to see the blood-splattered ghost of his sister.

## (3)

Weinstock had all of the information spread out in front of him. Videotapes from the morgue security cameras and from his clandestine second autopsy of Castle and Cowan, blood work and labs on both officers, photos and additional lab work on a half dozen other patients, mostly older folks who had passed on over the last few days. He still didn't have the reports from the independent labs in New York and Philly, but they were due tomorrow and he already knew what they would say. He had reports from two attendings and one intern in his own hospital for patients who had died, and reports and some lab work from primary care physicians who had reported deaths from among their patients throughout the region. Since he was the assistant county coroner, these reports routinely passed through his office and he had started doing database searches. There were a surprising number of heart attacks, and of those there were five fatalities. A whole family was wiped out in a house fire. Seven people had died in car accidents—a high number even with the increased amount of tourist traffic. Two deaths from industrial accidents, two farm-related fatalities. The local papers even remarked on it, ascribing the deaths to carelessness due to the stress of recent events, plus tension-related heart attacks. That sort of thing. It was on the radar, but no one was seeing it for what it was.

Why would they? He could not actually tie these deaths in with Castle and Cowan, and ordinarily no connection would ever have been made, even by him. Now, however, he was looking for that connection, grouping any recent death under the umbrella of his suspicions. Since completing the autopsies on the two officers, and reading the resulting reports from the labs, Saul Weinstock had created a very strange picture of what had happened at the Guthrie farm, and with each day he was adding more information to that picture, expanding it into bizarre areas and at the same time making it more clear—but clear in a way that was patently impossible.

If ever there was a time for a second opinion, this was it—but who could he consult? Who on earth would even listen long enough to his suspicions to hear it all the way through? Terry was out of the question. *He looks worse than I feel*, Weinstock thought, then for no logical reason wondered: *Does he know? Does Terry already know about this? Is that why he's so stressed out lately?* He thought about it, and then dismissed the idea. Terry had been showing signs of stress since long before Ruger and Boyd had come to town, and as far as he could tell that's when all of this had started. Was it something those bastards brought to town? Who else could he tell? Crow wasn't available until Saturday morning, but at least he would listen, so there was that to hold on to. As for the rest . . . well, Gus Bernhardt was a fool. Rachel? Could he tell her about this? No, probably not. Rachel would think that he was suffering from some kind of stress-related paranoia, and several times a day he wondered if maybe that was indeed the case. It would certainly be the best possible solution, because then he could just take a few weeks off and take the kids to Disney. But . . . no. This wasn't something he could run away from. Not if he was even only partly right about what was happening, and he knew that he was certainly right about some of it.

So what was the solution, then? If he brought it to his medical colleagues, how would they react? Weinstock tried to put himself in the frame of mind of someone else, a doctor like Bob Colbert who was great with a scalpel but had little imagination. Would Bob believe, even after all the evidence?

"No," he said aloud, and he knew that was true because too much of the evidence was speculation, and almost all of it could have been faked. Even the video. If they can make horror movies with special effects, then some clever kids at the film department at Pinelands could cook this up, and in Pine Deep elaborate Halloween pranks were run of the mill. Same with the tissue samples. Some jackass orderly or a nurse with a twisted sense of humor could have taken skin samples from a corpse in one of the anatomy classes and put it under the fingernails of Nels Cowan. It would be sick, but it wouldn't be difficult.

The wounds on the officers' throats could either be explained away as bites by a dog or other animal who happened onto the murder scene before the cops secured it. The fact that the skin bruising showed that some of the bites had been inflicted while the officers were still alive meant something, but could still be explained by animal attack. A dog or bear drawn by the scent of blood, biting the officers while they lay dying—it was a stretch, sure, but it was a hell of a lot more plausible than what Weinstock was thinking, and he knew that's where Bob Colbert would go. As would any medical professional, and Weinstock knew that if he made the case and was not believed then his reputation, his career, and his job would be shot to hell, along with any chance he had of ever convincing anyone of the truth.

If it was the truth, and the more he played devil's advocate with it, trying to see it from the outside, the shakier his own assumptions were becoming. "If you assume . . ." he murmured. So, where did that leave him? If every bit of the evidence, separately, could be disproved or cast into doubt, then what did he really have to make his case?

"Crow will be here Saturday morning," he said aloud. "He knows this stuff . . . he'll know what to do."

**(4)**

"You're here early," she said.

Crow smiled down at her from the porch. He leaned against one of the whitewashed wooden porch columns, arms folded, posture casual and relaxed, and mouth smiling as Val trudged toward him from where her father's Bronco was parked in the big circular driveway. "I left Mike in charge of the shop and thought I'd surprise you," he said simply.

"A nice surprise," she said as she came up onto the porch. She took a handful of his plaid shirt and pulled him toward her, and he came willingly enough. Their lips met softly, but with heat. After a long and delicious moment, she murmured, "Maybe Connie or Mark can fix us all some supper."

"Nope," he said. "They're not home. I convinced them to go to the movies."

"To the movies?"

"Uh huh. A nice, quiet Bruce Willis picture just opened at the Webster." He shrugged. "Hey, the guy's trying romantic comedy. No guns. No murder, not a drop of blood. Just him and Michelle Pfeiffer. Placid."

"They actually agreed to go? Alone? That must have taken some convincing."

"You stand in the presence of a master of the art, my dear, but truth to tell I bribed Harry O'Donnell and his wife to go with them. You know Harry . . . he's with Mark in the Rotary. I had coffee with him today and told him that I needed a couple of chaperones to make sure Mark and Connie actually have a good time together. Harry was actually happy to do it once I guilted him into it by explaining that it was good therapy for Mark and Connie."

"Ah. So we have a couple hours to ourselves?"

"I made them swear that they wouldn't come home until at least eleven."

"Must be a long movie."

"I made dinner reservations for the four of them, too."

"Really? Where?"

"The Vineyard Room at the Dark Hollow Inn."

"So, instead of taking your *own* gal out for dinner and a movie—"

"Ah, my duckie, you fail to grasp the subtlety of my scheme. With them out of the way, it leaves this big, old, comfy house to ourselves."

"So?"

"So, it's a chilly night, baby, and inside there is a warm fire and some other goodies, all laid out for my lady fair."

Her smiled seemed a little forced. "Look, Crow . . . if you're thinking what I think you're thinking . . . I don't think it's such a good idea."

"And why not? We already know it's not too soon."

She wasn't smiling. "It's more than that."

Crow kissed her forehead. "I know what it is, baby. You think I don't feel the weight of all this stuff pressing down on me, too? I know what you're feeling, and I know that living with Mark and Connie is wearing you thin."

Val leaned against him, kissed his chest and then rested her head against his shoulder. "I know . . . it's just that . . ."

"Besides, my dear," he said lightly, "you are presuming that you know my plans. I might have in mind a quiet evening of reading the Bible, drinking whole milk, and watching educational television."

"Oh, I'm quite sure," she laughed.

"My sweet baby," he murmured, kissing her hair. "What I have in mind is just a chance for you to turn off your brain and relax."

She snorted. "Relax? Maybe if I was shot with a tranquillizer dart."

"Just happen to have one inside. C'mon, it's cold out here." Taking her good hand, Crow led her inside and nudged the door shut with his foot. He touched her chin and kissed her once, very sweetly. The wind had blown and tangled her dark hair, but she looked wonderful to Crow. He helped her off with her coat and tossed it onto a chair. They stood together just inside the door, in the wide living room, which was lit only by the warm fire crackling in the fireplace. The room was sweet with incense and the darkness was soothing.

"Come with me," he whispered, and taking her by the hand, he drew her up the long flight stairs to the second floor. She saw, with wonder, that each stair was scattered with rose petals. The third floor was dark except for the spill of golden candlelight coming from the bathroom. Crow led her inside the spacious bathroom and smiled at her gasp of surprise. There were a dozen candles burning quietly, and wisps of jasmine incense wafted through the humid haze of steam rising from the filled and scented tub. A small CD player was playing serenades by Tchaikovsky.

"What's all this . . . ?" Val begin, but he touched his fingers to her lips to quiet her words. He kissed her again, and then began slowly—very slowly—to undress her. He did it with all the deliberate slowness of a sacred ritual, making the unfastening of each button a special act of beauty. He moved slowly, touching her face, her eyes, her lips with many small kisses that were as light as spring raindrops. He removed her bulky sweater and laid it on a chair, and then tugged the .45 out of her waistband, making sure not to comment on it as he shoved it under the sweater, and then gently tugged the ends of the blouse from the waistband of her jeans.

Beneath the blouse she was wearing a lacy peach-colored bra. The sensual awareness of the moment had made her nipples hard and they made small tents in the soft cloth of each cup. He set the blouse on the back of a small chair and leaned forward to kiss her bad shoulder, his lips brushing the nearly faded bruises. He knelt in front of her and slowly undid the zipper of her jeans, revealing inch by inch the pale flatness of her stomach, and the edge of panties of the same lacy peach pattern as her bra. Crow slid the pants down her legs, taking long, slow strokes of her legs through the cloth as he gathered them at her ankles. She rested her hands on him for balance as she stepped out of them, and he placed the jeans on the chair on top of the blouse. Reaching up, he unhooked the front closure of her bra and it slid off easily into his hand, he felt the shift of weight as her breasts came free from the material. He rubbed the soft material across his cheek and then lay it over top of her other clothes.

Val tensed, and he saw it, but didn't acknowledge it. She was never comfortable with being seen in the nude. Years ago Val had wrecked three motorcycles in as many years and each crash had left its marks. She had a four-inch scar across her stomach, a few minor ones on knees and elbows, and a whole bunch of jagged little ones dotting the curved landscape of her left shoulder, left breast, and the upper ribs. Those scars were linked by a few patches of healed burns. Val hated those scars, but Crow thought they were sexy.

In the glow of the candlelight her breasts were golden, except for her nipples, which were as dark as autumn roses. He bent forward to kiss her, only once, between her breasts over her heart, hooking his fingers at the same time in the waistband of her panties. He tugged them down and Val stepped out of them. The puff of dark hair between her legs had once been trimmed into a heart but had not been tended to since before the attack ten days ago; even so the heart shape was still visible and the dark hairs caught the light so that it seemed it was sewn with golden threads.

Crow kissed her stomach. Rising, he took her hand and guided her toward the tub. Val paused, looking uncertain and self-conscious, but Crow gently tugged her hand and she stepped over the rim; he continued to hold her hand as she settled, inch by inch, into the deep, hot water. It was one of the old-fashioned tubs with clawed feet, big enough for Val to stretch out her long, slender legs and immerse all of her body up to the delicate skin of her throat. The water was deliciously hot and a faintness of perfume rose from the mist.

Once she was submerged, she let out her first relaxed sigh.

Reaching over to a small table by the sink, Crow took a cut-crystal wineglass of very dark Shiraz and raised it to her lips. She drank gratefully of the fruity red wine, closing her eyes as she did so. She sank back against the tub and let the waters close over her body.

While she soaked, Crow positioned himself behind her and slowly, deeply began to massage her scalp, feeling where the tension hid and chasing it away with strong, deft fingers. The music soothed her, lulling her into torpor, and

Crow gradually slowed the motions of his fingers until they were barely more than a whispery touch. Time drifted past with a dreamy slowness.

After a while, once her skin had soaked up the richness of the water, Crow slipped one hand into a terrycloth mitten. Wetting it, he fetched a bar of scented wheat-and-lavender soap and worked up a good lather; then he helped her to stand up in the tub. Water sluiced down the lovely length of her, and pausing once in a while to kiss her glistening hide, he used the luxurious soap and the gentle roughness of the mitten to wash every inch of her glorious skin. He was diligent in his thoroughness, and then with a large bath ladle he poured water over her to rinse away the soap. He drained most of the water from the tub as he did so and quickly refilled it so that when he helped her down again, she lay in fresh water and that sloshed around her.

With the ladle he soaked her black hair and worked a rich shampoo into it, massaging the gel into her scalp until it foamed with a hearty lather. He used a gentle spray attachment to rinse the suds from her hair, and with a fluffy towel patted the excess wetness from her hair. He bent and pulled the plug from the tub, letting it drain away, rinsing her with the shower attachment until every bubble of soap was gone. Finally all the water was gone and she lay reclining, nude and immaculate, on the slatted wood Japanese grille inside the tub. She made no effort to cover herself with her hands, which Crow took as a good sign. He kept running the clean water for a long time. Then, switching it off, he reached for her and helped her up, wrapping her in a huge oversize towel that had patterns of moons and stars and swirling galaxies.

At first all he did was wrap the towel around her and enfold her in his arms, careful of her shoulder, nuzzling his face in the dampness of her hair. Then he patted her dry, missing no single inch of her skin, and kissing her here and there as he went about his task. When her body was totally dry, he helped her into a silky robe that he'd bought for her that very afternoon. It was a deep electric blue, a perfect color for the paleness of her skin and the deep black of her hair. The thin silk clung to her body in a particularly tantalizing way, and Crow was eminently aware of it.

He blew out the candles and led her out into the hallway, where he paused for a long and lingering kiss. Neither of them had spoken a single word since they'd come upstairs, and neither spoke now. Words seemed pale and weak, the wrong language for this country of soft touches, sweet kisses, and incense-fragrant air. They went downstairs, following the trail of delicate little rose petals to the large living room. The floor was polished hardwood, and the high ceiling was lost in a swirl of shadows. The fire logs were quietly chuckling.

In the center of the floor, Crow spread a thick mat of layered quilts, scattered with pillows, and onto this he lowered her, holding her hand until she was seated comfortably. He used the remote to start the CD player, and Loreena McKennitt began singing sweetly to them from the four speakers placed around the room. Sandalwood incense burned mildly and flavored the air with the aroma of exotic and faraway places, and Crow went around and lit a dozen long tapers, adding their golden glow to the light from the fireplace. There was an ice bucket with two bottles in it; Crow poured white wine for her and Perrier for himself into tall glasses and they lounged there listening to the music. The fireplace was cheerful but subdued, and the candlelight soothing to the mind and the eyes. Time just seemed to swirl, not really moving forward and not standing still. Time just was, and they were, and the moment was golden.

Crow touched her face and she reached and drew him to her, rising until they were an inch apart, both of them on their knees facing one another, bodies only a whisper apart. Crow took her hand and kissed her wrists, her palms, her fingers. He held her hand like a precious thing and kissed each fingertip, and then pressed her palms against his heart. Leaving her hands there, he reached and lightly touched her face, his own fingertips barely touching the softness of her cheeks as he bent to kiss her forehead, her eyes, and finally the sweetness of her mouth. It was such an innocent kiss, despite, or perhaps because of the intense purity of its passion.

He trailed his fingers down until he found the knot of her robe, and with the subtlest tug, the knot yielded and the ends fell away. The folds of the robe parted and candlelight touched her with gold: the curve of one breast, one thigh, the tips of her pubic hair. With infinite slowness and gentleness, he helped her to lie back on the soft mat. The folds of her robe fell in such a way as to cover her, and somehow that made his heart glad, as if all things in this night were conspiring to keep her safe.

Kneeling next to her, he kissed her lovely face and mouth, feeling the heat of her tongue. Her eyes were closed, long lashes sweeping down over her cheeks. Crow couldn't help looking at her, at the construction of bone and tissue and blood and heat that had combined into such a pattern of loveliness, and he marveled at the fortune that had allowed him to be the caretaker of that loveliness if only for a single night. His lips sought hers again, and then drifted away downward to chin and throat, tasting the different parts of her, the different textures of her. He traced the lines of her collarbones with kisses, as well as the hard flatness of her sternum, and brushed against the upswell of flesh where each breast rose away from her heart. With great care he peeled open the robe and looked at her breasts as if he'd never seen them before, as if beholding some new mystery. They reflected golden light from the candles, and he bent to them, kissing the contours of each, finding the hardness of each nipple and drifting away only to rediscover them again and again, touching the pebbly hardness with the very tip of his tongue.

Val writhed slightly, her back arching as Crow took one nipple in his mouth, his teeth nibbling on it very gently as the tip of his tongue teased the flat tip. The writhing of her body made the robe fall open even more, and he looked down the length of her, past belly and hips, down long legs to the feet and to each pink toe. To his eyes she was a collection of perfect curves and planes and angles, each part correct in its design and in its part of the whole of her. At the inward curve of her left knee he paused and pressed his mouth and teeth against a pressure point, drawing a line of sensation with teeth alone that made her body twist. Then he continued up her leg, kissing the inside of the long, soft, slender thigh, going higher until he could feel the feathery brush of her pubic hair against his cheek. He shifted, turned, and bent to bring his lips gently down onto the dark swirl of hair, drinking in the perfume of her body, the scent of her awakening passion. His lips explored deeper until they touched heat and wetness and softness. Val hissed and moved as his tongue found that tiny rosebud, coaxed it to hardness, and kissed it deeply.

He shrugged out of his own robe and settled down naked on his chest. Both of his hands swept slowly up and down the length of her, touching and exploring as his tongue began it rhythmic dance back and forth, back and forth, slowly at first, then faster as her breath came faster. Val knotted her fingers in his hair and arched her back as the sensations within her began to build and it was not long before the tremor began deep within her. Crow could feel it through his hands, through his tongue, and through every part of his body that was touching hers. It was a faint tremor at first, but it grew quickly, vibrating out from inside of her, blossoming up, becoming real and full and at a certain point, unstoppable. Her hips were bucking now, twisting and shifting under him, and Crow had to hold on to her to maintain that contact, to keep that essential rhythm so that she don't fall from that peak. When she climbed to the top of that mountain, her whole body arched, froze, held for a long moment, and then there was a release so violent and so total that Crow was buffeted by her. Val managed no words, just a continuous and inarticulate cry of pleasure and sensation. Her fingers knotted and twisted frantically in his hair, pushing Crow's face against her, forcing a deeper, harder contact until the relentless waves of pleasure begin slowly—very, very slowly—to diminish, each new wave reaching to a lesser peak and settling lower.

As her body began to relax, slumping bonelessly, exhausted for the moment, Crow kissed his way up her stomach, along the straight line of her sternum, up the graceful curve of her throat, and finally to her parted lips. They kissed, tongues darting and dancing, and he took her in his arms and held her, feeling her sweat mingle with his, feeling her breasts crushed against his chest, feeling the hammering of her heart so much in rhythm with his own. Gradually he rolled over onto his back and with infinite gentleness and care, he helped her slide atop him. It was a movement so skillful, so synchronously performed that even as she sat astride him they were joined. They both uttered small, almost inaudible gasps

There was a long time for silence, for doing nothing but holding that position, for maintaining that perfect contact. They lay in the candlelit darkness for a long while, and Crow felt a burning tear land on his cheek. He reached his hand up to touch her face, searching for a troubled frown and finding only a smile, and he knew that the tear was shed for beauty, and not for pain. He immediately felt his own eyes well up, and as they wept, they began that slow rhythm that is the pulse of all life and love.

# Chapter 22

## (1)

For a town like Pine Deep having Friday the 13th fall in October was a reason to celebrate. "Little Halloween," they called it. Schools were let out at noon, special football games were scheduled, there was a major party planned for the Haunted Hayride, and the town got into the party mood. The Harvestman Inn ran a special for groups of employees who showed company ID: thirteen beers for thirteen bucks. Motley's Steaks offered a special on thirteen-inch hoagies, and the Dead End Drive-In was advertising a thirteen-movie marathon of classic horror that kicked off with the entire Friday the 13th series, including a Jason Voorhees costume contest.

Tourists would be pouring in by noon, and by two o'clock there would be ten thousand people packing the streets and another five thousand at the Pinelands College stadium for the non-league game between the Scarecrows and the Temple Owls. Then the town proper would reverse course and start to empty as everyone cruised out to see Concrete Blonde or Los Straightjackets in concert at the Haunted Hayride, or went to the Drive-In, or crammed the bleachers for the Scarecrows-Owls game. The town bars would be full, of course, but shopping would drop off after five o'clock, which was fine since many of the vendors set up booths at the Hayride and in a carnival line around the campus parking lot. Little Halloween was planned for months, and never in Pine Deep's history had the holiday been as important to the overall financial survival of the community as it was this year. Terry Wolfe had been working to find ways of including the farmers in the town's nonagricultural activities so they could make a buck. Maybe a few bucks; enough to meet their mortgages and get through the rest of the season with their farm deeds still in their hands. For everyone it promised to be a great day in Pine Deep.

## (2)

Propping himself up on one elbow and watching her sleep. Crow thought that he had never seen anyone or anything as beautiful as Val looked at that moment. There was just the faintest rosy glow of sunlight painting the window and the softness of it caressed her cheek and jaw. He wanted so much to touch her face, to trace the line of her cheek, but he didn't want to wake her.

"I love you," he whispered.

She opened one eye, surprising him. "Good morning to you, too."

"Did I wake you, sweetie?"

"Just the frequent heavy sighs. You sound like you're deflating." She was smiling, though, and bent forward, kissing him on the nose. "I love you too, you goof."

He leaned toward her and gathered her in his arms. She was soft and warm and real and he covered her face and throat with kisses.

"Hey, slow down, cowboy," she said, coming up for air, "before you start something you don't have time to finish. Don't you have somewhere you have to be?"

Still nestled in her neck, he peered over her shoulder at the bedside clock.

"It's not even six and I don't have to meet Newt until seven-thirty. We got loads of time." He made Groucho eyes at her.

Val affected a yawn. "I should try and get some more

sleep. I have a long day ahead of me, too. I don't know if I should fritter away the morning with the likes of you."

"'Fritter'! I'll give you 'fritter,' you vixen!" He began to tickle her, or tried to, but she was quicker and jammed her fingers under his elbows and got his ribs, reducing him to helpless shrieks of laughter. He tried to get away, but she wasn't having any of that and climbed astride him, tickling him all over. There was pain—in her shoulder, her head, his wrist, his hip—but neither of them cared. Some things matter more than pain.

One minute later they were wrapped in each other's arms and though they were both smiling, neither was laughing.

### (3)

Crow was half-dozing on the hood of his battered old Impala Missy, his back against the windshield and his hands folded around a cardboard cup of Irish cream coffee that rested on his stomach. He wore six-stitch boots, faded jeans, and an insulated denim vest over a bright-red plaid flannel shirt. Eight inches of frayed thermal undershirt hung down below the rolled cuffs of the shirt. He wore white plastic sunglasses with opaque black lenses and had a Phillies cap turned backward on his head. The mangled end of a brown coffee stirrer hung from the corner of his mouth like a pool-hall Jim's matchstick.

At 7:35 Willard Fowler Newton's ancient Civic rolled to a squeaky stop in front of the Crow's Nest. Newton locked his Club snugly in place and got out, dressed in a blue Eddie Bauer padded jacket, 501 jeans, and Nike sneakers that had never seen the inside of a gym. Crow raised his sunglasses an inch and peered at him under the rims, one eyelid raised. "Did retro-Yuppie come back in and I miss the memo?" he asked.

Flushing a bit, Newton smoothed his jeans, and said, "Yeah, well you look like you're in a Marlboro commercial."

"I'm a manly man."

"And the sunglasses?"

"Keeps me in touch with my counterculture youth." Crow sat up and drained the last of the tepid coffee. He slid off the hood and did a hook shot that landed the cardboard container in the waste barrel that stood beside a streetlamp four feet away. "Yes! Two points, nothing but can."

Newton applauded ironically. "Who's driving?"

Crow looked pointedly at the squatty little Civic and then back at Missy. He said nothing. Newton fetched his gear, and they piled into the car and Crow popped a Flogging Molly CD into player. As Crow was pulling away from the curb and into the pre-business-hour flow of traffic, Newton said, "What about your store?"

"Mike's due in at noon. He has keys. Most of the Little Halloween weirdness won't get rolling until this afternoon, and we'll back by then, and by tonight all the action's going to be at the campus or the Hayride, and no one'll be shopping. Everyone'll be drunk. If we get delayed and the kid gets into a crunch, Val said she'd come down tonight and help with the rush."

"Oh." Newton opened a pack of Big Red gum and put a stick in his mouth. "I liked Val. She seemed nice."

A smile curled the edges of Crow's mouth as he drove. "She is."

"She forgive me yet?"

"Time will tell," Crow said mysteriously.

"Have you guys set a date yet?"

"We're thinking maybe a Christmas wedding—*next* Christmas, I mean—but really we haven't done that much planning yet. A bit too soon, you know?"

"I can understand that."

The morning had dawned clear and blue and cloudless, and there was a mildly cool wind from the northeast. Crow had his window cracked and crisp air blew into the car and made their cheeks tingle. They headed down Corn Hill to A-32, turned left, and within minutes they were out in the farm country. Groves of carefully tended shade trees gave way to acre after acre of geometrically sown cornfields, many cut to stubble that late in the season, but some still swelling toward the last corn harvest in November. There were fewer houses to be seen, most of them tucked far back at the end of winding dirt roads. Here and there a roadside stand stood fully stocked and ready for the influx of Little Halloween tourists. Barrels of peaches and apples stood in ranks; tall stands of decorative cornstalks leaned in bunches, tied with lengths of hairy twine; Indian corn hung from the rafters of the stands, cheery in their browns and reds and oranges; buckets of mixed nuts stood by the cash registers near jugs of dark, rich cider; and row upon row of pumpkins waited in patient lines, some painted with spooky or cheerful faces, some precut, some untouched and pumpkin-pie ripe in the early sunlight.

"See those pumpkins?" Crow asked, pointing with his chin.

"Uh huh."

"Imported. Most of them are from Berks County."

"Because of the blight?"

"Yep. We can't let it show, so on days like today—and really for the rest of the month—there has to be the appearance of prosperity and business-as-usual. Pestilence and hardship aren't big draws for tourists."

They drove on, heading south.

The Bone Man sat on a hay bale by the side of the road and watched the big brown Impala cruise by. All Crow and Newton saw was a line of hay bales stretching across the field, and on the one nearest to the road there were a dozen crows loitering in the morning breeze. The Bone Man knew the men couldn't see him. He had his guitar across his lap and he strummed a few notes as the car passed. One of the birds opened its scarred and splotched beak and cawed softly.

"Mm-hm," murmured the Bone Man, squinting in the sun's glare. His eyes were colorless in that light. "It's a bad business." The crow cawed again and the Bone Man played a few more notes, clear and sweet and sad. "A very bad business. Shouldn't be going out there, little Scarecrow. Nossir, not out there."

In the distance, the Impala was just a fading dot.

They rolled past several signs advertising the Haunted Hayride.

PINE DEEP HAUNTED HAYRIDE
**Biggest in the East Coast!**
*We'll Scare you Silly*!

Newton nodded to it as they passed. "The hayride? You helped design it, right?"

"Not initially, but I've done all the upgrades. I redid all of the traps—the spots where monsters jump out at you."

"Thinking of putting in a Karl Ruger trap?" When he saw that Crow's mouth had become a tight line, Newton winced, and said, "God! That was in poor taste, wasn't it? Sorry."

"Anyone ever tell you that you shouldn't be allowed out in public?"

Newton sighed. "My editor tells me that all the time."

Crow sucked his teeth and after half a mile said, "Skip it."

They passed a wrecker. Crow tooted his horn, and the driver of the wrecker raised a single hand in response.

"Friend of yours?"

"Not really. Guy named Eddie Oswald. Everyone calls him Tow-Truck Eddie. He's okay," Crow said.

A couple of cars passed going the other way, including a Pine Deep police cruiser, and then Crow slowed and drifted onto the shoulder at a crossroads where a dirt road lead away from the highway, forming the division between a vast pumpkin patch to the left and on the right a cornfield that sped away into the distance seemingly without a break. The road was small, but it looked well traveled, and there were deep wheel-ruts trailing away into the distance until the road jagged left and out of sight. Crow pointed. "That cornfield is the outer edge of Val's farm. Ruger's car was wrecked just a half-mile down the road. This pumpkin patch over here belongs to another family, the Conleys. They've been hit pretty hard by the blight. Worse than just about anyone."

"And the road?" Newton nodded down the winding dirt lane.

"This here leads down to Dark Hollow, or rather to the entrance to it. One entrance. At the top is our local Lovers' Lane—we call it the Passion Pit. I don't know how much *love* goes on down there, but I hear it gets pretty intense."

"Gee," Newton said dryly, "our first date and you're taking me to Lovers' Lane."

"No, dipshit, I'm taking you *through* Lovers' Lane. We'll park there and then go over the pitch and down the hill to the Hollow. I looked at the old maps and the old road that used to go to Griswold's place isn't even marked anymore. Don't know if it ever was, being a private road, but there's no way I know of to get a car in there. Going over the pitch and down the slope is no picnic, but at least it's a way that'll get us there." He nodded down the dirt road. "This is gonna get bumpy, so buckle up for safety, kids." Crow put the car back into drive and steered his way carefully down the dusty dirt road. It seemed to be comprised entirely of potholes.

"Nice road," stuttered Newton as his body fought to jump free from the seat belt.

"Thank God for shocks, huh?"

"This car has shocks?" Newton asked doubtfully.

Crow steered around a couple of sharp turns and then into a clearing that seemed to appear magically out of the dense green forest. He braked to a stop and as the dust settled, he switched off the engine. "Weeee're hee-eere," he said, the same way the little blond girl had said "They're here!" in *Poltergeist*. Newton gave him half a smile.

The reporter looked around the clearing and frowned. "This is Dark Hollow? It doesn't look like much."

Jerking open the door, Crow stepped out, saying, "This is the Passion Pit I was telling you about. Yonder," he said, pointing to the western edge of the clearing, where the pinelands were showing signs of recovering from an old forest fire, "is the pitch, and way down below is Dark Hollow. From here we walk."

Newton had brought a small backpack filled with sandwiches, juice boxes, PowerBars, and gum; it had a water bottle strapped across the top. He also had a walking stick he'd bought at a Natural Wonders store ten years ago and had never used. Crow popped his trunk and reached inside for his gear, strapping on an army-surplus web belt—vintage Desert Storm—then hung an authentic Boy Scout canteen over his rump, clipped a long, broad-bladed machete in a flat canvas sheath on his left hip, and from his right hip he slung a holstered automatic pistol. Newton stared at it for a moment, then looked at Crow and arched an eyebrow.

"Are we invading Cuba today?"

Crow gave him a big grin.

"Are you licensed to carry that?" Newton asked, nodding at the pistol.

"Sure. Businessman's privilege in this town."

"Does it matter at all to you that you look completely ridiculous?"

"Who gives a shit?"

"I hadn't looked at it from that perspective."

Crow hung a Maglite and a small compass to the web belt.

"What, no antitank gun?" asked Newton. "No lightsaber?"

Crow gave him a raspberry. He removed two long coils of rope from the car and laid them on the hood. He fished under his backseat and came up with a pair of work gloves and a pair of fingerless weightlifting gloves.

"What about your toothbrush, a Scotch-tape dispenser, and a Mr. Coffee? You forgot those."

"Keep it up, Jimmy Olsen." Crow took his cell phone out and tossed it onto the front seat and locked the car.

"You take everything except a fax machine and you leave your cell phone behind?"

"No reception around here," Crow said. "Check it out."

Newton looked at his own phone and saw that there were no bars.

Crow nodded. "This whole area's like that, and it'll probably be even worse down at the bottom of the Hollow. The cellular relay tower is on the other side of these mountains. Plus, it's rough terrain down there, so I'd rather leave my phone here than risk losing it."

"Swell." Newton patted himself down and tugged a small digital camera out of his jacket pocket. "For the article," he said and took a shot of Crow in all his gear, then walked to the rim of the pitch and took four shots of the long fall into the shadows at the foot of the mountains. He lowered the camera. "Charming."

"Cheer up, it gets worse. Come on." The first thing Crow did was to tie one end of each of the two lengths of rope to sturdy trees. He tied a complex series of knots and then jerked on them with great force to make sure they weren't going to slip

"Don't tell me we're rappelling? I failed the rope climb in gym class every year."

"Not really, but that pitch is too steep for you, and I'm not as spry as I used to be, so I'd rather we had a line to steady us down and then help us get back up again. Use these," he said, indicating the heavy canvas gloves that were old and stained with grease. He slipped his own hands into the weightlifting gloves and flexed them, adjusting the Velcro straps. He picked up the two coils of rope and hurled them out over the pitch, then took one rope, tested the tension again, and stepped to the edge of the pitch. Until now everything Crow did had cool efficiency about it, but now, poised—literally—on the brink of commission he finally paused and Newton could see strain showing in his face. His eyes were slightly squinted and he would look up at the blue sky and then down into the shadows of the Hollow and back up again, repeating the cycle every few seconds while balancing his weight against the pull of the rope. His mouth was tight, lips pinched, and he was breathing through flared nostrils.

Newton picked up the end of the second rope and came to

stand by Crow, and for a moment they both looked down into the Hollow, then Newton glanced at Crow. "You okay?"

"Nope," Crow said with a tight smile. "I'm scared out of my mind."

"We can still bag it and go catch lunch at the Harvestman."

"Can't," Crow said.

"Can't—why? No one's making us do this, man."

Instead of answering, Crow started singing under his breath. Words that didn't mean anything to Newton. "I got an ax-handled pistol on a graveyard frame that shoots tombstone bullets, wearin' balls and chain. I'm drinking TNT, I'm smoking dynamite . . . I hope some screwball start a fight."

"What's that?"

Crow turned to him. "Old Muddy Waters song, 'I'm Ready.' Great song."

"Okay. And—tell me again, why are we singing blues songs?" He grinned. "Hoping to channel the spirit of the Bone Man?"

"Keep it up, Newt, and I'll use you like a snowboard and surf down the mountain."

Newton was fishing for a snappy comeback when he paused, head cocked in an attitude of listening. For just a moment he thought he actually heard the chords of an actual blues guitar, impossible as that was, and he jerked his head around and looked over to the Passion Pit. The sound—just a couple of notes—was so clear, so strong, that he half-expected to see someone standing there with a guitar; but the clearing was empty except for Missy and the only sound was the murmur as the trees whispered secrets to one another and the crows chattered in the forests. When Newton turned back he saw that Crow was looking at him with dark eyes that glittered with amusement. A jumpy, corner-of-the-lip twitching amusement.

"You heard it," Crow said, "didn't you?"

"I heard . . . something."

Crow tugged on the rope that held him, but his eyes were steady and intent. "Tell me what you heard."

Newton just shook his head. "It was stupid. It was nothing."

"Come on, Newt—tell me."

Taking a breath and then huffing it out through his nose, Newton said all in a rush, "I thought I heard a guitar but it was nothing. Wind in the trees. Silly."

The wind had time to rustle ten thousand leaves before Crow said, "I heard it, too."

When Newton opened his mouth to say something else, Crow just shook his head and started down the hill. After a long stunned moment, Newton followed.

### (4)

Jim Polk slowed his unit and pulled onto the verge, waiting until a few cars and a farm truck passed, and then put it in reverse and crunched along the gravel back to the crossroads. He stopped with his rear bumper just this side of the dirt side road, put it in park, and got out, walking quickly to the edge of a screen of bushes and then peering cautiously around. He could just make out the dust plume left behind by Crow's car.

While the dust drifted on the breeze, Polk pulled his cell out of his uniform pants pocket, flipped it open, and speed dialed Vic Wingate.

"What?" Vic answered.

"It's me. I'm out on A-32 where it crosses Dark Hollow Road. Guess who I just saw driving down there toward the Passion Pit?"


Vic Wingate put his cell phone back in his pocket and leaned against the wall of the grease pit. The wheel of the big Ford Explorer was inches away from his head and he caught the tread and idly turned the tire, his eyes distant and thoughtful. At least three full minutes passed while he thought about what Polk had just told him, and about what it might mean. Pursing his lips, Vic pulled the cell phone back out of his pocket and called his own private office number. He let it ring once, disconnected, and then dialed again. It was picked up on the third ring.

"Yeah?"

"I just had an interesting phone call about your dancing partner."

"Crow . . ." it came out as a hiss.

"He's heading out to Dark Hollow like you thought, but if he's going all Sherlock Holmes on us then maybe it's time to put your plan for the Guthrie bitch into action. Be a nice way of distracting Crow from anything he might discover down in the Hollow."

There was a profound silence on the line. "It's daytime," Ruger said at last.

"No biggie—cloud cover's moving in. I'll pick you up in five minutes. Be ready."

Ruger's own laugh was low and jagged. "I'm ready now," he said, and hung up.

## (5)

The Bone Man was sitting on the hood of the Impala, his heels resting on the bumper, the guitar snugged against his belly. He had been playing some old songs, hoping Little Scarecrow would hear him, and not at all expecting him to. He'd heard Crow singing "I'm Ready," that great old Willie Dixon song that Muddy Waters had cut way back in 1956, and hearing those lyrics had made him want to play the tune. He'd picked out just a few notes when that reporter fellow pricked up his ears and rubbernecked so fast it looked like his head was going to unscrew itself.

*He had heard the music!* Had actually heard it. The Bone Man sat there on the Impala's hood and stared in total shocked amazement at the empty edge of the pitch.

## (6)

Climbing down from the pitch was no picnic and within a dozen yards Newton was sweating badly and his breath was coming in gasps. The slope started at a forty-five-degree

angle but went sheer to the point of a straight drop several
times, and Newton was glad for the rope. His walking stick
hung slantwise across his back, lashed in place, and was totally useless for the downhill journey. For the first fifty yards
the incline was littered with discarded beer bottles and man-
fully crushed beer cans, dozens of old shriveled condoms
and wrinkled condom wrappers, and scattered debris that
was now so ancient and sun-faded that it was impossible to
tell what it had originally been. Birds sang noisily in the
trees and the last lumbering flies of the season floated heavily by seeking quiet places to die.

The side of the Hollow was composed of slate, sandstone,
schist, chunks of granite, and lots of loose dirt and stone. A
glacial mishmash of rock of every kind, most of it hardwired
into the landscape by roots or packed in with hardened clay.
No part of it was safe, even the stones that jutted out like
sturdy steps, as Newton found out the first time he tried to
stand on one to catch his breath. The stone was undercut and
the loose soil gave way and Newton plunged down fifteen
feet, the rope hissing and smoking through his hand and his
limbs pinwheeling until Crow snaked out a strong hand and
caught him under the armpit and then slammed him belly-
flat against the pitch. Crow swung over and straddled Newton, the balls of his booted feet steadying him and his other
hand wrapped turn-and-around with his own line.

"You okay there, Newt?" Crow asked, and Newton just
flapped a hand. His heart was beating so loud he wondered it
didn't echo off the walls. "Catch your breath. We'll go again
when you're ready."

In a minute they started down again, going more slowly
now with caution learned from the fall. Newton was not
nearly as fit as Crow, not even as fit as a wounded and recovering Crow, and he had to stop several times. Once, he
looked over his shoulder and down just as his rope swayed
and he got a sickening rush of vertigo and had to close his
eyes and clench his jaws to keep from gagging. When he had
his gag reflex under control and the world had stopped spinning with such abandon, Newton braced his feet against a

big rock and used his free hand to dust himself off. As he did he saw something in the dirt by his knee glint dully, and he bent picked it up, thumbing away the clots of dirt.

"What's that?" Crow called from ten feet lower on the slope.

"Nothing. Just an old dime." The dime was dated 1966 and had a crude hole punched through it.

"Let's keep moving," Crow said. "It's not a treasure hunt."

Newton nodded and made as if to throw the dime away but without realizing that he was doing it put it in his pocket instead. Later on he would remember that dime and for the rest of his life he would wear it on a string around his ankle as a reminder of why he survived the autumn of the Black Harvest. Why he had survived while so many others died.

Dark Hollow was a deep depression formed at the base of one medium-size mountain and two huge sidehills and their steep sides kept most of the hollow in shadows except at noon. Farther southwest the land flattened out and even opened up in spots so that a rare beam of sunlight could reach down to the floor of the hollow, but there were also spots that never saw the light and it was toward one of these spots that Crow and Newton descended yard by yard. There was a clear division line where the mountain crest blocked the sun from reaching any farther down into the valley. It took the climbers twenty careful minutes to reach that point, and as they crossed that division line from sunshine into shadow, Newton felt a chill pass through him. Certainly the air was colder without the touch of the sun, but to him it felt as if he had stepped into a freezer unit. He blew out his breath and was surprised to find that it did not steam the air; it felt cold enough by far. He glanced at Crow, to see if he felt it, too, but Crow was reacting in a starkly different way to the shadows of Dark Hollow. Despite his jaunty baseball cap and grunge-crowd sunglasses, despite the affected spring in his muscular step, he was sweating bullets. Perspiration beaded his face and trickled in icy threads down his face. Unnerved by the sight, Newton said nothing and they kept moving, heading deeper into the valley.

They climbed down without conversation, silent and alert to the deceptive irregularities of the slanting landscape. Newton became more and more aware of the ambience of Dark Hollow.

Crow removed his sunglasses and stowed them away in a pocket. "Black as pitch down here," he said vaguely. "Come on."

Ten minutes later they reached the floor of Dark Hollow.

At the bottom they stopped and stepped away from the slope, their legs wobbly, and when they pulled off their gloves, their hands were pink and puffy. Crow took both pairs of gloves, then wrapped several turns of both climbing ropes around them and tied it all off so that nothing would be lost, weighting the ends with rocks to mark the spot. As he did this, Newton unslung his walking stick and shrugged out of his backpack so he could get to his canteen. He took a long pull and handed it to Crow. Then Crow fished a PowerBar out of his pocket and split it between them. They stood in the gloom, chewing, looking around them. The place was a bleak nothing, cold and damp and utterly still.

Crow consulted his compass and pointed northeast. "Griswold's farm is that way," he said. "I think."

"You . . . *think*?"

Crow shrugged as he put the last piece of the PowerBar into his mouth. "It's not like I've been there before, dude. I found it on the county surveyor's map. Its location is mentioned in some old borough zoning records."

The way ahead looked choked with brush and stumpy scrub pines and Newton gave it a dubious stare. "Is there a path?"

Crow shook his head. "I doubt it. Come on."

If there had ever been a path it was thirty years overgrown and as they went northeast they simply picked their way through the path of least resistance, and for an hour they crept forward with no feeling of having made any real progress. They clambered over rocks, crawled through coarse shrubs, slithered under fallen trees, and leapt gullies, feeling like they were running an obstacle course with no breaks in it at all.

Newton's legs felt leaden as he lumbered along behind Crow, and he struggled to draw chestfuls of air. He wanted to blame his breathlessness and tiredness on the sedentary life of a writer, or the arduous terrain, or the weight of his pack, but he was unable to manufacture any real belief in those fictions and tried to work it out logically, tried to pick apart his own nervous reactions and explain them away, using weather, lack of sleep, bad coffee, and cold air as culprits for each individual emotion. He tried, in short, to be a reporter and slant the story in a way that would favor a totally rational explanation for everything. For most of the trek he was happy with that, but as the shadows got deeper and the air got colder the farther into the Hollow they went he kept having to remind himself of his own logic. He really didn't want to openly acknowledge the grim and oppressive atmosphere of Dark Hollow, because to allow it to be a fact, or even a possibility, would be to accept that the place itself possessed some kind of negative energy, and to him that was preposterous. Crow was the one who believed in this freaky shit, not him.

Eventually even Crow's pace faltered and he stopped and leaned his back against a hemlock tree; he dragged his forearm across his face and examined the dark stains of perspiration on the sleeve. His chest was heaving, though he looked less like someone who was exhausted from exertion than someone from whom breath had been robbed by illness. His skin color was bad and his dark eyes looked faintly feverish as he sucked at the air like a gaffed fish.

"Jesus," he breathed raggedly as he unclipped his canteen and took a long pull, "this is like fighting your way through a jungle. Never seen such dense brush." Crow wiped his face again. "Man, I'm sweating like a pig."

"Pigs don't sweat," said Newton distractedly as he looked around at the high walls of shadow that climbed the steep sides of the hill.

Crow shrugged. "They would if they were down here."

There was a squawk from the branches of the hemlock

and Crow looked up to be a half-dozen ragged black birds clutching to the bare branches. Mostly female crows with their blue, green, and purple iridescent wings, and one fat albino male that was a sickly ash-gray. The jury of birds watched them with black intelligent eyes, and the albino squawked again, softly.

"Tell me something," said Newton, finally reaching for the canteen. "How come you never tried to come down here before? I mean . . . why now?"

Not taking his eyes off the birds, Crow said, "Thought about it a million times. Even drove out here twice, once got as far as the top of the pitch, and chickened out."

"You looked like you wanted to bug out today, when we were about to start down."

Crow looked at him, and though he laughed there was little humor in it. More of a nervous chuckle. "I came close, Newt. If I'd been alone—well, let's just say that Mike could have used some help at the store and I would have been fine believing that's why I turned around and went back to town."

"But you didn't. I find it hard to believe that you feel safer with me here." Newton said, and when he saw Crow's lip twitch, he said, "Yeah, it's okay to laugh at that."

"Nah, it's not that I need someone to protect me and hold my hand . . . it's just that I think I would have felt too ashamed to cop out with someone watching."

"You hardly know me. What would it matter if I knew that you copped out?"

Crow flicked him an appraising glance. "It's not that you specifically knew, it's that anyone would know." He sighed and took another hit from the canteen. "I'm the guy who killed Karl Ruger. I can't pussy out of climbing down a hill to visit a haunted house."

"Who'd think that?"

"Me. Oh, and don't give me that look, buddy boy, 'cause it's no great revelation that we have to believe in our own hype sometimes." He nodded toward the northeast. "Let's get moving."

"Well . . . I'm no psychologist, that's for sure," Newton said after they'd gone a dozen yards, "but I think you're being way too hard on yourself."

"I have a lot of personal work to do regarding my feelings about the guy who used to live down here. I've got enough personal baggage to open a luggage store, believe me."

"I know, you told—"

"Newt, ol' buddy, I've only told you part of it, and I've got to work up the nerve to tell you the rest." Crow gestured as if trying to grab the right words out of the air. "I've got to prove to myself that my fears and superstitions are as silly as Val insists they are. You see, she doesn't believe most of the stuff I believe. Oh, don't get me wrong, she believes that *he* was the killer all those years ago, but she thinks it ended there and then."

"And you don't?"

"And I don't." Crow shrugged. He tried to make it look lazy, offhand, even careless, and failed. "You see, it doesn't matter which of us is right, it just matters that I get this shit sorted out up here." He tapped his temple with a finger. "Besides, there's this old samurai axiom about facing your fears. If you're afraid of ghosts, sleep in a graveyard."

"Very pithy. So, are you afraid of ghosts?"

"Mostly, no." Sweat trickled down Crow's cheeks. "Sometimes, yes."

"One ghost in particular? Ubel Griswold's ghost?" asked Newton.

Crow stopped and turned, but for a moment just looked up above Newton's head at the leafless branches of the tall, black trees. "I would appreciate it," he said with exaggerated calmness, "if you would refrain from using that name while we're here."

Newton laughed. "Oh, come on! You're not going to tell me you're afraid of saying his name?" The reporter studied him. "You're . . . serious."

"As a heart attack."

"Then you're scared, is that it? This isn't just an AA self-realization exercise, is it?"

Crow looked all the way up to where sunlight dazzled the very tips of the trees, a pure light that did not have the reach to warm the shadow-darkened valley. "Newt, ol' buddy, I am so freaking scared right now I could cry. For two pins I'd run all the way back up the hill, get back in my car, and drive to the first bar I could find and drink it dry. That's how scared I am."

"I can't believe I'm hearing this from you."

"Why not? I'm just an ordinary guy, you know, not Captain Amazing."

"Even so . . . You took on Karl Ruger. You have all those black belts."

"Doesn't mean jack. Karl Ruger was just a man. This is . . . *him*, you dig? This is my nightmare for thirty years. This is the reason I started drinking, the reason I sometimes want a drink so bad I get the shivers and shakes and want to scream. This is the reason sometimes I wake up in the middle of the night so terrified that I want to eat my gun just to stop from seeing his face every time I close my eyes. You don't understand, and I hope to God that you never do, but what's out there, the thing that used to live out there, was a monster. Don't you get that? It was a *monster*! Not a man, not even an animal, but something unnatural, something that killed my brother, man. It ripped his throat out and tore his head off and . . . and . . ." Crow stopped and turned away, breathing hard, fists clenched at his sides. He drew in a long, steadying breath and tried it again. "You're right, I'm out here just to get some kind of Twelve Step closure. Newt, I'm out here to try and save my own sanity."

"Crow, I—"

"Hush. Just listen, man," Crow said and they started walking again, slowly, side by side. "I'm out here to try and exorcise some of my personal demons, and I have to admit that I brought you along as kind of a witness. Maybe I need to prove to myself that I really did this. Who knows, maybe it'll make a good sidebar for your feature. Maybe when we get out there all we'll find is some moldering sticks that used to be a house and nothing else. Man, that would be so nice!

But I needed to come out here, out to *his* house, just to see where he lived, to walk the earth he walked on, to touch things that he might have touched."

"But . . . why?"

Crow drew in a deep breath and held it and Newton could see that he was steeling himself for something. What he finally said was, "Because I think Ubel Griswold might still be here."

"What?"

"Yeah. How crazy does that sound? Now, you want to hear the really crazy shit?"

"I'm thinking no."

"Want to know what Karl Ruger said just before he died?"

"Not anymore. I think I'd rather climb back up that hill and find that bar you were talking about."

Crow stepped close and Newton could smell his sweat. "Right before he died . . . with his last breath, Ruger pulled me close and whispered 'Ubel Griswold sends his regards.'" He stepped back. "What do you think of that?"

Newton was very aware of the gun at Crow's hip and the machete in its sheath. He was aware of the stories he heard about how tough and dangerous Crow was. He was aware of his own heart hammering away in his chest. He was wondering what his chances were if he just turned and ran. The black forest around him was immense.

# Chapter 23

## (1)

"Hand me that trowel, honey?" Connie asked, holding out a gloved hand. She was kneeling on a rubber garden pad, her rump in the air, with her blond hair pushed up under a straw hat and a decorative smudge of potting soil on her cheek. Val handed her the trowel and watched as Connie set to work digging holes for some gardenias she'd had delivered from a greenhouse in Warrington. It was the first time since coming home that Connie had shown any real interest in doing something creative, and Val was taking it as a good sign. Last night Crow had arranged for Mark and Connie to go out for dinner and a show, and when they had gotten home there was just the faintest hint of something akin to romance between the two of them. Val thought that was even more hopeful. Maybe that was what it was going to take—real-world, ordinary stuff.

However, Connie wasn't entirely rational. Val had patiently explained that this was the middle of October and that there was likely to be a frost soon and besides it was way too late in the year to be planting flowers, but Connie had patted her hand—actually patted her hand—and told her that whereas Val may known how to grow crops she didn't really understand pretty stuff like flowers. Val had wisely shut up. It was better to sacrifice the gardenias than the moment. So far they had planted four trays of gardenias and three of marigolds. Val was amazed they had even found them this time of year, greenhouse or no. Connie was surrounding the front porch with colorful flowers and she was going about it with the single-minded relentlessness of a fanatic.

Diego had come up while they were still in the marigold phase and had even opened his mouth to say something, but Val had waved him off. Not wanting to call his boss crazy, Diego had just touched the brim of his hat, smiled, and melted back into the fields. The last of the late-season corn was being harvested and whole sections of the Guthrie farm were now bare.

"Is Mark going to be home for dinner tonight?" Val asked, trying to make it sound casual, but she could see the trowel falter for a moment.

"I think so," Connie said with only the slightest hesitation and her trowel chopped into the dirt with a bit more force. "He has a Moose luncheon thingee and then he'll be home."

"Okay," Val said. "Shall I cook?"

Connie laughed at that as if Val had just made a great joke, and Val had to grudgingly give her that point. Though she could rebuild the magneto on her 1973 FLH 1200 Electraglide Custom motorcycle or do a tranny job on John Deere 8030, she was no wizard in the kitchen. All thumbs and no sense of what went where. There were family stories about some of her classic dinners, including a brisket that everyone thought was tofu and pizza with cold tomato sauce and a runny crust. Val sighed.

When her cell phone rang she was delighted. It wouldn't have mattered if it had been a telemarketer.

"Val? It's Terry—is Crow there?"

"No, he's out for the day," she said as she stood up and dusted off the knees of her jeans and strolled out onto the front lawn.

"Val—he didn't really go out *there*, did he?"

She turned and looked back at the house, saw that Connie, still on hands and knees, was staring off in the direction of the stand of trees near the barn. Val glanced that way, saw nothing, and didn't think much about it. She often found Connie standing still, staring out a window or whatever. God only knew what she was seeing. What had Saul called it? Dissociative behavior?

"Val?"

"Yes," she said at last. "They left a couple of hours ago."

"Damn it!" Terry snapped, and abruptly hung up. Shocked, Val stared at the phone for several seconds before finally folding down the lid and putting it back into her pocket. "Asshole," she murmured, and then remembered her promise to Sarah that she would bury the hatchet, but the memory of his rudeness stung her again and she repeated her comment. Frowning, she strolled back to the porch. Connie was standing now, her face still turned toward the barn.

"What's up, Con? Is that fox back?"

At the sound of her voice Connie jumped, turned, and for a moment looked at Val as if she didn't know who she was. Then she blinked and smiled self-consciously.

"My . . . I was a million miles away." She glanced again at the barn. "I just saw the strangest thing. . . ."

Val stiffened. "What?"

"You'll think I'm crazy, but . . . I just saw a snow-white deer. A buck. You know, with all the horns? White as snow."

Val took a few steps toward the barn, but there was nothing to see and the trees were too thin to hide a full-grown deer. She looked back at Connie.

"Isn't that just strange?" Connie asked with an enigmatic smile.

"Yeah," Val agreed. "Strange."

## (2)

It looked like a nest, with the bodies of the creatures tangled and clustered together with no thought of comfort. There were fourteen of them now, all pale and bloated, gorged and somnolent, huddled in the darkness of the basement, secure in the shadows. An onlooker would have thought they were all dead, a mass of murder victims whose bodies had been carelessly disposed of out of sight in that forgotten, half-collapsed house, but every once in a while one of the bloated bodies would turn or shift, the movement inspired by some red dream.

Last night there had only been nine of them, but the number had grown, as it would continue to grow; just as it grew for each of the nests scattered throughout the town. Last week there had been two, but now Adrian and Darien lay sprawled there in the secret, silent darkness, wrapped in each other's arms, clutched together against the sleeping back of Dave Golub.

The bodies all slept on throughout the burning day. Once, just before noon, a bold and foolish rat scuttled into the basement, following the scent of spoiled meat and fresh blood. It minced down through the spiderwebs and shadows, driven by the nearness of food, hungry beyond caution. In its daring and hunger it came close to Adrian's outflung hand. The fingers looked fat and pale and full of meat, and the sleeper looked oblivious. The rat considered for a moment and almost fled out of natural fear, but the demands of its belly overrode the logic of its instinct. It darted in toward the little finger, its yellow teeth bared for the bite. . . but the white hand flashed so fast the rat was a broken-necked corpse before it was even aware that it was in threat. It twitched once, twice, and then lay eternally still in the killing grip of the boy. Adrian's eyelids never twitched, never opened, but he pulled the corpse close to his chest the way he once would have held a stuffed bear. Beyond the speed of his hand he made no other move. As the hours of the day wore on, he lay there with the dead rat clutched in his hand and a smile of hungry joy on his innocent face.

### (3)

"Crow . . . you're scaring the crap out of me, here. Why the hell didn't you tell me this stuff before?"

"Would you have come down here if I had?"

"Hell, no! And I want to turn around and go back right now."

"Why, do you think I lured you down here for some nefarious purpose?" Crow was smiling when he said it, then his smile faded. "Jesus Christ—you *do* think I lured you—"

"What am I supposed to think?" Newton shouted. "You talk me into coming down to the remotest place on planet-frickin'-Earth and then you tell me that Karl Ruger—who had never even been to Pine Deep before—used his last breath to give you a message from someone who's been dead for thirty years . . . someone you also think is some kind of monster. What the hell am I supposed to think about that kind of thing?"

"Calm the hell down!" Crow yelled back, amping it up a notch. "And don't get all paranoid on me. You wanted the whole story, right? Well, this is part of the story, and on that point—this isn't just a story to me. I *believe* this stuff. All of it. I know that Griswold was a goddamn monster because I saw his goddamn monster face, all right? He killed my brother, he killed Val's cousin, he killed Terry Wolfe's sister, he killed a shitload of other people in this town, and he *almost* killed me. I know this and you don't because you weren't even there. As far as Ruger goes—I faced him down twice and he nearly killed me and my fiancée *and* our baby and I can't just forget him or what he said!"

"Baby? What baby?"

That made Crow grind to a halt. He stopped, flushed and flustered and furious. He sputtered for a moment and then, just as loud, he yelled, "Val's pregnant! You happy? She almost died and that means our baby would have died. You think I'd invent what Ruger said just to impress you?"

"Crow . . . shut up." Newton said it quietly and it had the same effect as if he'd have belted Crow across the mouth. "Just dial it down, okay?"

He stood there, hands up palms-outward, facing Crow, who had clamped his mouth shut but was still glaring.

"I didn't know that about Val."

"Yeah, well, now you do."

"Congratulations."

"What?"

Newton held out his hand. "Congratulations."

Crow stared at him for a long minute and then took the hand and shook it, looking totally puzzled by the right-angle change of direction.

"Now," Newton said with a level voice, "look me in the eye, Crow, and tell me that you aren't completely off your rocker, 'cause I have to admit that this is all a bit hard to take and right now I'm more scared of you than I am of these woods, and that's saying something."

"Why the hell are you scared of me?"

"Because you're acting crazy and you have a gun."

That made Crow gape; then he turned and walked in as wide a circle as the brush would allow, flapping his arms and shaking his head. He stopped and turned and looked at Newton from a dozen feet away, and he was smiling a great big rueful smile. "Yeah, I guess it sounds pretty crazy at that."

"It's a healthy sign to admit it," Newton said hopefully.

"Oh, bite me." He came back over. "Look, Newt, here's the deal, I've told you almost everything now. So, am I crazy? No, or at least not in that way. But do I believe this stuff? Then, yeah, I do. I believe Griswold was a monster, I believe Ruger said what he said, and I believe one more thing, and if I tell you I don't want you to go running off into the woods to escape the crazy man."

"You could probably outrun me, anyway. Sure, love to hear what else you believe, 'cause as you know we sane people can't get nearly enough of this stuff."

"Yeah, cute, but don't push it," Crow said with a half-grin. "Okay, I've been working on a kind of theory about Griswold and Ruger. This should be right up your alley because I know you're a big conspiracy-theory nut."

"Pot calling the kettle black."

"Whatever. Anyway, I told you Griswold had a crew of cronies back in the day. Vic, my dad, a few others. Ruger would have fit in with that crowd pretty well. Mean, vicious, and probably the same kind of asshole who would have a set of white robes in his closet. So maybe it wasn't entirely an accident that Ruger happened to break down in this town. Maybe he was heading to Pine Deep."

"Why?"

"Well, this is the part you're not going to like."

"I haven't really liked any of it so far."

Crow snorted. "I think maybe somehow Griswold called him here."

"Yep, you're right. I don't like it. Shoot me if you're going to, but you're a fruitloop. You're describing an episode of *X-Files*. You're describing a Stephen King novel. This shit happens in stories and it happens in folklore, but this is the real world."

Crow held his arms out to his side as if embracing the dark forest around them. "Newt, if this isn't the sort of place where folklore gets its start, then I don't know what is. We're in the deep, dark woods near where a monster used to live, which in turn is in the center of a region that has had a reputation for hauntings going back three hundred years. If something like this was going to happen . . . wouldn't it be likely to happen someplace like Pine Deep?"

Newton took out his canteen and sipped at it thoughtfully, eyeing Crow.

"I wanted to come down here," Crow said, "because I need to solve the mystery of what Griswold was, and to prove to myself one way or another if there was a link between him and Ruger."

Newton nodded slowly, but he said, "Isn't that a lot to ask of a walk in the woods?"

"Not *these* woods," Crow said.

Newton glanced around. Despite the early hour, the light was gray and stained and looked like the glow from a feeble bulb ready to burn out. Shadows seemed to lurk behind every tree, crouch in every hole, hang from the long bare fingers of each branch. The twisted undergrowth was snarled around the base of the towering pines and oaks, and most of the tree trunks bulged with disease. Not one single bird offered even a distant song to diffuse the tension in the air, and the wind played a slow dirge through the trees.

"You have just succeeded," Newton said without humor, "in scaring the living shit out of me."

Crow nodded. "Welcome to Dark Hollow."

### (4)

Dr. Saul Weinstock poured three fingers of Glenfiddich into a chunky tumbler, quickly drank down a mouthful, then took another, his eyes widening over the rim of the glass as he drank and the gasses burned his mouth. When he set the glass down he was gasping like someone who had just been hit in the solar plexus, and the glass was nearly empty. He poured more of the Scotch into the glass, but did not take another sip just yet. As he set the bottle down he raised his hands and stared at them, watching their palsied tremble. He could no more have performed surgery with those hands than he could hover in midair. He had been barely able to tie his shoes. Then he wiped his mouth with the back of one of his hands.

His office was brightly lit, and the door was securely locked. The windows were shut and shuttered, and against each pane he'd hung flowers whose scent perfumed the air with a harsh pungency. Weinstock found the air cloying, the smell oppressive, but each morning he replaced the flowers with fresh ones. On his desk, lying next to the tumbler was a gnarled lump of metal that gleamed with an angry potential. Weinstock reached for it, as he had a dozen times since locking himself in for the evening. He curled strong fingers around the butt and picked up the weapon, slipped his index finger into the trigger guard, and exerted gentle pressure on the trigger. The hammer trembled. Weinstock squeezed harder and the hammer eased silently back, poised with intent, and then leapt forward, striking the firing pin with decisive force.

There was an empty, hollow *click*.

Weinstock sighed and set the gun down. Then he opened

his briefcase that lay on the side table. Inside was a crisp paper bag imprinted with the name *MARLEY'S METAL SMITHING—WE MAKE BEAUTY THAT LASTS!* He opened the bag and removed a small drawstring bag and upended it over the blotter. Twenty-four lumps of smooth metal dropped and bounced and rolled across the green face of the blotter. He stared at them, and drank some more of the Scotch as he watched the way the light played off the copper jackets that enclosed the rounded chunks of purest silver.

Weinstock finished his glass of whiskey, his third in the last hour, and then picked up the pistol again, opened the cylinder, and as he fed the .44 slugs into the chambers, he murmured prayers he had learned as a child, his Hebrew faulty but his prayers in desperate earnest.

### (5)

They kept walking through the shadowy forest, and for a while the brush thinned out and left them with a path that was easier to follow. Once in a while they would hear birdsong, but generally the place was quiet. The temperature, though, was rising as if they were nearing a hot spring, and the humidity rose with it. For several minutes they had walked in silence, each digesting their last conversation, but then Newton picked it up as if there had been no break.

"What kind of monster?"

Crow glanced at him. "What?"

"You said Gr— I mean *he* was some kind of monster. Exactly what did you mean by that? A serial killer? A psychopath?"

"Maybe I shouldn't have said it," Crow said primly.

"A little late for that. So . . . when you say 'monster' you mean that he was some kind of *real* monster? Not that I buy any of that, but I'd like to hear what kind of a monster you think he was."

"Answer your own question, Newt. The answer is right there in the facts I gave you."

"What facts? You recognized him as the man who attacked you. Okay. You assume he was the one who killed all the other people, including your brother, Mayor Wolfe's sister, and Val's uncle. You assume that Oren Morse killed him because he felt indebted to Henry Guthrie, and because the first victims were fellow gentlemen of the road, to use the old expression. Those aren't really facts. Mostly they're suppositions."

"Okay, get literal on me." Crow used one hand to vault a fallen oak and then reached out to help Newton over. The path was still clear for about a quarter mile and then looked like it faded into shrubs again. "Let's look at the circumstantial evidence, then."

"Such as?"

"Such as the cattle on his farm. Remember what I said about him raising a herd of cattle?"

"Uh . . . right, the cattle he never sold. So what?"

"So, what happened to the cattle?"

"You mean, why did they die during the Black Harvest?"

"No, you ninny, what happened to them in the years before? He raised cattle, he bred cattle."

"So, maybe he fancied himself a cowboy."

"Cute. No, his herd, small as it was, changed size from season to season. Sometimes he had a lot, sometimes only a few dozen."

"So what?"

"If he didn't sell them, then what was happening to make the herd dwindle during the times when he didn't have as many?"

"I don't know, for Christ's sake. Maybe he liked a lot of steaks."

"No one eats that much beef. Not even Gus Bernhardt," Crow said with a grin. He drew his machete to cut away some vines that blocked their way. "Plus, isn't it odd that the killings of the people in Pine Deep only started after all of Griswold's cattle had died off during the plague? Put those two facts together and you have a pretty odd pattern."

"What . . . you think he was amusing himself by killing

his cattle for years," Newton said, "and then when they bit the dust, he started in on the local citizenry?"

"Something like that."

Newton laughed. "Oh, come on! And people call *me* paranoid."

"You explain it."

"Why bother? Griswold probably really was selling off his cattle somewhere else."

"People in town would have known."

"How? Did you have twenty-four-hour surveillance on his property? Maybe he had a private arrangement with a meatpacking plant somewhere, just selling a couple here and there to supplement his income, or justify his image as a gentleman cattle rancher, Pennsylvania style."

"We would have known," Crow insisted stubbornly. "This is a small town, and it was a lot smaller back then. People know everyone else's business. Besides, in order for a person to sell off cattle they have to pay taxes on the sale, and Griswold never once paid taxes on a single cow or bull, not once in ten years. I checked. The only records show the cattle he bought to replenish his herd. I still think that he was killing them off himself."

"Hell, he wouldn't be the first farmer to shy his taxes." Shaking his head and smiling, Newton said, "But even if he wasn't, why on earth would he kill them himself? What would be the point?"

"Maybe he liked it," Crow said. "Or . . . maybe he *needed* to do it."

Newton blinked. "Needed? For what? Some kind of religious voodoo thing?"

"There are other reasons for killing."

"Such as?"

Crow cut away a thick vine, putting arm and shoulder into it so that the heavy machete blade sheared cleanly through it. His wrist and ribs had healed nicely and the exercise felt good. "For lack of a better term," he said, "call it a primal need."

"Primal need? That's a weird choice of words."

"It seems to fit."

"Why? What makes you so sure, so certain of all this? You seem bound and determined to pin all that horror and all that crime on Griswold. Why?"

"For the same reason I already told you. When he dragged me out of the bushes, I saw his face."

"Yeah, and you thought he looked like a monster. Come on, Crow, you were a terrified kid! Your brother had just been killed in a horrible and terrifying way. You almost certainly had nightmares the night before, and here it was, nighttime again. You were sitting in your yard, daydreaming, rocked by the loss of Billy, horrified by the other killings, too young to make any kind of sense of it all. Mix all that together and you have the perfect brew to warp a child's perceptions of what he sees. Then someone tosses you into a bush and before you know it strong hands are pulling at you. You say that the face you saw was a monster's face? Crow, with all that going on, how could you *not* have seen a monster?"

Newton sighed. "Look, I'm not trying to badger you, man, but try to see it objectively. All the evidence points to Oren Morse—none of it points to Griswold, except the cattle thing, and I could work up twenty good reasons for that. You were a little kid. Terrified, in shock, confused. What you saw was a man's face, his features probably distorted by shadows and moonlight and the leaves of the bush. There *are* no monsters, man. Truth to tell, there are enough rotten, bloodthirsty sons-a-bitches in the human race without us needing any help from things that go bump in the night. That's one of the reasons I don't believe in the devil. If there's a devil making people do it, or if there are demons possessing innocent folk and making them hurt other people, then it takes the culpability away from man himself. We have to be responsible for our own actions."

He gave Crow a reassuring nod. "When you were nine, you couldn't understand that any man, any human being, was capable of committing the horrors that were happening in town. You couldn't accept that a man had done those things to your brother. For a kid, it's much easier to believe in monsters—after all, monsters are supposed to do bad things, they're evil by their nature, so there is no betrayal of human morality. Crow, you *needed* it to be a monster, and so it *was*."

"You're wrong," Crow said simply. He stopped and slid the machete into its flat sheath and looked at Newton with humorless eyes. "There are monsters. I saw one. You make a really good argument, Newt, I'll give you that. Very persuasive, eminently logical, but you *are* wrong. I know what I saw."

"But—"

"It was pretty bright, despite being nighttime. It was two days past the peak of the full moon, there was a lot of light. I saw his face."

"Griswold's face?"

"Uh huh. Almost his face. Maybe in another couple of nights it would have been even more like his face. Maybe two days earlier it had been a lot less like his face—but on that night, it was somewhere between."

"Between . . . what and what? You're not making sense."

Crow's dark eyes glittered. "Between the face of a man," he said softly, "and the face of a wolf."

Newton opened his mouth to speak. Words utterly failed him.

Crow nodded. "Yep, that's exactly what I've been trying to tell you. There were two sets of murders, each spread out over a handful of days, separated by just less than a month. Both sets began just two days before the full moon and ended two days after."

Newton still couldn't manage the words.

"I think Ubel Griswold was a werewolf," said Crow.

# Chapter 24

### (1)

"Please tell me that you're just having a mental breakdown," Newton said, "and that you don't really believe that Griswold was a werewolf."

They had stopped walking and stood together in a natural clearing surrounded by wild rhododendrons and holly. A few crows were gossiping back and forth above them in the trees. Crow met the reporter's skeptical stare with his own flat and level one. "I know what I saw."

"You were nine!" Newton yelled.

"Yeah, I was nine!" Crow yelled back, "and at age nine I saw a fucking werewolf! I don't care if you don't believe it."

"I don't believe it."

"Well I damn well do!" Crow bellowed those words and they seemed to hang in the air around them like ozone.

Newton made a dismissing hand gesture and turned away, walking ten steps down the path they had come, saying, "This is nuts. How the hell I ever got talked into coming down here . . ."

"You can go back if you want to."

Newton wheeled and marched right back and, when he was close enough, jabbed Crow in the chest with a stiffened finger. "Tell me what you saw. Exactly, every detail. Put me in the scene if you want me to believe this bullshit."

Crow's face went suddenly scarlet and in a movement too fast for Newton to see he grabbed the reporter by the front of the shirt and spun him completely around and slammed him up against a pine tree and held him there, fists knotted in the cloth of his jacket front. Newton's hiking stick went clattering to the ground between them and Crow kicked it angrily aside. He leaned in close and his voice was a feral whisper. "Listen, asshole, this thing *killed* my brother and it damn near killed me. I was not hallucinating, and what I'm telling you right now is not me flashing back to the DTs. I saw *its* face, man, I looked right into Griswold's face and I saw it change. I saw bones *moving*, Newt, I saw his eyes turn from blue to yellow to red. I saw that snout and saw the teeth tearing through the gums, dripping blood, getting longer. I smelled its breath on his face. I *saw* Ubel Griswold change. I saw it. Not a man, not some jerkoff in a fright mask. I saw the *change*."

He took a breath and exhaled sharply, and then pushed himself away from Newton. "I saw it." He turned away, flapping an angry hand at Newton. "Val was right. You're really are an asshole and I should never have trusted you." He kicked a stone and it went skittering through the brush, startling the crows, who leapt into the air to find higher branches.

Then he turned back to face the reporter. "If you want to go back, then go back. You know the way. But I'm going on and I'm going to find his house. I want to look inside . . . I *need* to look inside. Maybe I'll find nothing but raccoon shit and thirty years of dead termites . . . but maybe I'll find some evidence of who he was, and what he was." He stopped and pointed to the northeast. "Did you even bother to look up Griswold's name on the Internet?"

Newton nodded, unable to speak.

"Did you look up what his name means?"

A shake of the head this time.

Crow laughed. "I told you that it probably wasn't even his real name. I told you that on Val's porch; well the other day I did a translation on it on Google and guess what I found out. You know what it means? You know what 'Ubel Griswold' means?" He didn't wait for an answer but stepped closer. "It's German for 'Wolf from the Gray Forest.'" He spat on the ground. "Don't you get it? He was screwing with us back then. It was a nickname, a stupid in-joke for him and that goon squad that hung around him. Wolf from the Gray Forest. This is the gray forest, you moron!" Crow shouted. "Look around you." Indeed the forest was perpetually gray, always in shadows. "And he was the wolf that lived here." He closed his eyes and shook his head. "He was telling us all along and we were just stupid yokels who didn't have a clue. God!" Once again he turned and stalked a few feet away, swiping angrily at the air and cursing.

Newton stood stock still, his back pressed against the gnarled bark of the pine tree, his face burning. He licked his lips and swallowed a dry throat, then slowly straightened and smoothed down the front of his clothes. He looked around at the forest—the gray forest—and felt very cold and small. "Crow . . . ," he began, but Crow waved him off. Newton pushed himself off the tree and walked tentatively forward. "Look, Crow . . . I'm sorry I mouthed off the way I did . . . but put yourself in my place for a minute."

Crow turned to look at him.

"Granted, I wasn't there thirty years ago," Newton said, "but I have a pretty open mind. Yesterday I didn't so much as believe in the tooth fairy and today you want me to believe that there are such things as werewolves. I mean . . . *were-wolves* for Christ's sake. How should I even react to something like that?"

"You could try a little trust."

"Crow—coming down that hill with you, coming out here with you—that's showing more than just a little trust, but believing in werewolves . . . at the risk of you slamming me into another tree, that's going to take a bit more than simple trust."

They stared at each other for a while and then Crow sighed heavily and nodded. "Yeah, goddamn it." A rueful grin twitched up one corner of his mouth and he bent and picked up the hiking stick and held it out. "Sorry about the whole slamming into a tree thing."

"Sure," Newton said snippily and snatched the stick out of Crow's hands and held it defensively in front of his chest. "Don't worry about it, but please don't do it again."

"Scout's honor," Crow said and held up three fingers.

A little breeze swept through the clearing and stirred some leaves. "So now what?" Newton asked.

"It's your call. I'm going that way," he said, nodding to the northeast. "If you want to head back, no harm, no foul."

"I should go back," Newton said. "I really should. But . . . what the hell."

A big grin broke out on Crow's face and he stuck out his hand; after only a moment's hesitation, Newton took it and they shook. "But," Newton said, not letting go immediately, "this doesn't mean I believe in werewolves, witches, goblins, or honest Republicans. All it means is that I'll go to his house and we'll see what we see. Fair enough?"

Crow pursed his lips, then nodded. "Fair enough."

They started walking again, heading farther up the road, and in a loud stage whisper that was meant to be heard, Newton said, "Werewolves, my ass." Then suddenly a memory kicked its way out of the shadows in the back of Newton's mind and he jerked to a stop and grabbed Crow's sleeve. "Holy shit!"

Crow wheeled. "What's wrong?"

"Ubel Griswold . . ." Newton stammered. "Werewolf!"

Crow blinked. "Um . . . yeah. We covered that."

"No, Jesus Christ, I just remembered something that you absolutely have to know. About Griswold."

"Newt—if you're going to reveal that you're his long-lost son or some B-movie shit like that I'm going to hurt you. A lot."

"No, shut up and listen. The other day when I was doing a Net search for my feature I searched on Griswold's name and—jeez, how the hell could I have forgotten this?—I found a reference to Ubel Griswold and werewolves. I totally forgot about it."

"And you're just telling me *now*?"

Crow whapped him on the top of the head with his open fingers. "You friggin' cheesehead. How the hell could you *not* remember something about Griswold and werewolves when we are in Dark-frickin'-Hollow arguing about werewolves while going to Griswold's frickin' house? Explain to me how that is possible."

"I don't know . . . I just forgot. I guess I just didn't pay much attention to it at the time. I'm sorry, okay? But at least let me tell you what I read."

"Yeah, useful information might be—oh, I don't know—*useful*?"

"Stop shouting. It was just a quick reference, and I guess it didn't really register at the time because it referred to something that happened in the late fifteen hundreds, maybe early sixteen hundreds. Something about a guy put on trial for being a werewolf. Peter something or other. Can't remember his last name. Point is, he was point on trial for being a werewolf and later executed."

"You lost me. Guy named Peter gets killed four hundred years ago, what's that got to do with—"

"They gave a bunch of aliases for him. One of them was Ubel Griswold."

Crow stood there and stared at him for quite a while after that. "Oh, that's just swell," he said.

"Maybe it's an ancestor of his," Newton offered. "If Griswold was descended from someone who was accused of being a werewolf—and a pretty famous one if the transcripts of his trial are on the Internet four hundred some years later—then maybe he played on that."

"What do you mean?"

"Figure it out. He took the werewolf thing from his ancestor as a gimmick to disguise the fact that it was just an ordinary man—albeit a serial killer—behind the Reaper murders. Or, maybe he was really nuts and thought he was channeling his ancestor. Didn't Son of Sam get messages from a dog or something?"

"I think that was something he made up to try and prove to the cops that he was insane."

"Well, he was a mass murderer . . . how sane could he have been?" Newton said. "But the point is that if you're a homicidal maniac and you discover that your ancestor was tried and convicted of being a werewolf, wouldn't you play on that? Use it to increase the terror and thereby increase whatever psychosexual pleasure these guys get from killing? Isn't that like a given here?"

"It would be," agreed Crow, "except for one thing."

"What's that?"

"During the Pine Deep Massacre no one even floated the word 'werewolf.' Not even me. I don't think I've even said that word aloud in conjunction with Griswold until today. I didn't even tell Val that's what I thought Griswold was."

"Balls."

"Yeah, so any connection Griswold had with the four-hundred-year-old werewolf trial was kept pretty well hidden until you found it on the Net. I never even made that connection, and believe me I have looked."

"Well, regardless of that . . . the original Peter what's-his-name is dead, and the Griswold of the 1970s is dead, so as spooky as this is it's all kind of academic."

Crow turned away and looked down the tangled path. "Maybe," he said.

"What's that supposed to mean?"

Crow turned back. "What if they're the same werewolf?"

"Oh, come on now, that's going too far. First you want me to believe you met a werewolf, now it's an immortal werewolf? Next thing you'll tell me that his real name is Dracula."

"Dracula was a vampire."

"Well, Crow, you want me to believe in ghosts and werewolves. Why not vampires, too?" Crow walked away from him and started down the path. Newton called, "Hey, while we're at it we can see if we can find a crop circle and maybe a leprechaun."

Crow held up one hand, forefinger raised.

**(2)**

Mark stood on the porch, leaning his shoulder against the pillar, the neck of a Sam Adams hooked between his index and forefingers. The sun was up but storm clouds were rising in a solid ring from every point on the horizon; they were closing like a camera aperture, shutting out the blue of the sky. In another half an hour it would be black as night. Weird weather patterns lately, he thought. When he heard the screen door open and then bang shut he knew it would be Val and not Connie following him out of the living room battle-ground.

He didn't turn to look, just said, "Don't start."

"I'm not going to say a damn thing." Val's voice was ice cold. Mark had heard his mother sound like that on those rare times when she and Dad were fighting.

"It's not your business anyway," he said.

"You're right, it's not."

"It's between Connie and me. So, butt out."

Val did not reply. He heard the boards of the slat bench creak as she sat down. Over beyond the barn an owl hooted, probably confused by the coming darkness, and there was the sound of some traffic on the road. Truck, by the sound of it.

The day had started okay, with Connie acting more like her old self, even to the point of doing a bit of gardening, but when Mark had come up behind her and wrapped his arms around her, pressing his loins up against her rump, she had screamed. Actually screamed, and then started struggling to get away from him like he was some kind of damn rapist. It made Mark sick and it scared him, and it also made him mad. He hadn't seen her struggle like that when Ruger was running his hands all over her that night, but when her husband wanted to cop a feel—her frigging husband who had *rights*—then she was all piss and vinegar, fighting for her maidenly honor. Well screw that. Then, of course, she had burst into tears and gone running off to cry on Val's shoulder. She cried all the damn time. There were times that he wanted to shake her, slap her, tell her to just get *over* it. It had been like that since they'd gotten home. Connie spent most of her time either crying or staring off into space like a zombie, and now they were sleeping in separate bedrooms.

Val was being a pain in the ass about it, too, always siding with Connie and treating him like he was Jack the Ripper.

"Mark?" He tried to ignore her. "Mark," she repeated, putting a finer edge to it.

"What?" he snapped, still looking out into the big dark. There was the sound of another vehicle out on A-32. A car this time.

"You need to get help, Mark."

Now he did turn and pointed at her with the half-empty beer bottle. "Yeah? Well you need to mind your own bloody business, Val."

Val sat almost primly on the bench, her legs crossed, hands folded in her lap, head cocked slightly to one side, appraising him. "I'm serious here, Mark. Connie's in therapy, and I think you need to see someone, too."

"Bullshit. The only one around here with a goddamn problem is my goddamn wife."

There was such a look of naked contempt in Val's face that even in the heat of his anger Mark couldn't look at it. He turned back to the gathering darkness, drank down the rest of his beer, and with a snarl of rage threw the bottle far out into the yard where it shattered against a stone.

"Mark," Val said, her voice softer as she got up and came to stand right behind him. "I understand that you're hurting because of what happened, but denial isn't going to—"

"Spare me the psychobabble," he hissed. Then he spun on his heel and shouldered past her into the house, letting the screen door slam emptily behind him.

### (3)

Crow stopped with a barrier-arm across Newton's chest. Since their last tête-à-tête they had walked for another hour, following a series of hills that appeared to be descending lower and lower into the roots of the mountains. Their path, such as it was, spilled out at the bottom of one of the longer hills and they stood completely shrouded in cloying shadows. Across from them, perhaps forty feet away, the other hill lifted tiredly on its long journey upward to find the hidden sunlight far above—sunlight that looked weaker now as clouds thickened overhead. To their right the valley between the hills wormed through some ancient glacial boulders and then widened into a thicket of gray and sickly trees. The undergrowth glistened wetly, as if covered in grease.

Slowly, Crow raised a finger. "Listen," he whispered.

Newton listened to the woods, to the air. It was like watching a movie with the sound turned down. "There's nothing," he murmured.

"Right," Crow said softly. "Absolutely nothing. No birds, no wind. Nothing. It's dead."

Crow nodded slowly. "Yeah. Good word for it."

They moved toward the thicket, entering a natural archway made from the laced fingers of empty branches. They took two paces into the corridor of black trees and then stopped, as still and silent as the forest around them. Both men blinked in surprise and alarm, both opened their mouths to speak; neither said a thing. If moving from sunlight into shadow on the hillside had jarred them, then entering the thicket positively struck them over their hearts. Both of them had stopped as if they had walked into some invisible barrier.

"Jesus Christ!" Crow gasped.

"Damn!" hissed Newton. They exchanged looks of shock.

"What just happened?" asked Newton in a hushed voice.

Crow just shook his head. He took a tentative step forward. His foot moved easily, there was no actual barrier, no specific tangible thing barring their way. He took a few steps, and then stopped and looked back to Newton, who seemed wholly unwilling to go any farther.

"Come on, Newt," said Crow in a hushed voice. "In for a penny. . . ."

Newton looked up, and the intertwining branches of the

skeletal trees made him feel as if he were inside some vast and monstrous rib cage. He followed slowly.

The archway of trees stretched on for nearly 150 yards, at times so narrow that they had to walk in single file while branches plucked at their coat sleeves, and sometimes wider, so they could stand side by side to leech confidence from the visible presence of the other. As they reached the end of the archway, they stopped again. Crow was still sweating profusely and he was breathing as heavily as he had during the long climb down the hill. Newton noticed, as he had before, that Crow's hands automatically and unthinkingly touched the butt of the pistol and the handle of the machete over and over again, like a pilgrim touching his talismans while in the land of the pagans.

Crow blotted his face with his sleeve and then froze, staring at the ground. He took two short steps and then squatted down. "Look at this." When Newton came over Crow pointed at a part of the dirt pathway visible through the fallen debris.

"Is that a footprint?"

"Yeah. Not too old, either. See, there's more of them. Someone's been down here, since it rained last." He brushed away some of the debris. "Couple of people. See? That set is all over the place. Looks like work shoes. But over here, smoother soles. Dress shoes."

"Could have been the cops. They were supposed to have come down to the Hollow, weren't they?" Newton asked.

"Maybe. Don't know if they came this far in, though." Crow shook his head as he rose. "Let's go."

They moved on for another ten minutes and once again Crow stopped. "That's it," he said, nodding toward the place beyond the archway, his voice low and as deflated as a flat tire. "I think we're here." He pointed to a spot just ahead where the path widened but was littered with grubby, stunted trees. Some of the trees were middle-aged, twenty-four years old or more, but not one of them looked healthy. Thick, hairy vines were wrapped like tentacles around nearly every trunk and sloped from one tree to its neighbor, and everywhere there were smaller vines with mottled gray-green leaves. Between the trees were fierce tangles of rough-looking shrubs and bushes, which combined with the vines to form wall after unfriendly wall between them and their destination. Along the ground moss ran like a poorly laid carpet, the dark green broken frequently by the bone-white caps of toadstools. Drifting sluggishly through the air was a sickroom smell of rotting vegetation and mold.

"Oh, man," said Newton, wiping his mouth. "What's wrong with this place?"

Crow's mouth was a tight line. "Everything," he said.

Pointing to the vines and bushes, Newton said, "How are we going to get through that? Can you see a path?"

Crow drew the machete with a rasp. "I'll cut a path. Stand clear and give me room to swing. I don't want to take your face off with this thing."

"Sounds fair," Newton said, fading back a few paces.

Crow moved forward, frowning at the imposing foliage, his eyes darting around, and then he slashed down with the machete. The blade sheared easily through the closest vine, severing it so that both ends fell away. Sap welled from the severed ends, like blood from a bisected snake, dotting the moss with black drops thick as syrup. Crow and Newton winced at the swinging, dripping ends of the vine. There was a smell like sulfur in the air. "Damn," muttered Crow. He looked at his blade, half-expecting to see the edge corroded as if by acid, but the flat blade was only stained with smelly sap. "Let's keep going. Stand back."

They cut their way into the forest that had grown up on Ubel Griswold's field, and it was brutal work. Within a dozen yards Crow was feeling tired, and he looked ready to drop. He moved his arm like it weighed about a thousand pounds and someone had poured concrete over both his shoes. Both he and Newton were splattered with dripping goo of a half-dozen shades and viscosities. All of the gunk from the unnameable plants stank like sulfur mixed with spoiled milk. Several times Crow had to stop to control his gag reflex, gulping down huge mouthfuls of air filtered by breathing against the folds of a sleeve he wrapped around his face.

"This is going to take forever," said Newton, exhausted from watching and beginning to get seriously worried for them both.

He looked at his wristwatch. "It's two o'clock already."

Crow wheeled around. "What?" he demanded. "It can't be that late!"

Newton showed him his watch, and Crow compared it to his own. 2:03 P.M. They stared at each other.

"It can't be that late already," Crow repeated.

Newton shook his head. "I know. I don't get it either. At this rate, we won't get back to town until past sunset, and let me tell you how much I don't want to be caught down here at night."

Crow cursed and drove the machete into the ground and drank some water from his canteen.

Newton pursed his lips judiciously and avoided eye contact with Crow. "So . . . you want to just bag it?"

"I can't," Crow snarled and then hacked the next vine, and the next.

### (4)

"If you don't stop that goddamned crying, Connie, so help me God, I'll . . ."

"You'll what?"

Mark stiffened and turned sharply. Val stood in the doorway to the bedroom, her dark hair tousled from the wind, her eyes narrow and cold. "You'll what?" she asked again. Her voice was as cold as her flat and level stare.

Mark stabbed a finger toward her. "You stay the hell out of this, Val. This is between Connie and me. It doesn't concern you. So butt out!"

Sprawled on the bed, Connie Guthrie lay with her face buried in her hands, her shoulders quietly trembling, her sobs faint against the louder rasp of Mark's agitated breathing.

Ignoring Mark, Val said, "Connie? Connie, are you all right?"

"No, she's not all right!" Mark spat. "She's on that crying kick again."

"Why don't you just leave her alone?"

"Leave her alone? That's all I've had to do since that night. She won't let me do anything *but* leave her alone! Christ! It's worse than living with a nun!"

Contempt showed in Val's eyes and the twist of her lips. "My God, you are a complete asshole, Mark," she sneered.

"Oh, kiss my ass! Besides," he snapped, "who are you to lecture me? At least *you're* getting laid. Oh, no! Don't try to deny it! Don't you think I know why Crow talked us into going out last night? He just wanted to get in your pants. Hey, I'm not criticizing, Val, don't get me wrong. I just think I'd like to know what it feels like. Shit, a married man and you'd think I can at least get a frigging kiss from my wife. Hah! Not with the Crying Game over here. I even look at her and she's all tears and hysterics and all that bullshit. Shit. The way she acts, you'd think it was *me* who attacked her."

"Isn't that what you were about to do when I came in?" Val said coldly, and saw the point strike deep, but Mark's anger was too big to let a little shame deflate it.

"No, Miss Know-it-all! I was not about to attack her. I'm just trying to get things back to the way they were. I mean, hell, there was a time—and it wasn't all that long ago—when I could actually touch my wife without her going to pieces."

"Poor baby," Val said. "Did you stop to think how she feels?"

Mark looked down at Connie, who still had her face buried in her hands, refusing, or unable, to look up. He slowly raised his head to face his sister and there were hot tears in his eyes. "Just what the hell is that supposed to mean? I was *there*, Val. I saw what he did. I went through it, too, you know. It wasn't just her. Ruger kicked my ass and tried to screw her right in front of me. Another couple of

minutes and I'd have had to watch my wife have sex with another man. Do you know how that makes me feel?"

Val shook her head in disbelief. "Listen to you. Do you
even know what you're saying? You said you would have had
to watch Connie have sex with another man. Is that how you
see it? That she was going to have sex with him?"

"Well, just what the hell do you think rape is?"

Val's voice dropped lower in both tone and temperature.
"Rape isn't sex, dumbass. He was going to hurt her, not
make love to her, not screw her, not have sex with her. He
was going to hurt her, inside and out. If you think what he
was going to do was have sex with her, then you are a total
jackass!"

"Oh, please, let's leave feminist propaganda out of this,
shall we?"

"Do you really equate rape with sex? Are you actually
that stupid? God!"

"You don't understand—" he began, faltering just a little,
but she cut him off with a swift chop of words.

"I don't understand? Kiss my ass! I'm a woman, and I
know what it feels like to be afraid of men just because
they're bigger and stronger. You just can't imagine it, Mark,
to be afraid of walking outside in the dark, of being alone
with a man in a parking lot or an elevator or anywhere. To always have to be on your guard! To always realize that your
body—your actual body—can be invaded by a man, just because he has the physical power to do it! That's something
every woman lives with all her life. You think women have
nightmares of monsters and ghosts? We don't. We have dreams
of being raped and abused because some nasty trick of ge-
netics decided we'd be the smaller, weaker ones, that we were
the ones to have vaginas that could be so easily invaded.
That's what almost happened to Connie. Another couple of
minutes and he would have invaded her with all his rage and
ugliness. Yeah, you would have had to watch, but that would
have hurt your male pride more than your heart. You actually
have the balls to tell me it would hurt you to have seen your

wife have sex with another man. How about imagining what it would have been like to have Ruger's hands all over your skin, his mouth on you, his cock inside of you, his sweat on your skin, and his semen inside of you. Do you call that having sex? Christ, you are a pathetic excuse for a human being, Mark!"

Mark Guthrie stood there, trembling with rage, fists balled at his sides, glaring at her, his mouth drawn into tight lines that showed a double row of clenched teeth. "Don't you *dare* talk to me like that!" he snarled in a deadly whisper. "This is none of your goddamn business! Who the hell do you think you are to talk to me like that? Who the hell do you—"

Val's hard left hand slapped the rest of the words into silence. It was a hard blow and so fast he never saw it, and it spun him halfway around. For a moment he stood there, eyes wide with shock, a hand pressed to his cheek, head ringing from the blow. He straightened and both of his hands became fists.

"What are you going to do, Mark?" Val asked harshly. "Are you going to hit me back?"

"If you ever do that again," he said in a fierce whisper, "I'll—"

"You'll what?" Val snapped. "Will you do to me what you were threatening to do to Connie if she didn't stop crying? Is that your only answer? To hurt women instead of being a real man and trying to help?"

He raised one fist, wanting with every fiber of his being to smash her into silence, to shut her mouth, to stop the flow of words. Val stood there and looked at him, ignoring the heavy fist poised above her, just looking at him.

She said, "If it will make you feel like a man, Mark, go on and hit me. You're bigger than me. Go ahead and do it. Be a man."

The fist trembled, shaking visibly as every muscle in his body strove one against another, warring with rage and confusion and a mindless compulsion to smash. Then, with a growl of inarticulate rage, he spun away and slammed out of the room. Val heard him stomp down the stairs, heard the sound of the hallway closet door opening and then banging shut, heard the front door slam open, then heard only the silence of the house and the soft sounds of Connie's sobs.

"Shit," Val said softly to herself as she sat down on the edge of the bed and stroked Connie's hair, listening to her tears. After a while, she, too, wept.

### (5)

The storm clouds encircling the sun closed ranks and blotted out the sky. They were thick clouds, swollen with cold rain and drooping low over the town. In just minutes day turned to an early twilight so thick that streetlamp sensors triggered and the sodium vapor lights flickered on. Drivers turned on their headlights. None of this stopped the celebrations. Little Halloween rolled through the town thicker and heavier than the clouds overhead.

Deep in the cellar of the house, down in the darkness below old floorboards, the white things in their nest *stirred,* knowing that the sunlight had faded. Sleep, for now, was ended. Night had come early to Pine Deep.

# Chapter 25

## (1)

As the sky darkened overhead with the coming storm Crow continued to hack his way through the dense vine-choked brush. Then he broke through a wall of stinking vines and beyond it the path abruptly widened and the way ahead was unobstructed. They walked around the bushes rather than battling them. The ground, though, was marshy, soft, and unpleasantly spongy under their feet, sometime yielding inches under their weight, sometimes unexpectedly firm, but always requiring care. Crow was troubled about Newton, who was clearly not a woodsman. The thought of having to carry a broken-legged Newton up the hill was unappealing.

"Move slow," he said, "this muck'll pull your boot right off."

Newton stopped and pointed. "What's that? Is that a wall?"

Crow stopped and looked where Newton was pointing. Their marshy path broadened even further and then spilled out into a field. On the near side of the field, crowded back against the forest wall, was a flat mass of gray-white. "Sure as hell is," he said, his throat going dry.

They moved through the forest with great caution, watching as the gray flatness took shape, became defined, resolved into walls and bricks and window frames. After a few dozen paces it was clear to them that they were approaching the place from the side, through a wall of trees that probably once stood as a backpiece to the house, in woods that would have remained untouched even as the forward acres were converted into farmlands and fields.

They crept closer, breathing shallowly, careful of the sound of each footfall as they studied the house. It was a huge old three-story pile of a place that looked like something out of a Charles Addams drawing, with a pitched and shingled roof surrounded by a decorative wrought-iron railing and improbable gables that looked like they had been attached as an afterthought. A broad-aproned porch ran completely around the house, the rail overgrown with ivy. Beginning at the edge of what had probably once been a path leading from the front yard and into the woods where they now stood was a wall made from rough-cut blocks that were about a cubic foot each; the wall began in the front as a knee-high double layer of stone and climbed, layer upon layer, until it reached its full height equal with the bottom of the house's rear windows. The effect was that the wooden part of the house looked like it had been fitted into a huge stone socket.

Ivy and wisteria climbed all over the stone and sent tendrils up the wooden planks all the way to the roof. Some kind of dense weed that looked like onion grass covered most of the visible parts of the roof, sprouting right up between the faded shingles. The wooden walls were brown with old paint and age, but they were still whole and looked strong. There were no holes in the walls, no crumbled sections of the wall, no evidence that any part of the roof might have collapsed. Except for the proliferation of the vegetation, the house might have been abandoned only a year ago, not three decades past.

"Are you sure this is the place?" Newton asked. "You said it'd be some kind of old hovel."

As they moved closer Crow started shaking his head.

"This can't be right," he said. "But—it has to be. The map I looked at only showed one house on this lot, and this whole parcel belonged to him."

They moved closer, stopping again within twenty yards. There were thick sheets of plywood covering all of the windows on their side of the house. The side yard was a tangle of rowdy pumpkin vines, and all the pumpkins were obscenely swollen with disease. Crow squinted at the house, said nothing, but when he moved closer he drew the machete again. Newton followed him, holding his hiking stick at an angle across his chest as if it formed some kind of barrier between him and what he was feeling because of that house.

The house stood almost in a clearing except for four huge oaks that leaned so close to the house that their outstretched limbs and branches effectively kept the whole place in shadow. The first sunlight Crow and Newton had seen since entering the Hollow came no closer than the front yard and they glanced up to see that the whole sky was an almost solid mass of purple clouds except for a single hole up in the southern quadrant, beyond the tree line. A solitary ray angled down and its light glimmered on the brown tips of the grass like a promise of hope, but it was surrounded by despair, and it seemed badly overmatched by the gloom.

Careful not to make any noise, Crow and Newton drifted toward the patch of sunlight and stood in it as they examined the house. Weak as it was, the warmth of the sun and its golden light seemed to soak into their skin all the way to their bones like a shot of good brandy. Some of the oppressive weariness melted away under its heat, but the caution and apprehension they had both felt as they stared at the front of Griswold's house obdurately remained. They lingered there and soaked up the warmth.

Now that they were closer to the house they could see that front porch had peeling whitewashed posts that held up a decrepit porch roof, which was the only part of the house that looked like it bore the ponderous weight of thirty years of disuse and neglect. The front windows were covered with plywood. Each sheet was larger than the window and appeared to be nailed right into the wooden front wall.

"Get your camera out," said Crow. "I want some pictures. Get the whole house. All four sides."

Newton pulled out his small Minolta digital, tucked his walking stick under his arm, and left the patch of sunlight to begin shooting. As he stepped out of the patch of sunlight he was amazed at the difference in temperature and humidity of the shadows clutched around the house. Crow headed to the left, prowling around the perimeter of the house, frowning at everything. When Newton reached the front of the house, he stopped, staring at the patch of sunlit ground where they had stood.

"You done?" Crow asked from right behind and Newton actually screamed. It wasn't much of scream, more of a yelp, but he did jump inches into the air and landed in a crouch, spinning around. He hadn't realized that Crow had circled the house and come up behind him from the other side.

"Don't *do* that! You about scared the piss out of me!"

"Oh?" Crow said with a snide grin. "Is this place getting to you?"

Newton flipped him the bird.

Crow moved past him and squatted down on the bottom step so that his line of vision was just above that of the porch floor. "Newt . . . don't put your camera away just yet. Take a look at this."

"What is it?" Newton climbed up onto the porch to where Crow stood in front of the boarded-up window to the left of the door.

Crow pointed with his machete. "Looks like footprints in the dust there on the porch. Can't tell how old they are, though. There's been a lot of rain . . ." his voice trailed off and he rose to his feet, brow furrowed in perplexity. "Oh . . . shit."

"What?"

Crow stepped onto the porch and used his blade to tap the wood covering the window to the left of the door. "What's your read on this?"

"Yes. Plywood. I have seen it before. Very impressive."

"Okay, smartass, you're a hotshot reporter. You're supposed to be a good observer, so observe. Tell me what's wrong with this picture."

Newton stepped closer, peering at the four-by-eight sheet of heavy three-quarter plywood. It had been securely affixed to the wall with at least fifty heavy-duty sixteen-penny nails. The nail heads were neatly spaced and hammered flush. Professionally done, no owl-eyes, no miss-strokes. There was a pale-blue stencil inked onto the surface of the wood sheet, repeated twice in the high left and lower right corners. The lettering read BILDMOR LUMBER—CRESTVILLE. "Well," he said, "I can say with some confidence that this, indeed, is plywood."

Crow made a disgusted noise. "No shit, Sherlock. Don't you think there's anything a little odd about it?"

"Um. No. Not really."

"Christ on the cross," Crow snapped. "Newt, this place has been deserted for thirty years. We know nobody owns it because I checked the deed yesterday. Look at the plywood, for God's sake. It's still *green!*"

Newton did look at it and his mouth slowly opened. "Oh," he said.

"Look at the nail heads. Shiny bright. They're brand-new."

"Oh . . . shit."

"I'll bet this hasn't been up for more than a couple of weeks. All of the windows are the same. I checked. All the lumber is new, all the nails are new."

"Oh," Newton said, "shit."

"Uh huh," Crow said and his eyes were bright and even a little wild, "but there's more, kid, and this is the kicker. This is the cat's ass." He pointed to the double front doors. They were heavy and ornate, and once had long glass panels, but the panes were covered over with neatly sawn strips of plywood as green as what covered the windows. But what Crow was indicating was the chain that held the doors closed. One hole had been drilled through each door and a heavy length of brand-new steel welded chain was laced through, effectively chaining the doors shut. Crow lifted the slack and gave it a shake to show how solidly the doors were held fast. The links were as thick as Crow's thumb.

"Damn," Newton observed, bending close to examine the chain. "We'll never break that."

"No shit. It's the same on the backdoor."

"What do you think? Caretaker?"

Crow felt like punching the man. "Jesus, Mary, and Joseph, Newton, are you friggin' blind?"

"What? I can see the chain. I can see that it's as new as the plywood."

"Newt," Crow said with as much patience as he could muster. "Where's the lock?"

"The, er, lock?" Newton looked blank, then he got it. The loop of chain emerged from one drilled hole and reentered the house through the hole on the other door. What Crow held in his hand was an uninterrupted length of slack. "Oh, shit," Newton said again, with greater emphasis.

"Yeah."

*The chain was padlocked on the inside of Griswold's house.*

"Back door?"

"The same?"

"Cellar door?"

"Uh huh."

"Crow . . . whoever slung those chains—"

"—is inside that house," Crow said and then gave Newton a ghastly smile. "Inside with all the windows all boarded up."

"So no sunlight can get in," Newton said softly. Even more softly he said, "Uh oh."

"Yeah."

"Crow, trite as may be to say it, I have a very bad feeling about this."

"Yeah. I've had a bad feeling since we came out of the woods. The place is in too good a shape, and that bothers the hell out of me." Licking his lips nervously, Crow stepped closer to the door and reached out with one tentative hand to touch the wood. The plywood was cool and felt slightly damp. "That's weird."

"Put your hand on the wood."

"I really don't want to."

Crow said nothing, but continued to touch the door. There was a faint tremble and he couldn't tell if it was coming through the wood or was the shaking of his own hand. He closed his eyes to try to focus his sense of touch and instantly the trembling became more pronounced, and it wasn't just in the wood. He could feel it rippling in waves up his arm as if the whole house was vibrating. Then, in the deepest part of his brain, the place where his fears lived, where those last words of Ruger echoed without end, he heard a voice whisper to him.

*She is going to die and there is nothing you can do to save her. Nothing!*

It was so deep, so tangled up with his own fears that he almost didn't hear it, but then the vibration in the wood spiked and he cried out and staggered back as if the wood had sent a shock through his skin.

Newton looked at him. "What's wrong with you?"

Crow just shook his head, looking pale and shaken.

"Why'd you call out like that? Why'd you call her name?"

Crow frowned at him. "What?"

"Just now. You yelped like you'd been burned and then said 'Val!' real loud. What's the deal?"

"I . . . don't know," Crow said. "I don't think I said that . . . did I?" He looked down at his hand and his palm was an angry red. In his mind the words replayed in a nasty whisper: *She is going to die and there is nothing you can do to save her. Nothing!* "Jesus Christ," he said slowly, "I wanted to come here, you know, to ease my fears, to put this shit to rest. I didn't come here for this shit."

"No argument."

"I think we should get the fuck out of here and I mean now!"

Newton only nodded and together they backed off the

porch, lingering at the top step just long enough for Newton to take a picture of the front door, but as he did so he dropped the walking stick that he'd tucked under his arm. He bent down to pick it up and instantly there was a tremendous *CRACK!* and the entire center section of the sagging porch tore free from the age-weakened supports and plummeted downward. Newton heard the sound and looked up but he was shocked into immobility, absolutely frozen to the spot; then something hit him in the side hard enough to drive all the air out of his lungs and he was swept off the porch and went tumbling down into the yard, banging elbows and knees as he went. Crow, who had tackled him, rolled over and over with him until they both lay sprawled in the weeds two yards from the porch. The sound of a ton of wood and plaster crashing down onto the tired boards of the porch floor was like a slow thunderclap that chased them down into the yard and washed over them to echo off the stone wall and the distant line of trees.

Sprawled among the weeds in a tangle of too many arms and legs, chests heaving with shock, hearts hammering like fists against the insides of their sternums, mouths dry with dust and terror, they looked up to where the bare porch should have been, but what they saw was a mass of jagged spikes of wood, torn plaster, ripped shingle, and splintered lath. A cloud of gray dust hung over everything like smog.

"My . . . God!"

Crow struggled to a sitting position and spit grit onto the ground between his shoes. "You almost met your God."

"That was . . . the roof?"

"Used to be," Crow said and winced as weeks-old aches flared up again. The wrist Ruger had nearly crushed was throbbing badly, and his palm felt burned.

"Oh my . . . it could have . . ." Newton sputtered. "I mean, it nearly fell on us."

"Yes, it sure as hell did."

Newton swallowed and they sat there, staring at the porch. He cleared his throat. "Kind of strange, it happening just now."

"Oh, you *think*?" Crow shook his head.

Another chunk of the roof sagged down, hung swaying for a moment, and then broke off and thudded down onto the mess, kicking up more dust.

"That's not normal," Newton said.

Crow said, "We left normal when we started down that hill."

Newton felt something warm on his forehead and wiped his hand over his face. It came away with a smear of blood across the palm. "Shit." He glanced at Crow, who was picking pieces of dust off his tongue. "Is it bad?"

Crow leaned over and peered at the cut. "You'll live." He dug a Kleenex out of his shirt pocket and handed it to him.

"You saved my life," Newton said, marveling at the idea. He had never been close to death before and the thought that he was actually in a real life-or-death moment excited him, despite his fear. He dabbed at the cut and then stared at the tissue, amazed at how intensely red his own blood was. "I don't know what to say."

"For the love of God, do us both a favor and save the gushy shit for some other time. Preferably after time ends. Besides, I was trying to save my own ass and I jumped off the porch. You were in the way, so you got to come along for the ride. End of story."

"Fair enough."

"So—let's go back to Plan A, which is hauling ass out of here." Crow crossed his legs under him and got to his feet, then bent and began slapping the dust off his trousers, glancing at the house as he did so. Newton was looking at Crow and saw his face change from annoyed to slack to a mask of total shock, and Newton whipped his head around to follow the line of Crow's gaze. What he saw twisted his heart like a rag and together they stared in complete horror as from the cracked and shattered timbers of the broad porch roof, from each little pocket of space between beams and shingles, through all the weather-worn holes in the lumber poured a seething, bristling, boiling black mass of roaches. Thousands of them. Tens of thousands, their chitinous shells gleaming like polished coal, their million scrabbling legs skittering and hissing over the debris. The whole black festering tide of them began sweeping down the porch stairs directly at them.

Crow grabbed Newton's coat and hauled him up, spun him roughly, and gave him a violent shove away from the house. "RUN!" he screamed.

And they ran. Both of them, very fast, as behind them a wave of insects swept after them with a hiss like foam over the hard-packed sand of a beach. They left behind the walking stick and Newton's camera, which he had dropped again during the fall from the porch. They left behind Crow's machete, buried now under tons of rubble through which a hundred thousand roaches were swarming.

Crow and Newton ran the wrong way at first, cutting in the most direct line across the large front yard, dashing through the patch of sunlight to the edge of the forest by the overgrown fields, tearing along the line of trees, moving fast despite the spongy ground. Crow risked a hasty glance over his shoulder. He was horrified to see that the roaches were spreading out across the field, the carpet of them covering dozens of square yards.

"Christ!" he said. They kept running until they were into the woods, then as one they realized they were heading in the wrong direction. Crow looked back again and saw that the roaches had reached the patch of sunlight. He skidded to a halt for a moment, stunned by what he was seeing. As the roaches reached the strip of sunlight, they parted neatly, going left and right around it, avoiding it completely.

He grabbed Newton's shirt and pulled him to a stop. "Newt! Are you seeing this?"

The reporter stood there, eyes bulging, mouth working for a while until he gasped out a single word. "God!" The roaches raced around the sunlit patch, reforming into a single seething mass as they reached the end of it, and the reformed tide of black bugs scrabbled and whispered on toward them. "They're still coming," Newton cried.

Crow nodded sharply. He glanced around to reorient himself. "This way—come on!" Moving as fast as their legs could carry them, they tore along the edge of the woods, making a wide circle back toward the side of the house where they had first left the forest. The roaches turned, following as if guided by radar; the change in vector gave them a shorter distance to cover and they seemed to devour that distance, rolling like a sheet of oil over stone and leaf and withered grass.

"They're going to cut us off!" yelled Newton.

"Shut up and run!" Together they raced to the entrance to the forest of old-growth trees and made radical turns, skittering on the moss and wasting valuable seconds trying to find traction. The roaches came in like a midnight tide, the gap closed to barely a few yards. Crow took the lead, his boots getting better purchase than Newton's sneakers. He reached back and again took hold of the reporter's shoulder and pulled him along until they ran side by side, sometimes guiding, sometimes pushing. Breath rasped and wheezed in their lungs, blood roared in the ears. They burst out of the grove into the thicker forest of diseased trees and dripping vines, running hard back up the path they had come.

Something moved at the edge of Crow's vision and he turned his head to see a second wave of cockroaches swarming out of the back of the house. They were not racing toward them but were almost heading in the same direction. Then Crow realized what they were doing and a knife of terror stabbed him in the heart. The roaches were not paralleling their course, they were racing forward at a converging angle. In seconds the way forward was going to be completely blocked.

### (2)

Mike Sweeney stood in the shop doorway and looked back into the store, his eyes roving over every aisle and rack of the Crow's Nest. Ever since he could remember he'd been coming into the store to spend his allowance—when he hadn't lost it as a penalty for accidentally breaking one of Vic's many household rules—or his paper-route money on the

stuff Crow sold. Mostly comics and half-priced old paperbacks, but also model kits and posters and science fiction
novelties. One summer he had managed to score the entire
Ace Books run of Edgar Rice Burroughs—the ones with the
Frank Frazetta or Roy Krenkel covers. The store had always
been the single most fun place in town, and one of the few
places where he didn't feel like a geek or an outsider. Hell,
no one was a bigger geek than Crow.

Now he was standing in the doorway with a ring of keys
in his hand, ready to lock the place up after having worked
there all day. He was now a part of the place, and just thinking about made his head a little swimmy and his feet feel
like they weren't really touching the ground. He was grinning so hard his face hurt, though considering the bruises he
still had, that wasn't saying as much as it should. At that moment he wouldn't have cared all that much if he knew he was
going home to another of Vic's beatings. Now he had somewhere to be, and some*one* to be. Now he had Crow.

Mike stepped out and pulled the door shut, locked both of
the locks, and pocketed the keys. He'd taken care of the re-
stocking, counted out the till, and put the cash drawer with
the day's take in Crow's apartment, fed his cats, and shut the
place down. It was Little Halloween, and though there had
been brisk traffic through the store all day, Crow had said
that it would die by sunset because there were so many things
going on just outside of the town proper—the movie marathon
at the Dead End Drive-In, parties on the campus, fireworks
up by the Crescent Bridge, and a rock concert at the Hayride.
Crow told him that he could close at five tonight, which left
him four whole hours before he had to be home. He wanted
to be on his bike—the War Machine—and be out flying along
the roads, feeling the wind and feeling the freedom. He walked
down the alley beside the store and unchained his bike from
the chain-link fence, rolled it back to the street, and swung
his leg carefully over it, though his wince was more a reflex
than a reaction. Though he still hurt in a hundred little places,
the aches were small and dull and fading. All of the big pains,
even his broken rib, had vanished over the last few nights.

*The fugue was a furnace—a forge—and he melted in it like iron ore.*

Mike thought that this speeded-up healing was due to puberty. He was almost fifteen and he was aware of the changes in his body, the thickening of his muscles, the hair growing under his arms and on his crotch, the broadening of his palms and the soles of his feet, the shadowy faintness of a red-gold mustache. He figured that as you got older you healed faster. Why else could pro ballplayers shake off those train-wreck collisions on the gridiron? Why else could boxers take hit after hit in the ring? It made sense to him.

*In the furnace of the fugue the impurities are burned away and the metal becomes denser.*

He had no idea at all that each night he was taking a short trip sideways out of his body, or perhaps just *winking out* for a bit. Not being there.

*The purified metal waits for the blacksmith's hammer to learn its shape and its purpose.*

Walking the bike to the top of Corn Hill, he paused for a moment, enjoying as always the colorful complexity of Pine Deep's many stores and galleries and shops, and then he kicked off and swooped down the hill and up the other side, banked hard right onto Orenda Street, and rolled past the Dark Hollow Inn and Corn Dolly's Bar, both bright with lights and activity, the usual late weekend crowd swollen with scores of people from out of town. He rocketed by Dragon's Lair Games, which was still packed with kids, and past the darkened windows of the town's biggest store, Gordon Python's Fine Antiques, closed now for the day. Little Halloween revelers were never known for antiquing of a Friday evening. Feeling happy for the first time in a long time, he kicked the War Machine into action again and stopped at Half-Baked to buy a couple of pumpkin muffins, still hot from the oven.

"Hey, Mike," said Hillary MacPeake, leaning out of the little sales window cut into the side of the store, "what happened to you?"

Mike constructed a sheepish smile. "Oh, I fell off my bike."

"Ooo, looks painful."

"It's not that bad," he said, his tone light, and in truth the bruises hardly hurt at all.

"Well, just be careful."

"Thanks." Chewing the soft, spicy muffin, he pedaled off into the darkness. *Be careful,* he thought. *Now that's a joke. How can you be careful when you live with a monster?*

He headed south, away from the lights and activity of town, and as he approached the turn onto Route A-32 he slowed, looking out at the long black ribbon of asphalt as it rose up and down the hills and snaked around out of sight. This used to be part of his regular paper route, but since the near-miss with that wrecker the other night he hadn't been out there. Then he remembered that he had planned to approach Officer Oswald about it and had been so caught up in Crow's attempts to make him the next Karate Kid that it had somehow totally slipped his mind.

*The chrysalis has only a few defense mechanisms, but it tries. It tries.*

Now that memory clicked back into place and he slowed to a stop, debating. He could turn around now and find Oswald . . . or he could finally own up to the realization that the whole tow-truck thing was not what he thought it was. It was a near miss with some drunk asshole who thought it would be fun to play chicken with a kid on a bike. That was all. Anything else, he told himself, was ridiculous. Besides, he had no witnesses, no proof.

He looked down the road. "Crow wouldn't chicken out," he said aloud. "He's not afraid of anything."

With those words in the front of his brain, Mike set his jaw, kicked down hard on the pedal, and shot the War Machine forward onto the black road.

(3)

The late afternoon gloom churned around Mark as he bulled his way through it. The shadows thrown by the big oaks and the tall barn resisted him, jostling his shoulders as he hunched forward into the stiff wind, stalking purposefully toward the empty nowhere of the farm road that led away from the house and eventually into the fields. His legs pumped like a fortissimo metronome, marking the rhythm of his furious pace. He paused once to angrily light a cigarette, sucking in fiercely enough to ignite a third of the Camel and fairly spitting the blue smoke into the night air; then he snapped his lighter shut with the metallic aggression of lopping shears and shoved it in his pocket as he resumed his march toward the end of his own anger.

The actual physical destination turned out to be the barn, not by any choice but merely because it loomed up in front of him and he stopped, startled, and looked up at it as if he'd never seen it before. His surprise betrayed the intense confusion in his mind: he hadn't realized he'd walked this far from the house or even in that particular direction. He stood in the road, smoking the cigarette in harsh puffs, whipping the butt out of his mouth between each puff and blowing the smoke out in a thin, forced stream as he regarded the barn. It was the same barn he'd always seen, the barn that had been there when he had been born, the same barn he'd helped his father paint red when he was ten and repaint twice since then. It was the same barn in which he'd smoked his very first cigarette; the same barn in which he and Val had spent many a covert hour leaping from the loft into the massive hay mounds that covered most of the floor. It was the same barn where he and Connie had first kissed almost thirteen years ago, and where he had first made love to her, nestled there in the soft fragrant straw of the highest loft, the two of them losing their virginity together in a few moments of sweet, clumsy fumbling that possessed far more passion than skill. It was the same barn where he had had his last conversation with his father prior to that terrible night. Mark had come home for lunch and had spent twenty minutes talking to Dad about Terry Wolfe's offer to lease a parcel of their land to build a Christmas Town attraction. Dad had said he'd think about it, and Mark had driven back to his office at the college. The next time he would see his dad would be while they were all hostages to Karl Ruger, and from that moment on everything had gone to shit.

Mark walked slowly up to the tall red sidewall of the barn. He reached out to touch it, drawn for some reason to the wooden planks, needing to feel the slightly pebbled surface of the thick layers of red paint. The paint felt cold, but it felt real, and it was an old and familiar texture. Mark leaned his forehead against the wood, closing his eyes and then screwing them up into tight pits of gristle as a wave of unbearably intense emotion crashed down on the shores of his soul. His lips writhed, trying to speak, trying to articulate what he needed to say. His chest ached with the burning need to scream.

In the end, all he could say was one word. *"Connie!"*

It came out as a whisper of mingled desperation, self-loathing, and fear that he had lost her forever. He stared inward across the vast empty landscape that stretched between his wife and his own impotent, damaged soul and wondered how he could ever make such an impossible journey back to her. With each beat of his breaking heart he pounded on the side of the barn with a balled fist. Inside the barn the echoes sounded like the amplified beating of a giant's pulse.

"Connie!" he whispered in a voice choked with tears. Slowly, his knees buckled and he sank to the cold ground, huddling against the barn, not cowering away from the cold, but sinking into his own defeat and failure.

He did not see the shadow rising between him and the distant cloud-choked sky. He was so lost in his grief that he never even felt the coldness of it, a frost harsher and deeper than the icy blast of the October wind. He never saw the pale white hand reach out of the shadows, and knew nothing at all about it until it was far too late.

# Chapter 26

## (1)

The first swarm of roaches swept toward them. Fifty yards away. Forty. The second swarm was still a hundred yards away but it was moving with incredible speed.

"Keep running!" Crow yelled and reached back to grab Newton's shoulder. With a growl of fury he propelled the reporter forward and then ran a half pace behind him, ready to shove him again if he slowed. "Run!"

They ran toward the rough path Crow had hacked through the vines, but by the time they had taken twenty steps it was clear that the second swarm would cut them off long before they reached it. Crow grabbed Newton's arm and they both skidded to a halt as around them the whole forest seemed to be rustling with the sound of a million tiny legs. Crow looked back toward the house and the field. There was still that one big patch of sunlight and there was the fact that the wave of roaches had split apart to avoid it.

"God, let me be right about this," he said and quickly squatted down to make sure his trouser cuffs were tucked tightly inside his boots. "Newt, listen," he said, rising and talking fast. "No questions, no arguments. Just follow me. Fast!"

With that he spun around and ran full tilt toward the field—straight at the oncoming mass of insects.

Newton goggled at him. "Are you *crazy*?" he screeched, but Crow was going at a dead run and within seconds had reached the wave of roaches and kept going. From twenty feet away Newton could hear the sound of Crow's Timberlines crunching on the shiny backs of the creatures, the carapaces cracking like pistachio shells. Crow ran fast, arms and legs pumping, heading deeper and deeper into the sea of bristling black bugs. Some of them turned to pursue him and collided with the wave of oncoming bugs, causing a rage of overlapping currents that bubbled up off the ground.

"RUN!" he heard Crow yell over his shoulder.

"Oh, Jesus," Newton said as the leading edge of the swarm flew toward him, "don't make me do this." Then he was running, too, and with his first step his sneaker crunched down onto the shiny black shells and he could hear the bugs pop wetly. He ran as fast as he could, and he stared at Crow's back twenty feet ahead of him. He fixed on that, not daring to look down, knowing without seeing that the roaches were milling in confusion as the leading edge of the wave was fighting to turn and follow while the main mass of them was still in motion forward. Their bodies boiled up around his ankles as he ran and he tried to pick up his knees so that his ankles would be as high off the ground as possible with each step. He was horribly aware of how low his sneaker tops were.

He ran and ran, and within a dozen steps his shoes were smeared with a sticky white-green goo of insect guts and still the roaches swarmed around him in their legions; the hiss of their bodies scraped against one another and the whisper of their legs over the rough ground was dreadful. He ran as the air burned in his lungs and pain blossomed in his chest like fireworks, all the time watching Crow's back as the man pelted down the path back the way they had come. Crow was running faster, pulling ahead yard by yard.

*We're going to die!* He thought as he ran. *We're going to die!* It was the only clear thought he could manage.

Roaches leapt at him, clung to his clothes, crawled up his pants legs as he ran, and Newton was uttering a high-pitched continuous cry of total terror. The field was still a hundred yards ahead and now Crow was almost up to the back wall of the house. Newton saw this and a fresh wave of terror struck him as he suddenly remembered that whoever or whatever had locked itself in that house could use their keys to unlock the locks, and then those doors would open. Front door, backdoor, cellar door. All of them would open, and what—dear sweet God, *what*?—would come howling out?

*We're going to die!* He thought, but deep down another, far more horrible feeling was growing. It had no words, no specific shape, but Newton was gradually becoming aware of the possibility that there might be things in that house worse than roaches, perhaps worse than death.

"Newt!" Crow's voice shook him into awareness and he turned away from the house and saw that ahead of him Crow had suddenly stopped running. Newton almost stopped as well, which would have been fatal because the roaches were gaining on him, coming at him from every direction, both swarms now joined into one vast bristling ocean, but Crow had stopped because he had reached the clear patch of sunlight. He whirled around, alternately brushing bugs off of his clothing and waving furiously to Newton. "Come on! Over here! In the light! Run, goddamn it, *RUN!*"

### (2)

"He hates me," Connie said hollowly, staring bleakly over the steam rising from her teacup. The kitchen was painted in shadows with only a single lamp on.

Val squeezed her shoulder. "No, he doesn't. He's just confused. I don't think he's gotten over Dad's death yet. He's rattled and upset and doesn't know how to react." She stroked Connie's hair.

"But you yourself said—"

"I was mad at him," she admitted, "and I was trying to shock him enough to snap him out of it. But . . . I seem to have only made him madder. We'd better give him time to cool down, sweetie. He'll come around." Her words did not match her thoughts, though. She prayed that Mark was out there now, wherever he was—sulking over a beer at the Harvestman, probably—thinking about those horrible things he had said and feeling bad about it. Maybe he'd come back soon, not crawling or abashed, but like a man, owning up to the things he'd said and done over these last couple of weeks, and ready to make things right. That would be great, but it was a bit too storybook and Val had her doubts. Maybe one day, but today didn't feel like it was going to end with a Kodak moment.

They sat staring through the kitchen windows at the golden sunlight shining on the autumn-colored leaves of the big oak in the yard. All day it had been cloudy and now, just before sunset, the sun had drilled its way through the gray and the yard looked beautiful. It made her wonder what the forest was like down by Dark Hollow where Crow was. Was he seeing the same sunlight all the way down there? He could use it, she thought. Crow had been sweating his little hiking trip for days. Unconsciously she touched her stomach, and to the tiny baby just beginning to grow inside of her, she said, *Your daddy's a crazy man.*

Connie said, "It's not that I don't want to . . . you know . . . *do* things with him. You know what I mean. In the bedroom and all—it's just that I can't. I just can't." Connie stared into the depths of her teacup as if there were answers down there. "Every time Mark tries to touch me, all I can feel is that man's hands on me, and—and—"

"Whoa . . . shhhhh, girl," Val said, reaching over to squeeze her hand. "Don't go there. Try to let it be. I understand what you're going through. I'm still going through some of it myself."

Connie looked at her, surprised. "You?"

"Uh huh. Nearly every night I see him in my dreams. Sometimes I wake up and imagine I can see him standing at my window. Pale, like a ghost. Scares hell out of me."

With a shudder and a nod, Connie said, "Yes! That's how I see him!"

Val laughed. "God, will you listen to us? We're worse than a couple of Girl Scouts around a campfire."

Connie tried on a smile, but it was too weak to hold. "I know . . . but I can't help it."

"Yeah, me neither, but I do remind myself that it's just dreams . . . and dreams can't hurt us. At least we have the satisfaction of knowing he's dead." Val stood up and gave Connie a quick hug and repeated, "He can't hurt us." She stepped back and smoothed her jeans. "Come on. Let's take a walk. I need to get out of the house for a few minutes, catch the last of the sunshine."

Connie looked doubtfully at the silent phone. "What if Mark calls?"

"Then he can damn well leave a message. Come on."

### (3)

Tow-Truck Eddie cruised the black road from Corn Hill all the way down to the Black Marsh Bridge and didn't see a single kid on a bike. There were plenty of kids out, but they were older, mostly college kids in crowded cars heading out to the campus for the Little Halloween parties. No child on a bike, no *Beast*.

At the bridge he turned around and headed back to town. His frustration level was mounting, but as he drove the slow miles the voice in his head kept whispering one immensely powerful word, over and over.

*Tonight!* it said. Eddie's hands held the steering wheel with a strangler's grip.

### (4)

Newton ran. It felt like ten miles to the light, but he ran. The roaches—some of them were actually leaping up at him—were piling over themselves in front of him, layer upon layer of them, and he had to plow shin-deep through them. Roaches were swarming up his pants legs—outside and *inside*—and as he ran he started slapping them off his clothes. One crawled down out of his hair and Newton screamed as shrilly as a little girl as he swatted it off his cheek. Suddenly Crow was there and he was reaching out with both hands to grab Newton and drag him into the patch of sunlight. Then he, too, was swatting and pawing at Newton, brushing away dozens of gleaming black bugs, knocking them down to the ground where they twitched and fled toward the shadows that surrounded them.

"Pants . . . pants!" Newton was yelling as he shook and danced in place and Crow grabbed his belt buckle, yanked it open, and then grabbed his pockets and pulled, tearing the cloth but also dragging Newton's jeans down to his ankles. His legs were covered with roaches and as the sunlight touched them they leaped off and raced for shadows, while others scuttled up under the hems of Newton's boxer shorts. Newton screamed when he felt them begin to crawl over his scrotum and try to wriggle between his buttocks. He tore off his boxers and danced a frantic jig and within seconds all of the insects had fallen off or been swatted away by his desperate hands. His legs were covered with tiny red marks from where some of the roaches had tried to bite through his skin. None of the bites had broken the skin, however, though Newton shuddered at the thought of what would have happened had the creatures had more than just a few seconds to gnaw at him.

They froze there—Crow with his chest heaving, eyes bugged out in terror, pants smeared to the knees with a paste made of insect guts and crushed shell, Newton with his pants and undershorts around his ankles, face white with shock. Around them in a circle thirty feet across the sea of roaches had come to a complete stop. Only their antennae twitched, but they did not move, did not mill around. They stood in their endless ranks and watched hungrily.

Crow stared at the insects for a moment and then slowly looked up at the cloudy sky. There were three beams of sunlight angling down and as he watched, a fourth broke through and its light touched the upper near corner of Griswold's old house. It was still gloomy but the false sunset was ebbing. Just a bit. He looked at his watch. Sunset—real night—was less than an hour from now. "Newt," he whispered. "Get dressed. Hurry up."

Tears ran down through the dust and grime on Newton's cheeks. "Crow—what's happening?" There was a hysterical edge to Newton's voice.

"The sunlight's keeping them back, so might have a chance here . . . but you gotta be ready."

The reporter looked at Crow, and then at the ring of light around them. The clouds were thinning and the circle of sunshine started expanding outward. Suddenly the insects began hissing again as they drew back away from it. "See!" Crow yelled in a voice filled with fierce triumph. "They can't stand the light."

"But . . . roaches always run when you turn on the light."

Crow shook his head. "That's because they don't want to get stepped on . . . this is different. I don't think they can *abide* the light." It was a strange word to use and it hung there in the air, both of them aware of it and of what it implied.

Newton looked up at the sky. There were a dozen beams of light—the pillars of heaven, he thought, remembering the phrase from an old book. The pillars of heaven, and these little monsters can't *abide* them. "No," he whispered, but he meant yes.

Around them the gloom was visibly diminishing as the clouds above burned away. Now there was a big central column—heaven's mainstay, Newton thought—and its light washed across the entire field. The sunlight, cold and raw with the humidity of a lurking storm, was still rich and pure and it washed over them and over the sea of roaches that instantly turned and fled in a swarm back toward the house. In thirty seconds every one of them was gone except the bugs that lay smashed and dead in the line from where they had first been attacked. How many had they killed? A thousand? Five thousand? It hadn't made even a dent in the ocean of them there had been.

Newton suddenly became entirely self-conscious about the fact that he was standing there with his pants down and turned with an absurd stab at modesty away from Crow and pulled up his boxers and jeans—checking to make sure there

were no roaches hiding in the folds—and zipped and buckled. As he slipped his belt through the last loop a huge shiver
of absolute disgust shook him from head to toes and he took
a step away from Crow and vomited into the brush. While he
spit and gagged the forest seemed to tilt and sway around
him.

"We've got less than an hour before sunset, Newt," Crow
said urgently. "We have to make it to the pitch long before
then."

Newton straightened, his face green and his eyes runny
with tears from straining to empty his gut, and he stared at
Crow for a long second, then looked up at the sky. The light
was slanting down from an extreme angle as the sun slid toward the southern treeline. They would be in darkness long
before the sun actually set on the region.

"Little bastards must have gone back into the house . . .
don't ask me how. Or why. But if they're regrouping or some
shit then it's our cue to haul ass."

They started running toward the forest and this time
Newton ran as fast as Crow.

### (5)

Vic punched the dashboard lighter in and when it popped
he lit his cigarette and then handed it to Ruger. They smoked
in silence for a long time, watching as the sun slipped below
the treeline. Vic's pickup was tucked back into a copse of
trees, safe within shadows as dense as the bottom of a well.
They could see the sun, but the rays did not penetrate even as
far as the truck's hood. Ruger's ski mask, hat, and gloves
were on the backseat. He wouldn't need them again tonight.
Vic looked at his wristwatch. "Sun'll be down in ten minutes."

"Vic," Ruger said softly, and when the man turned Ruger
said, "You know that I know about the sunlight." He smiled.
"Don't you?"

"I guessed."

"Why the bullshit?"

Vic shrugged.

Ruger said, "It bothers me, but that's it. I don't turn into the Human Torch."

"Some of your boys do."

"Most don't."

"Well . . . we don't know what we got all the time. It's pretty clear that there are a lot of different kinds of you sonsabitches."

Ruger said nothing.

"You got dead heads like Boyd. Like extras from *Night of the Living Dead*, Part Ten. I mean . . . are they even vampires?"

Ruger just looked at him.

"Then there's your core group—you and Golub, Gaither Carby, the twins, those guys. There's your true fang gang."

"'Fang Gang.' That's cute."

"But in between you got a bunch of weird spins on this thing, some of them I never even heard of before. I know you've been reading my books. Do you have an answer?"

Ruger looked out the window at the fading light. Turned away so Vic couldn't see his smile.

Vic waited for a moment, then gave it up. It's something he would take up with the Man. Too much of what was happening was not part of the Plan, and that made Vic nervous. Even within the Plan itself there were variations popping up, and for the first time in his life he wondered how much control the Man had. Were there things he didn't know, even about his own kind? Just thinking that made Vic's stomach hurt.

To hide his discomfiture, he said, "Wonder how things are going down in the Hollow."

"They're still alive," Ruger said, closing his eyes. His voice was tinged with surprise.

Vic stared at him, and the sickness in his stomach worsened. "Yeah, I can feel that, too. Son of a bitch!"

Ruger wore a knife-slit smile and was slowly nodding to himself. "I guess I'm not the only one who trips over bad luck when that asshole Crow is in the mix."

Vic shot him a vicious glare. "You watch your mouth!"

"Oh, face it, Wingate," Ruger snapped, "that little bastard has the luck of the devil, and you know it as well as I do. Even the Man couldn't take him down on the first try. Don't even try to tell me there isn't something else at work here. It's not just me."

They smoked in silence as the sun continued to fall. Vic gave a sour grunt and said, "Yeah, maybe. But at least that bitch'll be dead soon."

"Recruited," Ruger correctly mildly. "*Dead's* just a by-product."

"If Terry Wolfe hadn't been going off his nut, I'd have popped Crow weeks ago," Vic mused. "He's always been a pain in the ass."

"You think Wolfe would make it to Halloween if Crow was off the board?"

Vic shrugged. "The Man thinks so. He says he has the mayor on a leash, and maybe he is. Hard to say—talk around town is that he's really starting to crack."

"Crack or turn?"

"Not even the Man knows that for sure. Like I said, Wolfe's a wild card."

"Great," Ruger said with a sneer, "we got a key player we can't count on and a sawed-off prick who's too damn lucky. We're in clover here."

"Shit," Vic agreed and then peered up at the sky. The sun was almost gone. He said, "Luck doesn't last forever."

### (6)

The Bone Man sat on a fallen log just at the point of the trail where it widened to spill out onto Griswold's property, his guitar slung in front of him, his slender fingers moving with blurred speed over the strings, the bottleneck slide wailing up and down. The sound of furious, angry jailhouse blues filled the air around him. Birds shouted in the trees, lending a discordance that was somehow appropriate to the moment, and surrounding their noise and the music was a constant rising hiss from the tens of thousands of insects that clustered with fury before him.

The insects had swarmed back out of the house as soon as the sun began to edge toward the horizon, but at the first stroke of the Bone Man's fingers over the strings they'd crowded to a stop inches from where he sat. They milled and leapt but not one of them could cross the line from field to forest. The rustle of the bugs and the murmur of the trees in the wind of the Hollow both carried a tone of absolute surprise and total outrage.

The Bone Man played as fast as he could, but his mind was reeling from this. When he had strummed his guitar the best he had hoped for was to spur Crow and his friend to run faster. He had never expected this, could never have imagined this.

He didn't understand it, and even feared that it was all some kind of joke on Griswold's part—a trick to raise hopes before he closed his fist around Crow for real—but as the minutes passed and the sound of running feet diminished behind him, the Bone Man slowly changed his view. This wasn't any of Griswold's doing, no sir. This was something else— the sign of someone else in the game.

Who or why didn't matter right now. He played and played and prayed that whatever strange magic was at work here would last long enough.

### (7)

"Hurry—hurry—hurry!" Newton chanted in a frenzied whisper as he ran; next to him Crow ran in silence. Above them the clouds melted away but the forest did not brighten. The sun hung low and swollen above the far treeline, its fiery corona just singeing the treetops. Night was falling and they were miles from the pitch, with the whole of Dark Hollow between them and safety, and the devil knew what lay behind or before them. By now neither Crow nor Newton was much counting on the world being sane and predictable. That moment seemed to have passed for them, forever perhaps, when they had crossed the line from sunlight to shadows back on the pitch, or perhaps it was when they had entered that marshy swamp. Perhaps both. Two steps into hell.

Newton turned to look back the way they had come, half expecting to see the tide of roaches sweeping back, but all he saw were shadows. More shadows than when he had looked back only a minute ago. Darker, thicker, closing in on them as the sun began its fatal fall beyond the forest uplands on the far side of Griswold's farm. Newton could no longer see the farm, or the fields, or even the tall-tree line. He looked at his watch. 6:11. What had Crow told him? Sunset was at 6:24.

"The sun's going down!" he shrieked, but Crow didn't waste breath replying to that.

A tiny pain flared against Newton's thigh and he stooped and began smacking hysterically at it, thinking that another of those bugs had crawled up his pants and bitten him, but this was different. A small burning spot three-quarters of the way up the top of his thigh, but when he dug into his pocket to see what he could feel all he brought out was the tarnished old dime with the hole cut through it. Newton peered at it as he ran, looking to see if there was a sharp edge or anything that could explain the sudden pain, but it was just an old dime. The burning in his thigh faded and he raised his arm to throw the dime away, but for the second time that day he made the decision to keep it. He put it back in his pocket and raced to catch up with Crow as the shadows coalesced behind him.

Fatigue was a huge fiery dragon that breathed hotly in their flushed faces, sat on their chests, and bit them in the sides. They slowed from a dead run to a staggering walk and Crow pulled the canteen from Newton's pack, took a pull and handed it to the reporter. Newton opened his mouth to say something but Crow held up a hand to silence him and stood there, head cocked in an attitude of listening. He thought he had heard something impossible, something they had both heard before starting down the hill. Was it the ghost of an echo of music on the sluggish breeze?

"Is it the bugs?" Newton hissed.

Crow listened a moment longer and then shook his head. He let out a chestful of air. "No . . . I guess it's nothing. I think we're safe." But doubt was evident in his voice. "Either way, I don't want to wait around to find out."

"Why didn't they come after us again?"

"I don't know. Come on, let's keep moving."

At a quick walk—both of them were now beyond running—they set out down the path, picking their way along by starlight, fleeing from the marsh with its methane vapors and stink of rot, far along the valley floor toward the foot of the pitch. It seemed to take hours, days. They didn't stop again until they saw the great slab-sided slope rise before them, then they rested, drinking the last of their water. The climbing ropes were still there, leading up through shadows and becoming invisible in the gloom far above them.

Crow found his gloves where they had left them hours ago and slowly fitted them on as he studied the angle of the slope. He nodded to Newton with an uptic of his chin. "What shape are you in?"

"I'm a wreck."

Crow gave Newton a reassuring slap on the back. It was going to be a total bitch of a climb, and Crow didn't think he had enough left to manage it. He was certain Newton didn't. He turned and looked back, scanning the forest, listening for the sound of skittering insect feet. Their absence should have been reassuring, but strangely it wasn't.

"We'll have to try and rest along the way up," he said, knowing it sounded lame. Newton just nodded, his eyes glistening in the darkness and he turned away. Crow was sure he was crying. He pulled tension on his rope and raised his leg to brace it on a snarl of root a foot above the forest floor, then with a sigh that spoke of his sadness, his fear, and his exhaustion, he began to climb. Sniffing back his tears, Newton followed.

Dark Hollow had defeated them.

# Chapter 27

The sun was almost down and the first stars were igniting overhead as Mike sped on through the darkness, going away from town, riding with no specific purpose along the highway, seeking the loneliness of the farmlands. As he rode, the aches of his body and the aches of his soul seemed to fade as the War Machine devoured the miles. A rare few cars hummed along A-32 but the heaviest congestion, he knew, would have turned off onto College Road, which cut west between the Dead End Drive-In and the Haunted Hayride and then emptied onto the campus of Pinelands College. Overhead a single dark bird flapped lazily, easily keeping pace with him, and he and the bird soared along for nearly two miles, keeping perfect station with the other until they crested the hill that led to the sharpness of Shandy's Curve. Mike slowed, not wanting to race around Shandy's Curve again, not since his close encounter with Crow's old Chevy two weeks ago. He reached the curve and coasted around it, the bird now circling overhead. Mike felt a strange chill as if the air around the curve was colder than along the rest of A-32. It was a moderately cool night anyway for the middle of October, but on the curve it felt like March.

Mike pedaled a little harder, wanting to be past the spot. He heard the night bird screech and he looked up to see it thrashing erratically, trying to change direction, fighting for control as if caught in a whirlwind. It squawked and dove down toward the forest leaving the road and the boy and the . . .

. . . *gleaming wrecker that squatted in the middle of the road just around the last part of Shandy's Curve.*

Mike grabbed the hand brakes and squeezed with all his strength, brake pads squealing. His tires stuttered for purchase along the pebbled surface of the road. The War Machine skidded to a smoking stop, stripes of black rubber burned onto the hardtop, and the momentum slewed him around so that Mike was sideways to the huge wrecker.

He froze there, turned to ice by the shock of it, at the impossibility of it, feeling his heart hammer in his chest, staring in total disbelief as the wrecker sat there, huge, incredibly massive, totally black, dominating the road. It was as if time itself had become frozen with shock. The world was totally still. Nothing moved, nothing dared make a sound. Mike lungs clutched tight, holding in his breath.

*This can't be happening.*

Though he knew that he had actually encountered this same wrecker two weeks ago, seeing it again was totally unreal. One encounter—okay, a drunk behind the wheel or an asshole playing chicken with some random kid—but this . . . this was a trap. Deliberate, calculated. It was here *waiting* for him. Waiting. For *him*. Specifically him. This thing was here to kill him. All of this processed through his brain in a furious second as his logic circuits accepted the impossible and made this reality the only reality. Crazy as it was, the wrecker was right here, and right here was where he was going to die.

Very slowly he began to walk the bike backward around the curve, hoping that in the darkness the driver hadn't seen him, that maybe the trap was still poised, not yet sprung.

Then the lights of the wrecker flared on. Headlights, running lights, fog lights—all came on in a blinding luminous assault, driving white needles of pain into Mike's eyes. He cried out, throwing his arm across his face; then there was a unspeakable roar as the wrecker's powerful engine howled to life, rending the air with teeth of sound, clawing at the stillness with talons of pure noise. The driver gunned the engine once, twice . . .

Mike knew for sure that he was going to die.

Using strength he did not possess, he wrenched his bike around and stomped down on the pedal, propelling himself and the War Machine back onto Shandy's Curve, away from the huge, gleaming monster, away from the thunder of its engine. Behind him, it seemed as if the engine howled with rage at his flight, but Mike knew that was just the driver shifting gears, shifting from park to drive, from waiting into full-bore attack. Mike tore along the highway, using the dips in the road to give him speed, steering small and smart, pumping his legs like pistons. Behind him the wrecker followed; slowly at first, rolling at a strange creeping pace around the Curve, seeming not to pursue, just to follow. But Mike wasn't fooled. He knew that the wrecker driver was just giving him a head start, making the hunt more interesting. Mike took the chance for what it was worth and pedaled the bike with every ounce of his desperate strength, fighting his bike back up the hill. At first he didn't look back, knowing that to do so would be to lose maybe a precious second. Instead he switched into a lower gear and his knees pumped up and down and he willed the bike to climb the tall hill. He widened the gap—a quarter-mile, a half-mile, almost three-quarters of a mile, the space of two medium hills. Then the wrecker's engine howled with a furious delight and the chase was on.

Mike crested a hill and finally dared to look back, knowing what he would see. And he did see it. The wrecker was flying down the farthest hill, its massive bulk soaring into the pull of gravity. Mike could hear the driver giving it gas as it came up the other side, pressing the pedal down to keep the speed it had won from the freefall, devouring all of the precious lead Mike had earned.

"No!" Mike pedaled so hard that his legs blurred and his muscles caught fire; it felt like he was breathing flame. There were still two small hills between him and the wrecker, but he could hear it now, coming closer, closer. Where the hell were all those news vans and tourist cars when he needed them? He was halfway up the next hill when the lights of the wrecker pinned him to the macadam. Mike gasped. In the time it had taken him to go down and halfway up the next hill, the wrecker had taken both hills. It was going to catch him. Soon.

Which is when Mike Sweeney, the Enemy of Evil, came up with a plan. It was simple, it was obvious, and it was right there in his mind, fully formed. He almost smiled, but the terror was still too big for that. Still as he reached the top of the mount and vanished over it, he did smirk. Just a little.

Tow-Truck Eddie grinned as he saw the demon on the bike disappear over the nearest hill. *Got you,* he thought. *Did you really think you could get away from me? Know you so little of God's power and glory?* He stamped down on the accelerator and rocketed down the hill, feeling the jolts as he bounced over patched sections of highway, feeling his own excitement build and dance in his mind. *I am the Sword of God!* The very thought made him feel wonderful, made him so proud, so purely joyous to be a part of his Father's plans. This second chance to do his Father's will. It would be a starting place, a cornerstone on which he could build his church.

He had it all worked out. He would run him down but not kill him immediately, take him to a quiet place, and with his own hands wrest the truth from his flesh, discarding the polluted skin of evil that was simply shaped like a boy. He would reveal the demon within, then he would cast it out, banishing it into the darkness where it belonged. This was the first truly great mission of his ministry.

In his mind the voice of his Father hissed, *Yes! Slay the Evil one!*

Tow-Truck Eddie grinned as he raced down the slope, gunning the engine as he clawed up the other side. The boy was close, just out of sight on the other side. He reached the top of the crest and peered forward, hungry for sight of his prey. Suddenly something shot by him from the side of the road, something small and dark and fast, heading in the other direction.

*The demon!*

Tow-Truck Eddie saw it flash past, heading back down the slope. He slammed on the brakes and tried to stop the turn, jerking the wheel hard over. There was a horrific squeal of tires, plumes of smoke puffed up from the road; the whole chassis of the wrecker snarled in protest as too many forces fought to control it at once: thrust and gravity and angle, all working for that moment in the service of the Beast. Tow-Truck Eddie screamed aloud as he manhandled the wheel, his mind black with fury, and he could feel almost at once that he wasn't going to make it.

The wrecker slewed around and actually slid sideways, burning smears on the hardtop. Immediately the angle of the turn became warped and the back wheels skidded all the way around and then swung completely clear of the road as they spun out over the deep drainage ditch. With neither weight nor traction the wheels raced at insane speeds, sending up a banshee cry, and then Eddie let loose his own howl as the whole back end of the wrecker canted into the ditch and he was bounced around in the cab like a rag doll in a clothes dryer. The front wheel jumped high off the ground and the massive machine slid down five feet into the drainage ditch, front wheels spinning madly in the air now and dirt spraying up in huge clouds as the back wheels touched down again, but the rear tires only dug themselves a trench. The wrecker continued to slide backward until the towing bar thudded with finality into the mud wall on the far side of the ditch.

Eddie was slammed back against the seat but he was at an

angle and his head missed the headrest and smacked against the rear window with a sound like a fist hitting a door. At the same time his right knee jerked upward and he hit the underside of the steering wheel hard enough to send hot lightning through the joint. The engine continued to roar, but now there was a frustrated, almost petulant gripe to the motor.

Squinting through pain, teeth clenched and bared, Tow-Truck Eddie stared in stupefaction at the improbable angle of the wrecker. He was looking almost straight up at the darkening sky over the cornfields. He could not believe it. It had all happened so fast. He was in the ditch! The engine whined on, and Tow-Truck Eddie reached out, jerked the stick into park, and wrenched the key over to kill the noise. The engine died along with his confidence. He gripped the knobbed arc of the steering wheel and let out a howl of pure frustrated rage.

Mike skidded down the hill for thirty yards, wobbling and swaying and almost going off the blacktop into the ditch himself. When he heard the crash of the wrecker, he squeezed the brakes and slid to a long, slow stop and then crouched there listening, ready to flee, panting, feeling sweat running in cold rivulets down his face. He heard the whine of the engine, and then the silence as the engine was abruptly turned off.

*Got you, you son of a bitch!* he thought, smiling fiercely, and a dark wave of malicious glee soared up through him. *Got you!*

He wondered what to do next. Later he would have to try and sort out what was going on with this nutcase in the wrecker, but for right now he needed to decide what to do next. *Go!* his instinct told him. *Get the hell out of here.* The wrecker was now between him and home. He needed to go get the cops. He needed to tell Crow. Would Crow be back from the hike he was taking in the woods with that reporter? Maybe Val would be home. He turned and looked into the darkness that stretched away from the wrecker. Val's farm was pretty close, a couple miles. He could go there. All of these thoughts banged around in his head with all the noise and distraction of a silver pinball. Getting the hell out of there, no matter where he went, was the only smart thing to do, he knew that much.

But first . . . he had to go back up and look over the top of that hill. He had to find out what had happened to the wrecker. He *had* to.

*This is stupid,* he thought, and then said it aloud. "This is really stupid."

Sweating icy rivers, his body aching, he nonetheless turned his War Machine around and pedaled slowly, carefully up the hill, all the time listening for the engine to start again. Nothing. Just silence.

Twenty yards to go, and he wondered if maybe the guy had really cracked up the wrecker. Maybe the guy was hurt. *Screw him if he is.* Maybe he was dead, that was something to think about. Mike didn't want to be responsible for killing anyone, even if the guy was some kind of nutcase who liked to try and run down kids on bikes.

*Get the hell out of here. Go. Now.*

Ten yards to go, and he wondered—not for the first time—if maybe it was Vic himself in that wrecker after all. *Jesus, is he really that crazy? Is it him up there?* He felt terror grab at him, but he fought for control. *No,* he told himself, *no. Vic is probably at home. Vic is home getting drunk and probably slapping Mom around. Or maybe doing whatever it was he did to her in their bedroom that made her scream like that.* Mike knew that Vic did things—bad things— that made his mother scream and cry out at night, sex things that Vic wanted Mike to hear because he knew it would hurt to hear that stuff. *But . . . was this him?*

Five yards to go and he could see the glow of the wrecker's headlights, pointing upward at a weird angle. Pointing crookedly at the sky. Mike frowned. No, Mike thought. *Vic may be crazy, but this isn't Vic. This is someone else.*

Three yards to go and then someone leapt out of the shadows at him. Mike screamed as the huge bulk, a mass of shadows silhouetted by the wrecker's headlights, sprang at him, huge hands reaching, his mouth shrieking with a sound that tore the night to rags. Mike jerked the handlebars hard to one side and leaned over them, throwing his weight to the left and down, kicking down on the pedals, mixing all his weight and muscle as he veered desperately away from the monstrous form. The hulking shape had only a few yards to cross and he'd have him, but Mike had a deep slope, the constancy of gravity, and the iron in his legs put there by total terror. Mike shot past him, down the slope that pointed back to town. It was way too close, though.

It was so close that as the demon fled down the hill Tow-Truck Eddie felt cloth and hair teasing the tips of his fingers; then there was nothing but cold dark air at the ends of his fingers and the demon shot away down the hill, picking up speed so fast that he seemed to shrink instead of go farther away. If it had been on flat land, Tow-Truck Eddie might have had him, but as he tried to run down the steep slope his bruised right knee buckled with each step.

Mike belted down the hill and up the next. He didn't stop until he was nearly a mile away, and at that distant, lofty perch he finally stopped. He literally fell sideways off the bike and lay there, gasping, barely able to breathe. His chest was a howling red-hot mass of pain, his lungs were burned raw, and lights danced all around him in a mad fireworks display. Even at that distance, Mike could see the figure of the man. He appeared to be jumping up and down in place, tearing at himself in a fit of such awful rage that it scared Mike. He stared in shock and confusion, in growing horror at the realities of the situation. Who *was* this madman? He was too big to be Vic.

Then it hit him, and he could not believe that he hadn't seen it before. A big man, a wrecker—both with ties to Vic.

The man who had just tried to kill him had to be Tow-Truck Eddie.

Knowing it still didn't help him make sense of it. Why would Tow-Truck Eddie be trying to kill him? It made no sense, none. Everyone knew Eddie as being super religious. And, besides he was a . . . cop. Mike lay there, unable to move, shocked to a vigilant stillness, watching the man dance with rage, watching as he sank slowly down to one knee, burying his head in his hands, becoming part of the shadows of the hill for a moment; and then saw the man throw back his head and let out a howl of such pure bloody rage that the whole night was torn by it. It rose above the hills and the trees and into the starfield above; it was a terrible thing to hear, and it struck some primal chord of fear in Mike that came near to choking him. The howl rolled over the hills at him, a cry of frustration as much as it was an awful promise.

# Chapter 28

## (1)

Val and Connie strolled quietly down the lanes between the corn as stars blossomed and wheeled overhead. It was dark, but Val had the pistol snug in the back of her waistband and Diego and two of the hands were still on the property, working one field away on a tractor that had broken down. The glow of lanterns and the hum of a portable generator where the men worked was a comfort to both women.

Mostly they didn't talk, and when they did it wasn't about Mark or the recent violence. The safest subject for Connie was a discussion of Val's wedding plans. Connie warmed to that subject immediately and was filled with ideas for making the event the talk of the season. Most of Connie's suggestions were frou-frou nonsense that would have had Val in too many layers of Italian lace with her hair in curlicues, but Val let her ramble. It was refreshing to hear Connie enthused about something.

Several times, however, she stole covert glances at her watch, wondering why Crow wasn't back by now. *If he's fallen down the mountain and broken his damn leg I'll break the other one for him,* she decided. When her cell phone rang she looked at it, expecting it to be him, but frowned at the number on the LCD display. She flipped it open.

"Hello . . . Terry?"

"Val? I've been trying to call Crow all day but he's not answering and I need to speak to him but he doesn't pick up the—"

"Whoa, Terry, slow down. What's wrong? Are you okay? Is something wrong with Sarah, the kids?"

Terry's tirade ground to a halt and he barked out a dry, totally humorless laugh. "Wrong? Shit. What isn't wrong?"

Val blinked, still surprised by Terry's recent vocabulary shift. Back when they had dated he would never have used a vulgarity. "Terry? Jesus, what is it? Tell me what's going on." Connie raised her eyebrows to ask what was up but Val held up a hand for her to wait. "Terry, *tell me* what's happening? Is it something with you and Sarah?"

"No, no, not that. Thank God, it's not that, too."

"Then what? Are you sick?"

There was that dry laugh again. "Sick? Yeah, I guess you could say that."

"Are you hurt? Do you need a doctor?"

"I've *been* to doctors. I've been to a dozen doctors. Frigging quacks, all of them, Val . . . you just don't know. . . . Nobody knows."

"What, Terry? What don't I know? Tell me."

"Val," Terry breathed huskily and Val realized with a start that Terry was crying. Softly, but wretchedly. "I think I'm over the edge, Val," Terry said in a tortured voice. "I think I'm gone."

"Hey . . . hey, now . . . ," she said.

Terry's voice broke into pieces and collapsed into ruin, and Val thought she knew the shape of this. Crow had told her about Terry's dreams and delusions. They must be intensifying, ganging up on him. Val stood there for a long time, just listening to the big man cry like a lost child. She tried to say soothing things, but felt hamstrung. She opened her mouth to speak and then abruptly there was the sound of fingers fumbling on the receiver. A voice said tentatively, "Who is this, please?"

"Sarah?"

"Val? Oh, thank God!"

"Sarah, what the hell is happening? What's wrong with Terry?"

"He's in the bathroom now. Oh, Val—I just don't know what to do."

"What's *wrong*?"

"He's . . . well, he's not well." Sarah lowered her voice. "Remember what I told you—the dreams and all? It's gotten so much worse lately. I have a call into his doctor."

"Oh, sweetie, I'm so sorry. Is this because of the blight and all? Or the older stuff? From . . . when we were kids?" She didn't want to say much more with Connie standing close by, but Sarah caught the drift.

"I—think so." She paused. "He's told me this morning Mandy has been following him around."

Val echoed softly. "I know . . . Crow told me a little, but—"

"He said that she's been trying to get him to kill himself. The medication's not helping. I'm so scared, Val. I've . . . sent for an ambulance." Sarah was starting to cry now. "He's falling apart. I can see it happening but I can't do anything for him."

"Hey! Listen to me, Sarah," Val said, putting some steel in her voice. "Believe me when I tell you that you don't want to break down right now. Later, but not right now. This is going to sound really harsh, but suck it up because you can't let him see you fall apart. Not now, not until he's under *care.* You hear me?"

Val could almost hear Sarah take a steadying breath. "Right. Right . . . but . . . *shit!*"

"Sure, get mad, honey, that's good, it'll help—but stay focused."

Sarah gave a funny little laugh. "God, I wish I had your strength, Val."

"Honey, I don't even have my strength. It's all smoke and mirrors."

"Bullshit," Sarah said, but she sounded like she was standing on firmer ground.

"Should I come over? I can be there in fifteen minutes."

Then she caught sight of the look on Connie's face. "Connie's with me. We can both come. Get some girl power going."

"No," she said sharply, "but if they want him to check into the hospital could you come over there later, sit with me for a bit? Can I ask that?"

"Sure. Call me once you know what's happening and I'll scoot on over. Me and Connie. Crow should be back soon, too. We'll all come over."

"He keeps asking for Crow."

"Yeah, I know, but Crow's out of touch right now, but he should be back soon. Look, you get him ready and we'll all see you later. And . . . Sarah? I love you. Both of you. Tell Terry that he's not alone."

"Thanks, Val, I'll tell him," Sarah said, and hung up.

Val closed her phone and looked at Connie, then told her the bones of the conversation.

"That poor man," Connie said in a motherly way, but her eyes were nearly vacant. After a moment they started walking again, taking the long way around that would bring them up past the barn and then back to the house.

*I think I'm over the edge, Val, I think I'm gone.* There had been such pain, such terrible fear in Terry's voice as he said it. Such awful conviction that the observation was true. "Damn . . ." she said softly.

### (2)

Just as Sarah set down the phone there was the sound of a blow and shattering glass from upstairs. "Terry!" She tore out of the kitchen, raced up the stairs, and burst into the bedroom just as Terry Wolfe brought the golf club down on the glass of a framed Warhol litho. The head of the sand wedge chopped noisily through glass and matboard and took the top of John Lennon's head clean off. Sarah skidded to a halt by the edge of the bed, turning away to dodge the spray of little glass needles.

Terry turned a face toward her that was a snarling mask of animal rage.

(3)

Mike Sweeney got home just before seven, well before his curfew. He walked his bike around back and chained it up by the garage door, then went inside.

"That you, Mikey? You're home early. Want some dinner?" Her voice floated from the living room, which was dark except for the blue flicker of the TV. There was already a gin slur to her speech.

Mike stood in the hallway, not wanting to go into the living room, not wanting to see his mother drunk, though nowadays she almost always was. He turned toward the stairs, calling over his shoulder. "I'm not hungry. I'm gonna go study."

"It's Friday!"

"Big test on Monday."

"Oh. Okay." She sounded more relieved than disappointed that he didn't want her to cook anything. "If you want something later, we can order. I have some coupons for Pizza Palace."

"Yeah. Sure. Whatever." He pounded up the stairs and into his room, where he locked his door. He was no longer sweating, but his clothes were damp; his skin still felt feverish and strange, so he stripped the clothes off and headed into the bathroom. He was in the shower for a long time, first just standing under the spray, eyes closed, running and rerunning what had just happened out on the road. It was all so weird, so unreal.

*Tow-Truck Eddie tried to kill me*, he thought. Twice now. And tonight he had caused the guy to crash his wrecker in a ditch. As the water pounded him he replayed each moment—the way the truck was lying in wait for him, the way the big driver had let him get just far enough ahead so that it would be a good chase. The way the bastard had nearly caught him when Mike had gone back to look. The way he had howled after his truck had been wrecked. It was all so unreal. He took the soap and washed himself and shampooed his hair and used a nailbrush to scrub his fingers. He wanted to be clean, *needed* to be clean, as if by washing so hard he could sponge away the unreality of what had happened. Of nearly dying. The water was as hot as he could stand it and he lingered under it, loving the feel of the thousands of tiny impacts, feeling his muscles become gradually looser, feeling the tension go, letting his mind drift . . .

*Fugue.*

The water rained down on him but Mike Sweeney no longer felt it. He stood there, eyes closed, his skin red from the heat.

*Inside the chrysalis the pupa undergoes slow change.*

On his face the last of the bruises faded to green and then to yellow and then vanished as if the water had washed them away. The cartilage in his knees that had suffered microtears while he raced uphill away from the wrecker mended itself. Internal bruises from cramps deep within his calf muscles relaxed and the tissues mended.

*Transformation continues along predetermined pathways following a biological imperative.*

The water pounds down on him, but Mike Sweeney has stepped out. No trace of him exists within the chrysalis of young flesh.

*Transformation is inevitable now.*

When he opens his eyelids Mike Sweeney does not look out through those blue eyes, and indeed those eyes are not quite blue. Not pure blue. They are blue flecked with red and the irises are rimmed with gold. Mike Sweeney does not see the water, or the steam, or the shower walls through those eyes. They are not his eyes. Mike Sweeney, as he has been, is almost completely gone now.

It is the *dhampyr* who sees through those eyes.

### (4)

Terry bellowed in rage and lifted the golf club like an ax, standing with legs braced wide, his naked body bathed in sweat, his muscles rigid with tension as the club reached the apex of its lift, and then with a ferocious convulsion that carved definition into every muscular inch of his body he smashed the club down on the largest remaining piece. Splinters leapt up around him, adding to the dozen small cuts that bled sluggishly on his calves and feet and thighs. The glass settled quickly into stillness on the carpet, not only adding to the litter but substantially increasing the number of mocking glass surfaces. He raised the wedge again, not even remotely aware that Sarah was standing in the doorway, her face white with shock. All he saw were the thousands of splinters of that picture glass spread out in a fan-pattern on the thick blue bedroom carpet, each polished surface dispassionately reflecting his face and body. Each little sliver was a funhouse mirror, distorting blue eyes and red hair and strong limbs into feral yellow eyes, stiff reddish-brown fur, and the twisted, hulking musculature of something impossible. When his mouth opened to yell in protest, the muzzles of the myriad mirror-image mouths wrinkled to show dripping fangs. If his hand wiped angrily at the tears on his face, the reflected mockery swiped at its bestial face with a furred paw that ended in black talons. A thousand tacit accusations glared at him from the glittering debris.

"Terry! For God's sake!"

He spun, the club still raised, glaring at her with mad eyes. "*Get out!*" he roared.

"You're going to hurt yourself," she pleaded. "Look at you. You're bleeding!"

"Get out! Get away from me!"

She took a tentative step into the bedroom; her movements slowed by fear for him and fear *of* him. Until now Sarah never would have believed Terry would ever hurt her, but the closer she got to him the more she doubted. At that moment there was nothing in him that was not polluted by torment—and she did not trust that he really knew who she was. "Terry, come on now," she soothed, holding her hands out in a gesture of nonhostility, empty palms turned toward him, half to calm, half to plead, the way you would calm a dog.

He stumbled a step back, his big feet crunching on the

glass. There were smears of blood on the carpet. He pointed the club at her. "You stay away! You don't *understand*!"

"I'm trying to understand, Terry! Let me help, Terry." She kept deliberately using his name, calmly, soothingly, hoping that it would in some way anchor him, bring him back to himself.

He jabbed the head of the club at her. It was less a threatening gesture than it was a barrier for him to hide behind. Then he spun and pointed at an old armoire across the room. "It's all her goddamned fault! She won't leave me alone. She's been driving me out of my goddamn mind for a month. Every day . . . every *goddamned day*!"

Sarah turned to look. The japanned armoire stood silent and alone between the twin doors to their clothes closets. Slowly, she turned back to Terry. "Who, Terry? Who is she?" She knew he was talking about Mandy, but did not know how to approach that concept.

"*Her!*" he snapped. "She's blamed me all these years . . . all these years. But—damn it to hell, I did what I could. I was just a *kid*! What else could I do have done? It all happened so . . . fast! What *could* I do?" He glared with anger and hurt at the wall. "Why can't you get that through your head?" He paused, as if listening and then picked up the conversation as if he was replying to a statement. "Well, if you don't blame me for what happened, then why are you doing this to me? Why do you keep making me see *that*!" He pointed the club at the broken picture glass.

There was a looking pause and then, "Bullshit!" he snarled, but there was an ocean of doubt in his trembling voice. "He's as dead as you are!"

Terry stood there and listened just as naturally as if someone were really speaking. Sarah watched in awed fascination, seeing his expression undergo a series of slow changes: at first his face held a challenging look, then his features went slowly blank as if he was hearing new information that was taking some thought to digest; then it was indignant disbelief that curled his lips to tight thinness; then a slowly dawning look of profound horror; and finally a sad despair that made his fall into sickness. "*No*," he said, and his voice was a hoarse whisper.

"T-Terry?" Sarah ventured.

"But I'm nothing like that!" he cried, arguing with empty space. "I'm *nothing* like that." Tears fell coursed down his cheeks. "I *can't* be like that. . . ."

"Terry, talk to me!" She might as well have been a million miles away.

"It's not fair," he mumbled. "Not fair, not fair, not fair . . ." Each time he repeated it his voice diminished, sounding further and further away as if somehow inside his own head Terry was moving farther away from Sarah, from the room, and from himself. It was utterly chilling to watch.

There was the faint cry of a siren in the distance.

"Not fair, not fair, not—" Abruptly he lifted his bowed head and looked again at the empty wall by the armoire. "What can I do?" A pause. "I don't *want* to do that. I can keep control of it. I never gave in, you know that. I'm a good person! I'll never be like *him*. I can stop it!"

Sarah took a small step forward, close enough to touch him if she dared, but she did not. Part of her mind was suddenly screaming at her to run, to get away from Terry before . . . Before . . . what? She had no idea what her instincts were trying to tell her, so she slammed the lid down on them. She watched as he reached down and picked up the largest remaining piece of glass from the Warhol lithograph, a triangular spike four inches wide at one end and tapering along eleven inches to a dagger-sharp point. Sarah's heart seemed to freeze midbeat, but Terry held it between his fingers gingerly, not like a weapon but truly like a mirror, angling it to increase the reflective surface. Just for this moment all he seemed interested in was his reflection—the twisted reflection he apparently saw and she did not. His face was filled with a dreadful fascination, as if he no longer doubted that what he saw was completely real to him and could now, in at least a marginal way, bear to examine it, as if he now understood some of the awful answers.

A chill, like a brief icy breeze, brushed along Sarah's

side, and she turned to look, but the room was still empty, still desolate. Terry turned, too, looking in the same direction as if he, too, had felt the chill; then Sarah felt her stomach turn to ice as he addressed that spot of air from which the coldness seemed to radiate. He no longer addressed the wall by the armoire. "Is it real, then?" he asked with such crippling hurt in his voice that the sound of it broke Sarah's heart. "Is it true?"

"Oh my God . . . ," she whispered, and for the first time wondered if what he was seeing was really in the room with them.

"God . . . no," he pleaded, letting the glass fall from his hand. "Don't let it be. Please God, don't let it be like this!" More tears fell from his blueberry-colored eyes.

Sarah was weeping now, too. She reached out to touch him, but he saw her hand and jerked away from her as if she had come at him with a knife.

"Don't touch me!" he hissed, falling over onto his hip, scrabbling and crawling desperately away from her. Red blood blossomed from several long gashes that opened as he scrambled away through the jagged litter. "Don't touch me! Can't you see?"

His rejection of her stabbed into her with terrible force, producing not more despair but an anger that leapt up from her broken heart and escaped through her mouth.

"Goddamn it, Terry! There's nothing *to* see!"

"Yes! Look! For Christ's sake—are you blind?" He held up another piece of glass, turning it to show her.

"No!" she snapped. "No more of that!" She stepped forward and slapped the glass out of his hand, but her angle was bad and immediately she felt a burn across her palm and looked down to see blood flood outward from her palm. She stared at it and then held her hand out angrily to Terry. "Now see, damn it! Do you want to keep this up until we cut ourselves to piece . . ." Her voice died abruptly in her throat, choked to silence by the look that had appeared suddenly and intensely on Terry's face as he stared at her welling blood. It was a look of total, naked hunger. A horrible, lustful hunger. He leered at her blood and his mouth began working, lips and jaws moving as if tasting the air, as if tasting her blood.

With a cry of horror, Sarah reeled back, whipping her hand away and hiding it behind her back like a starving child hiding a scrap from a scrounging dog. Terry leaned forward as if to follow her, his weight dropping down onto his palms. When she moved back another step, and then another, he moved forward, walking on knees and hands in a mockery of a dog, and with each step forward his body movement changed, becoming comfortable with the posture, moving with a strange grace that was so much at odds with his naked, bleeding state.

Sarah's back struck hard against the edge of the door frame. Terry advanced again, then darted forward in a lunge that brought him to within a yard of her. His eyes glared up at her, and in them Sarah saw no trace of Terry. The eyes that looked at her were the hungry eyes of an animal.

The strange wave of coldness that had touched her earlier swept past again, passing between her and Terry. Sarah shivered involuntarily, but Terry turned suddenly, lunging at the cold air as it passed, actually snarling at it and biting the empty air. Sarah wanted to run, to scream—but a stronger urge kept her there, in that room, with Terry. Not this Terry, but the one she loved, however much he might be damaged, might be submerged beneath all of his sickness.

Terry slowly turned back toward her. The muscles in his arms and back began to ripple with an unnatural spasm, and pain danced in Terry's eyes. He tore at the carpet with his fingernails, and a line of drool slipped from between his lips to hang pendulously below his chin.

Sarah could have run, could have been out the bedroom door, down the steps, gone from the house in seconds. The ambulance wail was closer now and she could run toward it, toward safety, but she stood her ground for love of him. The twisted, snarling knot of muscle and bone that inched toward her had madness in its eyes and enough physical power to easily break her apart. She knew that if he attacked her she could not—and would not—fight him. She held her ground as he stalked to within inches of her, his face wrinkled in a grotesque parody of an animal's silent scream, like a tiger's face before it kills, like a wolf as it leaps. Sarah believed it, knew the threat, felt that her life was measured now in seconds. Slowly, slowly, she lowered herself down to her knees in front of him, bending until she sat on her calves, her head level with his, feeling the sharp bit of glass into her knees but not caring, not reacting to that—pain and blood were nothing to her at that moment.

His eyes watched her, alight with hunger. Sarah reached out with her hands and touched both sides of his face. At first he jerked away, growling low in his throat, but she tried again, saying a single word, "No." Just that one word, said softly.

The places where her palms touched seemed to crackle with energy, though whether it was real or not, she couldn't tell. She knelt there, touching his face, and said it again, "No."

The moment was unreal. He was there on all fours, transformed in a broken moment from a gentle man who had held her and loved her to a damaged and incomplete imitation of some predatory thing—a beast of indefinable nature. She was there, kneeling on a glass-strewn and blood-splattered carpet, touching madness and denying its power with a single word. "No."

He looked at her with the eyes of madness. In the uncertain light by the open bedroom doorway, his eyes no longer seemed blue at all, but appeared to glow with a bizarre red-gold glow. Animal eyes. He turned his face toward her bleeding palm, sniffed at it.

"No, Terry." He leaned closer toward the flowing blood. An inch away, less. The smell of salt and copper filled his nostrils. Sweat burst from his forehead. He was shaking all over as if he had a raging fever. His tongue wormed from between his lips, reaching, needing, almost touching the blood, almost tasting it.

*"NO!"*

This time it was Terry himself who said it. Yelled it. Screamed it—and the words were ripped out of him, bellowed with horrible and inhuman force as he reared up and shoved at her, knocking her into the hallway, knocking himself back against the bed.

*"NO!"* he screamed again and the red-gold glow of his eyes burned with incandescent fury. Sarah fell heavily, her head rapping hard against the banister. Dazed, she watched as Terry rose up from the floor, first to his knees and then slowly, with terrible struggling jerks and spasms to a crouch, and finally all the way to his full height. Naked, crisscrossed with bleeding slashes, bathed in sweat, he was an awesome sight. Every muscle in his body was locked in battle, one against another, evidence of some titanic internal struggle.

*"NO!"* he roared, and he wept, too, his tears burning bright in his eyes. "No, you can't take that away from me, too! You can't make me, you bastard! You lose, Griswold, you fucking *lose*!" He laughed with weird triumph, though his laugh became a sob.

He wrenched himself around to face Sarah, his mouth working as he tried to speak, but only choked sounds came out of his constricted throat.

*"Sarah!"* was all he could manage, and then he spun around, ran straight across the room, and threw himself headfirst out of the window with Sarah's horrified, despairing scream following him all the way down to the garden flagstones.

# Chapter 29

## (1)

Diego saw them walking along the back road and cut through the rows of corn to intercept them, pushing his John Deere cap back on his forehead and smiling. "Little dark out here for a stroll, ladies, dontcha think?"

Val shrugged affably. "Taking the shortcut back to the house. How's the tractor?"

"Axle's shot, but we're going to tow it in back to the shed and José and Ty can fix it tomorrow."

"Okay. I have to go into town for a bit. You guys should knock off for today."

Diego grinned, his teeth very white against the deep black of his mustache. "Okay, we'll wrap it up as soon as the tractor's moved. Besides, it's Little Halloween and there's a keg party at the campus. Ty and the others were planning on heading out there."

"Not you?"

"Too old for that crap. Gonna order a pizza, watch *Dawn of the Dead* on cable, and fall asleep in my La-Z-Boy. At my age that's partying."

"Sounds like a plan."

"Hey," he said, "if you two are going to be out prowling around you should take this." He tugged a Maglite from his back pocket, turned it on, and handed it over.

"We're just heading back to the house. I need to get my purse and leave a note for Crow in case he comes out, and then we're taking off. Thanks, Dee."

He sketched a salute and headed back across the fields to where José and Ty were hooking the tractor up to the tow-rig on Diego's big Tundra. The moment he was out of sight Connie's mental focus seemed to snap back on as if someone had thrown a switch. "I know!" she said brightly. "Maybe before we go see Sarah we can bake her a pumpkin pie." Like most of her recent remarks it was as much of a non sequitur as if she'd suggested they set themselves on fire and jump off the roof. Val was learning to roll with them, but it took effort.

"Sure, honey," she said, "but let's do that later. C'mon."

As they walked the strong white beam of the Maglite picked out their path through the corn on one side and the harvested field on the other, and then caught a splash of dark red as the barn loomed out of the darkness in front of them. In the field they could hear the Tundra's engine growl to life as Diego and his men began hauling the tractor back to the shed that was down the road from the barn. Val and Connie walked without hurry, and Val figured that if an ambulance was coming to take Terry in to Pinelands, then Sarah would be busy for a while getting him settled. No need to be there for that; it was those long hours of waiting and fretting in the lounge while the doctors ran their tests when Sarah would need allies.

"Maybe we should put together some fruits and things and take a basket," Connie rattled on and on. "I have a lovely basket in the pantry and we could use some of that ribbon that—"

Then the flash caught something shiny lying in the dirt just outside the barn door and Val bent to pick it up. It was a small diamond-shaped medallion with a length of broken silver chain. Clearly stamped on the front was a six-armed cross painted bright red and set with a tiny caduceus in the center.

"That's odd . . . that's Mark's MedicAlert necklace," Connie said with surprise, "for his peanut allergy."

"I know," Val said, turning it over to see the warning notice and phone numbers. "He must have dropped it." She looked around and then skimmed the flashlight beam along the dirt path that led from the barn to the house. A line of footprints, clearly Mark's smooth-soled Florsheims, was visible heading toward the barn, but no overlapping prints led back. Frowning, Val slowly followed the footprints, and saw a second set of prints—shoes of a different size but still city shoes—also heading toward the barn and these were overlapped by Mark's. Was he meeting someone there? That seemed very odd. The prints led right up to the door, and the last visible print was cut off by the door that had been pulled almost all the way closed. Obviously Mark had gone into the barn and pulled the door shut behind him.

Connie shifted to stand next to her, her eyes following the same path and the same logic Val had used, and there were twin vertical lines between her brows. "Is Mark in the barn?" she asked, as if that was the strangest thing in the world.

"I think so." Val took a half-step toward the door, and then paused. Did she really want another screaming match right now? She was shaking her head in answer to her own question when Connie said, "Open the door."

"If he's still in there, Conn, then maybe he wants to be alone for a bit. Let's leave him be."

It was at that moment that they heard something move inside the barn. It was a soft, shuffling sound—a scrape of a shoe on the hard-packed dirt floor just on the other side of the big plank door. It froze Val in place and she stood staring at the nearly closed door, at the black line of inky darkness between the door and the frame. *Was Mark right there, listening to them? Listening and saying nothing? Standing there in the dark?*

She glanced at Connie, who had also heard the sound. Her frown lines had deepened. "Mark . . . ?"

Another sound—a shift again and this time Val was sure that it was the scuff of a shoe on the floor, just on the other side of the door. It had to be Mark, of course, but why was he standing there in the dark? It was so—she fished for the word. Weird. Especially for Mark, who was not the type to be loitering in the darkened barn. Farm-bred or not, Mark was a city boy, and this was just not his sort of thing. It was—prankish; even a little mean. That part—the meanness—that could be Mark, but not prankish.

A third scuff and now there was a second sound. A more organic sound, like a grunt. Not a middle-register grunt of a pig—there were no pigs on the Guthrie farm—but a deeper sound, almost a cough, or maybe a single short snort of laughter.

"Mark?" Connie asked again and started reaching for the door handle, but Val instinctively caught her wrist.

"No," she said quietly, staring hard at the door, at that vertical line of darkness that showed a total lack of light inside. "Don't." She hadn't liked that grunt, whether it was a cough or a snort, it just didn't sound *right*. "Let's go back to the house," she said. She took Connie's wrist in her free hand and then took a single backward step, drawing Connie with her. Connie resisted, her gaze lingering for a moment on the door before finally turning around to give Val an uncomprehending stare.

"But—it's Mark," she said, giving Val a frowning smile of confusion.

There was a second grunting sound and then a light slapping sound as if someone had placed their open hand flat on the inside of the door. The heavy door trembled and opened maybe half an inch, broadening the line of darkness. Val pulled Connie another step back. This time she was sure she had identified the kind of sound coming from behind that door. It was laughter. It just wasn't Mark's.

"Let's go back to the house," she whispered harshly. "Now."

Connie tried to pull away and as she did so she turned toward the door and shouted Mark's name.

"No!" Val yelled as the door suddenly swung open. She shined her light on the face of the man standing there. It wasn't Mark.

It was Kenneth Boyd.

(2)

They struggled up the last few feet and collapsed onto the grass that fringed the Passion Pit. The sun was long down and the sky was bright with a billion stars. It was warmer up there and a rowdy gaggle of geese was waddling around the clearing, honking contentedly and poking into the grass for bits of stale hamburger buns and cold french fries. In the trees the last finches of the season were chatting noisily. There were even some elderly fireflies drifting lazily through the air. Newton, lying on his back, recorded these things. "Is this even the same planet?"

Crow shook his head. "Don't ask me, son, I have long since lost the capacity for rational thought." Crow struggled to sit up and reached over to pat Newton's leg. "We're going to have to talk about this. I mean we'll have to *think* about it some, and then you and I are going to have to talk about this."

"Well," Newton said, "there's one thing I can tell you now, and that's you can pretty much go on the assumption that I am somewhat less skeptical about this town's reputation for being haunted."

"How much is 'somewhat'?"

"Like maybe a hundred percent."

"That's all?" Crow tried on a smile, but it didn't fit. Even the muscles of his face hurt from strain. He took a breath, exhaling as he forced himself to sit up, and after a moment stood up, reaching a hand down to haul Newton to his feet. Then he walked over and unlocked his car. He reached in for his cell. "Still no bars. I'll have to call Val from the road. Come on, cowboy, let's go." He lingered by the open door, looking at the black edge of the pitch. "Let's get the hell out of here."

Crow fired up the engine, did a three-point backing turn, and then headed back up the bumpy dirt road, away from Dark Hollow. Neither of them spoke as the car bounced over the ruts, and when Crow reached the crossroads, he turned right toward town. Away from the Guthrie farm.

(3)

Boyd stood there in the doorway, framed by darkness, shadows behind him, his skin gray-white in the glare of Val's flashlight, grinning at the two women. His eyes were sunken into desiccated sockets, his cheeks gaunt, his nose askew with splinters of cartilage and bone poking through the flesh like cactus needles. But it was his mouth—his awful mouth—that held them in an immobility born of total horror. Boyd's lips were curled back from his teeth and those rows of teeth, top and bottom, were twisted and elongated, set crookedly in the gray meat of his gums, and each one ended in a wicked point. Those teeth gleamed wet and dark and red in the flash's light. Blood dripped from his mouth onto the filthy tatters of his suit. He snorted again, a bestial grunt of laughter that caused a bubble of bloody mucus to form between his rows of fangs. It swelled and then burst with an audible *pop*, seeding the air with a mist of blood.

Val was frozen to the spot, unblinking, unable to process what she was seeing, but then Boyd stepped to one side and turned, allowing the light from her flash to slide off him and shine in through the open barn door. He turned his head and held out one hand, gesturing inside like a magician revealing a clever trick. Just inside the door, only a yard beyond where the last of the footprints had ended, was a body slumped in a shattered, rag-doll sprawl, with arms and legs flopped away from the torso, and a head thrown back, mouth wide as if caught in the midst of a great scream, tilting away from the red ruin of a savaged throat.

Connie Guthrie stared past Val, past Boyd, through the open door, and into the wide and sightless eyes of her husband. And screamed.

"MARK!"

That scream—a tearing screech that tore her throat and flecked her lips with her own blood—galvanized both Boyd and Val. With a howl of furious delight he flung himself at Val. The sound of both screams broke her paralysis of shock and she hurled the Maglite at Boyd and threw herself at Connie, knocking her sideways and down so that Boyd's lunge missed them both. Connie fell hard and Val crashed down onto her and there was a loud *snap!* as Val's hip landed on Connie's ribs. Connie's scream modulated upward into a shriek of agony; Val rolled off her just as Boyd came scrambling off the ground and she tried to dodge the swing of his open hand, but he clipped her as she moved—not a whole-hand blow, just the flats of his fingers, but it was hard enough to send her reeling against the side of the barn. She struck it with her forehead and the pain stabbed through the healing eye socket where Ruger had similarly struck her. Her right eye went black and the other exploded with white light and the whole barnyard spun around her in a sickening reel. She collapsed into an awkward heap as Connie's screams continued to rip holes in the night.

Because of the blow to her head everything was suddenly muted, and Connie's screams seemed to be coming from a hundred miles away. Val tried to crawl toward her, but she couldn't see. She kept blinking, trying to clear her sight. The right eye stayed black and blind, but there were images now in her left one—fuzzy shapes cavorting in the indirect glare from the fallen flashlight. She saw a hulking shape—Boyd, it had to be Boyd—rising to his feet a half-dozen yards away, and he had something in his hands. Something smaller. Connie! Struggling, still screaming, kicking and flailing. Fighting back. Fighting back against Boyd the way Mark had said she hadn't done against Ruger.

*Mark! Oh God!*

Darkness wanted to close around her, to smash her into nothingness, but she fought it with a snarl of heartbroken rage, fought it with hate for what this man had done. Val pulled herself to her hands and knees and supported herself on one palm while she reached behind her back and pulled out her father's big .45 Colt Commander; she sagged back onto her heels, racking the slide with trembling hands. Her one eye was clearer, but it was like looking through oily glass, and as she raised the gun Boyd lunged his mouth toward Connie's throat. The sound of his teeth tearing through the softness of her skin was lost in the cannon-loud explosion of the gun. The bullet took Boyd in the hip and the heavy slug's impact spun Boyd around; he lost his grip on Connie. To Val it seemed like he fell to the ground in exaggerated slowness, trailing a thin arc of blood as he collapsed into the dirt.

"Connie!" Val yelled—or tried to, but her voice was a choked whisper of pain.

Boyd had been knocked off balance, down to one knee, but he turned, whipping his white face toward Val, baring those awful teeth that were smeared now with Connie's blood as well as Mark's. Val shot him again as he rose and this time the bullet punched through his stomach and burst out the other side. The impact barely made Boyd pause. He flinched, and that was all; then his snarl became a smile as he rose to his feet.

Val's mouth formed the word *No!* as she fired again, taking Boyd in the meat of his thigh and she could see the pant leg puff and blood and bone splatter against the fence post beyond him, but he kept rising, getting to both feet now and starting to move toward her. She fired again, a chest shot that surely punched a hole through his lung.

All Boyd did was smile as he lunged toward her.

### (4)

Crow drove the rutted twists of Dark Hollow road, his mind churning over everything that had happened down in Dark Hollow. The sensations as they had crossed the line, the swamp, the chains with their locks inside the house, the new boards, the roaches. Even for him it was all too weird, too . . . *real.* Not tainted childhood memories, not alcohol-induced DTs, not the result of repeated head trauma courtesy of Karl Ruger. This had just happened, and unlike when Ruger had said those enigmatic last few words there was a witness this time. He cut a glance at Newton, who had his arms wrapped around himself as if for warmth; the reporter's head was bowed and he was shaking it slowly from side to side. *Oh boy*, thought Crow, *there's my credible witness going bye-bye on me.*

He braked to a stop where the dirt road emptied out onto A-32, and for a moment he sat there. Turn right and head to town, drop off Newton, then come back here to Val; turn left and go see Val first. He pulled out his cell, got enough bars, and hit speed dial. Val's phone rang five times and then went to voice mail. He tried her house, same deal.

Then all at once two things happened that changed everything forever.

First, his mind—still replaying everything that had happened that day—tripped over the buried memory of that bizarre thought he'd felt when he had been on Griswold's porch, when he had touched the wood with his palm and felt the odd whispering tremble beneath his skin. A voice—maybe it was the voice of Griswold's ghost, dead these thirty years, or maybe it was the voice of his own fears—hissed at him from the shadows.

*She is going to die and there is nothing you can do to save her. Nothing!*

Crow jerked upright in his seat and snapped his head around toward Val's farm. At that moment he heard the gunshots. And the screams.

### (5)

Boyd lunged at her and Val fired two more shots, catching him in the upper chest. It didn't stop him, but the force of the two heavy-caliber bullets turned him while he was in mid-leap, spinning his mass so that he crashed beside her rather than on top of her. He landed with a hiss like a scalded cat and turned toward her, clawing at her with his white fingers, the black nails tearing at her sleeves and chest as she lay on her side, but she brought her feet up and kicked at him while trying to steady the gun with both hands.

"Val!"

Val and Boyd both turned as three men came pelting around the side of the barn. Diego was in the lead, with José Ramos and Tyrone Gibbs close behind. "We heard screams—" Diego was saying and then they took in the tableau. Connie writhing on the ground, her face and throat splashed with blood; Val on the ground with a pistol; and a crazy-looking man grabbing at her. All three men put it together at once— they had all seen the news stories; they'd lived through the aftermath of the murder of their boss and the savage killings of the two cops not eighty yards from where they now stood. They *knew* who this son of a bitch was, and in the space be- tween one footfall and the next their faces changed from concern to fury.

"Get that son of a *bitch*!" Diego yelled, and the two younger men—a twenty-year-old heavy equipment mechanic with ropy muscles and a twenty-five-year-old farmhand who once played halfback for the Pinelands Scarecrows—rushed in with hate in their eyes. They were big men who had dealt with their own grief over Henry's death, and loved Val like a sister, and they wanted a piece of this South Philly wiseguy white trash. Shoulder to shoulder they raced toward Boyd, who had stopped pawing at Val and was rising to meet them; and from ten feet away both younger men threw themselves at him, leaping high and low as if they had practiced the move a thousand times. José slammed his shoulder into Boyd's thighs and Ty braced his forearms in front of him and took Boyd in the chest, and they crushed him back against the barn wall. Bones snapped, Boyd howled in rage and there was a huge muffled echo from inside the barn.

José clung to Boyd's legs, trying to pull him down, but Ty landed on his feet with old football reflexes still in his mus- cles. He pressed Boyd back with one forearm and started hammering him with short overhand rights that pulped what was left of Boyd's face, splintering his nose, cracking his si- nuses, ripping skin along his eyebrows. The sound of his blows was like an ax hitting wet cordwood.

Boyd endured the hits and just shot out one hand to catch

Ty's throat, and with a jerk of his wrist tore the whole front of it away. There was a massive spray of blood that shot like a hose from Ty's arteries, drenching Boyd, splattering the wall, splashing Val's face as she struggled to her feet. Ty tottered back, clawing at a gaping red nothing of a throat; his eyes went wide with the impossibility of what was happening, awareness sinking in even as his mind went red and then black. He fell backward, blood geysering up for a second before settling down to a dribble as shock shut down his heart.

"*¡Dios mío!*" Diego cried, skidding to a stop, his own fist raised for a punch, unable to comprehend what he had just witnessed.

Boyd reached down and grabbed José by the hair and jerked his head up and back, and there was a sound like a rake-handle breaking. The young man flopped to the ground, his chest and shoulders jerking, his feet kicking spasmodically.

Screaming in horror, Val fired two more shots, catching Boyd in the side and staggering him away from where José lay. The young man was staring upward, eyes wide and bright, feeling nothing at all below his neckline but a fiery emptiness as if he had been separated from all of his nerve endings.

Boyd crouched and spun, hissing as he began to advance toward Val once more, but Diego snapped out of his shock and waded in to land a single wide haymaker on the side of Boyd's jaw. It was a powerful punch, backed by all of the sturdy foreman's mass and turn, and Boyd's head snapped so far around that there was an audible snap somewhere in his neck, but he just twitched his shoulders and turned his head back toward Val, lashing out with one hand almost as an afterthought and catching Diego on the cheekbone. This was a far more powerful blow and the foreman spun like a dancer on the ball of one foot and landed facedown, his eyes rolling high and white.

Grinning with his bloody mouth, baring his jagged rows of teeth, Boyd lunged once more at Val and she fired again, standing in a shooter's crouch now, the gun held in one hand, the other one clamped around her wrist to support its weight, one eye seeing nothing but black and the other staring right into Boyd's hideous face. Her first bullet punched through his mouth, clipping the tips off several teeth, like a missile flying through a cave and snapping off stalactites and stalagmites. That slowed Boyd by no more than a half-step.

She put the next round through his right eye and the next through his forehead.

The force slammed him back against the barn, but this time he seemed to freeze in place. His one remaining red-within-black eye stared at her with such profound shock that Val didn't pull the trigger again. Instead she watched as that dark eye lost its clarity and slowly rolled upward as Boyd slid down into the wall, toppled over into the bloody dirt, and lay still.

Val stood there, her muscles locked and trembling, pain continuing to detonate in her skull and in her bad shoulder, but she still held the gun tightly in both hands. She took a single step forward, barrel aimed at the killer's head, but there was no movement. Another step, remembering how Ruger had fooled Crow that terrible night. She wouldn't make the same mistake. She took another step, and risked a glance around her. Ty was definitely dead. José—she thought his neck must be broken, but she could hear him breathing . . . and crying. Diego was out, but didn't look that bad. And Connie. Dear God . . . Connie was alive, her hands clamped around her throat, her eyes open and glassy with shock. Inside the barn, Mark lay silent amid the shadows. She looked back at Boyd and took a final step until she was standing over him, the gun barrel pointing down. He had two black holes in his face. One where his right eye should be—which was now a dark mass of jelly—and another in the center of his forehead. He was definitely dead.

But she emptied the rest of the magazine into him anyway, each shot punching through his skull and into his brain.

The slide locked open, the magazine empty.

Val staggered back, lost her balance, and fell just as the

first sob broke from her chest, and abruptly the whole yard—the house, the path, the barn, and all the bodies—were washed into a cartoon of harsh blacks and whites by headlights as Crow came tearing up the road toward her.

# Chapter 30

## (1)

Crow sat with Val, both of them wrapped in the blanket the paramedics had draped around her shoulders. The cartoon black and white of the scene had been repainted with the red and blue of police lights, and ambulance sirens were a constant wail. Diego, Connie, and José had all been taken away. Ty Gibbs still lay where he had fallen, his dead face still registering amazement; inside the barn, Mark was being photographed. Crow could see the white flashes of the camera as they documented the scene. Crow had done it himself once upon a time; he knew the drill. He looked up and saw Newton standing nearby talking into his cell phone, calling in the story, scooping everyone else. Crow almost hated him for it, but just couldn't spare the energy.

Crow kissed Val's face, her hair. "It's over," he murmured.

"He was dead," she whispered.

"He's dead, baby, it's okay. You killed the bastard—"

"No!" she had snapped, pounding on his chest with her fist. "He was dead. I shot him over and over again. I didn't miss once. Not once. He was dead."

Crow looked at her and saw the truth of it in her eyes. Not shock, not delusion. He stood up and walked over to where Boyd lay, ignoring Dixie McVey, who was writing in his notebook. Crow squatted down and counted the bullet holes. Fifteen of them from Henry's old .45. But it was worse than that, worse than even Val knew, and sometime soon he'd have to tell her. As Crow knelt there, using a Bic pen to lift the folds of Boyd's clothing, he saw other bullet holes. Old ones. Nine of them. In belly and groin and chest. Nearly healed over. Nine shots. The number of bullets that had been fired from Jimmy Castle's pistol. Nine. Nine and then Val's fifteen, the last of which had been head shots. Twenty-four shots all told. It was, of course, impossible.

He looked at Boyd's mouth, the jaw hung loose, twisted askew, the lips slack over the teeth. With hands that were starting to shake with a palsy of rising terror, Crow reached out and pushed back Boyd's upper lip, looking at evidence of what he did not want to find; but the bullet had done too much damage and what was left of the teeth revealed no dark secrets. Crow got to his feet feeling no relief.

He turned and walked slowly back to Val and waved away the paramedic who was trying to usher her into the back of an ambulance. The paramedic must have seen something in his face; he held up his hands, palms out, and retreated to his vehicle.

Crow took Val in his arms, careful with her.

She leaned into him. "He was dead," she said again.

He nodded. "I know."

### (2)

When they heard the shooting and saw Crow's car pull into the driveway, Vic started his truck and he and Ruger drove without headlights down the farm access road all the way to the river, then Vic turned his lights on and headed first north then west until they had circled above the town proper. Most of the way they didn't say anything.

Vic's cell phone rang when they were just north of town. It was Jim Polk. Vic put it on speakerphone. "All hell's breaking loose at the Guthrie place. Is that your stuff?" he asked.

Vic had to take a breath before he answered. All he said was, "Boyd."

"Yeah, well that reporter from Black Marsh called in that Boyd was dead."

Vic and Ruger exchanged a look. "What do you mean 'dead'?" Vic said.

"I mean dead, what do you think I mean? I was the one that took the call," said Polk. "Mark Guthrie's dead, too, and someone else, some guy works at the farm."

"What about Val Guthrie?" Vic asked hopefully. "She dead, too?"

"Not as far as I know." He told Vic everything Newton had said. "What the hell happened out there?"

"None of your business."

"There's one more thing, Vic. We got a report that Terry Wolfe tried to kill himself."

"What?" Vic yelled.

"Yeah. Threw himself out of a window . . . he's in critical condition. They're not sure if he'll make it. Vic . . . what the hell's happening?"

"I'll get back to you. Keep me posted." He hung up, slammed the cell phone down hard on the seat, and then punched the dashboard. "Shit!"

"Let me get this straight," Ruger said in his whispery voice, "that bitch killed Boyd? How the hell did she manage that? I thought you said no one would know how to kill us. I mean . . . it's not like that stake-through-the-heart shit actually works. So what happened?"

They stopped at a light and Vic pushed in the dashboard lighter and fished in his pocket for a cigarette. "I don't know!"

"Oh, that's just peachy. You got this great big master plan, you got wheels spinning within wheels, you own dozens of key people, and you can't kill one woman?"

Vic stabbed the air in front of Ruger's nose with his forefinger. "You can shove that up your ass, sport, because this was your plan, not mine. I should have just dragged her ass down to the swamp and fed her to the Man. But no, you gotta be some criminal mastermind and screw with their heads. This is your fault."

Ruger turned away and looked out at the darkness. "This should have worked. With anyone else . . . it *would* have worked." He turned back to Vic. "There's something else going on here."

The lighter popped and Vic pulled it, held it to his cigarette and the glow of it painted his face a hellish red. "Listen to me, sport," he said. "These two are standing in the way of the Red Wave, and now they know that something hinky is going on around here." He leancd close. "We can't have that."

"No, we can't."

"If Boyd's really dead, then we have to get his body before they can do an autopsy. Let's call that Priority One. I mean, if we have to burn down the shitting hospital, then that's what we do. Accidents happen."

"We can work something out," Ruger said. "There are a lot of us now."

"The thing is . . . Crow and that reporter were at the house. They were in the Hollow. How or why the Man couldn't stop them I don't know, but they were there, they got away, and they have a story to tell. Plus, that Guthrie bitch saw Boyd—she had to see what he was. All of them now know more than they should. Shutting them up or shutting them down is Priority Two. Problem is . . . with Wolfe out of action we can't actually kill the son of a bitch anymore. Damn it."

"Then we're screwed."

Vic sat in silence while the light turned yellow and then red again. A smile grew on Vic's face like the slow spread of a disease. "Maybe not," he said softly.

The light turned green again and Vic drove them both back home.

### (3)

Crow's cell rang while the paramedics were examining Val. He saw that it was Saul Weinstock and flipped it open. "Saul—thank God it's you. I guess you heard . . ."

"I know, it's horrible," Weinstock said, sounding ragged. "I just can't believe I didn't see this coming."

Crow hesitated. "What do you mean? How could you have foreseen something like this?"

"Well, come on, Crow," Weinstock said, "we've all been watching him come apart for weeks now and—"

"Saul—what the hell are you talking about?"

"I'm talking about Terry. What are *you* talking about?"

Crow told him.

"Holy shit!" Weinstock yelled. "My God. I didn't know—I've been in the ER for the last hour working on Terry."

"Terry? What the hell happened to him?"

"Crow . . . about ninety minutes ago Terry Wolfe threw himself out of his bedroom window. I've got a team of residents picking glass out of him, and he has forty broken bones, including a skull fracture."

Crow took a wandering sideways step and sat down hard on the fender of his car. He looked wildly across the driveway to where Val was being tended to, and over at the bodies that crime scene investigators were examining. And at the *thing* that Val had shot fifteen times. Then he looked up at Newton, and all of that hit him, too.

"Crow? Crow—are you there?"

"Y-yeah, Saul . . . it's just all . . . it's too much."

"You don't know the half of it."

"Believe me—I think I do."

"Believe *me*," Weinstock insisted, "I think you don't. We have to talk."

"Not now, Saul . . . Val . . . I—"

"No, not now—but soon, Crow, as soon as we can. I need to talk to someone about what's happening around here. I was going to tell you tomorrow morning. Crow, I've never been this scared before in my life!"

"I have," Crow said hoarsely. "But not recently."

"Crow—Pine Deep's in real trouble," Weinstock said softly.

"Yeah," Crow agreed. "I think so, too." Crow cleared his throat. "Look, they're getting ready to bring Val in. I'm going with her. I'll . . . see you at the ER."

"Okay," Weinstock said, and hung up.

Crow tried to walk calmly, normally, over to Val, but every third or fourth step he staggered, just a little. The paramedic was reaching down to help her up, but Crow gently pushed him to one side. "I got it," he said and drew Val to her feet and then pulled her close, wrapping his arms around her. "Let's go."

There was a look of hurt and panic in her eyes. "Mark—"

But Crow shook his head. "Sweetie, they'll take care of him. We can't do anything here, and Connie's going to need us at the hospital when she wakes up."

She searched his face with her one good eye; the other was once again wrapped in gauze. "What's happening, Crow? Everything's gone crazy." Tears ran down her face and he bent and kissed her forehead, her cheek, and then her mouth, and as he did so a sob broke in his chest. They clung together, both of them crying as the paramedic fidgeted nearby looking greatly embarrassed.

# Epilogue

## (1)

Midnight. Little Halloween was over. The night around the hospital was immense, painting the windows a featureless black. Crow sat in the guest chair of what would become Val's hospital room once she was finished in the ER. Crow had seen Weinstock for only a few seconds. Not enough time to talk as Weinstock ran alongside the gurney team that was wheeling José into surgery. Crow knew that he wouldn't see him at all, probably not until tomorrow.

Newton came in and sat in the other chair, and they sat there in silence for five minutes, watching the black night beyond the glass. Finally, Crow said, "You file your story?"

Newton shot him a cautious glance. "Yeah. You mad?"

"I should be, but—screw it. It's your job." He made a face. "After all . . . this is news."

Newton cleared his throat. "Crow . . . I only called in the basic stuff. The shootings. Val's brother and the guys who work for her. I—left out some stuff."

Crow digested that. "The Hollow?"

"Yeah."

"Just that?" Newton was quiet for so long Crow turned to look at him. "Newt?"

"Crow—I saw that man's body. I was looking over your shoulder. I saw what you saw."

"And what did I see?"

A pause. "I saw something that can't be real."

Crow drew a breath, let it out, said nothing.

Newton said, "I heard what Val told you, too. I heard her tell you how many times she shot him. I read the police reports on Castle, too, and I know that he fired off nine shots. Crow—you found every single one of those bullet holes. Every one. I was there, I saw you. I saw them."

"Okay."

"No—no, it's not okay. We both know it's not frigging okay." Newton looked at Crow. "And I know what you're thinking."

Crow gave him a crooked smile. "What is it that I'm thinking, Newt?"

"You're thinking that Boyd was like *him*. That somehow, impossibly somehow, Boyd was like him. Like Griswold." Crow was silent. "That somehow Boyd was a—" Newton stopped and turned away, unable to say the word.

So, Crow said it for him. "That somehow Boyd was a werewolf?"

"Yes. Jesus—this is impossible. I can't wrap my head around it."

"You're wrong, Newt."

The reporter swiveled around to stare at him. "What?"

"I said that you're wrong. I don't think that Boyd was a werewolf. That's not at all what I think."

"But—the gunshots. He—"

"What I think, Newt," Crow said, his eyes reflecting the great dark nothingness beyond the window, "is that Kenneth Boyd was a vampire."

To that, Newton had nothing to say.

"I think Ruger was, too. I don't know how, I don't know why. I just know what I saw." And Crow told him everything. The attack in the hospital, Ruger's eyes, his unnatural strength. Newton kept shaking his head throughout, but it wasn't that he thought Crow was wrong. He just did not want to believe it.

They sat there in silence for a long time, oblivious to the

hospital sounds close at hand or the traffic sounds outside. Newton sniffed, wiped his eyes on his sleeve. "We're all going to die," he asked, "aren't we?"

Crow had no answer for him. None at all.

### (2)

He sat on the rooftop, legs folded Indian fashion, old guitar laid across his bony knees, singing blues to the night. The wind had turned cold and fierce and it blew around him and through him. On that gale he could hear the voice of the creature in the swamp. The wind was filled with his rage.

The Bone Man smiled. He felt great sadness that Henry's boy had died, but he also felt great pride that Henry's daughter, Val, had stood up and stood tall. Henry would be proud of her. She'd done what no one—certainly not him, and probably not Griswold—had thought anyone *could* do with just an ordinary gun. She'd brought down one of them. One of *his* soldiers. Griswold's fury filled the air around him, and it tasted just fine to the Bone Man.

He strummed his guitar. So much pain downstairs. So many folks hurting and dying. So many folks *changing*, in good ways and bad. So much death.

Yet it wasn't all dark, not even up here in the wind, and he ran his fingers over the strings, picking out a tune. Val had taken her stand, and now for the first time in thirty years the thing down there in the wormy dark was not so sure, not so cocksure by a long mile, and that was good. Now there was a little more hope mixed in with all that hate and rage on the wind. Not much, maybe, not enough almost for sure, but some—and for tonight that was going to have to do.

He slipped his bottleneck out of his coat pocket and fitted it over the forefinger of his left hand, sliding the smooth glass down the strings as he plucked a note and then another. Downstairs they were doing their trying and their dying, their sewing and their praying. The Bone Man was no sage, he didn't know who was going to make it through this night, or who was going to make it through till the coming of Griswold's Red Wave. He didn't know if anyone would be able to take another stand, like Val did tonight. Maybe Crow would, but that was something the Bone Man would have to see. Crow . . . and maybe Mike. He played some notes, finding his way into a song. The old one that he used to play on Henry's porch. The one about prisoners walking that last mile to Old Sparky down in Louisiana. The one he played on that long ago summer. "Ghost Road Blues." He played it and then he started to sing the words in a voice no one could hear.

As the wind shrieked its fury around him, the dead man sang his song.

# BAD MOON RISING

The Bone Man was as thin as a whisper; he was a scarecrow from a blighted field. He stood on the edge of the hospital roof, toes jutting out over the gutter, his pant legs fluttering against the stick slimness of his legs. His coat flaps snapped vigorously but silently around his emaciated hips. The only sound the wind made as it whipped by him and through him was a faint plaintive whine as it caressed the silvery strings of the guitar slung behind his back.

Far below the parking lot faded back from the glow of the emergency room doors, spreading out in a big half circle that had been cut acres-deep into the surrounding sea of pines. Even this late there were dozens of cars down there, dusted with moonlight but asleep. All around the town there was a ring of black clouds that were invisible against the night, but above the Bone Man the stars flickered and glimmered by the thousand.

For three hours he had sat cross-legged on the roof, playing his songs, humming and sometimes singing, coaxing the sad blues out of the ghost of an old guitar that Charley Patton had once used to play "Mississippi BoWeavil Blues" at a church picnic in Bentonia, Mississippi. Another time the Bone Man's father, old Virgil Morse, had used that guitar to play backup on a couple of Sun Records sides by Mose Vinson. The guitar had history. It had life, even though it was no more real than he was. A ghost of a guitar in a dead man's hands, playing music almost no one could hear.

He'd sat there and played and listened to the whispers and cries and moans from inside the hospital; hearing the beep of the machine that breathed for Connie Guthrie. Hearing the sewing-circle whisper of needles and thread as the doctors sewed stitches in Terry Wolfe's skin, and the faint grinding sound as they set his bones. He heard the whimper of hopelessness from the throat of José Ramos as the doctors stood by his bed and explained to his mother that his back was broken; and then the scream as the enormity of that drove a knife into his mother's heart. He heard the dreadful terror as Doctor Weinstock murmured, "Dear God," over and over again as he knelt alone in the bathroom of his office, hands on either side of the toilet bowl, his face streaked with tears and his lips wet with vomit.

He heard all of these things while he played, and then he heard the hospital slowly fall quiet as drugs or shock or alcohol took each of them into their private pits of darkness. That's when the Bone Man had stopped playing and rose to stand on the edge of the roof, staring across blacktop and car hoods and trees at the moon.

It was an ugly quarter moon, stained yellow-red like bruised flesh, and its sickle tip seemed to slash at the treetops. The sky above the trees was thick with agitated night birds that flapped and cawed, hectoring him like Romans at the Circus.

**(2)**

"Where are you now?"

Jim Polk cupped his hand around his cell and pitched his voice to a whisper. "At the hospital, like you said. Back loading dock."

"Anyone see you?"

"Jesus, Vic, you think I'm that stupid?"

Vic's voice tightened a notch. "Did anyone *see* you?"

"No, okay? No one saw me."

"You're sure?"

Polk almost mouthed off again, but caught himself. A half beat later he said, "I'm sure."

"Then open the door. We're here."

The hallway was still dark and empty. He'd already disabled the alarms and the video cameras, permanently this time per Vic's instructions. He pocketed his cell and fished for his keys, his fingers shaking badly. His nerves were shot and getting worse every time Vic asked him to do something like this. There was no letup, always some other shit to do, always something that was tightening the noose around his neck. The McDonald's fish in his stomach felt like it was congealing.

He turned the key but before Polk could push it open the door was whipped out of his hand and Karl Ruger shouldered his way in, pausing just enough to give Polk a slow, hungry up-and-down. He smiled a wide, white smile that showed two rows of jagged teeth that were wet with spit. The greasy slush in Polk's belly gave another sickening lurch. Vic was bad enough, but looking into Ruger's eyes was like looking into a dark well that was drilled all the way down to Hell. He fell back a step, stammering something useless, and twitched an arm nervously toward the morgue door halfway down the hall.

Ruger's mouth twitched. "Yeah," he whispered, "I know the way."

Polk flattened back against the wall, not wanting to even let Ruger's shadow touch him. Two other men came in—beefy college kids in Pinelands Scarecrows sweatshirts—their faces as white as Ruger's, their mouths filled with long white teeth. Vic was the last to enter and he pulled the door shut behind him and stood next to Polk, watching the three of them pad noiselessly down the hall.

"Yo!" Vic called softly and the college kids turned. "Quick and dirty. Mess the place up, paint some goofy frat-boy shit on the wall, break some stuff, and then haul Boyd's sorry ass out of here." He looked at his watch. "Five minutes and we're gone."

The college kids grinned at him for a moment and then pulled open the morgue door and vanished inside. Ruger lingered in the doorway.

Vic said to him, "They can handle it, Sport. You don't need to bother."

Even from that distance Polk could see Ruger's thin smile, and he felt Vic stiffen next to him. *Jesus Christ,* Polk thought, *Vic's afraid of him, too.*

"Mark Guthrie's in there." Ruger's tongue flicked out and lapped spit off his lips. "I want to pay my respects."

With a dry little laugh Ruger turned and went into the morgue.

Polk looked at Vic, who took a cigarette from his shirt pocket and slowly screwed it into his mouth, his eyes narrowed and thoughtful. Absently Vic began patting his pockets for a match and Polk pulled his own lighter and clicked it. Vic cut him a quick look, then gave a short nod and bent to the light, dragging in a deep chestful of smoke.

"Vic . . . ?"

Vic said nothing. Polk licked his lips. "Vic . . . is this all going to work out? I mean . . . is this all going to be okay for us?"

Vic Wingate exhaled as he turned to Polk, and in the darkness of the hallway his eyes were just as black and bottomless as Ruger's. "Couple hours ago I'd have told you we were screwed. Royally screwed." He plucked a fleck of tobacco from his tongue-tip and flicked it away. "But a lot's happened since then." He took another drag.

"Does that mean we're okay now? Does that mean we're safe?"

A lot of thoughts seemed to flit back and forth behind the black glass of Vic's eyes. "Depends on what you mean," he said with a smile, and then he headed down the hallway toward the morgue.

# When Darkness Falls
# Grab One of These
# Pinnacle Horrors

# Scare Up One of These
# Pinnacle Horrors